THE SKY
MANIFEST

THE SKY MANIFEST

BRIAN PANHUYZEN

MISFIT

ECW Press

Published by ECW Press
2120 Queen Street East, Suite 200,
Toronto, Ontario, Canada M4E 1E2
416-694-3348 / info@ecwpress.com

LIBRARY AND ARCHIVES CANADA
CATALOGUING IN PUBLICATION

Panhuyzen, Brian, 1966–
The sky manifest : a novel / Brian Panhuyzen.

"A misFit book".
ISBN 978-1-77041-081-7 (PBK.)
ALSO ISSUED AS: 978-1-77090-453-8 (PDF);
978-1-77090-454-5 (ePUB)

I. TITLE.

PS8581.A638S59
2013   C813'.54   C2013-902487-5

Editor for the press: Michael Holmes
Text design: Tania Craan
Cover image: Stev'nn Hall
Cover design: Carolyn McNeillie
Typesetting: Troy Cunningham
Printing: United Graphics   5   4   3   2   1

The publication of The Sky Manifest has been generously supported by the Canada Council for the Arts which last year invested $157 million to bring the arts to Canadians throughout the country, and by the Ontario Arts Council (OAC), an agency of the Government of Ontario, which last year funded 1,681 individual artists and 1,125 organizations in 216 communities across Ontario for a total of $52.8 million. We also acknowledge the financial support of the Government of Canada through the Canada Book Fund for our publishing activities, and the contribution of the Government of Ontario through the Ontario Book Publishing Tax Credit and the Ontario Media Development Corporation.

Ontario
Ontario Media Development
Corporation

ONTARIO ARTS COUNCIL
CONSEIL DES ARTS DE L'ONTARIO
50 YEARS OF ONTARIO GOVERNMENT SUPPORT OF THE ARTS
50 ANS DE SOUTIEN DU GOUVERNEMENT DE L'ONTARIO AUX ARTS

Canada Council
for the Arts

Conseil des Arts
du Canada

Canadä

PRINTED AND BOUND IN THE UNITED STATES

for
Arina Janna Panhuyzen
1938 – 2013

Why, I ask myself, should the shining dots of the sky not be as accessible as the black dots on the map of France? If we take the train to get to Tarascon or Rouen, we take death to reach a star. One thing undoubtedly true in this reasoning is this: that while we are alive we cannot get to a star, any more than when we are dead we can take the train.

— Vincent van Gogh, letter to Theo van Gogh, July 9, 1888

I kissed the hatcheck girl
It was the end of the world.
— *On the Rocks*, Loudon Wainwright III

DECEMBER 21ST

In the distance a dome of white radiance, strange monument in the black of a solstice night. It shimmers beneath cloud and swirling snow, perched atop a cyclone pulsing red and blue. Snowflakes swarm in the car's headlights like stars, like flies, and the highway is a rift gouged from the rolling farmland by the blades of snowploughs. The husky thrum of tires plying the road's slush. Seatbelt intersecting my breastbone as I crane forward, staring into the light.

An ambulance overtakes us. Strobes as it retreats into the distance illuminate the falling snow, forging a multihued halo.

Something bad ahead, she says.

My eyes remain fixed on that light. I can still taste her mouth, eggnog and brandy.

Yes, I reply.

Looks like we'll drive right past it.

I think you're right.

But of course we don't.

CHAPTER I

- - - - - - - - - - - - - - - -

Nathan pulled the car onto the narrow shoulder. He drew from beneath his seat a spiralbound notebook, plucked a pencil from the steel coil. Every few seconds the wipers swept across the windscreen, cleansing away a spatter of rain. He wrote quickly, trying to capture the scene before it transformed, as it always did, as it already had.

OCTOBER 5TH
Plump cloud cruising westward across chinablue sky, churned from the ruffled face of the Atlantic, summoned by the howl of an autumnal gale. In the east, fixed between sky and earth, a curtain of rain and sleet turning the distance to jelly. Clouds the colour of bleached denim, fissured with light. In the northwest a sunbeam has punched through, a searchlight trolling the landscape beside the road, slicing across a paddock, powering the grass an electric green. Two horses near the fence. Nuzzling in the sunshine.

Imagining Lisa's eyes drifting across those words, Nathan felt lightheaded and almost weightless. Momentary lucid connection. He brought the chewed pencil-end to his mouth and listened to the rain, watched the scene blur before the wipers sawed past, restoring the view. A tanker roared by, shook the car, retreated into the distance, its wheels skirted with spray. He rested his fingertips on the base of the steeringwheel and closed his eyes. The pain almost obscure through this padded hush, like thunder beyond the horizon. But a car horn sliced through the quiet and he seized the handle, rammed through the door, stumbled onto the road, fist aloft, shouting curses at the escaping taillights. The car slowed and he felt a gush of adrenaline behind his breastbone, felt the need to twist and smash, wanting that sensation of ribs collapsing beneath the concussion of his fists. A hand emerged through the window, finger extended, and then the car accelerated beyond a rise, leaving Nathan within a quilt of silence pleated by the patter of rain and the periodic sweep of the wipers.

He looked at the horses, sun gone, rain falling harder. The larger of the two, a sorrel stallion with a broad chest and ivory pall, seemed to nod at him, and the mare pressed her cheek to the stallion's throat and nickered.

He slid into the car and lifted the notebook, leaned across the gearshift with an elbow on the passenger seat to better study the sky, and the rain surged, a frothing deluge against the windshield. He tossed the notebook onto the heap of foam cups and muffin-bags on the floor and sat up, pondering the cascade on the glass, the view momentarily reopened by the swab of the wipers. Clarity every seven seconds. Twin diamonds approached, hard and bright, scooted past, a van's wheels hurling a gout of rainwater against the car's door. The sky dimmed. Night falling earlier every day.

Nathan saw his own sad eyes in the rearview mirror. Recalled a woman in a Yarmouth roadhouse, a slurring, halfdrunk nymph with butterscotch hair. You know, she'd said, You're a bit like an animal you find bleeding on the roadside. You stop to help, but it snarls and tries to chew your fucking hand off. She cackled, and Nathan turned to study her, his cheek pressed to his fist, and she averted her gaze, let it fall to the bulge of his bicep, which flexed involuntarily, as if awakened by her attention. He excused himself to use the washroom and slipped away into the stormy evening, letting the chill rain drench him.

Nathan's body, which in his teens and twenties was doughy and pale, had transformed. He'd developed limbs like twisted wire, his frame defined by flat, taut muscles built by relentless exercise, the jerk and pump of freeweights and the Nautilus. He didn't know what had pigmented his skin, age or sorrow or fury, but he now appeared mildly tanned, at times almost sunburned, face flushed, the backs of his hands brown and sprung with coarse tendons, knuckles scabbed from a punch he'd thrown into a man's teeth on the sidewalk outside the Split Crow pub in Halifax three days before. He touched the welt on his ear where the man's wife had bitten him. She'd pounced on Nathan's back and chomped down there as he'd wound to strike again. He'd been defending her from her husband's assault.

He clicked the wipers to fast mode and stepped on the clutch, rocked the stick into first. The clouds were rushing dusk down and he needed a place to sleep, but first something to eat, a diner-motel combo would be best, eat and then crash into bed. He accelerated along the slick pavement.

An oncoming truck flashed headlights and he switched on his own, punched and punched the radio seek button, caught the tail of the CBC news. Weather next, a cold front tearing through, ploughing away cloud, polishing the sky to opaque azure, so familiar he could almost write tomorrow's entry now: blue blue blue, cooling to hazy aquamarine against the horizon, bleached by pale aerosols. He'd read somewhere that pre-industrial skies curved in unfettered blue from rim to rim. If we saw that today we'd sense something was amiss and panic. Our familiar poisons.

Nothing but forest and gas station towns here, the car's broken antenna an impotent stub, so he hopped along an archipelago of CBC transmitters, stations snuffed by the horizon, leaving him in barren troughs of reception, the digital display careening through the FM band, bottom to top, pausing before repeating the trek at 87.5 megahertz. He tuned to the AM band, found it bloated with signals, cranky parades of 50s and 60s tunes, the hoarse shout of a football commentator, and there, crystal clear among the abrasive frequencies, the cool twang of a preacher somewhere in the mid-western U.S.

. . . keep thee from the evil woman, from the flattery of the tongue of a strange woman. Twenty-five: Lust not after her beauty in thine heart; neither let her take thee with her eyelids. Twenty-six: For by means of a whorish woman a man is brought to a piece of bread: and the adulteress will hunt for the precious life.

Nathan stabbed the power button and tried to unravel the relationship between bread and whorish women.

A car on the roadside, hood open. He slowed, saw a figure

huddled in the cabin, drew onto the shoulder ahead of the vehicle. Stepped into the rain and walked to the driver's door, tapped the window which cranked open a few inches, a young woman in a handknit toque peering through the gap.

You need help? Nathan asked.

Are you CAA?

I was just driving by and thought you might need help.

I already called CAA. They said they're backed up some but should be here shortly.

Nathan heard a voice from the backseat and peered past the woman to see two boys, one about five, the other two or three, both strapped into boosters, watching him. Nathan felt a sting of grief, had to swallow before he could say, Hey there, boys.

I appreciate your kindness, the woman said. But CAA will be here any minute.

Pretty dark and lonely out here, Nathan replied. You alone and just your little ones.

He saw the immediate panic his words struck in her, was searching for a phrase and tone to reassure her when she cranked the window shut. He heard the thunk of the powerlocks. He spread his hands in a helpless shrug, but she turned away, stared straight through the windshield. Nathan stepped backwards onto the blacktop, looked up and down the deserted highway, then called loudly, Listen. I'm going to get into my car and just sit there. Wait for the towtruck. Okay? She ignored him and he strode to his car, stepped in, shut the door. Gripped the steeringwheel, rainwater trickling onto his neck. Hating that his presence was terrifying to the woman and her children, but unable to drive away, to leave them unprotected in this dark night. Wanting to help. Not helping. He bent until his forehead rested against the steeringwheel. Clenching his eyes shut. Listening to rain pound the car.

A hard rap on his window. A man in his twenties, wearing a Canadian Automobile Association jersey, smoking. Nathan rolled down the window.

You want to move your fucken car, bud? Can't get the truck in place to hook er up.

Nathan glanced back and saw a white towtruck idling on the highway beside the disabled car.

Did you – does anyone need help? Nathan asked.

It's all under control, bud. You can screw off now.

A wave of anger swept over Nathan. In a flash he'd calculated the next moments of action: launch open his door, catching the man in the knee, and while he was staggering back Nathan would be out of the car, swinging a fist into the man's face . . .

All right, Nathan replied, crushing the steeringwheel in both hands to prevent them from acting. Though I believe I'll stick around until they're safely on their way.

The driver put a hand on the roof of Nathan's car and bent to eyelevel. He shot smoke from his nostrils and said, Bud, she says you're freakin her out. Best to screw off now and leave her be. Bud. Hey bud, you listenin? My next call is 911.

Nathan looked straight ahead into the night, felt a bead of sweat run down his forehead. He could put this guy down in seconds. Assessing the situation. She'd made a call to the CAA. There'd be a record of the dispatch. The greatest risk for her was being ripped off by the garage to which the car would be towed. And then, without taking his eyes off the road, he started the engine, revved it hard, and peeled away, spraying the grille of the disabled car with gravel. He fought to bring his car under control on the slick pavement, then shot away.

He drove too fast, raindrops slamming into the windshield, the grip of the old tires tenuous in every curve, oncoming headlights flying at him with alarming speed, and still he kept on, converting rage into fear, wanting, begging for the ecstasy of destruction, until at last the car entered a sharp bend with too much speed, quartering away from true and drifting. Nathan steered into the skid, swearing as the car slewed, pressing the brake lightly, and the car still moving without regard to the tires' orientation. He cranked the wheel, overcorrecting and skidding onto the shoulder of the oncoming lane, ballast pelting the undercarriage, steep drop to a gutter along the treeline and the car raking the edge and somehow remaining atop the berm, spurring avalanches of gravel.

A transport truck was oncoming, the tail of Nathan's car in its path, and he heard the truck's horn as it came on, aligned to smash the car's rear quarterpanel and send Nathan spinning off the embankment into the forest, until the driver at the last instant hauled the truck to the left and as the tractor came abreast the car it veered out far enough that the truck's front bumper clipped Nathan's rear bumper so narrowly it was a collision of nothing but paint. Then the truck roared past, driver fighting to bring the vehicle safely into the bend through which Nathan himself had blundered, Nathan craning in his seat to watch even as his own vehicle was grating to a halt, watching the strings of orange lights toppling slowly towards the bend's apex, Nathan holding his breath, bending his body against the tilt. There was a moment at which the tipover seemed inevitable but the driver in a display of skill pivoted the tractor in such a way that it rocked the trailer back onto its wheels, a shudder running through its frame, and then it rolled on, assuming the lane.

A sudden quiet in the car. Nathan opened the door and stepped into the rain, watched the truck slowing as it worked through the bend. He went around to the rear of his car, bent to look but saw nothing in the dark, ran a fingertip along the bumper where it wrapped the fender and felt a shallow abrasion in the finish. Panting, realizing how close it had been. He straightened, noticed that the rig had stopped, heard the throb of its engine. The cab door opened and a figure climbed onto the blacktop. Nathan raised a hand to signal he was okay.

Hey! came a shout across the distance. The figure began to walk his way. Hey, fucker!

Nathan squared himself and balled his fists, took a step towards the approaching figure before he recognized how his yen for combat would aggrieve Lisa. He wanted to fight, wanted desperately to throw punches, to take blows, to settle the apparent indignity he'd dealt to this truck driver. But giving in to an impulse had delivered him here, to the dark curve on this rain-slicked road. He'd pledged to resist. He blamed the adrenaline coursing through his body from the near-collision. That he was responding only to chemicals made his rage easier to resist, to disarm.

But to avoid this fight he had to act. His opponent closing the distance. Nathan, hearing the fast knock of the driver's boots on the blacktop, exhaled and bolted around to his door, threw himself into the seat. The engine had stalled, he tried to start it but neglected to push the clutch, the engine croaked and the car surged forward and died. As he saw the figure approaching at a run he jammed the clutch to the floor and twisted the key, starter cackling and the engine at last stirring. But it failed to start, flooded, and he stomped the gaspedal and cranked until at last the engine exploded to life. He moved the gearshift, unable to find first gear and finally struck home, gave too much gas as he popped the clutch, rear wheels churning in the gravel, a dark shape in the sideview obscuring view of the stopped rig, and then he was away, again screeching and yawing down the highway until he was able to regain control, the array of truck lights receding in his mirrors.

He let up, drove reasonably now, hoping the driver was not so inspired by revenge that he would bring his rig about and make pursuit.

Wiping his soaked brow, panting. He slammed the heel of his hand into the steeringwheel.

He had no consciousness of driving the next fifty kilometres, his mind busy replaying the events that had almost led to two fights and a crash. It had started, as usual, with his attempt to help. If he wasn't meant to help, what was he for? Tried to remember his life before the philanthropic impulse had overcome him. He'd been carefree and cavalier once. It was a long time ago.

The rain streaking the windshield and the lustre of oncoming headlights on the wet road made Nathan's eyes throb. But he had no choice but to push on, rubbing his fatigued eyes, struggling to remain alert.

At last a light appeared above the treetops, filling the sky as if from a stadium or a city, but as he closed he found it was nothing more than a strip motel and a diner fronted by high windows. He was grateful for it, pulled onto the gravel of the lot and shut off the engine.

He listened to the rain against the roof and felt instantly refreshed. Tempted to try another hundred kilometres. Almost forgetting he had nowhere to be. He opened the door and stepped into night.

Cold drops pelted him as he strode to the diner's door, pulled it open. No one inside, but music on a radio behind the counter, big band, a compliment to the diner itself, a relic from the 40s or 50s. Pitted chrome, split vinyl in burgundy hues, peeling veneer. He sat at the counter and called, Hello?

A woman of thirty in a stained apron entered and without asking turned over a cup and filled it with coffee. She had a hard, bony look, slategrey eyes, cheeks hollow, a scar under her lip. Hair the colour of dandelions. She pushed out her bottom lip like she'd practised it in the mirror. He looked at the coffee, saw in it a greasy rainbow.

You got anything fresher? he asked.

She turned and dumped the carafe into the sink, poured fresh grounds into a filter, started the machine.

Be a few minutes, she said. You hungry?

I'd look at a menu.

He ran his thumbnail down the typed card.

How's the omelette? he asked.

It's fine. But it's breakfast.

This says allday breakfast.

It's night. And I don't do omelettes. How about a burger.

I kinda want an omelette.

Special burger. I'll lay a fried egg on top.

You'll lay an egg? he asked without smiling.

On top. Fries too?

All right.

He thumbed through a local newspaper while she cooked the burger. The tang of hot fat stirred his appetite. He discovered from the paper's masthead that he was near Cumberland Bay, New Brunswick.

A story about a baby drowned by its stepfather caught his eye. The account nauseated him, summoned a raw fury of helplessness, forced him into that scene as witness, desperate to throw the villain aside and pull the struggling infant from the bathwater. He came out of this fugue with a gasp, the paper's margins crushed in his fists, pivoted on the stool and looked into the dark of the lot, panting, watching the rain.

Goddamn pissing down again, the waitress grunted, and Nathan twisted, regarded her, and she stuck out that lip again and turned away, squatted at a cabinet and rummaged inside. He saw his own expression in the mirror behind the counter, forced himself to soften it. He glanced down, studied the burger. The yellow eye of a sunnyside-up egg stared back. He blinded it with condiments and crushed the bun down with enough force to rupture the cornea. He picked it up and shook yolk onto the plate before taking a bite. He was hungry and ate fast. Pushed his plate away with his thumb and stood, unsteady with fatigue.

What time you open for breakfast?

Six.

Somebody be here to make me an omelette?

Somebody.

He paid and went outside and stood beneath the overhang and watched rain falling like meteors through the sphere of vapour cast by the lone lightpole.

His navyblue Toyota Supra hunched before him, gleaming, sporty and mean, the scars of twenty years on the road obscured by darkness: skin bubbled and peeling, bones salt-rotted and rusting, suspension soft and palsied. Lately when he stepped off the clutch he would grind his molars in sympathy with the slipping clutchplates. The only exception to these debilities was her engine, which had been tuned and modified by its previous owner to a state of scarcely constrained fury.

This car a distant relative of the vehicle it had replaced, a pearlgrey Toyota Prius. Inverted, roof crushed, nose punched in, and the cabin blighted with pellets of safetyglass. Bladders of spent airbags strewn about like jellyfish.

He jerked up his collar and stepped into the rain, opened the trunk. Among empty oiljugs and a set of dumbbells lay his old suitcase. He lugged it to the office door, stepped into the panelled interior. No one at the desk, but a cigarette idled in a dish beside the telephone, a cylinder of ash sagging from its tip and smoke unravelling towards the ceiling. He cleared his throat, waited a few moments and noticed a button on the counter, pushed it, and a doorbell rang in the back. A girl came in, she looked about twenty. Nathan blinked. High, polished cheekbones, honeycoloured hair bound in a ponytail, eyes like blue candy. Nathan was immediately vexed by her beauty, the obligation it inflicted when it colluded with his singleness.

Hello, she said, barely glancing at him as she drew a card from beneath the counter and put it on the desk along with a ballpoint pen. Just the night?

Yes.

He lifted the pen and filled the card, used the Toronto address where someone else now lived.

And your fortune? she asked.

My what?

Your fortune. She threw a thumb over her shoulder at a sign on the wall, silver script against midnight blue: Psychic Fortunes Foretold. $5.

Who does the fortunes?

I do.

How do you qualify to tell fortunes? You go to school for that?

It's a gift, she replied, clicking the pen with agitation.

What kind of things will you tell me?

Where you been.

I already know where I've been.

Where you're going.

You can see all that?

Uh-hum.

What if I don't want you to know about me?

Too late, she said, smiling. I knew when you walked in the door.

Really. You didn't even know I was here until I pressed the bell.

Her gaze faltered.

Sure I'll take that fortune, he said quickly. Please.

He sat on the edge of the bed and untied his shoes, kicked them off. Went to his bag and withdrew the book he was reading, a fat paperback, sat again and opened to a dogeared page, read until *But in that gale, the port, the land, is that ship's direst jeopardy; she must fly all hospitality; one touch of land, though it but graze the keel, would make her shudder through and through.* That dizzy torque of language, stirring the impulse to douse himself in words, in sentences. Turning away, shutting that book, trying to steady his mind, to reconstitute himself in the now. He set it on the sidetable and lay back, fingers laced behind his head, eying the room. Bland walls, freshly painted. Two framed prints, paintings, trees rising above a mosaic of fallen leaves. He sat up, surprised that these were Austrian forests, painted by Gustav Klimt. Buchenwald, Tannenwald. Tranquil scenes, treetrunks retreating into the depth of the canvas. The kind of place he sought. Except something distressing in the paintings' titles. One was the name of a Nazi deathcamp, the thought of which raised in him again that terrible helplessness of inaction.

After charging his creditcard she'd taken his right hand across the counter, traced the creases with a fingertip, her head lowered. Studying his life. He'd felt an abrupt panic, wanted her to stop. He closed his palm but she pried it open, gave him an admonishing look. He watched the top of her head, golden hair drawn into an elastic.

Is it . . . no, she muttered. Oh. Oh no, but why would you . . . ?

What do you see?

She didn't look up, muttered almost inaudibly, Oh, oh I get it. It was all about . . . But then why didn't you . . . when you could've . . .

Nathan saw stars and pinwheels shuttle across his vision, felt the floor pitch, forcing him to grip the counter's edge with his free hand.

. . . because you should've . . . because you didn't . . .

Do you want to come to my room? he barked.

When she raised her eyes they were brimming with tears.

What would your wife say?

My wife? My wife is dead.

I know. What would she say?

He retrieved his hand, drew a five from his billfold and flattened it on the counter.

It's five sixty-five, she said, scooping tears from her eyesockets with a fingertip.

I thought it was five.

You know, she replied, sniffling. Tax.

He pressed his head into the pillow and looked at the ceiling. After a moment sat up, realizing that a dark stain above the bed roughly the shape of Australia was wetness, and a legion of waterbeads was amassing along the southwestern coast. One broke free and fell, striking him on his cheek below the eye, a cold tear. He pawed it away and rolled off the bed and stood, looking up, listening to rain hammer the roof. Got down and rammed his shoulder into the bed, shoving it to the front of the room.

He awoke once in panic at a sound he thought was the door's lock, but after a moment recognized it as the plick of waterdrops onto the carpet. He was fearful not of thieves or murderers but the fortuneteller, using her passkey to enter the room, slipping naked into the bed, accepting his offer. The warm delight of her skin, of human touch, what he longed for but could not accept. Must not accept. He gathered the pillows against him, clutched them in his arms.

A band of sunlight on his cheek, warming it. He looked into the room's centre and saw a swampy pool on the dun carpet between divots from the bed's feet. A pillow crushed in his embrace. He let it go, rolled onto his back and reached up, pulled the blind's drawstring, took it hand over hand until sunlight bathed the bed. He threw back the blankets and lay nude in the warmth. Dozed, awoke when a shadow passed across him. He sat up and looked out, but there was no one.

He showered and dressed and stood in the room's doorway, assessing the day. Much colder, even with the sun on him, the sky a crystal of unmarred blue. High up a checkmark formation of Canada geese, their honking like the stridor of a distant traffic jam. Leaf smell, the spice of decay. Cars and pickups were clustered around the restaurant, two tractortrailers parked along the highway's shoulder. He stepped onto the mottled gravel, each stone shining pale and grey, the shaded side still wet. He put the suitcase in the trunk, went on to the restaurant.

He entered a babbling din and the reek of frying bacon, burned toast, cigarettes, body odour, lurid perfume, coffee. Scanned the room for an empty table and spotted alone by the window the fortuneteller working the newspaper crossword, shrouded in the vapour of her cigarette. An empty seat across from her but Nathan turned away, watched the backs at the counter, saw a man in an oilskin coat settling his bill. Nathan moved behind him to claim the seat. As the man rose he ripped a percussive fart, turned his head and threw Nathan a grin, then lumbered out. Nathan sat.

A pudgy boy with a mop of red hair stalked behind the counter, banging down plates, refilling coffeecups, collecting dishes. An Asian man laboured among clacking crockery in the kitchen, smashing a bellhop's bell with his palm as each meal slid beneath the heatlamps, whacking the instrument into a stuttering peal if a plate languished more than a few seconds. A plump and harried waitress with a broad vocabulary of sighs dashed about and bellowed reproaches at the cook's impatience.

The boy cleared the dirty dishes and set down a coffeecup and filled it. Nathan ordered the omelette. He gazed down the row of diners, seven men, men who worked outdoors or with heavy machinery or both. Nathan watched a chorusline of heads nodding above plates, saw a fork punch through a stack of thick pancakes smothered with butter and syrup; a chunk of toast used to mop the last yellow sap of a fried egg; a toothpick adorned with a spray of blue cellophane drawn from a Western, the sandwich crushed between stout fingers, lifted to a bearded maw.

The man on his right bowed his considerable torso over his

plate as if protecting it from rain, and gripped his fork in his fist as a child does, scooped egg into his mouth. His hands were rimed with engine grease.

On Nathan's left a slight fellow with sparse hair on a shiny scalp was reading the *Globe and Mail*. The waiter served him a saucer of coins and a breathmint and the man muttered his thanks, scooped up his change, left. Nathan leafed through to the sports section, saw that the Leafs had shut out the Sens 6–0.

His omelette arrived – the yellow crescent oozed orange cheese when he broke it with his fork. He ate it, the toast, the bacon, left the homefries for last. As he was salting them someone took the vacant seat. When Nathan looked he saw the fortune-teller watching him.

I'm sorry about last night, she said.

Which part?

I beg your pardon?

Nathan squeezed ketchup onto the fries. Which part are you apologizing about?

Your wife.

He looked at her, swirling a homefry in ketchup.

I'm sorry I reminded you of something painful.

It's not like a day goes by I forget. I'll take the cheque, he told the waiter. He ate the fries quickly, eyes fixed on his plate, could feel her gaze on him.

There's something else.

He regarded her, said, What's that.

I don't know what you need.

Oh. I thought you could see it all.

But you don't either, she replied as if she hadn't heard.

He opened his mouth to answer, closed it.

And that makes you dangerous, she continued.

He waited for more, but she pressed her lips together and looked away.

Well, he said, finding his voice. That's not psychic. It's psychiatric. And you need more than a handlettered sign on the wall to be practising that.

I wanted to warn you, she said without looking at him.

He was going to snap back at that, but saw that the man on the stool next to her was eavesdropping. Nathan downed the rest of his coffee. The bill came and he paid it.

I have to go.

I know.

Oh, your powers. What do I owe for that bit of shrewd clairvoyance?

Goodbye, she said, and before he could stand, she did, leaving through the door to the kitchen while Nathan sat wincing at his own asperity.

He sped northwest through the brilliant day along a four-lane highway. The spectrum of fall pigments. He'd intended to drop in on his brother Rex, professor of English literature at the University of New Brunswick, but just ahead of the Fredericton exit Nathan threw the car into third to pass a semi, gnashing the gears while tormenting the engine into a plaintive wail and flinging the tach into the red. The car shuddered and decelerated and the offramp shot by on the truck's far side. He missed the subsequent exit while fiddling with the radio, and the third was closed for construction. As Fredericton dwindled behind him and he hurtled towards the Quebec border Nathan succumbed to a feeling of powerlessness. Rex's gruff voice, fading. Nathan would have to phone and explain. Not while driving, of course, but at the next convenient stop. Criticism delayed, filtered through the gauze of distance.

He gassed up after Edmunston, pissed, bought a shrinkwrapped tuna sandwich, a jug of lemonade, a box of Smarties, gorging himself like a bird before a seacrossing. He knew just enough French for it to be useless in Quebec and intended to cross the province in one mighty leap. The car could do almost seven hundred kilometres on a full tank, if he kept the speed down and constant, stayed in fifth. With a tailwind.

He was halfway across when he realized he'd forgotten to call Rex. Opened his phone and keyed in a good part of the number before he snapped it shut and tossed it into the seat beside him. The first risk was that Rex's wife Hester might answer. Last time Nathan had called she'd buttonholed him, demanding to know when he intended to move on with his life, put his dead family behind him and find a new mate. Her word. Like he was a zoo animal, caged for the purpose of procreation. Rex wasn't much better. There could come from his brother only criticism, no comfort. So like their father, that frank tyrant who insisted that people – especially his sons – were all of a particular hue, and for them to behave outside that character – for example, to try to be generous if you were at heart greedy – could lead only to woe. Be who you are, he always said. Nathan had been many things in his life, and each had brought its own joy and misery.

He drove relentlessly eastward, past French signs, the motels advertising free xxx movies, the towns a procession of saints along the highway: Saint-Octave-de-Métis, Saint-Eugène-de-Ladrière, Saint-Paul-de-la-Croix. The Toyota's engine grumbling beneath the hood. His greatest fear was breakdown, suffering the injustice of a mechanic's cultural resentment. If the engine persevered, nothing could stop him.

He was wrong. Near Quebec City a plume of chalky cloud rose into the noonday sky, and somewhere above ten thousand metres the slicing torch of the west wind struck it, forcing a great curling plate of vapour towards the Atlantic. He drove with his head lowered to evade the strip of cobalt tinting along the top of the windshield. He spied red lights at the perimeter of his eyesight, had to jam the brake to avoid striking the car ahead, which had slowed to allow a fueltanker entry onto the highway. He pulled his notebook from the floor of the passenger seat and sequenced his attention between it, the sky, and the traffic, paging to a fresh leaf. He grasped the nub of the pencil's eraser to draw it out, pressed the notebook to the steeringwheel's hub.

October 6th

It was as far as he got before the car before him braked hard. Nathan dropped the notebook, drove his foot into the brakepedal.

The wheels locked and the car twisted nauseatingly away from true, the hood's corner driving towards the tailgate ahead like an axe towards a block. He threw his head into the headrest, bracing for impact.

The car stopped. A cloud of smoke continued on the car's abandoned vector, struck the Volvo ahead like some presage of what could have been, then split around its chassis, dissipating. Tang of cooked rubber.

The car ahead paused and Nathan braced for – hoped for – confrontation. But the car took off and Nathan followed numbly. A sideroad ahead and he threw on his blinker, took the exit at speed.

The road wound uphill, past a dealer of docks and rafts, wares laid out on a dry lot, a speedboat parked on gravel and moored to an aluminum pier. He crossed railroad tracks, drew into a dirt lot beside a railway spur where rusting boxcars stood in their frocks of graffiti. He shut off the engine and got out, spread the notebook on the car's roof, and gazed up to watch the towering cloud as it was lazily scalped by the shear of wind across its crest.

OCTOBER 6TH

Rare autumn cumulonimbus, a fat, undulating column decapitated by the westerlies, torso shuddering in a slowmotion seizure, writhing eastward. His heavy belly bruised, bleeding rain, a long arras of stained light draping the countryside. Snagged on hilltops, drawn taut above hollows and swales. Soaked in the blood of the sky.

Nathan's vision of Lisa's hands clutching the notebook as she assessed his words was interrupted when a threewheeled ATV leapt from the brush on the lot's far side, sprawled on the dirt, and rumbled towards him trailing a plume of dust. It slowed as it passed, the driver's helmeted head cranking around to look, a sinister apparition with chrome eyes, oval grille mouth, a blister of polished acrylic for a nose. A gloved hand rose, thumb raised, and the craft sped away over a crest and into the scrub. Nathan got into the car, corkscrewed it about in a spray of dirt, and recrossed the tracks before racing down to rejoin the highway.

He hit Montreal's rush hour, boxed in by transport trucks and minivans, sporadic accelerations before taillights flashed on in the long snake of vehicles before him. Fatigued clutch foot, drumming the wheel with fingertips, rolling down the window to combat claustrophobia.

By the time he reached La Station-du-Coteau the fuel gauge was sagging below empty. He stopped reluctantly at a service station, was relieved to be spared the nuisance of human interaction by the pump's automated creditcard reader.

He got back on the highway and crossed into Ontario, where a sign showing the distance to Toronto sent a wave of dread ripping through his core. A hole in the map to him, a smoking crater offering nothing but the fallout of his destroyed life. So he turned north, zigzagged along rural routes and highways, north then west, north then west, as if tacking into a gale.

He tore along a sideroad of fissured and bleached pavement, crested a swell where the sun low in the sky blinded him through the dusty scrim of the windshield before the car plunged into the shadow of a hill. He passed a leaning henhouse, its boards weathered and roof blushing green beneath a mantle of moss. The car climbed again and the road banked northward then shot straight and flat between the boles of naked burr oak and willow, the sun stuttering through branches. Nathan cracked the window and chill air poured into the car, and he drew deep lungfuls, cooling the heat in his belly. An abandoned structure surrounded by a parkinglot appeared on the side of the highway and Nathan slowed and ducked to study it through the passenger window and saw mounted to an iron pole the sign, an ice cream cone. He drew into the lot in front of the structure's glassfaced serving counter and shut off the engine. He opened the door and stood, an elbow on the roof and his foot on the doorsill, and sucked in the autumn air, the sweet rot. The quiet interrupted when a gust of wind stirred the poplars, the sound of their jittering leaves like surf on a beach. The little shop appeared handbuilt, framed in wood, sided with strips of stained board, roof of painted tin. He stepped away from the car, shut the door, pushed his hands into his pockets and approached the window, the counter a slab of varnished oak, the wood ornamented with initials and hearts and dates. A crack in the window, its source an impact point like an exploding star surrounding a dimesized hole. Nathan moved an eye over it and peered through, saw a crater in the board on the back wall on which flavours and prices had been handpainted. He turned and looked into the forest across the highway.

Tiger Tail. Bubblegum. Pralines 'n Cream. Low on the back wall a tarnished outlet and a snake of dust, residual path of the freezer's powercord. Everything pillaged or sold for scrap.

Sydney never tasted ice cream.

This thought burst uninvited into Nathan's head. Never tasted ice cream. He'd bought her a cone only once, from an ice cream truck that had lumbered stiffshocked onto their street one summer evening bellowing a lurid melody, but as the tip of the girl's tongue was about to make contact Lisa had plucked it from the girl's hand and tossed it into the greenbin. Sydney had shrieked in blind outrage while Lisa quietly rebuffed Nathan. He knew better. Refined sugar, absolutely not, this little girl raised on organic applesauce and brown rice. A year and a half of life and never tasted ice cream. What good had it done her, that calculated diet of quinoa and kale?

No, Nathan said aloud. No.

He pressed a palm to the counter in front of the sliding window where cones were once traded for coins, and sensed the ghost of his daughter on his hip, longing for a taste. Nathan watching her first tentative lick. Shocked first by the cold, then as she pressed her tongue to the roof of her mouth and the cream melted and the taste bloomed, the startle of chocolate-peppermint.

Nathan bowed his head, filled it with whitenoise and blaring nonsense to drown those images polluting his thoughts, pictures of the two of them inside their rotting boxes, bodies succumbing to the corruption of death. The tongue for tasting ice cream a blackened stub within the rictus of her jaw.

Nathan reeled backwards into the parkinglot, came charging with his shoulder as a ram, crashed into the shack with such force it shuddered to its foundation. He backed and launched himself again, struck the same spot, and this time the structure took the blow and leaned backwards, creaking and popping. The third time he struck he was rewarded with a traumatized crack, and the thing began to topple slowmotion away from him before it settled on its broken haunches, a kneeling parallelogram. Nathan jogged away and was ready to rush again to deliver the coup de grace when he heard a car approaching on the roadway. He ran, but this time passed the broken shack and raced between the poplars and into the bush, his shoes slashing through the carpet of newfallen leaf, red whips of dogwood snapping against his jacket and face as he bolted for the forest's heart, for that silent cradle of forgetting. He ran until a purling grew distinct, and he was brought up on the bank of a river, a rapid of churning buttermilk, and he squatted on a flat boulder slick with translucent slime. He watched the flow, felt the bruised cramp of his shoulder as he unfocused his eyes and let the sight of foaming water drone into his subconscious, scouring away thought. He knelt on the rock, wet cold soaking through his jeans, and plunged his hands into the river. The icy water sucked heat from his fingers, made them throb and ache as the cold penetrated to bone, but he maintained them there, froth spuming over his wrists and wetting his jacket's cuffs, and when the pain grew immense and the impulse to rip his hands from the punishing water surged, he instead jerked his head skywards and bellowed his agony, and only when his back began to spasm and he nearly pitched facefirst into the deluge did he withdraw his hands and fall back on his heels and study his fingers, seized into talons with skin that looked boiled.

When he stood and tucked a hand into each armpit and looked to the west, the sun lay low beyond the treetrunks, illuminating a pale mist shrouding the forest floor. He stepped from the rock into the sea of leaves and walked towards the road, shading his eyes from the sun. A moment later it fell from view and he felt immediately cold in the shade that rose to fill its absence. The sound of the river diminished and when he stopped walking the hushing of the sibilant leaves left a deep and restive quiet, and when he looked up he noted that sunshine still gilded the trunks and branches above. Fog huffed from his mouth with each breath, and he watched the boundary between night and day against the bark of a birch, saw it slide towards the tree's crown like a waterline, darkness inundating the woods, drowning him. He went on with growing dread that he might find waiting at that shack its owners, ready to prosecute him for his vandalism. But when he arrived it stood as he'd left it, alone and glum and purposeless, leaning back from the spectre of his car as if with aversion. He had to resist a powerful impulse to finish it off. He got into his car and started the engine, cranked the heater, blew and rubbed his hands. He moved the lever to the defog setting and watched heat from the vents erode the drifts of moisture illustrating the glass. Looking at the structure he felt a sudden rage that it remained a standing, purposeless wreck. Thought about ramming it but feared damaging his car, instead peeled away, leaving its conclusion to rain and wind and rot.

He found a convenience store a few kilometres down the road, bought pop and potato chips and a jellyroll, paused at the magazines and took down the latest *Vanity Fair*.

He sat under the car's domelight, chips cracking between his teeth as he flipped through ads and features, reading halfheartedly of ostentation and outrage, skimming bumptious predictions of the next fad, turned the page and was heartstruck by a woman in a perfume ad. She was naked and barely concealing with a bowler hat her alabaster breasts, while a bolt of amber silk snaked across her belly and between her legs, and the sight of her lovely face and perfect skin invoked a nauseating ache in his chest. Without thought he pried open the sample flap and was punished when a toxic vapour of vanilla and lilac flooded the car's interior. He pressed the flap back and shut the magazine, scrolled it tightly to contain the odour but it was too late, the air was caustic with it, and as he started the car he tossed the magazine into the backseat, the reek his penance.

The approaching headlights along the highway bloomed into spheres of haze and he knew he had to stop, but the two motels he'd passed were closed for the season, so he turned onto a secluded roadway and rushed through a corridor of trees, his own headlights casting a meagre glow on the dirt road until the discs of retroreflective markers along a picket of white palings guided him through a curve and down a slope. The road ended at a steel gate beyond which a trail continued into the forest, and he parked, shut off the engine, levered back his seat. Squirming on the cracked vinyl, trying to find comfort. There was none for him, but he was used to that, and he slept.

A clunk awakened him, and he bolted upright, pulse racing, and he saw in the dawn light a fat raccoon tottering on the car's hood, staring through the glass at him.

Shoo, he said, waving.

It leaned forward until its nose met the glass, then sat back and pondered the smudge it had left. Nathan struck the horn, the sound of it braying through the forest and startling not just the animal but himself. The coon reeled back and bared its teeth, then leapt off the hood, hobbling into the brush.

He looked at his watch: coming up on seven. He put on the domelamp and drew a map from the doorpocket, unfolded it. Stay north, through Algonquin perhaps, on up to North Bay, Sudbury, Elliot Lake, the Soo.

The girl at the drivethrough gave Nathan a wary assessment as she handed him a jumbo coffee and a sack of muffins.

He paused at the parkinglot's exit to peel open the hatch in the cup's lid, and he craned the rearview mirror towards him, studied his bloodshot eyes. He passed the back of his hand across them, combed fingers through greasy hair. He appeared to be translucent, studied his hand to gauge his solidity, looked back and realized he was seeing himself reflected in the mirror's secondary plane, the one for night driving.

He met Highway 60, drove westbound and passed through the eastern gate of Algonquin Park. He grew addled by the caffeine and the signs that warned of crossing moose, deer, bear.

He slowed to the speed limit, eighty kilometres per hour. It brought a tranquility he rarely felt. In Ontario, where only the decrepit or insane drove the speed limit, Nathan now felt the soothing approbation of Lisa's gaze. It had twisted her into knots, the highway rush of thirty over the limit, the "speed of traffic," people called it. Like a universal constant, like pi, but really just a threshold tolerated by the Ontario Provincial Police. Speeding raised her ire not for its illegality, but for the fact that pollution increases significantly, startlingly, with speed. Exponential drag or some such nonsense, Nathan never paid attention, he was too busy speeding. Why don't you close your eyes, honey, and let me drive. He'd seen her speed herself when her mind wandered, and her sister told him before she'd learned of its environmental impact she was a demon of speed – her good looks enough to convince most traffic cops to excuse her with a wink and a warning.

Now, for Lisa, for the untold legion of wildlife he imagined crouched in the underbrush ready to spring onto the blacktop to be crushed in bloody sacrifice, he kept to the posted limit. Within moments he'd incurred a tailgater, an enormous blue suv. Nathan watched the driver in his rearview, saw no apparent expression of frustration, but at the first clear straightaway the driver swung into the left lane and passed in an explosion of acceleration and exhaust.

Sorry, Earth, Nathan said.

A minivan took its place. When it passed in a similar manner, Nathan again muttered the apology. The van was replaced by a car, then another, and another. The procession extended by car and van and truck until he could see when he rode through a curve a snake of vehicles stretching out of sight. Every clear straightaway resulted in a swarm of passing vehicles, and as each drew abreast Nathan's resolve to stare straight ahead faltered, and he glanced sideways into glowers and handgestures. These only enhanced his defiance. You want something to get riled at? he shouted. How about poverty? How about famine and genocide!

The road began to twist, the passing lines remaining solid, yet many drivers were willing to risk death for twenty more kilometres an hour. So fucking sorry, Earth! Nathan shouted, glancing at the entourage accumulating behind him.

Sweating, furious, he struggled out of his jacket and threw it into the backseat. The speedometer's needle glued to the eighty mark. The flesh of his knuckles stretched taut and bloodless over the bones as he gripped the wheel. Rage felt good. He wanted to haul the steeringwheel over, jerk the handbrake so his car pivoted sideways, making a barrier into which that tailgating throng would plough, car and van and truck, in a massive pileup of greedy speeders, his last act, a mortal lesson for those mindless pursuers of velocity. His right hand curled around the handbrake's stalk, ready to pull.

But he met in his mind's eye Lisa's expression of disapproval. For she'd also been a pacifist, a subscriber to the philosophies of Buddha and Gandhi. He realized as he tried to suck calm into his lungs with oxygen that wrecking his own car along with countless others would hardly qualify as an environmental act.

He saw a picnic area ahead, thought it best to shed that great parade. He guided the car along the gravel ramp past bearproof garbage bins, drew up before a pair of outhouses and got out, watched through the treetrunks the surge of vehicles accelerating along the highway like auto racers revelling in the withdrawal of the pace car. Quiet here, feeling the fury drain from his limbs. He drew a breath of air and it was sweet. He spied motion from the corner of his eye and reeled to see a black towtruck rushing at him. He froze as the cylinder of his vision cinched around the sight of the approaching bumper. He thought he might die, and it surprised him to discover his ambivalence at the prospect. In the last year he'd experienced moments when he'd been eager for death, had considered suicide more than once. At other times he'd felt it his duty to live, to survive, to earn penance, to mourn, and, as he had just now with his speed reduction, to propagate Lisa's good works. But he'd never felt such a clear balance between the two states. Well, he thought, as the truck bore down, this will go one way or the other.

The grille halted a halfmetre from his chest. The driver reeled out, a burly man in black with a meaty gut and an unkempt beard.

He wore a baseball cap with the brim to the back, and he drew a wheezy breath.

You fucken fucken fuck.

Nathan remained motionless before the grille, felt the heat from its radiator.

You slow fucken fucker. What the fuck are you fucken doin drivin so fucken slow, you fuck. You slow fuck.

And so on. The man's harangue went on for a minute or two and ended with a series of questions – do you think you own the fucken road? is your head full of shit? you like guys like me riding your fucken ass? – and as no opportunity to respond was provided, Nathan determined that each was rhetorical.

The man finished, his chest heaving. Nathan hadn't budged. The driver opened his mouth to continue, but something halted him, perhaps Nathan's failure to react in any way. They stared at each other for a moment and Nathan felt a sudden inexplicable fellowship with this man, and since grief occupied the foremost chambers of Nathan's spirit he figured that grief must be something that they shared. Maybe there exists a physiognomy of woe, something recognizable only by kinship of the stricken. Nathan was reaching for words to introduce this topic when the man whirled and climbed into the truck. The hot grille withdrew and as Nathan watched the man's face through trees and sky reflected in the truck's windshield he witnessed it again, the grim mien of sorrow.

Hey, Nathan said as the truck pivoted and began to roll towards the highway. Hey, I want to talk to you!

Nathan panicked, watching the truck go. He squatted and cast about on the ground, found a lemonsized rock. The truck was accelerating, already fifty metres away, but Nathan had years ago fielded for a hardball team, had nailed more than one runner at the plate with a colossal hurl from the rightfield fence. He threw hard, expecting the rock's irregular shape to send it awry, but the throw went true; the cab's rear window flashed white, a keen crack sounded across the distance, and the glass poured like coarse liquid into the truck's bed around the tow rig. The vehicle hadn't quite stopped when the driver tumbled out of the cab and sprinted towards Nathan brandishing a tire iron. Nathan crouched, his mind struggling with how best to ask his attacker if he was also suffering from sorrow and loss. As the man arrived Nathan rose, sidestepped the descending iron, and shot out a turned foot, felt his heel connect with the man's kneecap. The man pitched forward and Nathan heard the concussion of the iron striking the ground beside him, saw it eject a divot of earth. Nathan's own knee rose and struck the man's face with the plate of his patella. The man stumbled backwards, wobbling on his damaged knee, then clamped a hand over his nose, faced Nathan while hefting the iron. He stepped forward, and in a gesture of curious elegance, as if bestowing a blessing, he swung the instrument in an arc which cut the air before Nathan's eyes. A practised manoeuvre, Nathan thought, backing away.

I think I know the pain you feel, Nathan said, mortified at his choice of words. The pain of a broken nose? The pain of a shattered kneecap? The man released his nose, wiped it with the back of his hand, smearing blood and mucous across his cheek. When he looked up again Nathan saw in the narrowing of his assailant's eyes that he was entirely possessed by rage. Fury, Nathan knew, is sorrow's antidote. The iron swung, swung again, a lethal pendulum. Even without the weapon his attacker had fifty pounds on him and probably dozens of brawls. It was tempting to answer with his own anger, tempting not just because of its effect on grief, but because it made combat a pleasure rather than a chore. But it made you lose.

Nathan stepped through the iron's orbit as the weapon rose to his attacker's right, knowing that the man's control and power were weakest at the outside of the swing. Nathan formed his left hand into a flat fist, fingerjoints sharpened, and fired two fast jabs into the man's wrist. The hand opened as if Nathan had pressed a button, and the iron fell, struck the ground with a clang. The man was still reacting when Nathan threw a series of swift punches, starting in the soft paunch, rising to the solar plexus. Just as he struck the hollow below the breastbone he boxed the man's right ear with the flat of his palm.

A torchlight of pain erupted in Nathan's right foot, and as he reeled away he realized that the man had stomped on his instep. The pain was spectacular, and for seconds his mind seized and anger threatened to erupt, but he took a breath and limped in a semicircle outside his opponent's reach. His attacker went for the iron.

Nathan kicked with his injured foot because he knew he couldn't stand on it while kicking with the other. It was a fast, cheap move, less of the judo kick he intended and more like what in the schoolyard would constitute fighting dirty, but they had no audience, and the iron factored in the potential lethality of this contest. Nathan's shoe caught beneath the man's chin and fetched him up off the ground. The man rolled onto hands and knees, crawled towards the weapon, and Nathan kicked again, sent him sprawling. A shock of pain ran up Nathan's leg with each kick that followed, and the man rolled and grunted helplessly. Nathan stopped and the man curled into a ball like a woodlouse rolling into its louvred shell.

Nathan hopped on his good foot, spotted the tire iron, bent, lifted it. He saw the man's eyes shift, following the motion of the tool. Nathan kneeled and lifted it high above his head, thought the man would rise to parry but he lay still, panting, bleeding into the soil. Nathan brought the tool down hard, struck the earth a hand's breadth from the man's ear. The iron's elbow lay embedded in the soil. He drew it out, climbed wearily to his feet, tested the weight on his bad foot. Then he spun, made two rotations, and released the iron like an Olympic hammer, watched it arc through the trees.

He hobbled to the outhouse and went in, letting the spring-loaded door whack shut behind him, stood panting in the noxious dark, his eyes upon a slice of daylight penetrating through a gap in the boards. At last he pissed into the rank hole and when he came out he hoped to find the man gone but he lay where he'd fallen. Nathan squatted beside him.

Listen, he said. I'm sorry about what happened here. I didn't want to fight. I didn't even expect to hit your truck with that rock. A fluke.

The man panted, porcine eyes shifting.

I want to know something. About you.

The response a vicious grunt: Fuck off.

Nathan wet his lips, said, I sense something. I know it's weird to say, but I have this feeling about you. I think you're grieving.

Fuck off.

It's a kind of mutual recognition.

Fuck off.

But that's just a theory. I'd need to know if you really are in the same state as me. Then I'd know.

Fuck off! the man roared, and lunged, a fist flying out and cuffing Nathan' nose, not hard, but enough to knock him back and send his hands to his face, probing for blood.

Nathan stood, brushed off his jeans, eyes watering.

Well, Nathan said. You have a nice day.

The man let out a guttural wail, and twisted so his bloodied face lay in the dirt, and began to howl with great whooping sobs. Nathan stepped back, watching for a moment before he backed away.

He pulled onto the highway, flipped his cellphone open against his chin, dialled.

Yes, I'm calling to report an injured person. He's at the rest stop on the north side of Highway 60, just inside Algonquin's west gate. A towtruck driver. No, I don't know his name. He appears to have been beaten. He's conscious. I don't know. Maybe a bear attack? No, I am no longer at the scene. I understand but I'm no longer there.

He snapped the phone shut, realized he was offering an incriminating amount of information. Wondered if they had his cell number. Or could they pinpoint his location with the signal? At this last thought he crushed the accelerator to the floor. The speedometer shot through 120, 130, 140. A backhoe was cruising the shoulder ahead, one great wheel turning on the asphalt, and he jerked the car around it, heard the shriek of rubber as he jolted back into his lane. A few minutes later a police cruiser crested a hill and ripped past, lights flashing and siren wailing. Nathan tightened his grip on the wheel. He had to get off this route.

He saw a sideroad ahead and stood on the brake. The magazines strewn across the backseat scuttled into the backs of the chairs. Tires hit the road's gravel and slid towards the ditch. There was a yellow post and Nathan forced himself to look not at it but in the direction he wanted to travel, and the car's rear flank struck it with a whump. Then the car was following through the manoeuvre, centring on the new road. A pall of dust rose behind him. He ripped along the gravel road, speeding through sickening descents and rising again to crest hilltops, briefly airborne before crashing down on the suspension. Drifting through turns, scattering gravel, past cottage driveways and mailboxes, the force of concentration and fear required to maintain the road blending with the adrenaline of the fight. When the road t-boned a highway he blew past the stopsign and drifted onto the asphalt and drove hard until he came upon a minivan plodding along at the speed limit. He swung into the oncoming lane and tore past, kept at it until the geography abruptly changed, forest replaced by rolling farmland. He took another sideroad. The country surged in great rolling hills like the backs of whales, the next progressively higher than the last, and when he reached the height of land he stopped the car, launching a hail of gravel into the undercarriage.

He got out and limped around the car and looked at the dent in the rear fender, a smudge of yellow paint filling its trough. He looked at the sky. The silence after the road pressed against his eardrums, and the breadth of the heavens seemed to suck him skywards. He was shaking, panting, sweating, replaying the last hour in his head as he tried to determine what had gone wrong. Holding to the speed limit and suddenly fighting for his life against a madman. Or a man gripped by sorrow, like himself. Or so he'd thought, and he'd thrown the stone to find out, escalating the confrontation. He'd done terrible violence to another human being. In self-defence. Should he have stood passively as that man attacked him with that tire iron? He looked down and saw his own hands splayed, palms up, as if he was pleading for under-standing. From Lisa. What way back into her heart?

He studied the clover and crabgrass in the ditch. A farmhouse with a derelict barn stood below him, and as his ears settled he heard the seethe of wind through the grass. He got out his note-book and smoothed it on the car's roof.

OCTOBER 7TH

Grainy blue sky. Rushing from the southwest like a fleet dis-patched to quash that azure audacity, a flotilla of corrugated cloud. In the gap between sky and land, instances of rain, maybe sleet or snow, falling like a heavy gas. One cloud is a bunched fist, knuckles punching through the heavens. A cold wind climbing to meet me now, smell of rain, scented like earth from an upturned rock. Earthworms and millipedes sprinting for cover.

Eyes shut in the tight whirlpool of his thoughts. Knew he was trying to distract Lisa from that fight. A strong gust of wind poured across the hill, cooling his hot face, and he raised his eye-lids, panned the landscape, gnawing the pencil-end. A sparkle of sunlight drew his gaze to something rotating on a distant field, bigger than a windmill, a great turning wheel like a piece of exposed clockwork, like a mechanism of the spinning Earth.

He got in and drove, down now, down, down along washboard roads, past farms and sheds and machinery for sale, heading blindly in the direction of that wheel. He stopped once on a low hill and looked west but he'd lost it, got in and kept driving.

He rounded a bend and there it was, a ferris wheel rotating against the blueblack cloud, lamps threading its frame like gem-stones. He followed a sign for Fairgrounds Road, found its margins clogged with parked cars. He slowed, looking for a spot. The entrance gate, where two codgers in toques and sweaters stood chatting, each identically posed, arms hugging their torsos. One of them waved him through the gate.

It's seven dollars. You can park on through there.

He drove slowly over the grass past a steel barn, a chain of temporary fencing beyond which teams of horses trotted past, driven by men in canvas coats. Families marched by, heading for the midway, the food concessions, men with eyes like nailheads, hands plunged into jacket pockets, their softfleshed and sulky wives grasping in each hand the hand of a child.

Nathan piloted the car up a slope and through a gap in a treeline to a field of pickups, minivans, horsetrailers. He parked and got out and opened the back door, donned his windbreaker, ambled back through the treeline and into the midway.

He trod the flattened grass past games backdropped with stuffed toys crucified on display racks. Airgun balloon pop or toss a ring onto a jarneck or two-dollar roulette spin on a clacking wheel. Stepped over cables fed by the chug of generators. Diesel oil, onionrings, frenchfries, cooked meat, trailers and vans with side-hatches propped to make awnings, and beneath them curlyhaired matrons doling out hotdogs in foil, slim packs of mustard, relish, ketchup. Garbage cans overflowing with cardboard and styrofoam, the stubs of hotdog buns, fries in a slush of gravy, pop cans, patrolled by regiments of coldstunned yellowjackets. And then the spinning rides, toddler motorboats in a trough of milky water, mini tractortrailers, motorcycles, gyring cupshaped buckets, tiny dragon rollercoaster, derelict carousel and the clangour of its calliope, horses frozen in jaunty poses, oblivious to their marred and peeling skins. And there the Ferris wheel, less substantial than it had appeared from the hilltop. Every ride he realized beginning and ending at the same point, as if an incrimination of leisure, nothing accomplished, no distance conquered. The Conklin clown's grinning, deadeyed countenance everywhere, the cardinal of some jolly cult.

People here, farmfolk and townfolk, people in workclothes or untidy bests, husbands and wives, kids and teens, grandmothers ambling on their canes or walkers. Nathan met eyes boldly as he walked, he was searching for contact, for acknowledgement of some kind. Some held his eye, most didn't, and he grew grudgingly resigned that there would be no human touch for him today, maybe ever. The heartpang at this thought sucked the breath from him.

Then Sydney at his knee, taking it in, the little wedge of her hand in his, straining, but when he releases it and she is allowed to surge ahead she pauses, waits for him, springing through her knees in a series of unresolved hops, head whirling with excitement, what next, what next?

Wind rising, whipping from every compass point, bringing first the pink sweetness of cotton candy, then rain. He bought some coupons and waited in the brief line for a ride called the Sizzler, three arms branching from a hub, and upon each arm four cars above which rose fans of yellow lighttubes. He wanted to spin. As he waited with his hand on the galvanized fencerail he watched an acnefaced boy operate the levers that controlled the ride. Anything could happen. The thought exhilarated him. He watched the riders as their cars were thrown towards him in sequence, saw their desperate delight. The ride slowed and stopped, security bars unlatched, riders disembarking. Then the boy opened the gate and collected tickets, muttered Thank-ya identically to each patron. Nathan walked to the far side of the ride and climbed into one of the cars, drew the bar shut. The padded bench was worn along the fore-edge, and on the siderest ballpoint initials and hearts scarred the cushion.

He gazed into the fat clouds above. Sunlight slanted beneath them, warming him through the thin coat. He saw high above him raindrops falling like marbles, each gob of liquid burning with sunlight. They struck around him. One hit the oxidized shell of the car, and when it broke it was nothing but water.

The operator was arguing with four girls in the car ahead of Nathan's. He could see only the backs of their heads. The boy's hands shot around him like he was directing traffic as he explained some kind of violation. Finally he popped the safety bar and one of the girls stepped out. The boy approached Nathan with the girl following.

Excuse me sir, but would it be okay if she rode with you?

The girl looked horrified. She turned and saw the other girls with their heads craned around, their coarse grins.

Yes. Certainly, Nathan said, and the boy opened the bar and the girl reluctantly clambered up.

No, sit on this side, Nathan said, moving. Otherwise I'll squish you.

The girl slid to the far end of the car and Nathan rested his hip against the sidepad.

Thank-ya, the boy said, secured the bar before he returned to the controls.

I'm Nathan.

She crushed her eyes shut then opened them wide and stared imploringly at her friends, who taunted her with gestures before turning to face forward.

The ride powered up, began a slow rotation. Nathan studied his ridemate; she looked to be about sixteen, but who could tell? She might be twelve or twenty-four. She had a chubby face, dirty-blonde hair, much of which was tucked beneath a woollen hat, though strands had struggled free against her cheeks. She wore hoop earrings and dense makeup around her eyes. She turned and saw his study, bit her lip, then looked straight ahead as they accelerated. He liked her nose in a way he didn't usually like noses.

He turned his gaze outwards as centrifugal force began pressing him into the cushion, throwing his mass towards the fence before drawing it back into the ride's hub. He abruptly felt the girl against him.

Sorry, she giggled as she grasped the bar and hauled herself towards the bench's far end. The next rotation threw her back into him and again she struggled away with a laugh. He looked out at the midway, the sequence of flashing bulbs atop a haunted house, the stop and go of the Ferris wheel as passengers disembarked and boarded. The lights on its frame brilliant against a backdrop of menacing sky. She was there again and panting from the effort.

It's all right, he said. Better that you just stay there than keep crashing into me.

Her laughter ceased and she looked away. The raindrops came frequently now and he gazed into the sky, enjoyed the vertigo of those careening drops, felt the pressure of her body against his, the corporeal warmth of her through her jeans and his. That touch felt good, feeding such a terrible longing that it seemed his entire consciousness was gathering along his flank at the points of contact – shoulder, arm, thigh, knee – desperately soaking it in like parched soil drinking rain. Even now mourning his losses, and the loss that would happen when the ride finished. And he loved the ride's swirling drunkenness even as he wanted to be sober, to be alone with his fury and sorrow, back in his car and driving. And then oh god no, chewing his lip when he found himself getting hard, his cock crushed uncomfortably within his jeans. Furious at the intrusion of sexuality, trying to govern the response with deep breaths, then realizing she could feel every one of them. On an outside orbit he discovered no operator at the controls. He swung his head around, searching the perimeter of the fence, the pockets of people standing on the grass. Panic rising in his belly. Around and around. Nathan's arm trapped between his body and the girl's. He pulled it free, stretched it out atop the back of the car, felt the chill of aluminum through his sleeve. The sun vanished behind cloud and a shiver went through him. His cock painfully erect.

The girl raised her head to him and said, Trippy! Only then did he smell the booze on her breath, a sweet aroma of rum.

The kid, he said. The operator. Where is he?

Looks like he fucked off, she said, and cackled. So we ride forever.

Oh hell, he muttered.

After a minute they slowed and Nathan saw the boy again at his station, drawing back the control stick. The pressure of the girl against him subsided, and she scooted down the car away from him. They stopped and the boy made his rounds, opening safety latches and liberating the riders.

Come on, open it up, the girl called as her friends approached.

Nathan's arms were numb, as on nights when he awoke on his belly clutching his pillow.

She reached over the bar and undid the latch, threw the barrier aside. Her friends were there, babbling, and when Nathan stood he twisted on the footrest as if to step backwards onto the earth, but really to conceal from the girls the distinct bar of his penis within his jeans.

He saw the girl's eyes light upon it before she looked up, her mouth slightly agape. He stepped down, pushed his hands into the windbreaker's pockets to conceal his erection, and shuffled out of the ride's pen. He moved fast, trying to escape the mob of girls. Arousal subsiding. Raindrops against his face. One ran into his mouth. He bought a Coke in a plastic cup, drank half before tossing it into a wastebin. A carnie gestured at him with an airgun. Someone tried to sell him a raffleticket.

He rounded a concession and there they were, in a bunch, chattering and laughing, prodding each other, and then a flask made a round, disappeared. She saw him and he pivoted, strode away. He entered the steel barn he had passed on the way in. The tang of manure filled his nose and beyond a yellow rope a heifer ambled past followed by a teen with a cattleprod. The boy tapped the cow's haunches as she moved around the ring. The arc-lamps hummed in the ceiling, and a scattering of spectators watched from plank bleachers. He heard the pop of rain on the roof.

The floorboards shifted like piano keys beneath his feet as people walked past. He passed into a bustling chamber with row upon row of tables crowded with produce. He pressed through the crowds, the din of voices submerging him in a fog of dislocation as he looked at the vegetables and fruit on display, much of it oversized or grotesquely deformed. Apples the size of cantaloupes, carrots as long as his forearm, pumpkins and squashes either of elephantine proportions or malformed into hideous, tumorous shapes, blotched skins erupting with barnacles. And there were ribbons adorning some of these, purple, red, gold, Biggest Cucumbers, Ugliest Pumpkin. He moved slowly among them, came to a display of tomatoes that were each as big as his head.

A voice was speaking to him, directed to him but he could not make out the words above the shout and chatter of the room, could not even detect its vector, until he turned and looked down and saw the girl from the ride looking up at him smiling.

Hey, she said. I said how's it goin?

Nathan looked around, hunting for her friends who were no doubt spurring her on this dare, but she'd come alone into this bellowing mob and when he looked down she was staring at him in breathless expectation.

I didn't tell them, she said. What I saw.

What did you see? What do you want?

Just, you know. She moved closer and ran her knuckles against his thigh. To do that to you again.

He seized her wrist, pulled her hand away.

What do you want? she asked, not drawing her arm from him, letting it dangle limply in his grasp.

This, he said, pushing his hand into her palm, lacing his fingers through hers. He squeezed her hand staring intently into her eyes, and after a moment she squeezed back. He looked away, looked out above the tables and heads bobbing as people shuffled through the aisles, gazed up into the faint fog shrouding the lights, and felt the quickness of her skin against his, his heart hammering in his chest, and he held on until the precise moment his libido awoke, and then he let go and moved away, shuffling against the crush of bodies, not looking back, hearing above the voices and laughter the clatter of rain on the roof, pressing through to the room's exit and manoeuvring through the crowd standing in the barn's entrance. Drops fell in streaks like tracers, beads of hail erupting from the grass. People stood in clusters beneath the game or concession awnings, gazing out at the rain.

He noticed the Ferris wheel was still in operation, the gondolas each protected by a canopy. He still had ride coupons, and as there was no lineup he handed a strip to the raincoated girl at the console and climbed aboard. He rose into the turbulent sky, gazed down upon the other rides, tractors and trucks, horses driven by their masters towards trailers, saw into the parkinglot where his own car glinted with raindrops. In the west a breathtaking view, the sun shining defiantly as clouds approached like a mob of bullies. Rain spilling from their guts. He looked away from the sun, and over the landscape arched a rainbow of such insubstantiality he had to blink to be sure it didn't exist only on the cones of his retinas. He reached the apex of the ride and his cellphone rang.

Hello?

Where are you?

It's you.

It's me. Where are you?

There's a rainbow. Barely there.

But where are you?

You'll never guess. I'm at the top of a Ferris wheel.

As the gondola dropped a spray of static filled the phone.

Hello? Hello?

Halfway up again the wheel stopped to discharge passengers.

Nathan? Nathan? a voice muttered through the hiss.

I can barely hear you.

The gondola rose one position and the static subsided.

. . . any better? she asked.

Yes. Not perfect, but yes, he replied.

I want to know how you are.

I'm fine.

How are you handling things?

I'm just driving. Mostly driving.

Are you ready to come back yet?

To what?

The car rose again, and the connection cleared completely. He could hear her breathing.

Mabel?

The ride moved again, reached its peak. The rainbow was gone. Rain falling harder. Wind blowing it beneath the canopy. Hitting his jeans, cold, each drop like a driven nail.

Someone called me dangerous today, he said with a laugh.

She was right.

Who said it was a woman?

Wasn't it?

He was quiet.

Nathan, there are people who care about you.

Yes.

Lots of people.

I know.

Isn't that what you need? Nathan. Nathan, are you still there?

Mabel, why do you call me?

Because you need me to call you.

Ah. It wouldn't make any difference.

Do you want me to stop?

Silence. The wheel turned, paused. He would lose her soon.

Nathan?

I better go. We're going to lose this connection.

Okay.

Goodbye.

She hung up but he didn't lower the phone, pressed it harder to his ear, imagining her standing at her kitchen window, looking down the long gravel drive to the highway. Mabel. Who saw them die.

CHAPTER 2

By the time he reached the car the rain was hammering down, drumming against the roof. He got in and stripped off the soaked windbreaker, balled and tossed it into the backseat, started the engine. The car's tires churned through the quaggy earth of the slope and figures in raincoats or clutching umbrellas darted past his headlamps. He got on the road and when he reached the stopsign at the highway he saw in his rearview mirror two OPP cruisers approach from the north and round the corner to enter the fairgrounds. Nathan turned onto the highway and headed west at eighteen kilometres per hour over the posted limit.

By late afternoon the rain had subsided and he pulled up before the Choo Choo Roadhouse, a single car in the lot. A rusting caboose of sunbleached orange stood against its east wall, one window shattered, the other boarded with plywood. The sign above the bar's entrance displayed a steam locomotive screaming through the countryside, greasy smoke pouring from its stack. Someone had spraypainted a grinning mouth and dots for eyes around the headlamp nose, like Sydney's videos of petulant steamengines with static faces and rolling eyes.

He got his ragged paperback from the trunk, went inside into the smell of stale cigarettes, alcohol, meat. As he stood in the doorway he heard a whine and clatter and looked up to see a locomotive the size of a shoebox pass over his head towing a retinue of boxcars. The rails circumscribed the deserted room and Nathan watched the train make one revolution, over the booths along the right wall, the bar at the back, the jukebox, doors to kitchen and toilets, the pooltables in the left corner, more booths and tables. When it passed again over his head he started for the bar and sat with his feet on the rail. He studied the bottles behind the bar.

Like glass trophies, they were flushed with light from below. The rich ochres of whiskey, the incandescent clarity of vodka and gin, the florid vista of liqueurs. Like his father, he was salivating at this spectacle of spirits, bottles of liquid stupor. The haze, he realized. Today, in this dark room, away from the sky's volatile palette, he craved the haze of forgetting.

The kitchen door opened and a paunchy woman of sixty with a head as round as a honeydew entered from the back carrying a platter of sliced lemons and limes. She halted when she saw Nathan at the bar, said, Sorry, we're not open yet.

How long?

Twenty minutes.

Twenty minutes. I can't just get a drink?

Not yet, sir.

Mind if I just sit here?

She came forward, stepped behind the bar saying, You're cute. So I don't mind.

It's twenty minutes.

It's my liquor licence, she stated as she slid the fruit into their stainless pots. She sucked the citrus from her thumb and said, No hard feelings, eh? I'm Claire.

Nathan.

She watched him briefly, then drew a quarterglass of beer from one of the taps, swirled it, watching how it lathered the vessel's sides. She sniffed it and tossed it into the sink. He opened *Moby-Dick* to a dogeared page and read until he found himself in the throttle of words, *For as this appalling ocean surrounds the verdant land, so in the soul of man there lies one insular Tahiti, full of peace and joy, but encompassed by all the horrors of the half known life.* He recoiled from the storm they stirred in his viscera, opposite to what he wanted to achieve in this place, and he closed the book, and looked around at the railroad paraphernalia on the walls.

Why so glum, Nathan?

He looked at her, annoyed to think he was broadcasting his emotion, said, Glum. I'm not glum.

Aren't you.

No.

Well you look like maybe you been fighting.

Fighting.

Yeah. Like you just gone a few rounds. She raised her fists and boxed the air.

Oh, Nathan stated flatly, his face hot.

I'm just teasing.

I know.

You're sensitive. I'll stop now, you're way too sensitive.

She busied herself behind the bar like a magician preparing her implements. Abruptly she stopped in front of him, said, Well, that's twenty. Thanks for your patience. What'll it be?

He had to ponder a moment what she was asking before he replied, Jim Beam. Straight up.

She set a shotglass on the bar and got down the bottle, poured.

He tapped the rim said, One for yourself.

That's generous, but I couldn't. I'd be asleep by dinnertime.

Later then.

You plan on staying?

Does it get good here?

Saturday night? It gets crazy.

All right. Today I need crazy.

The train circumnavigated the room. Every few minutes a gambling terminal at the end of the bar played a tinny rendition of "Rawhide" and a cartoon cowboy strode onto the screen, presented the barrels of two revolvers, and fired. A prodigious stream of pixelated coins spilled from the bores. The train clattered past again across the trestle above the bar.

Does that toy train drive you crazy? he asked Claire.

What toy train? she replied with a grin.

As he sipped he felt the alcohol soak into his brain, each heart-pump surging it through the arteries in his neck, permeating like a rich, brown syrup. He downed the rest and shut his eyes, imagined his conscience slipping off behind him, now at arm's length, retreating, making for the door.

Let's have another, he said.

It wasn't long before people began to collect around the bar, and a heavyset man with wireframe spectacles and a nose like a boxcutter sat beside him and ordered, then aimed his bleary eyes at Nathan.

Hey, he said.

Nathan nodded.

The man passed a hand roughly down his face from forehead to chin, his lower lip flapping wetly. He sighed loudly, said, Debugging.

What? Nathan replied.

Debugging. Computer program. Sixteen hours. Step away from your keyboard it takes forever to get back in.

Claire tossed down a coaster, set upon it a pintglass of cider.

Thomson Barlow, the man said, stuck out a hand.

Nathan. What's the software?

Java. For a poker website. You know, Texas Hold 'Em. I created this new hunt-and-retreat algorithm, learns from the player in six hands how much losing he'll tolerate, adjusts itself accordingly to keep the guy in the game.

Isn't that cheating?

Not cheating, Thomson replied without offence. It's nothing human players don't do unconsciously.

Seems like cheating, Nathan said.

It is, a voice at Nathan's right called. He turned and saw a woman with pale skin and straight hair dyed the colour of plums perched on the stool beside him. She wore a v-neck sweater and a burlesque lace choker, gothic in its filigreed design.

Then reading a tell is cheating, Thomson said. Get out the blindfolds. Nathan, this here is Nina. Nina, Nathan.

Hey, blindfolds, Nina said. Now you're talking.

Nathan looked at her again, said, What are you drinking?

Nothing at the moment, and it's pissing me off. Claire!

I mean I'll buy you one, Nathan said. When Claire arrived Nathan told her, I'll have another. And the usual for Ms. Nina.

Aren't you a fancy gentleman, Nina said. And she added in a drawl: I do declare. Bartender, make it a double.

Like he said, Thomson muttered through the side of his mouth. The usual.

Fuck off, Nina barked. I'm talking here to Mr. Nathan. She pivoted her barstool and put a hand on his forearm, continuing with the twang, It's awfully nice to meet you, kind sir. Are you here to stay or just passing through?

Through, Nathan replied, and their drinks arrived, hers a rum and coke.

Stay awhile, she said, and sipped.

I might just do that, he replied, drinking.

Aw, make me puke, Thomson said, lifted his drink, and went off to join an elderly couple at a nearby table.

Nina stirred her drink with a finger, sucked it, then lifted out an icecube and set it on the bar. I should be nicer to him. Probably gonna be rich, the fucker. How about you, Nate? What are your plans?

Nathan said nothing for a moment, attempting with his increasingly impaired brain to determine his direction this night. She lit a cigarette, blew a beam of smoke over his head, offered him one. He took it, accepted the flame from her lighter, and inhaled, felt instantly that sweet nicotine buzz. He said, I'm seeing the country.

What's it look like?

A lot of trees.

She pushed the icecube about on the varnished bartop, said, What do you do? Or what did you do before you started cruising?

It's not interesting.

I want to know.

I was a fundraiser.

A funraiser? I like the sound of that.

Fundraiser. Money for not-for-profits.

Oh. You're one of those annoying people on TV. With all the starving kids.

Yeah. What about you?

Schoolteacher.

One of those annoying people at the front of the class, Nathan replied.

She poked his shoulder with a fingertip, laughing.

I teach grade one. Teach. Ha. It's babysitting. Hey Cowboy Joe, she called, looking past him. A widechinned man with melancholy eyes and a cowboy hat sat beside Nathan.

Evenin' ma'am, he replied, and touched his brim, then added in a tightlywound English accent, Fucking cold in this place.

I actually think it's getting kind of hot, Nina said, tugging at her sweater.

I'm not referring to the building's interior. Out there. Is it going to get much colder?

Oh yeah, Nina laughed. Today was practically tropical.

Shit and fuck, Joe replied. He looked at Nathan. Sorry mate, I'm Joseph Caston.

Cowboy Joe, Nina corrected him.

Only in your class. And at birthday parties and bar mitzvahs. To Nathan he asked: Hey, you need a cowboy?

Everybody needs a cowboy, Nina giggled.

What kind of cowboy are you? Nathan asked.

Oh, a singin', sawin', twangin' cowboy, y'all, Joe replied in a florid drawl. I sing "Home on the Range" and other canticles about kitchen appliances. Haw. Barkeep!

Claire looked up from where she was filling a glass at the beertaps, called, What can I get you, Cowboy Joe?

Oh shit and fuck. A Glenlivet, neat. Double. No, better treble it.

The room's din began to thicken, fuelled by alcohol and nicotine, inspired by weekend abandon, and Nathan let it buoy him, did not retreat from the pressure of Nina's knee against his thigh. Joe proved to be eloquent as he groused about the country he'd found himself in, lured by an Internet romance that had turned sour and left him marooned. In Britain he'd happily played a cowboy, but his arrival in North America had destroyed his confidence even here in Ontario's near north, as if he'd been billed at the Grand Ole Opry. He'd turned to children, who wouldn't care if he sang Hank Williams like Prince Philip.

After an hour and four scotches Joe slipped into a blue funk, and his voice fell to near inaudibility beneath the hubbub so that Nina had to pitch forward to hear him, which brought her shoulder and breast into frequent contact with Nathan's arm. He could smell her perfume, a sudsy, floral odour like restroom handsoap.

At half past ten Cowboy Joe took a final swig and left his glass upturned atop a small stack of bills, slipped away. Nina seemed ashamed of her advances, withdrew, retreated to the washroom, leaving Nathan abandoned at the bar flanked by vacant barstools. He stood up and stretched, stiff from driving, from sitting on this chair all evening. He scooped peanuts from a bowl on the bar, they were salty and good and he realized he was mightily drunk. He'd had nothing but bourbon for supper. He scanned the room for prospects. Around the pooltables women in miniskirts, tights, lace and appliqué showing under the hems of blouses or cresting bra cups. One woman was in a tubetop. Their hair feathered, bobbed, curled, streaked. Wearing pumps or cowboy boots, stilettos, ballet slippers, makeup like greasepaint, menfolk circling the tables in waltzes of machismo, brandishing cues like rifles, eyeing each shot with the grim focus of a sniper, relentlessly cool, reacting not at all to success or failure. Dancers in awkward gyrations to the stiff beat of the jukebox, longhair rock of the 80s, a 60s hit, then something recent Nathan didn't recognize. Parties of four, six at a booth, a long table littered with beer pitchers, men in hockey jerseys and t-shirts bellowing at the TVs. He was finishing his sweep when he locked eyes with a pale redhead alone at a booth. He looked away but when his eyes came back she was still watching, her expression not of sexual engagement but rather more analytical, almost anthropological. She held a pen poised above a notebook as if conducting an audit or survey, and she was dressed in a beige jacket, a blouse buttoned to the neck. Pretty in a wholesome way, like a sunflower, like pie.

Nina returned, demanding, You're not leaving – are you leaving?

No, he replied. Stretching.

Her hands fluttering along his lower back, saying, I give a wicked backrub.

I need to . . . you know, use the . . .

Okay, so go, she said with irritation. I'll be here.

He focused on simulating a sober gait as he aimed for the door of the men's room. No memory of passing through the door, vague recollection of a long, heavy piss, eyes wet, while a succession of men visited the neighbouring urinal. His forehead against the cratered plaster, and as he draws it away the graffiti resolving.

Nina sucks.

And beneath it, in another hand: and sucks

And again, in marker: AND SUX

He blinked and read it again. Cock stirring in his hand.

All wrong, all wrong, he thought, cramming it back into his jeans, squirming his hips to manoeuvre it into place. Turned and saw the man beside him jerk his head away and stare into the pitted wall.

Need help with that? the man muttered into the plaster.

Nathan pretended not to hear, backed away, zipping his fly, staggered to the sink, ran the cold water. He swabbed his hands on his jeans, escaped. When he hit the room's din he froze, disoriented by the smoke and noise, the heady flux of pheromones. A figure brushed past, muttered something indeterminate into Nathan's ear, a proposition, it was the fellow who'd spoken to him in the washroom, rejoining his buddies at their pitcherstrewn table, merging his voice with their gruff tumult.

In Nathan's spot at the bar a chunky man, red bandana tied around his bald head. Nina bending into him, pawing his arm with such undiminished enthusiasm the man might be Nathan's understudy. The show must go on. The barstool on the man's right vacant, but Nathan thought this usurpation a sign. Still unsteady he rotated, gazing at the tables, until his vision again met with the redhead in the booth. He strode to her, almost succeeding at maintaining an appearance of steadiness and poise. When he arrived he faltered, his thighs pressed to the table's rim and his mouth ajar, nothing to tell, and she watched him in merry stillness.

At last he said, I have a notebook like that.

Spiralbound? she asked.

Yes, he replied. Yes, spiralbound. Cardstock cover. Lined pages.

What are the chances? she wondered.

Minuscule, he said.

Infinitesimal, she added, and then, when he didn't reply, Well. You'd better sit down then.

He slid onto the bench opposite, squared himself before her. They sat regarding each other, and at last Nathan said, Hello.

Hi, she replied.

I'm Nathan.

Victoria.

A waitress with blonde highlights and a lipsticked grimace brought a drink for Victoria. For you? she asked Nathan.

One of those, he said, nodding at Victoria's glass.

Victoria crushed her lime and dropped it in. Nathan watched her. She was startling, not beautiful in a conventional sense but compelling in her selfconfidence and composure. When she smiled it stirred a warm hymn behind his breastbone.

Are you here alone? he asked.

Of course not. Just look at everybody, she said, waving at the room.

All right, Nathan laughed.

Two women passed the table, eying Nathan with suspicion. Marcy and Lee, I hope your mum is feeling better this week, Victoria said boldly, yielding from each a timid nod before they shuffled away.

What are you working on? Nathan asked, pointing at the blank page.

Victoria chewed her pen and looked across the table. A speech I have to deliver in a couple of days, she said.

A speech? On what?

You probably wouldn't be interested.

Sure I would.

You're new to Abbey Grove.

Well. I'm passing through.

His order came and as he folded his left hand around the bedewed glass his gut clenched at the thought of more booze.

You don't seem married, she said abruptly.

What?

She reached across the table, poked his wedding band.

He stole the hand away as if she'd stung him, then cautiously returned it to the glass.

She's dead, he said softly, and when she leaned across with a hand cupped behind her ear he had to repeat it. The words knocked her back in her seat, and she apologized with practised proficiency. He had a crazy thought she might be an undertaker.

The presence of death humbled them each into reticence, until Victoria reached across the table and took Nathan's hand in hers, pressed it firmly while smoothing her thumb across the ring's polished arc, and when her eyes rose she looked at him with such intimacy that it brought to Nathan's diaphragm the impulse of a sob. Something menacing must've clouded his expression, for she let go and dropped her face to the notebook, flipped a page back and pretended to read what she had written there.

The speech, she said without looking up. It's on the topic of philanthropy. On doing right in the world.

Seriously?

She looked up, said, You think that's silly.

No, not at all. It's just. That's what Lisa did. Lisa, my wife. Well, she worked for the Ministry of Community and Social Services, but that was only part of her passion. Being on the boards of a bunch of humanitarian organizations ate up most of her time. United Way, Casey House Hospice, Amnesty International.

Providence then, that we meet.

Yes, Nathan said. Fate. It's because of her that I became a fundraiser. Was. Am. Was.

Are you or aren't you?

I don't know what I am anymore. A fundraiser. A husband. A father.

A father? she asked, and he looked at his drink. She cried, Oh Nathan! and when he looked up her eyelids were squeezed shut. Then she opened them and broadcast their full intensity into his own, asked, You lost them both? Together? When?

Almost ten months. Sydney. Lisa and Sydney.

How old was she? Your little one?

A year and a half.

I'm sorry. Nathan, I'm so sorry.

It was a car accident. Wintertime. There was a snowplough and . . .

For some seconds they were both silent, until he looked up at Victoria and smiled, and he was now wary of her ability to provoke confession. Though he couldn't accuse her of trickery, for all she'd done was ask.

And suddenly Nathan was talking, words pouring out like a testimony, prattling to this stranger about Lisa, about her potent intellect, her tender nature counterbalanced with intimidating fervour. Her infectious compassion.

Not that I recognized that in the beginning, he admitted. And not, he added, lowering his voice, Not that I would even have cared, in the beginning. I wasn't much good before I met her.

How's that?

I was a son of a bitch. He laughed to mitigate the contempt with which he'd said this, then sat forward, explained, Sorry. I don't mean to insult my mother. She was also a saint, so I question, given the way I was, that she could have given birth to me. My father, my father is a bastard, so maybe that's the dominant trait. The way the world is, you'd think so.

Victoria seemed prepared to answer this theory, then closed her mouth and folded her hands. A roar rose from the assembly of men below the televisions, and handshakes and beer toasts were exchanged to celebrate the accomplishments of distant players with whom these men were affiliated by nothing more than pledge and commerce.

Still watching their blearyeyed elation, Nathan muttered, I was that. A cog. A gear. A consumer. Mindless participant. Nathan dropped his voice to a savage whisper, said, All I saw when I first met Lisa was that she was fucking hot. He fell back, face flushing, muttered, Sorry.

It's okay, Victoria said.

I've said too much.

Nathan. Please. I'm just listening.

It wasn't just behaviour. It was me. My character. Who I was. My attitudes. The poor? They're just lazy. The environment? Why should I sacrifice my fun and get nothing useful in return?

He thought back to that other Nathan, how he was defined by everything he wanted from life: hockey, action flicks, girls, driving fast, and a world of merchandise he was forever trying to finagle for cheap or free: booze, cigarettes, junkfood, porn, grass, gas, gadgets. He didn't want to think of landfill or starving kids or pesticides or atrocities committed by the West in the interest of big business.

Hell, life was a lot more fun then, he said with a laugh frayed by hysteria. He lifted his drink and jiggled it so the icecubes rang the glass like a bell.

Is that what they're like? Victoria asked, nodding towards the hockey spectators.

Yes! No. I don't know. I also learned not to generalize, he replied. So I don't know. I can only say that's what I was like.

How did you do at school?

I did well, he said almost mournfully. I did well, until it no longer served my purpose. It alienated people I wanted to impress. And I loved books, until someone called me a bookworm, and I started to see that they were interfering with fun.

I adore books, Victoria said.

He sat up suddenly. My book. I left it . . . He glanced at the bar where Nina was tipped against the bald stranger.

Victoria followed his gaze, said, Do you want to go back over there?

No, he said quickly. But my book is there. *Moby-Dick*.

Moby-Dick? Gosh, you're serious, she laughed. Don't worry. I'm pretty sure no one will steal it.

I suppose, he said, noting that Nina had hooked her finger into a beltloop on the back of the man's jeans.

So you're reading again.

Yes, he said, facing her. Actually, I have been for a while. It was the hockey strike, if you can believe it. In 2004 the NHL players went on strike.

Well, not technically a strike, she replied. A lockout. More than three hundred days. A year without hockey.

Oh. I'm sorry, I didn't mean to suggest that everyone who likes hockey . . .

Nathan, relax. Really, you try too hard. So the lockout made you start reading again?

Yes. Exactly. I was moping about one evening during what should've been the playoffs and Lisa suggested that I pick up a book. So I did. *The Sheltering Sky.* I got hooked again. Even started to write things.

He thought about telling her of his first, infantile attempt to describe in writing a sunset. They'd been visiting Lisa's grandmother on the west coast, it was in White Rock, British Columbia, the windwhisked waters of the Georgia Strait lacquered with sunlight. Lisa standing barefoot in the surf, Sydney on her hip, both of them watching him scrawl upon the back of a café receipt his fervid rendition of the scene. Desperate to capture this moment of utter perfection, for it seemed at the time, and even now, the pinnacle of his life. The voluptuous calm it had brought him to record it. And later, in the guestroom of Lisa's grandmother's house, Sydney asleep in the playpen so they were both forced to whisper, Lisa reading the piece, the transformation of her features into awe.

You're a writer! she'd hissed.

I'm not a writer, he replied.

You are, you are. This is sublime!

I am not a writer, he repeated with force.

Say what you will, she said, smiling, her eyes drawn back to his words on the chit. Only a writer could put words together like this.

I can be or not be what I want, he'd cried, and Sydney woke, and Lisa gave him a reproving look and went to the playpen to rub the girl's back.

My father's a writer, he said so softly she didn't hear. His father, newspaper writer, editor, failed novelist. His father and the inescapable edict of fate. Be Who You Are. Choice is a fiction. You can try to be something else, but like a weight on a string energy must be expended to draw it away from plumb. And to plumb you shall always return. How to explain to her that he must prove his father wrong, that he could be what he wanted to be, or not be. And he would certainly not be his father.

The next day she'd bought him that spiralbound notebook. Write, she'd said as she handed it to him.

Why?

Save the world.

Writing can't save the world.

It can better than anything else. If you write the right thing.

And what's that?

The truth.

He'd snorted, and she'd replied, When you write the truth, people will want to read it. And when people read, they stop talking. And when they stop talking, they start listening. And listening leads to compassion. And compassion can save everything.

Nobody reads anymore.

And look at the world. If you write the right thing, people will read it.

The right thing. What a cinch.

Start with the sky. Write about the sky. See where it goes.

He hadn't, not once, until . . . after. That original chit with the description pasted into that notebook. Page one. And now he couldn't stop. A bridge back to that transcendent moment, a pipeline to Lisa standing ankledeep in seawater, holding their child.

Instead of all this he described to Victoria meeting Lisa for the first time, he was thirty years old, a wedding, his supervisor Jason from his job, his old job, reaper of the city's ailing trees, days spent suspended in a bucket above street or park, pruning with a chainsaw what they affectionately referred to as lawsuits. Standing beneath some deciduous victim Jason might say as he indicated various treelimbs, That thick lawsuit will have to come down, and that one too, that bit of litigation with the bark coming off.

Lisa was a bridesmaid, he told Victoria. She was in this hideous green dress made from an odd twill, the other bridesmaids all looked ludicrous, like shrubs in a school play, but Lisa – Lisa was something else, another species, mostly because she wore this expression like she didn't give a damn what she looked like. Though, that's not really it, because it's hard to remember a situation in which Lisa didn't care in some way. Like she was incapable of indifference. In that green dress it was more like she knew she was dazzling. A self-fulfilling prophecy. I think I am beautiful, therefore I am beautiful. I couldn't stop looking.

Show me a picture, Victoria said, and Nathan drew his billfold from his back pocket, lifted a flap, pushed the wallet into her hands. You're right, she said. She's breathtaking. And this is Sydney? She looks like her. And you.

Nathan winced at the use of present tense. He took the wallet back, hadn't looked at the picture, did not look now. He thumbed out a card, said, I still have her birth certificate. Sydney's. Health card. Social insurance card. You're supposed to send them back, but I didn't. Couldn't. I claimed they were lost. In the accident.

Victoria was silent as he folded the wallet, stowed it back in his pocket. Then she said in a way which sounded reflexive, They're with God.

He nodded, said, She made me better. They made me better.

Nathan thought he should tell Victoria about the fight with the towtruck driver, but he compressed his lips and looked into the room's bustle. The bar's cacophony seemed to surge, music roaring, voices collectively rising to a crescendo, as if this moment had been appointed the evening's climax, but all of it reached the booth as if from some immense distance. He looked at Victoria, her green eyes, her face powdered with freckles. Jolted by the realization that she was wearing no makeup.

Her eyes rose to look past his shoulder and Nathan turned and saw standing uncomfortably close behind him an emaciated young man, not much more than a boy except for the violent tapestry of tattoos on his arms, and his bruised, reproachful expression. His chin bristling with stubble and the hood of his ragged jacket pulled up on his head.

Hello Edward, Victoria said cautiously.

Edward stabbed his hands into his pockets and bent over the table, eyeing their drinks.

Hiya, he said.

Nathan smelled the metallic tang of the alcoholic, and bile filled his gut. He looked into the boy's fissured eyeballs, then looked past him as a figure charged across the barroom. It was Nina, her expression livid.

No one's buying you a fucking drink, she hissed, taking Edward by the elbow and pivoting him towards the door. The boy jerked himself free, hinged forward on his bony hips, landed the flat of his hand on the table, and focused his gaze on Nathan.

She's hurtin my self-esteem, he said with a halfgrin.

You got to get lost now, Teddy, Nina said, and Edward's eyes jittered under the shrill fury of her voice.

I been lost before. Didn't like it, he told Nathan.

Maybe you didn't give it a chance, Nina said.

Nathan glanced past the scrawny stalk of Edward's arm at Victoria, who was watching with a look of serene curiosity, watching, Nathan thought, like a scientist.

Edward brought his sweating face to Nathan, croaked, Listen friend, if I could get one drink, one drink, then everything would be okay.

A drink will solve everything? Nathan asked, suppressing the seethe that crept into his voice.

Ya, Edward grunted. Is it so much to ask? To fix a guy's life for an hour?

The waitress was passing and Nathan flagged her.

What are you doing? Nina cried.

You like whiskey? Nathan asked Edward.

Jesus Christ, Nina said.

Who's paying? the waitress demanded.

Get this man a whiskey, Nathan said. Canadian Club.

Now just a goddamn minute, Nina said. He's not even allowed in here!

He's only banned because he can't pay, the waitress said. If this guy's paying then what's the diff?

The diff, you sullen bitch, Nina stated quietly, is that he's a goddamn junkie.

Oh for chrissakes, Edward cried. One drink! One drink and I leave all you fuckers alone.

The waitress was soon back with the whiskey. She set it on the table.

Hey, hey, the waitress huffed as Edward's hand shot towards the tumbler. Someone pay for this first. It's five forty.

Nathan paid while Edward drank, the muscles in the boy's throat jerking with each swallow. Even when the glass was dry he kept his head tilted back, and Nathan saw through the facets of the glass the boy's black tongue roaming the glass's interior, lapping remnants of liquor. Then he rapped the glass onto the tabletop and barked, Another!

There was a stunned silence at the table and Nathan looked for the first time in some minutes at Victoria, who was sitting forward in her seat, lips parted, staring rapt as if at some staged drama.

More? Edward whinnied into the pause. Just one more, mister.

I said one, Nathan replied mildly.

Ah shit, just one more, okay? he grunted, his hand closing on Nathan's forearm. Do a guy a favour. Can't you do a guy a favour?

He just did, Nina said as she gripped Edward's arm and tried to pry it away.

Mind your own business you cocksucking slut! He squirmed out of her grip and lunged at her.

Nathan slid off the bench and caught Edward around the waist, and the boy twisted around, fists rising. Nathan took a few weak blows to the chest and chin before he moved the boy away with an assertive shove. Edward reeled and stumbled, then raced at Nathan, bellowing. Nathan delivered a quick jab to Edward's stomach. The boy sagged to the floor, gasping and bawling. Nathan had meant only to immobilize the boy, but Edward was clutching his belly as if he'd been gutted.

Look, I'm sorry, Nathan said, crouching. The boy lifted his tearstreaked face. Nathan proffered a hand. Let me help you up.

The boy struck like a viper, closing his teeth around Nathan's hand just above the root of his thumb. Nathan had to swing his left fist twice into the boy's face to knock him loose, and Edward fell whimpering to the tiles. Nathan rose, gripping his hand, examining it. A crescent of florid toothmarks arched along the inside of his palm, and he turned his hand over to see the bite's antipode. He grazed with a fingertip the stutter of near-punctures, wincing. Then another hand was on his, and Victoria stood before him, and she brought an icecube to his skin, passed it along the little indentations, and she turned the hand and repeated the treatment on the back.

Any trouble here, Miss Victoria? a gruff voice asked, and Nathan looked up and saw two sandyhaired brutes in hockey jerseys standing before them, arms akimbo, straining minutely as if containing the impulse of violence, yet throwing deferential glances at Victoria.

It ought to qualify as trouble, Marvin. But it's done now. Maybe you and Jeffrey could help Edward up, she said, her attention focused on Nathan's hand, and the two men brought Edward to his feet and held him upright between them. The boy's head lolled and Victoria lifted his face. She placed the icecube against his cheek and the boy winced. Hold it there, she told him, and he brought his hand up, cupped it over the cube.

Nina, Victoria said, maintaining her gaze on Edward's wet face. Nina, take your brother home.

Nina looked momentarily vexed and was about to protest, but the two men were already manoeuvring Edward towards the door, and Nina followed, her stilettos clacking on the floor like gunshots. Nathan glanced at the bar and saw her bald companion watching the exit with a frown. As soon as she was gone his eyes shifted to the crowded room, and he began a slow scrutiny of his remaining options.

Well, that was something, Victoria said, taking her seat. She gulped her drink. Nathan remained standing, looking at her. Sit down, she said.

He did, drew ice from his own glass and clutched it.

Who are you? he wanted to ask, but remained mute.

Are you sulking? she asked.

No, he replied, looking up and trying to laugh.

What then?

Ashamed, he replied.

Why?

Because of what I did.

You bought that boy a drink. It's what he wanted.

Altruism, he replied. Not that simple.

Nathan didn't mention the rage he'd felt at Edward's request, nor did he describe the scent of the alcoholic – the scent of his father – that had prompted his specious act of generosity.

You knew what would happen, he said after a long silence.

I didn't know you'd buy him a drink. Or that he'd jump at his sister. Or that you'd defend her, and end up getting bitten and then punching him.

But you knew what would happen, he repeated. Like you know clouds bring rain. Nathan flattened his hands on the tabletop, said, I hit him gently. I only wanted to stop him.

I know that Nathan. You're not looking for a fight.

He thought of the towtruck driver, passed a hand over his eyes. He said, Fights look for me.

Rage attracts rage.

Do I seem angry?

She didn't reply, just watched him. Yes, he wanted her to say. Yes, Nathan, you're furious. Incandescent with rage.

You're fit and handsome, she said at last. Oh, don't pretend you don't know it. But there's also a damaged look in your eye. Perhaps to men you appear desperate or threatening. Though it can have the opposite effect on women, as I'm sure you've discovered. It arouses a nurturing instinct.

Is that what it arouses? he said with a laugh. You've got me all figured out. I guess you're some kind of psychologist?

Not professionally, she chuckled, and started to slide out of the booth, said, I'll be right back.

He began to rise and she held up a hand.

Relax, Nathan. I need to use the ladies' room. Don't move,

okay? She stood and walked to the washroom door, glanced at him, went in.

Nathan sat, feeling flushed and lightheaded, trembling. He looked at his drink, thumbing the condensation from the glass, studied his injured hand. Violet toothmark sickle. He flexed the thumbjoint, felt nothing. Then he glanced around the barroom, as he hadn't done in some time, and was startled to face a legion of caustic stares. His behaviour with Edward would've seemed shameful to uninformed spectators, but there was something else to those expressions that made him sense they were reproving him for a different violation, and he couldn't think what that could be until he looked across the table at Victoria's half-finished drink. Was she some kind of local celebrity? A singer-songwriter or the weathergirl, maybe the mayor? He returned the glares defiantly and they faltered, faces dropped, stared into drinks.

Their disapproval bolstered his determination and as he sat rotating the glass on its saucer of condensation he composed in his head phrases he would use to ratify the seduction of this woman. But he immediately faltered at this thought, ashamed, and he put his head down on the table and threw his arms over it, trying to shut out the hubbub, wishing he wasn't so goddamn drunk. She was lovely and smart, but that wasn't enough. How could he know her heart, how could he know if she was good? Take a chance? As Lisa had with him. Before they'd even traded a word. And not a hundred more, any of consequence, before their intimacy.

Remembering. Perched on the lip of a foldup chair on a lawn among the groom's kin and friends, parboiled in his tuxedo beneath the July sun, and upon a dais before them the minister in his black vestments, perspiring as he lectured bride and groom regarding their marital responsibilities, Lisa beside the maid of honour, clutching her bouquet, standing erect and seriousfaced in that queue of fidgeting green maidens, dutiful and attentive, Nathan's gaze unwavering upon her in breathless rapture, until at last she sensed the fire of his study and swung her eyes to meet his. And in that moment she was changed. Her eyes left his as quickly as they'd arrived, but her stance shifted subtly, it began with a slackening of her posture, but in a moment she grew rigid again, her breasts outthrust, and now her pelvis, which had been locked in balance, canting slightly so the fan of her hip stood out against the taut fabric. Minutes passed with her gaze fixed on the ceremony, and he thought that she was done with him, until at last her eyes flicked back to his and she granted to him a hint of a smile. His hand tightening on the chair's legpost, congratulating himself on arriving without a date. If anyone asked, his explanation for his unescorted state was engineered to solicit sympathy: she was supposed to come with him today but she'd dumped him a few days before. He'd even RSVPed for two, knowing that the empty chair at the reception table would emphasize his singleness.

But after that smile she deprived him. For the rest of the ceremony she did not once look back, and even at the ceremony's conclusion, with the wedding party processing down the aisle between the chairs and up the freshmown grass and through the banquet hall's door, she did not look at him. When he and the rest of the mob entered the airconditioned hall she was already seated at the head table, her face bowed to the best man, immersed in such serious discourse Nathan thought they must be here as a couple. She didn't look as Nathan was directed to his own seat at the rear of the room, at a round table with an octet of guests he didn't know: an IT guy at a film school and his lovely wife in communications, a coffeeshop clerk studying at OCAD, someone from Aboriginal Affairs, and a woman from the Ministry of Transportation. And Nathan beside the unused placesetting of his fictional date, with his back to the room, wanting to crane about to look but unable to or maybe just fearing that she would not have a glance to return. Trembling from the airconditioning or nerves or both. Suddenly aware of the cost to bride and groom and family of his deception, the exorbitant price of a placesetting at an upscale wedding. Though it was wrong to say he'd been unaware of this cost. He'd been indifferent. And suddenly wasn't. Suffering now a flare of guilt, he grew introverted and morose.

There were toasts and speeches and he hoped she would speak

but she did not nor did she cast even an accidental glance his way, and he felt absurdly like he was being punished for his costly deception, but how could she possibly know?

He fought his funk with drink, which fed back upon itself as he added to the newlyweds' bill the cost of each pilsner. He was leaning on the granite bar loosening his bowtie as he waited for the bartender to pour him another when she sidled up and ordered a cocktail and said to him simply, Hi, but with such conviction it could be interpreted in no way but as an overture, and they'd moved outside into the humid dusk and stood smoking, swatting mosquitoes, chatting aimlessly about the wedding and the weather. At a lull in their conversation she sighed as if accepting something inevitable, took his hand, and drew him across the dewsoaked lawn and into an opening in a twelve-foot cedar hedge which was in fact the entrance to an artful maze. They negotiated the path only briefly before blundering into a dead end. As Lisa turned to seek an alternate route he put his hand around her waist and drew her body against his and kissed her while her hands flailed in surprise before she surrendered, pushed an arm into his jacket and pressed her palm to his spine through his sweatdamped shirt. She'd known nothing about him but how he looked and moved, and he was certain that had she been capable of gazing into the slue that was his soul she'd have dismissed him for the cad he was. They rode silently in the taxicab's backseat, limbs entwined, speeding to his apartment, where they joined in the wordless dark, and he awoke at dawn to the sound of her voice from the next room, saying, Yes, uh-huh, I see. It's okay. No, no, I'm still at his place. Hey, it's okay. Anyway, you'd better go. I love you. Have a fantastic time. She returned naked and entirely unselfconscious, shutting her cellphone, and he ached for her, threw back the covers to invite her back into his bed. That was Penelope, she told him as she hunted for her panties, found them behind the television. She stepped into them, said, She was calling from the airport with important information.

What, he asked, hearing the doom in his own voice.

Oh, you know. Girl stuff, she said, putting on her bra, taking her wrinkled green dress from the back of a chair and wrapping it around her body.

He wanted to ask what this meant but couldn't speak.

Who goes to Vegas for their honeymoon? she wondered aloud as she stepped into her shoes. She was hunting for her purse when Nathan finally summoned his voice and offered to make her breakfast, but she gracefully declined, told him she was scheduled to participate that morning in a ten-kilometre run in support of a hospital. Then she was gone and he lay suffocating in the vacuum of her absence. After a moment he burst from the bed and dressed and chased after her, but when he reached the street she was nowhere and he wandered like an amnesiac, unable to recall his life before her. As he stumbled along his eyes swung left and right hunting not just her but one of those posters for the event in which she was today to participate, which he'd thought were everywhere but now he couldn't find even one. After an hour of this he bought a newspaper and rifled through until he learned the race started in less than an hour on the island across the harbour. He went straight to the docks vigilant for her among the passengers, then stood on the ferry's deck gripping the varnished rail, the harbour glazed with sunshine and the breeze smelling of iron oxide and algae, the drone of light planes practising touch-and-gos at the airport, all of it viewed through the intoxicating memory of her caress. A terrible anxiety in his belly, he'd not eaten, couldn't, had drunk too much coffee, now hyperalert, delirious, desperate. The ferry careening towards the concrete dock, he thought it would be smashed to flinders but the engines changed pitch and froth boiled beneath the craft's prow, slowing them as they slid between the guanostained tires, and in a moment they were moored and the gate was down and he was charging onto land, following signs to the startingline while thoughts of the last twelve hours spun in violent eddies. She hadn't said Call me or I'll call or anything of the sort and there'd been no exchange of phone numbers. But there'd also been in her departure no sense of finality, which at first gave him solace until he realized it probably meant that their fling was completely meaningless to her.

What had Penelope told her? Penelope must know some of Nathan's history, via her new husband Jason, who was Nathan's co-worker. Their past together included any number of unflattering episodes, most having to do with drink, some with women, and one, as recently as two weeks before, at Jason's stag, with both. Nathan couldn't remember much more than that they'd finished the evening in a private room at a stripclub. It was all a blur of flesh and perfume and restrained groping while cash vanished bill by bill into a stripper's tasselled beltpouch.

Nathan's pace slowed as these thoughts coursed through his mind, until he came to a complete stop within sight of the participants and banners and tents of the fundraiser. The Hospital for Sick Children. Recognizing now that Lisa was a woman who thought about sick children, how to help sick children. He almost turned and fled. Wanting to hide away his polluted psyche of selfishness and greed and apathy and contempt, but desperate to see her, certain that here she would meet another, a man of philanthropic heroism beside whom Nathan would never stand a chance. Unless he became that man.

And so it was that he found himself at the registration table, where he learned that the minimum sponsorship to participate was $500, and just as he was backing away with a mixture of embarrassment and relief someone at his elbow stated, I pledge two hundred for this good man, and he turned to look and it was her.

Oh hell, he choked.

Nathan, what are you doing here?

I came to run.

In this? she asked, looking him up and down in his dress shirt rolled to the elbows, bluejeans, sandals. He didn't know what to say, and they stood apart from each other in that cautious aurora of new lovers, he wanting to touch her but not touching her, feeling every moment he didn't that he was losing her.

Let me look at you, he said at last, and pored over her not pruriently but realizing it might seem so, in her running tights and Sick Kids t-shirt laden with corporate logos, the paper tag with its boldface number safetypinned to her breast, runningshoes, long yellow hair drawn into a ponytail, her body – so recently nude and pressed to his own – now concealed in this attire and he longing to touch her, to hold her, and yet maintaining that aching distance. He turned back to the table. Can I sponsor myself? he asked the woman, and she said, Of course, and at that he pledged $300.

But you can't run in those, Lisa said, kicking at his sandals.

Does it matter how long it takes? If I come in last? he asked her.

No . . . but you'll kill yourself.

I don't care, he said. It's for the kids.

She laughed, which surprised him, for he'd meant it, but when he considered his mawkish reply he laughed too. A few minutes later he was standing among men and women in their racing gear arching and stretching and Lisa had friends there, two middleaged women and a man with a goatee and sideburns for whom Nathan felt instant hostility, and they were all assembling at the starting-line listening to the distorted bark of the announcer's megaphone explaining rules and directions, and then they were off. Nathan kept up with the pack for the first half kilometre but he wasn't in shape and his sandals rapidly degraded into instruments of torture and he was shortly left behind, most distressingly by Lisa, who explained that she'd hoped to break last year's time. He was left alone among stragglers, some of advanced age, and a group of pregnant mothers and two boys in wheelchairs and a woman in her twenties with her leg in a cast and hobbling on crutches. He thought he should feel humiliated but he didn't. At the two-kilometre mark he abandoned the sandals wondering why he hadn't done so earlier, and his feet were blistered and bleeding and still he walked with the brokenlegged woman as companion and they talked of films recently seen and in a silence that followed he found himself explaining how he'd come to join this race while confessing to her a brief account of his daily sins, from the hash and booze and the drinking and driving and pilfering from convenience stores and racing his motorcycle on country straightaways and harassing other drivers and shooting squirrels with a friend's illegal handgun and seducing girls who may or may not have been underage and cheating on his taxes and cheating on girlfriends with the girlfriends of his friends and one time vandal-izing the car of a former boss and once, only once, participating in an incident of gaybashing, to which he added, The fags started it. It was at that point she said almost kindly, I think I'd better hang back a bit you go on no really it's fine please go on I'll be fine. And she slowed and he slowed until she stopped dead. Please, she said almost in tears. Please, leave me alone will you leave me alone? He'd stood before her with his hands fanned, said, Don't misunderstand, all that's not me. They're just things I've done. And she replied: What's the difference.

Then he was just walking, alone now, off the asphalt path through the grass while race marshals cheered him along. When at last he looked up from the chasm of his thoughts there she stood, ahead on the path, waiting for him, her face flushed and her t-shirt dark with sweat.

You waited for me, he said.

I finished, she said. I came back.

He had no reply for this explanation, just stood there barefoot in his jeans and pleated shirt, arms hanging slack from his shoul-ders, powerless to move. She studied him a bare instant before she stepped forward and folded her arms around him, crushed her face against his chest and by the pressure of her body recharged him, until he was able to lift his own arms and wrap them about her body. The air cooled as a wind came up and thunder growled in the west and there was a sulphurous cast to the light.

Come on, she said at last. It's going to rain. They walked with arms linked. When the rain came they endured it until it poured, and then they ran to a picnic shelter, were soon joined by a Japanese family with their blankets drenched and the children shrieking and scooting about while a miniscule obasan shouted at them to behave, rain and hail pounding the tin roof and light-ning flickering continuously with the thunder above the harbour echoing in twin reports off the downtown skyscrapers. The rain soon ceased but the sky maintained its threatening aspect with thunder growling sporadically, and they resumed the race, the air sweetened and mercifully cool as he hobbled along on wet grass and pavement with her arm about his waist and his across her shoulders. When they made the finishline the tents and brochure stands were dismantled while crews loaded chairs and tables onto a trailer and an organizer shook the tarpaulin from his desk and located the roster and entered Nathan's time of one hour and fifty-three minutes. It was only then that Nathan looked at Lisa and said, I forgot to ask how you did today. In the race.

Oh, she said. Ninety-third. I came ninety-third. But you know what's strange? She lifted herself onto her toes, and into his ear she whispered: I still feel like I won.

He sat there among the rabble of the Choo Choo Roadhouse on a Saturday night, feeling at that moment completely excavated of substance.

Victoria, accosted by a garrulous couple at a nearby table, raised her eyes to him and lifted a finger as if to pin him there. She edged away, deftly escaping the conversation and returning to the table.

I apologize for that, she said, sliding into the booth.

It's all right, he said, watching her, aching with a desire he'd not felt in so long. It wasn't a raw salaciousness but a visceral need to touch and be touched, to be lost in the timeless whorl of love. Move on, he'd been told recently. Move on, he thought bitterly. As you would be instructed when slowing to regard an accident on the roadside. As he himself had been told by a police officer when he'd come across the wreck of his own car in a snowstorm.

Victoria, listen, he said quickly. I want to thank you for listening to me.

It's okay. I like to think it's what I do best, she replied, sliding an arm into a sleeve.

It's just I'm awfully tired and I have to get on the road early.

She stopped her bustling, looked at him with a sly smile.

Nathan, what are you telling me? He felt the dull mortification of miscalculation. As he was collecting his wits a figure stepped to the table, an elderly man wearing a purple Legion jacket, hands deep in the pockets. He had a wide, flushed face and he watched Victoria, the cord of muscle along his jawline working.

What is it, Charlie? Victoria asked.

Mick and me was in back playing snooker and I just seen you. I know this could wait till tomorrow but I got the rectory key and wasn't sure where to leave it. He drew a brass key from his pocket.

Victoria took it. Did you find all the chairs? Some are in the furnace room.

Yeah, I got those. Mick's been in before, knew where to look.

Of course. I forgot he was with you.

How's that piece for Sunday shaping up?

I didn't get much done, on paper anyway. But my friend Nathan here has set my mind whirling.

Charlie fixed Nathan with a glare. You're not from here, he said.

No, Nathan said.

You trying to get her?

Charles!

What do you mean? Nathan asked through clenched teeth.

I mean lure her. You want her, I can tell. Yes sir, I can tell. Everybody wants her.

Everybody? Nathan replied.

They been trying for three years to get her up to Huntsville.

Charlie, I've told you. I'm staying here.

Charlie grunted, narrowed his eyes at Nathan, said, I'm telling no secret the congregation here went from a dozen to full house in a month when Vicky came. Everybody wants her. I don't blame them. She's the best.

Congregation? Nathan felt the world buckle and pitch, and yet somehow managed to maintain his composure while his mind re-evaluated her every word and nuance of the last thirty minutes. Providence, she'd said. And, They're with God.

Vicky, you want a ride back? Charlie asked.

That'd be fine. Nathan, do you need a lift? Where are you staying?

There's the Sweet Rest Motel cross the highway, Charlie said.

Nathan nodded, lifted his glass and drank. Plain soda water. He swallowed it all, set the glass down hard.

I've got an early start, he said, rising. He drew a twenty from his billfold, pressed it to the table. That cover you? he asked Victoria.

Nathan, that's not necessary, she said, rising, opening her purse.

I appreciate your kindness, he said.

Well, she said with a hint of exasperation. That's nice of you to say.

Let's go, Charlie grunted, and they made for the door.

Night Claire, Charlie bellowed to the bartender.

She looked up and called to Nathan, Wait mister, your book. Catch! She lifted it from the bartop and hurled it across the room. Nathan saw it pivoting end over end in an arc towards his head, his hands flying upwards to block it, but Charlie snatched it from the air a foot from his face, hefted it while glancing critically at the cover with its illustration of whaleboats thrashed in the lather of the white whale's flukes, and handed it over with a vague leer.

Nathan followed Victoria and Charlie out to the parkinglot. They stopped before a grey sedan and Charlie opened the passenger door, waited with a hand clamped to the windowframe.

God bless, Victoria said, and she caught Nathan's hand and gave it a firm squeeze. If you're still in town on Sunday you must come. Ten a.m. St. John the Evangelist on the main drag.

She got into the car and Charlie shut the door, rounded the tail, gave Nathan a nod before he got in and started the engine. Nathan bowed to Victoria's wave as the car backed out and mounted the highway and sped into the night.

He stood in the silence, watched the dark highway long after the taillights had vanished. The night was very cold but utterly windless, and he found himself standing within a tenuous pocket of his own heat. Even a slight motion of his head violated the warm corona, and he felt the chill of night air on his ears, cheeks. Someone emerged from the bar behind him, staggered past, and climbed into a car. The engine turned reluctantly over and the car drew away, faded rapidly. A flicker of light caught Nathan's eye and he looked up. Pale energies billowed across the heavens, pouring from the north. Appallingly silent. A green so pale he imagined the flesh of ghosts.

He considered retrieving the notepad to record these wonders, but they seemed too swift to capture. Aurora borealis. Somehow more satisfying in Latin.

His eyes fell shut, and during a heartbeat of slumber he dreamed. He was kneeling on the bank of a tumbling river, but when he pushed his left hand into the current he felt instead of water a savage deluge of glass, as from shattered windshields, lacerating his flesh. He drew his hand out and found it shredded and destroyed, a pale rake of chipped bone. His wedding band still in place, encircling the twig of his fingerbone.

He started awake, staggered on the gravel, righted himself. Cradled his left hand in his right, worrying the ring's smooth arc. Looking up he saw that the sky's display had diminished, showing only momentary and sporadic tongues of light now, each shorter and less intense as they withdrew into the north.

Nathan went to his car and opened the trunk, picked up his bag and crossed the blacktop to the motel. The deskclerk, a youth with a ring through his nose and a Game Boy in his lap, barely raised his eyes to acknowledge the checkin.

The room's bathroom window stood ajar, cold air pouring in. Nathan shut it and cranked the heater. He splashed his face with hot water and unwrapped a glass from a paper sheath, ran the tap and drank cold water, refilled the glass again and again before he crawled fully clothed between the sheets.

He awoke sweating to the drone of the heater's blower, threw off the covers, and lay staring at the ceiling. He got up and turned off the heat, stripped, sat naked on the edge of the bed. Light from the bathroom navigated the stale carpet, cut across his thighs before hitting the floor again and rising up the blinds in the front window. He picked the remote off the TV, sat down, turned it on. He watched the end of a *Bewitched* episode. He flipped past infomercials, highlights from a baseball game, a chef dicing liver. He found previews of Sunday's NASCAR race, watched for five minutes. He turned off the TV, lay on the bed and closed his eyes. Opened them when he heard voices next door, a man and a woman's, the words indistinguishable. Perhaps they would make love. He listened, engulfed in a pall of loneliness. Now silence. Then the man's snore like a twostroke engine.

Something woke him just before sunrise, his head a throbbing vessel, bladder bulging. He moved not towards the bathroom but the front window, where he parted the slats of the blind and looked out. Across the highway in the tavern's parkinglot sat an OPP cruiser, the driver's door open and an officer pacing warily around Nathan's car as if circling a sleeping panther.

Write a ticket, just write a ticket for parking overnight, Nathan whispered, his mind on his recent crimes.

The officer turned and looked across the highway at the motel, and Nathan let the blind snap shut. When he looked again the cruiser was gone. Nathan squinted in the grey light, thought he saw a slip of paper trapped beneath the wiperblade.

He showered and dressed and checked out, trotted across the highway. The sun was easing itself out of the spiny limbs of pine on the highway's south side and the air was terribly cold. Weeds fringing the lot rimed with frost. The Choo Choo Roadhouse forlorn among the elongate shadows.

He plucked a square of paper from the windshield, tilted it to the light. In purple ink a woman's handwriting so full of swirl and dazzle it was virtually unreadable. The first word began with a capital N. Nathan. And the signature: a great flourish of a V, the rest a series of whorls, a tiny mast cut by a crossbar, a dot over the penultimate vowel, and that could be an a at the end. Victoria. Why on earth would a cop deliver a note from Victoria? The letterhead was printed in a crisp copperplate: St. John the Evangelist Anglican Church, Abbey Grove, Ontario. After his name, a comma, then: Core nisit lelore you lere. It might be Latin. Some kind of benediction? I hone sorethiny to yire you. I have something to give you. Instant lascivious interpretation, and he mentally rebuffed himself. Yes, yes. The Anglican minister is offering you a blowjob. He laughed aloud at his own foolishness. For all he knew it said, I hate you and everything you stand for. Lisa thought it a mental deficiency, this inaptitude with handwritten text. She'd early on stopped leaving him notes in anything but a ponderous uppercase.

He turned the slip in the waxing light, folded and pocketed it. He drove west with the rising sun burning through the fogged rear window. Minutes later a green sign welcomed him to Abbey Grove. Houses on the outskirts meagre, a few ramshackle, but in town a row of century homes in red brick with ornate dormers. Downtown populated with the standard tourist shops, banks, restaurants, a clocktower for the town hall, then IGA, Tim Hortons, a liquor store, a few more houses, an iron bridge freshly painted, then the church, St. John the Evangelist, a squat structure of red brick, and beside it the rectory, also red brick, three storeys, in the yard the footprint of an elaborate garden, the kidneyshaped beds heaped with bare soil, the grass raked and stark. He drew into the driveway, shut off the engine and sat, tapping the steeringwheel, then brought out the note, studied it. Trying to recall if Anglican ministers were celibate. And if not, what about a fling? Rubbing his face. There would be no fling. Annoyed at this sudden bout of carnality. Best to get back on the road now.

A knock on his window drew his eyes from the note to Victoria standing outside his door, clutching a lavender bathrobe to her breast, orange hair drawn into a band. He rolled down the window.

I have coffee, she said.

He sat rigidly at the centre of a sofa, gripping a mug of rancid coffee between his palms while she sat across from him in a wingback, legs crossed. Nathan wondering why she hadn't got dressed. A slipper dangled from her foot, and he tried to keep his eyes elsewhere. He mimed drinking the coffee, but recoiled from its sour reek.

The conversation – about the house and furnishings and the redecorating improprieties of her predecessor – provided no illumination of the note's intent. The first sentence may have read, Come do me on the sofa. This sofa. He let a hand fall to the fabric. Was she wondering why he sat there, immobile, blowing his cold coffee, grimacing a smile?

I'll get that thing now, she said, rising, going to the kitchen from where she called, More coffee?

No! he called.

She returned with a small stack of paper and handed it to him. To Nathan's horror it was handwritten. The entire first page was a baroque scrawl of unreadable violet ink.

Well, he said. Isn't this something.

I was up for the rest of the night writing it, she said as she sat beside him.

Up all night? he asked, looking at her.

You inspired me, she whispered.

I did?

Oh, yes, Nathan, she said breathlessly, and lifted the manuscript from his lap, paged through it. I typed it first, she explained, And was just going to print you a copy, but that didn't seem right. So impersonal. You can't communicate essential truths through an inkjet.

Pithy, he said, and inhaled briskly, trying to suck the word back into his mouth. He cleared his throat said, You're right, of course, and he hoped with such effort that she would not ask him to read from it that his armpits grew damp. He looked into her eyes, and asked, Would you read it?

What, the whole thing? she asked with a laugh, fanning through it.

No, of course not. A section.

She rifled quickly through the document and without clearing her throat began to read in a rich contralto, A drowning man needs a lifebuoy, but for a wet man a towel will do. A man walks into a bar. She looked up at him, said, That will get a laugh. People only pay attention if they anticipate humour or tragedy. She turned her eyes back to the page, said, A man walks into a bar. He buys a drink, and another man, a young man, comes to him and says, I have no money, and I need a drink. Will you buy a drink for me? He asks the question as if he is drowning, but really he is only wet. Will you give him a lifebuoy or will you give him a towel?

She went on for a time with quotes from scripture, then ran

the gamut from St. Thomas Aquinas through Maslow's hierarchy of needs, even stranded Ayn Rand on a roadside with a broken timingbelt and no one but fellow egoists out driving that day. He lost focus, hypnotized by the music of her voice, watching her lips, there was something about sacrifice, he couldn't follow it, he found himself thinking of Sundays in his childhood when he would stave off sermon slumber by thinking about military hardware, tanks and frigates and bombers annihilating their targets, but then her voice softening, the pitch altered, he thought it polite to follow now but just then she stopped, her finger tapping the page where she'd ceased reading, her face averted, but from what Nathan could see it was flushed to deep crimson.

Of course, she said, not looking up, That last part won't be in the sermon. She lifted her eyes, smiling. I don't think my congregation is quite ready to know that much about me.

I guess not, Nathan laughed, trying to conjure an allpurpose expression. Then into the subsequent silence he said, It's nice, and sipped the coffee for penance and almost gagged. But your coffee stinks, he added.

She looked up with a sharp laugh. Honestly?

How long has it been on the burner?

I made it around three this morning. So, about five hours. Is that too long?

Too long, he said. Twenty minutes. At most. So. I guess this is my selfless act, my sacrifice for today.

Educating me about my coffee?

Drinking it.

She glanced at a carved clock on the mantle, stood and stated, You have to go.

I do?

Yes. Quickly.

All right. But why?

My brother will be here.

Nathan rose, asked, What does that mean? He imagined some brutish sibling arriving to defend his sister's honour.

My brother is an officer with the OPP. I had him put that note on your windshield. After he came to me last night. Somebody told him we were talking.

This is about the fight.

So there was a fight.

He started it, Nathan replied, and bit his lip with shame. I mean. He wanted to fight. I didn't. Look, I was just driving the speed limit and this guy –

She put a finger to his lips. Shh. Nathan, I know. From what Lionel told me this man has troubles. He suffered a recent tragedy. The police know him well. He fights now, and when he loses, the law is his recourse. Lionel says the attempted murder charge is just a formality, that it won't hold up.

I could have . . . I mean I was the one who . . . Nathan was overcome by a blend of indignation and fury.

It doesn't matter. You have to go.

Wait, just wait. Why didn't your brother just come and arrest me?

Nathan, there's no time! Here. She pressed the manuscript into his hands, then took his elbow and ushered him towards the door. He didn't want to go, felt for the first time in months a hint of peace, of safety. Her simple kindness, the grip of her hand on his arm. Touch. O, touch.

They reached the porch and she glanced up and down the street. Go, she said, and gave him a light shove towards the steps. Contact broken, a swell of gloom in his breast.

Just tell me why he's letting me go.

He's not letting you go. I am. So go!

Nathan trotted down the steps, darted to his car, got in, and reversed into the street, tires chirping on the pavement. Victoria watched from the porch, didn't wave.

He threw the stick into gear and peeled away, eyes watching his mirror as he raced out of town. There was little traffic. He drove for fifteen minutes and after speeding through a long curve took a dirt sideroad. It climbed a grade into an opening in the rockface which had been blasted to make way for the highway. He parked in the trees, collected his notebook and from the backseat a bag, its paper translucent with grease leached from the muffin within. He got out and walked back to the bluff, turned once to make sure his car was concealed. Then he sat on a stone outcrop against a kind of backrest of red granite overlooking the highway. Its warmth soaking through his shirt. Trucks and cars cruised by below, and with each he heard the dirge of tiretreads on asphalt. The stillness reinforcing his feelings of isolation and purposelessness. Realizing he could be here or not, and it didn't make a damn difference to anyone. Except, he thought wryly, Victoria's brother.

Resting his palms on the warm stone. Starlings vacating and repopulating the wires slung pole to pole along the roadside. He ate the muffin and opened his notebook.

OCTOBER 8TH

Ribbons across blue, some narrow and taut, others dissolving into pale, textured mist, loosedrawn, rolling and breaking with the wind's persuasion. A tiny silvered delta, spider running its web, labouring, strand of ice from its spinnerets, cabin crew ten kilometres away serving applejuice and Zinfandel to blearyeyed passengers, oblivious to their jetscrawl across heaven.

He slid a fingertip along the words to simulate the motion of Lisa's eyes, immediately conscious that he was trying to distract her from Victoria. But then horror when he realized he'd written for Victoria too, and thinking of Lisa's jealousy about him and other women – fierce, irrational, and excepting one fateful misdemeanour, always unfounded – he swung his thoughts away from this blasphemy. Wondering where his vinylback pocket thesaurus had got to. His head ached for coffee, but he pressed the back of it hard against the rockface, notebook spread on his lap. Ran his palm against the granite until it met the ridges of a borehole into which they'd packed the explosives. Imagining the blast, that moment of focused violence. A rustle of leaves drew his eyes to a bower below, and he watched a rabbit nosing about, brindled pelt shining in the daylight, its nostrils pulsing as it skittered, sniffed, ate.

In the distance the fervid whine of an engine, and a police

cruiser ripped into the curve, lights flashing, siren mute. A bead of sunshine sliced up its windshield, across the roof and light-rack, and down the rear window, and in a moment the car was gone.

Nathan sat listening to the sound drain away, then slapped the notebook shut and scrambled up the hill back to his car. He fired up the engine and backed recklessly down the slope and onto the highway, was still rolling when he jerked the stick into gear and popped the clutch, jammed the pedal to the floor. The tires squealing and smoking as the car shot forward. His plan all along had been to escape in the opposite direction, return through town and exit by an alternate route, but it felt cowardly at this point to evade his fate, to escape responsibility for what he'd done, or so he argued to himself as he ran the tachometer into the red, shifting rapidly until he reached top gear. His pulse quickened at the thought of confrontation, but whether in dread or zeal he could not decide. This engine still had plenty of vigour, and in a few seconds he passed through 190 kilometres per hour, the tires a fraction away from losing grip in the curves. It felt good, this speed, the thunder of the engine, the acute focus required to maintain control. A pickup in the lane ahead and a solid passing line, the route ahead obscured beyond a curve, but he switched lanes, shot past like the truck was standing still, returned to his lane. He thought he would reach the cruiser soon, hadn't considered that it was also moving at a significant clip. Traffic was light, and when he did encounter other vehicles, passing was like evading stationary objects. This went on for a time until he was climbing an incline while overtaking a dumptruck, and a schoolbus crested the hill from the opposite direction. It was suddenly there in front of him, yellow grille filling his windshield, the expression on the driver's face as clear as if Nathan were sitting across a dinnertable from her. Unmitigated panic. Were she his dinner companion he might've leaned forward and asked with concern, Are you going to be sick?

There was only one thing to do, and Nathan, without time to make a rational decision, did it instinctively. He did not brake, which would have either locked the wheels and made steering useless, or retarded the impact and destruction only negligibly, nor did he nudge the wheel to the right, which would have steered him into the flank of the dumptruck, likely knocking his car back into the path of the bus. Instead he nudged the wheel a degree to the left, a move of such precision he would calculate later that had he deviated by a fraction of a millimetre in either direction, he and possibly others would have died that day. As it was, the car moved out of the bus's path and flew onto the shoulder, gravel bellowing inside the wheelwells, the bus flashing past on Nathan's right, and he saw or imagined he saw children's stricken faces looking out at him as he ripped by, and for an instant the three vehicles were abreast on the two-lane highway, Nathan's Supra, the schoolbus, the dumptruck. In a heartbeat he was past and careening across the lane cutting through the path of oncoming traffic and aligning himself on the lane ahead of the dumptruck. He heard the repeated whoops of its horn as it shrank in his rear-view mirror, headlamps flashing in rebuke.

Nathan's first thought as he sped away was that he was a very good driver. But he had to be because he was, in fact, a terrible, reckless driver. These recognitions did not slow him down. He shot along the winding road, and soon caught the cruiser as it slowed to pass through a hamlet. Nathan careened towards its taillights, waited too long on the brakes, felt the wheels lock as he pressed the pedal, and to avoid a collision he had to repeat the move he'd performed to miss the schoolbus, let off the brake, draw to the left, so when he'd assumed control he was beside the cruiser, the young constable cranking his window down shouting commands, face flushed with anger.

Nathan rolled down the passenger window, called out, I did not, did not attempt to murder that man. He tried to murder me, with a tire iron. I only just managed to disarm him and could've hurt him very badly but . . .

But it was no use, the constable was screaming at Nathan to Pull over sir, pull over right now. I order you to pull your vehicle over now!

They were moving together abreast down the hamlet's main

street and a van was coming at them in Nathan's lane, so he geared down and stomped the gas. His car shot forward, he swung in front of the cruiser, and sped off. In a few seconds the cruiser was on his tail, lights flashing and siren wailing, and as they left the hamlet and passed a sign showing a resumption of the highway speed Nathan quickly took them through the limit and beyond. The unreasonable screaming of that police officer, his voice like the shriek of a sawblade through tin, face flushed with fury, convinced Nathan that the law was not the reasoned institution it ought to be, but another human construct governed by violent emotion. There would be no consideration of his side of the story regarding the fight with the towtruck driver. Nathan discovered that what he most feared was incarceration, however temporary, because his grief was a relentless pursuer, dogging him across kilometres of open road, and to cease would allow it to catch up. He saw himself trapped in a cage as his hunter found him, slipped like a ghost through the bars, swallowing him in its suffocating vapour.

As it was though he had no escape plan. The cruiser riding his bumper could likely outperform his own car, and the cop was certainly calling for reinforcements who had any number of tactics at their disposal to stop him. The road twisted and curved, shot between blasted rockfaces, and Nathan expected to soon see cruisers bearing down from the opposite way, or parked as a barricade across the highway. He knew it would happen. What he didn't know was how he was going to react.

They rode into a sharp curve, Nathan thinking of NASCAR racers riding bumper on bumper around the track, and the message on a yellow sign which Nathan had not consciously read as he passed it suddenly resolved in his mind: WATCH FOR FALLEN ROCK. For there was, lying on the highway in their lane just such an object, a rock of red granite the size of a housecat. It was just there, surrounded by flint, recently broken from the granite wall that rose above the curve. Nathan bore down, leaning forward in his seat, resisting until the last possible instant the compulsion to steer around it, and then he jerked the wheel so the tires squawked and his wheels and flank skimmed past the rock. The cop had no such chance to react, as Nathan's car had obscured view of boulder until the last instant. Nathan heard the impact as a muffled explosion, saw when he looked in his mirror debris raining down on the blacktop while the cruiser slewed sideways, a crater in the right side of its face, and he saw within the car's interior the pale apparition of an inflating airbag. Nathan zoomed away, the cruiser pirouetting and shedding fragments. In seconds it was far behind, and Nathan kept an eye on it as long as he could, slowing, prepared to turn his car around to offer help if it appeared that the driver had suffered injury. He was down to a reasonable highway speed when the cruiser came to rest facing the opposite direction, and instantly the officer was out of his cruiser and running, as if it did any good, in pursuit of Nathan's car. Nathan jammed the pedal to the floor. In seconds he rounded another curve, the scene gone from view.

He knew that radio calls had been made, that other cruisers had been dispatched, but as OPP stations were sparse in this part of the province there was no way of knowing from which direction they might come. He pulled his map from the doorpocket, unfolded it hastily, still accelerating, alternating his view between road and map, trying to orient himself. Here was Abbey Grove, the highway he'd followed west, the hamlet of Proudfoot Corners they'd just torn through. An intersection ahead. In a few minutes he saw it, a regional highway running north and south. He slowed, took the corner too fast, tires bleating and slipping on the pavement, and headed north. As he drove he stretched a hand out to rest on the passenger seat and it landed on Victoria's manuscript. That was her brother back there. A terrible sting in his gut when he realized he could never return.

He drove away from her, took every sideroad he encountered, west then north, west then north, gradually slowing to an inconspicuous speed, vigilant for police cruisers. He saw none, finally allowed himself to visit a drivethrough where the coffee he bought failed to ease his headache. He drove on, squinting at oncoming cars, looking for the telltale silhouette of a police lightbar.

Later in the day he spotted in the north a surreal object,

something so grand and distant it had the character of a natural object like an escarpment, like a mountain. It was an enormous smokestack spreading a grizzled plume across the heavens. A cloud factory. He drove towards it for twenty minutes before he reached Sudbury's limits, city gouged from living rock, subdivisions and malls chewed from the Canadian Shield, all of it hunched in the shadow of that superstack. Blackstone and weed, a watertower with the city's name freshly painted on the blue vessel. The city was patrolled by its own police force, which put Nathan out of the OPP's jurisdiction, for awhile anyway. Wondering if his apparent crime would justify a wider warrant for arrest.

Avenues of doughnutshops, gas stations, food chains, auto parts shops, hunting supply stores. SUVs, pickup trucks crowding the roads, Inco paycheques, Inco pensions. He passed the featureless four-storey structure of the income tax office where his annual return went to die. Dark coming on. A Sudbury Saturday night. Bingo parlours and bowling alleys. He sat on a stool in the window of a pizzeria and ate two slices and drank Pepsi from a can. A violent malaise building in his heart, his escape, losing Victoria, the fight with the towtruck driver, and all of it beneath the black sky of grief and guilt. He had to head it off. Before he left he asked the girl where a liquor store was and she said with a frown that she wouldn't know, and then she cackled and provided detailed directions.

He bought a bottle of Jim Beam and carried it back to his car and unscrewed the cap and took a swig. The woman in the passenger seat in the car next to his who was combing her blonde hair with a joyless smirk rolled down her window.

Gimme that, she said, her hand outstretched.

Nathan wormed out of his window, handing the bottle across the gap and she took a long draw and hacked and sent it back.

Jesus Q. Christ, she said. You're fucken serious.

Her boyfriend returned with a sixpack of vodka coolers and shot Nathan a glare before getting in and screeching out of the spot, narrowly missing a pickup trolling for a free space. The truck driver pressed his horn and the boyfriend responded in kind and

Nathan took another swig and hit his horn too. Symphony of assholes.

He drove a wide strip lit by bluewhite streetlamps, carwashes and doughnutshops and then deserted baseball diamonds and after that enormous refineries corroding in their spotlight glow. He turned around and aimed his car at the base of the superstack, found himself in a neighbourhood of steep streets, renovated houses set at odd angles standing shoulder to shoulder while that concrete phallus towered above ejaculating sulphur dioxide into the atmosphere, the cloud a broadening peninsula illuminated from beneath by city lights, gobs of smoke pouring forth on a grotesque scale, like Niagara rushing skywards.

He cruised the downtown strip with the bottle between his knees and saw Lisa and Sydney, hand in hand, moving away from him along the sidewalk. It was the usual punch in the gut, and then he slid past and craned about and saw the faces of strangers. Convinced that it had been them, walking happily along. Only at the moment of Nathan's perception did some higher power snatch away his beloveds and substitute these obscene replacements.

Nathan pulled over and took a long draw from the bottle. He looked crosseyed down the bottle's neck as liquor decanted into his mouth. He let the bottle fall and wiped his mouth with the back of his hand. This was not the first time he'd seen them, not the first time they'd been snatched away like that. It happened only in cities, and while he was drinking. He avoided cities.

He capped the bottle and pulled away from the curb and he drove and ended up in a stripclub with stucco walls where dancers gyrated to Bachman-Turner Overdrive. "You Ain't Seen Nothin' Yet." He sat at the brink of the stage where the table dancers with their wooden stepstools wouldn't harass him and watched a girl of twenty squat on a lush and gorgeous handmade quilt of abstract heliotrope and pretend to masturbate while casting imploring looks at the deejay. A caesarean scar across her belly. The deejay faded the song – the Guess Who's "These Eyes" – halfway through it. While his voice thundered from the speakers soliciting a hand for sweet Katrine the girl leapt up and seized the quilt's edge and gave it a firm shake and the fabric thundered and in four practised moves she had it folded and tucked under one arm and still nude she exited the stage. This folding operation strangely erotic after the banal performance. Nathan thought sadly of some nearsighted nana labouring over that quilt. He drank a beer, which mixed unfavourably with the pizza and bourbon in his gut. He wanted sleep. He drove east and found a motel on the city's outskirts, put the bottle on the bedside table, crawled under the covers, and turned off the light. Tormented by his demons, he switched the light back on and turned on the television and poured himself a drink and drank it and poured until the bottle was dry. He awoke on the floor to the sound of Ontario's legislative assembly debating photo radar. He turned off the television and the light and lay awake in the bed listening to the swish and howl of traffic on the highway twenty metres past the window.

The maid's key in the door woke him and he didn't move as she stepped inside and saw him curled on his side with the empty bottle on the table. Sunlight pouring in through the open door igniting a corona around her robust shape. She excused herself in French and shut the door. He slept more and awoke with hazy eyesight in the midafternoon. He lay for a long time looking at the ceiling. At last rose and dressed, went to the office braced for conflict as he laid the key on the desk in front of the elderly woman reading a bible but she just nodded and smiled and solicited from him future business. It was 3:30 in the afternoon.

Nathan's head boomed with each step as he walked to his car and stowed his bag in the trunk. An unusually warm day, sunny, haze above the horizon. Thoughts and motions gelatinous. Swinging onto the highway he felt like the pilot of a bathysphere moving his craft through crushing ocean depths. He passed a turnoff for Falconbridge and went on through town. He hated to stop at a chain restaurant but saw a Golden Griddle, felt a need for grease. The coffee was weak and he drank cup after cup and bit into stubby sausages and relished the hot oil as it doused his nausea.

He took 17 west past Espanola. Trees and bush and faces of

pink rock abutting the highway, graffitistained and pockmarked by the wormholes of the blasting drill.

In Blind River he stopped at a drivethrough for coffee and the voice through the speakergrille asked him to hang on a sec. He tapped the steeringwheel, looking at the van ahead of him idling at the window, wondering what kind of complicated order was holding things up. When he looked in his rearview he saw an OPP cruiser.

He slid down in his seat, emptied his lungs. Looked into his sideview mirror, waiting to see a door open, an officer emerge with billyclub unsheathed. He reached up and tilted the rearview mirror so he could see the cruiser's occupants. Two young officers, not glaring at him or calling into the radio mike for backup. Chatting and joking with each other. Here to pick up coffee. In an instant he realized how stupid he was, visiting doughnutshops when he needed to avoid the police. They hadn't yet run his plates. Wouldn't unless he gave them cause to. He heard an imploring, faroff voice, discovered it was the drivethrough attendant's.

Hello. Hello? Your order please, she called with irritation.

Coffee. Extra large. Double-double.

Is that everything? Two-twenty, drive up.

Nathan stepped off the clutch and stalled the car. Face burning, he started the engine and moved with care to the window and received his coffee, then drove with conspicuous caution towards the exit, watched the cruiser draw up to the window. When he got back on the highway he hammered the gas, staring at the rearview mirror more than the road ahead, thinking he'd better hasten his westward progress and escape Ontario.

He sped late into the night, camouflaged by darkness. But the roadmarkers were fuzzy, and when he saw a sign for a place called the Blue Hotel the name in its eponymous neon colour was bloated and blurry. Trying to remember when he last had his eyes checked. He avoided doughnutshops, was forced to fuel himself with gas station coffee. By midnight he was jittery and paranoid, grew to resent the sharpedged diamonds of oncoming headlights, flashed his highbeams severely at those who failed to promptly cut their own. The percussion of his tires in the gravel of the shoulder woke him once, and he drew wide, deep breaths to keep awake. He finally parked in the lot of an abandoned service station, the advertised gas price a fraction of the current rate. He levered back his chair and closed his eyes. After some hours he erupted from sleep, hands flying to the steeringwheel and wrenching it to the left while his feet scrabbled for the brake.

He reluctantly loosed his hands, wrapped his arms around his quaking body. In the light from a passing truck he saw his breath. Windows fogged. The dream evaporating: speeding, chasing a vehicle in which Lisa and Sydney were riding towards certain doom. He was almost upon them when a phalanx of emergency vehicles, mostly police cars but a few fire engines and ambulances among them, leapt out of the brush, lights flashing and klaxons blaring, and stopped in front of him, blocking his route. He was standing on the brake with no effect, about to slam into that wall of vehicles, when he awoke.

Blinking now in the darkness, shivering. He started the engine, threw the climate levers into the red. Cold air blasted from the vents, but in a few minutes the heat came. When finally the temperature seemed reasonable he got back on the highway. Less traffic now. He felt calm, calm and alert at the same time, aftermath of adrenaline, as he moved westward and the sky in his back window turned grey, bloomed through violet, red, orange. He kept going, past Thessalon, skirted the Soo, and started up the northbound leg of Lake Superior's shoreline.

CHAPTER 3

In the afternoon, after passing Wawa and the big Canada Goose standing sentry over the highway, he saw a pair of OPP cruisers shoot past in the opposite direction with their beacons flashing. He ducked as they careered past, lifted his head slowly to regard them in the mirror as they disappeared down the highway. When he looked at the speedometer it read 140 and it took an act of supreme will to let off and return to the limit. The calm of an uneventful morning destroyed. Nathan became nauseated with panic when a few minutes later a third cruiser whipped past. Never mind that they were headed in the opposite direction; he felt certain that in some way he was the object of their pursuit. The next two hours were fatiguing as he threw his attention from mirror to mirror and squinted far down the highway. He was past Marathon when he saw far behind him a cruiser heading his way, lights off, but closing fast. Without thought he threw on his turn indicator, had to travel with the flasher going for almost a kilometre before a sideroad presented itself, and he took it with apparent calm. Heading south on a gravel road, watching, watching the mirror, then the slam in his gut when the cruiser took the turn. Heard a moan that was his own. But then he saw the car's flank as it came fully about; it was using the mouth of the roadway to turn around, though as he watched he saw it stop and not re-enter the highway. Nathan wondering why, why? To block him in, to wait for backup?

Shit, he said. Shit shit shit.

In a moment the cruiser was gone from view and he drove along a descending road and saw after a time the vast grey expanse of Lake Superior. Fretting, wanting to turn around, to see if the cop was just pausing or setting up a highway speedtrap or sitting there in wait for him. He kept driving, the lake expanding before him, a barrier which he could not pass, knowing there was only one exit to this road and the cop likely blocking it. In a moment he might see a convoy of police cars surging down the hill after him.

In the midst of this terror he saw at the roadside a small restaurant made from yellow logs, was surprised to discover he was hungry. Thought: if they're going to get me, I may as well have a final lunch. There was nowhere to park but conspicuously out front, so there he parked.

He went in and found the restaurant with its rustic walls and wooden tables vacant. He startled the lone waitress out of the reverie of her iPod as she sat behind the cash, and as he did so he thought casually what an interesting break in her monotony if an OPP SWAT team arrived to capture him. He ordered a plate of breaded fish with rice and coleslaw, ate it slowly and thoughtfully, gradually adandoning his trepidatious glances out the window. When he was finished he felt full and weary and reluctant to face the confrontation waiting up the road. Thought he may as well wait things out, let them come to him. He asked the waitress about accommodations and she told him of cabins by the lake.

Old Onion Peters rents them, she said.

Onion, Nathan said. Onion? Is that his given name?

Nope. It's Ian. But everyone calls him Onion. Almost blind too, though he sure don't want anyone to know it.

Nathan drove to where the roadway ended at the lake and a handpainted sign advertised Onion Pete's Housekeeping Cottages. He rode a dirt track until he reached a house clad in sootstreaked siding. A halfdozen compact cabins faced the lake. He opened his door and heard surf. It was as good a place as any to make a stand.

A sign swaying in the wind directed him to the office. Nathan opened a screendoor and found himself at a desk of whitewashed plywood. On it sat a bell and he rang it. He smelled beeswax, Pine-Sol, pipesmoke. He heard something shatter on the floor in the next room, then a mutter of oaths. A crosseyed man with a white beard and a misshapen head entered. His skull was narrow and long, as if it had been flattened in a vice, although a shelf of cartilage above his right ear showed that the crown of his head had been partially spared, so it was like he was wearing a hat fashioned from bone. He had a lean, hollow face, flesh drawn tight and shiny along the hard cheekbones, a series of straight, shallow scars laddered along his left cheek, the pintles of his jaw visible beneath the stretched skin, the expression so skewed by injury that he looked to be perpetually pondering some difficult mathematic. Denim overalls, flannel shirt. He carried a clipboard, placed himself at the counter, set the clipboard down, gazed at a spot somewhere to Nathan's left.

You want a cabin?

Please.

For how many weeks?

Just tonight.

Tonight, the man replied with something like annoyance. Fill this in.

Onion set down the clipboard. Affixed beneath the spring-clip a registration card already completed by a former lodger, Mr. Jim Meyerhold of Bowmanville, Ontario. The man turned and fumbled along a cabinet until he found the knob, drew it open to reveal keys, above each a tiny, handprinted number. The man pushed his face close.

Nathan lifted the card, but there was nothing beneath it. He pretended to fill it in. The man returned with a key, placed it on the counter.

Take Cabin One. It's the nicest.

Nathan looked and saw a six printed on the cork fob.

How much? Nathan asked.

Eighty-five dollars.

Eighty-five? Nathan asked shrilly.

What day is it?

Monday.

Okay then. On account of it being a weekday, seventy-five.

That still seems like a lot.

They're nice cabins. They have kitchenettes and fridges and airconditioning.

I don't need any of those.

I still got to charge you for em. They all got em. If you don't smoke you still gotta pay for that ashtray they put in your car.

It just seems unreasonable. A motel on the highway might be fifty.

Lake view?

No.

Here you got a lake view.

And if I promise not to look?

It's still there. Just like that ashtray.

A dog came from the other room, a broadshouldered husky with a white face and a russet back, claws clicking on the floor. It rounded the counter and sniffed Nathan's feet, then looked up with iceblue eyes.

That's Scorp. He's okay.

Nathan rubbed the dog's head and the dog pressed its cheek to Nathan's thigh.

Look, since I'm your only customer, maybe we can work something out, Nathan said. He had money, a fair amount, since the insurance policy. Since selling the house. But it felt dirty. A sum exchanged for Lisa and Sydney. The avails of death. He said companionably, Maybe you could give me a break, Ian.

The man jerked as if struck. Ian? he said. Who the fuck is Ian?

I'm told that's your name.

You making fun of me?

No. The woman at the restaurant told me your name is Ian.

It's Onion, you jackass.

I'm sorry. She said it was Ian.

Onion. Goddamn it, it's Onion!

All right.

Fucking Ian. You call me Ian? Jesus, he muttered. How you gonna pay?

The dog was nosing along the baseboards, snuffling. Nathan tried to raise in himself enough ire to call the whole thing off, but he was trapped here, and weary, discovered he was looking forward to the novelty of a cabin.

I think I'll put this on my creditcard, Nathan replied, thinking he'd at least screw this guy on the percentage. Nathan slipped the card from his wallet, moved it into Onion's outstretched hand. The man lifted an imprinter from beneath the counter and located the brackets through touch, settled the card between them, then spent some moments manoeuvring a slip into position.

Maybe you could give me a hand, he said.

Sure, Nathan said, and pressed the slip's corners into place, then drew the clattering roller across it.

And fill it in, please.

All right.

Nathan hesitated with the pen's tip poised at the price column. He wrote $45.00, signed it, tore off his copy, and pushed the imprint across the desk.

Appreciate it. Here's your key.

The dog gave a muffled yip, lifted its muzzle. A furry little sausage writhing in its teeth. Nathan thought it might be a mole. The dog jerked its snout at the ceiling and swallowed.

He walked out to the cabins with their sparse lawns, looking at the numbers screwed into the doorposts. They started at number one, which made his the last. All vacant. He got to number three and went back and got in his car and drove along the dirt track behind the cabins and parked behind Six. He got his bag from the trunk and went around to the front door, unlocked it and went inside. A room panelled in pine with a double bed pushed against the left wall, on the right a counter with a hotplate and a kettle. Bar fridge. CorningWare mugs, translucent white. The floor made from painted boards. In the back a washroom with a pedestal sink, a halfsized bathtub, the drain a rusty, hairclogged hole.

Above the kitchen sink a sign in marker, Positivly No Smoking! The room stinking of must and stale cigarettes. He dropped his bag on the bed and opened the windows fore and aft, and the lake's cold breeze drove in through the tattered screens.

He went to turn on the television. There was no television. At the foot of the bed an orange La-Z-Boy.

He went to the car and got his notebook and dumbbells. He took off his shoes and lay on the bed. The room was cold and he climbed under the quilt and drew it to his chin. The chill air whipping around his face, sound of the surf. He would not hear the approach of the cruisers. The scent of the water – iron and lime. He slept.

He awoke after an hour, still daylight. He pushed back the covers and lay looking at the nailheads in the drywall ceiling. Like stitching, like the quilted pattern of farmers' fields viewed from above. How many ceilings, he thought, in the world? A game he used to play with Sydney. Though she'd been too young for it, he'd played it for his own amusement. Rehearsing for when she was old enough. How many of those in the world. Items for which no census would ever be taken. How many bricks? How many mushrooms? How many staples? How many meatballs? How many ceilings? How many nailheads?

He kicked away the quilt, sat on the bed's verge, put on his shoes and jacket. He picked up his notebook and went outside and stood on the small porch, looking towards the road. Almost disappointed to see it vacant. He looked at the lake. A black wall of cloud rose from the line of the horizon and halfway up the sky.

He went down to the water's edge, already flipping through the scrawled notebook to the next blank. Sunshine above, the water a milky jade where the light struck. Further out, beneath the shade of that cloud, the water grey, seething with strands of foam.

Nathan sat on a rotting picnic table, its frame jigging on the axis of each bolt. He spread the notebook on the scarred surface and drew out his pencil, sucked on the end and looked at the sky.

OCTOBER 9TH

Autumn sun pouring into the lake's shallows where a great bio-luminescent whale threatens to break. Waterdrops from the wavecrash on stony shore each like molten punctuation. The season pitches towards winter in the character of cloud, cloud like a great slab of pigiron pushing up from the horizon, blotting the sky, slicing with its scalloped edge across the vault. Extinguishing day. Those objects yet touched by sun – the near-naked trees, the scoured grass, stone and crag – all of it painfully bright, as if lit from within.

As Nathan sat with the pencil-end in his mouth the cloud cut across the sun, throwing darkness over the land, chilling him. He crossed his arms, clamped his legs together, wondering if the cloud meant something. Not that he believed that persons beyond the grave could influence weather. Though such influence would explain the unreliability of meteorological prediction. He smoothed a palm along the page, felt the faint filigree of graphite. The sun re-emerged within a bight of cloud, but the light seemed diluted, transitory. He'd need something for dinner. Had to know if they were coming for him or not. He shut the notebook.

He drove up the road, past the restaurant where he'd lunched, now shut, went on slowly as dark fell, killed his headlights as he approached the highway, was upon it unexpectedly, stunned when a transport truck ripped past immediately ahead of him. No cops. He put on his lights and entered the highway, drove warily westbound until he came to a town, found a convenience store. He parked and went in. The old Asian woman behind the counter stood up, and he nodded as he passed into the store's depths. A can of beef stew, saltines, cheese, a jug of rootbeer. At the counter he studied buttertarts under plastic wrap.

Are these local? he asked, lifting a package.

Local?

Yes. Are they made around here?

The woman nodded slightly.

Or from some factory somewhere?

She nodded again in the same manner. It was something Lisa would've asked. Nathan put them back and the woman rang up his purchases.

He drove, expecting cruisers to explode from the underbrush. A few cars and trucks. He turned down the road, sped back to the lakeshore. As he walked around the cabin to the front door a squall of pinhead snowflakes swarmed him. He stood in their swirl, watching them melt on the coat's leather, on the porchplanks. He went inside and put the groceries on the counter and stripped to his underwear. He performed a series of curls with the dumbbells, watching the slab of his bicep grow taut and relax. He finished the workout on the floor with a hundred abdominal crunches, his belly contracting into a halfdozen hard pouches each time he drew himself up. When he was done he lay on the floor, sweating into the cold room. He lifted himself on his elbows and looked along his body, his broad chest and the rippled plane of his stomach, the waistband of his briefs a flat, horizontal line, shadows in the hollows where the elastic stretched across his hipbones.

Hard knock on the door. He leapt up, tugged up his briefs, his heart squirming in his chest, swinging his eyes to the windows, expecting the masked faces of a SWAT team, snickering at him.

Who is it? he shouted.

Who do ya think? Open up! a voice called.

Hang on.

He pulled on his jeans, fastened the button. Shirtless, still sweating, he opened the door. Onion stood on the porch and a ram of cold wind struck Nathan's chest. The snow had ceased but the lake gave a strident roar, waves blasting against the rocks. Nathan felt spray on his skin. Onion was holding a flashlight by the lens, proffering the butt end to Nathan.

Trouble finding you, he said. I thought you wanted Cabin One.

This one's fine. What's the flashlight for? Nathan asked, accepting it.

Sometimes we get a good wind the power goes out. Scorp! he shouted, and the dog rounded the cabin and trotted up the steps. Onion bent and seized the dog around the torso, worked his arms up and grabbed the dog's collar.

You need anything you holler. Night.

Night, Nathan said, wondering how the old man would locate the house, realized as he watched him hobble away with his fingers anchored to the dog's collar that the animal would guide him. Nathan shut the door, got a flannel shirt and a pair of socks from his bag and put them on. He shut the windows and the wind began a plaintive skirl through the cabin's frame. He squatted at the baseboard heater and found the knob and turned it on. It clicked and pinged as the fins warmed.

He turned on the hotplate and got out a saucepan and found a canopener among a drawerful of mismatched cutlery. It pierced the stewcan's top but slipped free after two turns of the butterfly crank. He repositioned the blade, closed the handle. The blade sank into the steel, slipped free with another turn. In fits and starts, with nicks orbiting the lid's circumference, Nathan got it open. He turned the can over and a plug of broth slid into the saucepan, a perfect form of the can's mould, ribs and seam and the concentric impressions of the base. The hotplate's coil glowed orange, and Nathan warmed his hands over it. Then he positioned the pot and jabbed a spoon into the melting fist of stew and whipped it until it relaxed into a brown gob. It smelled like dogfood.

While it heated he arranged crackers on a plate and cut slabs of cheese and put one on each cracker. He poured himself a glass of warm rootbeer and lifted a cracker, and holding the cheese in place with his thumb brought it to his mouth.

He sat on the bed and ate out of the saucepan. The room didn't have a radio. Or a telephone. Snarl of the wind, thunder of the lake pounding the shoreline. He could distinctly feel each smash through the soles of his feet and resonating within the bedsprings. He scraped the scales of burned gravy from the bottom of the pan.

A place he'd never expected. Not the place so much as the circumstance. Eleven months ago he was thinking about mortgage payments and property taxes and daycare lists, and when could they arrange babysitting so he and Lisa might have dinner, see a movie. And what's Sydney's new word, or what silly phrase did she say today. Showing to him a cookie that Lisa had just handed her from the cooling rack. Mama is *cooker*, she make *cookie*. Nathan's own explosion of laughter startling the child, so she ran back and clutched Lisa's leg and bawled.

Thinking about her future. How can a future vanish? Where does it go?

Not that he hadn't expected to lose Sydney at any moment. Those occasions when the girl slept later than usual, Nathan waking to see the alarm clock nearing 8:30 a.m. Lying paralyzed, watching every sixty seconds the changing digits on the display, straining to hear her breath on the baby monitor as he gripped the bedsheets. Living out the scene in striking detail, striding down the hall to her bedroom, throwing open the door, and seeing the pale face on the pillow, mouth agape, lips blue. Is that how she would look in death? It didn't matter – he now knew the answer to that question, and it was nothing so peaceful.

Wind slammed the cabin, jolting the prints of wildfowl on the walls. Nathan's hand clamped around the spoon. He set it gently in the pot. He was nowhere. Except for a blind old man, no one knew he was here, and no one cared. Nobody needed him. And he needed no one. A state of perfect equilibrium. He sat, shuddering with the perfection of it all.

He took a long, deep breath, put the pot in the sink. He drank his rootbeer, licked the lather from his lip, poured another.

He awoke sweating, unable to determine if his eyes were opened or closed, so dark was the night. With lids in either state he witnessed in the blackness flares of distant light. Moments later, like the reports of thunder, came a series of agonizing spasms in his gut. Outside the cabin the bluster of wind and waves. Some rational fragment of his mind attributing the pain in his stomach to flu, food poisoning, appendicitis, ebola. He tossed onto his side, drawing knees to chest, shivering. He pushed off the quilt and felt the room's chill, sweat evaporating. Unsure if he should stay warm or cool down. And then the maddening swirl of nausea, the gurgle and churn of his bowel. His stomach seized and he pressed a hand over his mouth, pawing away the sheets. He rolled onto the floor, the boards booming. Consulting a mental map of the room. Where was the wallswitch? He scrambled to his feet, lurched through darkness, one hand extended, the other pressed to his belly. Wanting to vomit, dreading it. He stepped forward, puke rising. He tried swallowing but it blew out in a burning rush, and he bent forward and felt it propelled through his mouth and splayed fingers by the clench of his abdominals, heard it slop on the floor, felt the splash on his feet. Teetering now, smears of sweat on his face. More coming and he stepped across the puddle, heel squishing on its far shore, and he felt the rim of the countertop and the puke came and he missed the sink. As he groped along the cabinets towards the bathroom something toppled and rolled and thumped to the floor. He squatted and felt about until he came up with the flashlight, turned it on, aimed it behind him at the mottled pool. He located the switch for the overhead light and flicked it repeatedly but nothing happened. The flashlight's beam careening around the room and like a weapon, suddenly destroying all it touched, cutting rifts in the wallboards, charring away fragments of ceiling. He turned it off before it completely destroyed the cabin, flailed through the dark in the direction of the toilet. The sound of surf louder than ever, and he thought it must have overcome the shore and was now engulfing the structure. Pouring through the gaps in the walls, welling from the floorboards. Fearsomely cold against his fevered skin. It grappled with body, fought to sweep him away, he fell to his knees, took hold of an oblong object, smooth and cold and difficult to grip, and he realized that it was an ear, a tremendous ear, and to survive he must shout into it the extent of his sins. They exploded from him in a burning rush. He exclaimed them again and again, and in expressing them felt vague mitigation of the cramp in his gut.

There came a segue, and he found himself seated, folded forward with chest against thighs, shivering violently. Glazed with sweat, panting and damaged, his bellymuscles slack and abused. He rose and blundered about in the dark, caroming off walls and bathroom fixtures while outside the wind and surf became the cheers of an enormous crowd, rising to a fevered pitch. Still the lightning flashed, but the pain came in lesser stabs. He was standing now, it was raining, it started cold but grew obscenely hot before it subsided and he stood awestruck in the bathtub, naked and wet. He had to get to the bed, slammed against the doorframe, kicked something on the floor, the flashlight, he squatted and felt about and found it and turned it on with caution, testing the beam's destructive power against the far wall. It was just a flashlight. He stepped around the pool of puke on the floor and pitched onto the bed, lay sprawled with barely the energy to draw up the blanket. He set the flashlight on the mattress, turned it off. Through careful manipulation of his legs he brought the sheet and blanket into reach and tugged them to his chin. When he closed his eyes, he realized with horror that he was desperately thirsty, his throat acidburned, his body plundered of fluid and salts. He knew he had to drink, water at the very least, but better still something to replenish his leached minerals.

He closed his eyes, seducing sleep, but it would not come. The voice of his body demanding hydration. He pushed himself up on his elbows, flopped back, the impact against the pillow resonating a pain in his head.

He thought about his cellphone. In the car.

Help, he said softly. Help.

The crowd outside had dispersed. There was just the lake, the wind's indifferent howl.

He slept, but briefly, and was awakened by the sound of a dog barking. A hard rap on the door.

Yes, he whispered.

Again a knock, louder, like pistolshots in Nathan's throbbing skull.

A key in the lock and the door swung wide, admitting a stinging breeze. Nathan saw a shape in the doorway.

You in here? Onion asked.

Help me, Nathan said.

He heard the panting of the dog, then the chatter of its claws on the floor. Then the sound of lapping.

Aw Scorp, did you find something? Onion asked, shutting the door and moving into the darkness. Nathan wondered why the old man hadn't brought a flashlight, then remembered his blindness.

Onion came closer, ran into the bed. Nathan felt for the flashlight, turned it on, projecting a pocked sphere of light on the ceiling. The dog was circling the pool of vomit, sampling from various points as if from a buffet. Onion loomed over the bed, his flawed skull further warped by the weak light.

Well, I know you ain't dead. That light helps a little. Scorp, for chrissakes I'm going to knock your brains in. Get over here.

The dog trotted to Onion's side and the old man grabbed its head. He sank to the floor and the dog tried to lick his face. Christ, if your breath weren't bad enough! Go on over there. And sit. And lie down. Good dog.

Onion pressed his hands to the mattress, shuffled on his knees to the head of the bed, a pantcuff dredging through a fringe of the vomit pool. His hand found Nathan's face, moved to his forehead, and Nathan felt the scales of antique callus.

It better not be catching, Onion said.

Food poisoning, Nathan whispered.

Could be. You have the skitters too? Well, don't really have to ask. I can smell that too. Hope you at least made it to the john for that. How do you feel?

Thirsty.

I'll get you some water. Though there's gingerale in the fridge. That might be better. Scorp, get back over there and lie down! Listen, you guide me around that barf. I don't need to step in it. Just point that flashlight and I'll follow the beam.

Nathan aimed the light at the wall and the old man shuffled towards it. Nathan drifted it forward and Onion followed, circumnavigating the vomit until he reached the fridge. He opened it and withdrew a can of gingerale and shook it vigorously and held it over the sink and cracked it. *Spiff.* He poured off the foam and set the can on the counter.

Better let it flatten out some.

Nathan heard above the clash of wind and surf the crackle of bubbles bursting in the can.

Christ is it on the counter too?

Nathan struggled to voice an apology, emitted a pathetic croak. He must've slept then for Onion's hand on his shoulder awakened him. The man was sitting on the bed holding a glass of gingerale.

Drink this now.

He helped Nathan rise onto his elbows, then with a hand to the back of his neck held the glass to Nathan's lips. It was sweet and cold and it scoured his throat as it went down. An unguent's sting, electrically refreshing. Nathan drank eagerly, felt the ball of his epiglottis buck painfully in his throat. Onion tipped the glass away when it was half empty.

Slowly. Don't want it to come back up. Can you take more?

Nathan nodded and Onion restored the glass at his lips. Nathan drained it and Onion let his head back down on the pillow.

Better?

Nathan nodded.

Sleep now.

Weak sunlight entered through the window above the bed, quivering as it percolated through the windblown branches of the trees above the cottage. Nathan looked up through the filthy glass. He felt beaten, every muscle wrenched and bruised, a rancid taste in his mouth, his throat pickled. But the nausea gone, and he suffered a broad lust for drink, applejuice, or better still a mango lassi. How far to the nearest mango lassi?

He lifted his head, which hummed with a distant ache, and saw Onion asleep in the La-Z-Boy, a crocheted blanket across his lap. Scorp on the floor with his head on his paws. He raised it, looked at Nathan, and yawned. His tail thumped a few times on the floorboards and was still.

The vomit on the floor was gone, a wet blot on the wood where the puddle had lain, a mop and pail by the door. The counter cleansed too, his dishes washed and resting in a wire rack beside the sink. A basket with sponges and brushes and cleansers, the air ripe with the scent of Pine-Sol.

Nathan got up, pulled on his jeans, was winded by the time he reached the bathroom. Arms propped on the sink, looking at his pale face, eyewhites the hue of old ivory. While he brushed his teeth Scorp came in and nudged Nathan's thigh, then lapped noisily from the toilet bowl. Nathan spit, rinsed his mouth.

Come on out, he said, pulling the dog's collar.

The bathtub also cleaned, vomit sluiced away. Nathan felt the deck of the world listing, saw turbines of light at the periphery of his vision. He stumbled back into the room and crashed on the bed.

When he awoke the room was empty. He felt better, put on his shoes and a shirt and coat and went out. It was afternoon and the sky was a bleached blue, wafers of cloud stacked in the southwest, the lake below it choppy and teal blue. A freighter balanced on the horizon's edge, its deck a stiff dash between the superstructures on prow and stern. Moving almost imperceptibly eastward against the chop.

He walked slowly to the house, pausing when surges of exhaustion threatened his balance, entered the office. He stumbled to the counter and threw his arms on it and rested there, panting. He rang the bell, heard motion in the next room and while waiting for the old man Nathan took out his billfold and drew two twenties, folded them into his palm.

Onion came in with a pipe clenched in his teeth and carrying the clipboard.

It's just me, Nathan said.

Onion stopped, drew on his pipe. You should be in bed. I was just planning on coming down there with tea and toast.

Look, I underpaid yesterday.

You what?

On the creditcard form. I . . . I cheated you. Entered forty-five instead of seventy-five.

Mmm.

And I'm sorry.

Well I knew that.

You know I'm sorry?

I know you underpaid. I got this big magnifier with a lamp. I use it to read.

Nathan wanted to ask if he'd discovered the deception before or after venturing out to rescue his poisoned guest.

Why don't you come on in here and I'll fix you some toast.

But the bill. I want to settle up.

Nathan held out the bills but Onion's sight remained fixed on the wall.

That's all right. I usually charge thirty-five offseason.

What?

Sure. Who's going to pay any more for these dumpy shacks? Don't even have TVs.

But you said seventy-five.

Just come on in here. I think I got some bananas.

Nathan pocketed the bills, lifted the hinged board that gated the counter and followed Onion into his livingroom. It was a foul little chamber, lit only by daylight through the rainstreaked windows and the bleached glow from a television. Couch and easychair threadbare in their tartan casings, knickknacks and framed photos on every surface, the coffeetable, endtables, the television, the windowsill. Faded photos of longdead forebears. A fatlegged wooden dinnertable behind the chesterfield, and clamped to it a saucersized magnifying glass on an articulating arm with a loop of fluorescent tubing encircling the lens. Junk on the table, buttons and scraps of fabric, paper, and under the lens a hardcover book, largeprint edition. Behind the table a doorway led to a kitchen, and Onion headed in this direction.

Sit down. I can hear you puffing from the walk.

Let me help you in the kitchen.

I know better than you where everything's at. Sit.

Nathan perched himself on the sofa's lip. He could not discern the program on the mistuned television screen. Accusatory voice of a woman, shrill, then the outraged growl of a studio audience.

You can change the channel if you like, Onion called from the kitchen.

Framed on the wall the front page of an old *Globe and Mail*, and under the headline ALLIES LAND IN FRANCE a photo of soldiers crouched on the deck of an amphibious craft, rifles at the ready.

Nathan stood and approached the picture, stared through the greasy glass at the faces of the men. He read the caption: Michael Welch and Ian "Onion" Peters preparing for Juno. Nathan's eyes moved to the date: June 6th, 1944.

Nathan circled the room, saw on the mantle a sepiatoned photo of a patriarch seated beside his sourfaced wife and their brood. They were arrayed in what appeared to be a barnyard, for a rooster stood arrogantly on a fencerail at the edge of the frame. Eleven children and one shaggy mutt. Was one of these kids Onion? All heads normal. Something about the smallest boy, in front on the right, his head hazed by motion as he turned to regard the dog.

Also on the shelf an old nautical clock displaying an hour not even remotely accurate. Silent. A key of brushed nickel beside it. Nathan picked it up, opened the glass face, and put the key into the keyhole and wound, heard the leaves of the mainspring draw tight, but after only a few turns it resisted and Nathan, determined to wind it fully, clenched his teeth, and gave a hard crank. Heard a pop, and then the flutter of the leafsprings. He felt a bomb of dread explode in his belly, spun the key, spun it, spun it, but now there was no resistance at all. He withdrew the key, set it down, closed the clockface, moved to study other photographs, grainy daguerreotypes, early Kodachrome, colours pale now, nearly pastel, men and women, children, a softfocused portrait of Onion in uniform, head still intact.

Nathan turned to see the old man standing in the kitchen doorway holding a tray with toast and a teapot and cups. Let me get that, Nathan said, approaching, lifting the tray from Onion's hands.

Thanks. Any luck with that clock?

I – I think it's broken, Nathan replied.

Dammit. I know who it was too. That drunk son of a bitch Jeff Howatt. Brings me groceries. Just dumps the stuff on the kitchen floor and takes off. Drank a bottle of my brandy last month.

It was me, Nathan said.

Well that'd be quite the trick. Do ya siphon it off long distance?

I mean the clock. I broke the mainspring. Overwound it.

You're just liable to take the blame for everything. I know it was him. That son of a bitch.

Nathan set the tray on the coffeetable and Onion lowered

himself onto the sofa where sallow foamrubber bulged through the fabric's mesh.

Nathan, feeling woozy and poisoned, sat hastily in a chair. He tried to pant silently, but Onion turned his head, listening.

You participated in D-Day? Nathan asked.

Yes. Don't believe that newspaper photo, though. It was snapped the day before we landed, right in the docks at Dover. Photographer told us to look scared and proud at the same time. How we do?

You look scared and proud.

Course, that was a week before my accident.

Accident?

Tank run my head over.

A tank? Hell. Was this a common German tactic?

Germans nothing. It was one of ours. A Yank. A Yank tank. We were trying to dig it out of a trap. It'd been raining all morning, earth a complete quagmire. I'd got my shovel under the front tread and was trying to haul some mud out when the machine ran forward. I was under a good three minutes before they dug me out.

Nathan couldn't avoid imagining the horror of it: crushing pressure, mouth and nose crammed with muck, drowning while shovelblades jabbed around you. Nathan's guts churned, and he had to breathe deeply to maintain control.

You okay? Onion asked.

You were lucky the ground was wet, Nathan said.

Lucky nothing. Wouldn't have been anywhere near the thing if it'd been dry that day. Course I might've bought it elsewhere if that hadn't taken me out of action. Sniper got the other guy in that picture, Mikey Welch, the day before my accident. Put one right here. Onion tapped his forehead with an index finger. You never seen such a mess. Everything come out the back.

Nathan focused on pouring the tea.

You stay another night? Onion asked.

I've got to get on.

But you're sick.

I'm all right.

Where you off to?

I'm just . . . I'm heading west.

To what?

Pardon me?

Or from what?

I'm not sure what you mean, Nathan said, sipping his too-hot tea, trying to siphon off a little caffeine to salve his aching head.

Well, someone travelling is usually going somewheres or getting away from somewheres.

I'm heading west.

Okay. Don't mean to pry.

They sipped their tea. Nathan squirmed in his chair, set his cup down, lifted it, drank. Onion sat with his head tilted, as if listening.

How did you know to come last night? Nathan asked, his voice louder than he'd intended.

What?

To my cabin. How did you know I was sick?

I come cause the power was out.

How did you know it was out? Weren't you sleeping? And why did you think I'd need your help for that?

Now who's prying.

I'm just curious.

Onion turned his head as if to catch a distant sound and Nathan held his breath, also listening. The wind, the lake's foaming wash. Onion said without turning, I learnt long ago you can't wait around for the right person to help. You help whoever's about.

Nathan waited for a sardonic postscript, but there was none. He stood, cleared his throat, said, Well, goodbye.

Onion said nothing for several moments, and Nathan was about to leave when the old man said in a voice almost jovial, Hard to know what it would've been like without the accident. His face was aimed squarely at Nathan, as if he could see him clearly.

What's that? Nathan asked.

If I hadn't been run over by that tank.

You never . . . you didn't marry? Nathan asked.

Almost. I come back from France like this she didn't want me anymore. Funny to think though. If I'd had a son he'd be your age.

Yes, Nathan replied. More or less.

Onion looked away, and his gaze seemed to fall on something impossibly distant. When he spoke again his voice was hoarse and reedy, like he couldn't catch his breath, and he said quietly, Without the accident.

Nathan was frozen to the spot, seized by the bleak expression on Onion's face, the faint tremble of the old man's jaw. Nathan wanted to settle the debt, but he could think of nothing meaningful. At last he fished from his wallet a pair of hundred dollar bills and the twenties he'd pocketed, to cover the clock and the shortchanged bill and the labour of cleaning up his mess. Except for the change in his car's ashtray it was all the cash he had. Not nearly enough. Not even enough to cover the gingerale.

What are you doing? Onion asked.

Well. Paying you back for that brandy I stole.

Aw, you don't need to do that.

Nathan set the bills beside the sugarpot. He walked to the door, paused, waiting for Onion to acknowledge his departure, but the old man sat as before, his eyes focused on a place far away.

Nathan went outside and drew deep breaths of the cold and leafspiced air, the metallic reek of the lake. He went to the cabin and collected his things and when he came out a light rain was falling.

He drove up the gravel road, bracing himself for a police confrontation, but the way was clear and he got on the Trans-Canada and drove west, past Terrace Bay and Schreiber, Rossport and Lake Helen. Unable to bear it any longer he risked a drivethrough to buy a jumbo coffee, with six creams to blunt the brew's acidity. He parked and pried off the lid to cool it quicker, lifted the cup to his nose and inhaled before sipping. It was delicious as he poured it into the void of his craving, his head ringing like a gong as caffeine leached into his bloodstream. His stomach grappled with it, but in a few minutes a wide, flat serenity climbed into his skull, and he pressed his head into the headrest and closed his eyes. Panicked when he opened them and saw a car with a gold crest on its door slink past, relaxed when he saw that it belonged to a private security firm.

He drove until he crossed the Nipigon River Bridge, stopped at an ATM in Nipigon to restock his wallet, and in the parkinglot unfolded the map on the car's hood. He was at the northernmost crest of Superior, where Highway 17 turned southwest towards Thunder Bay. That city stirred in him a vague dread, and he lifted his eyes to study the cataclysmic expanse of Ontario's north, a sprawl of white fissured with blue and here and there patches of green: provincial parks, great roadless blotches with names like Wabakimi, Otoskwin-Attawapiskat, Pipestone, Winisk River. A dozen towns flung across the map's vastness like peppercorns – Muskrat Dam, Sachigo Lake, Kitchenuhmaykoosib – each clinging tenuously to an airport, and half of them displaying a tiny red cross, remote waypoints where ailments – bloated appendix, fibrillating heart, or the injuries of the bush: bear attack, falling timber, lightningstrike – might be treated, if you survive the transport. And still Nathan longed for it, longed to be airdropped into solitude. The bush, cradle of the north, the ultimate retreat, with only commercial jets and satellites crossing the open sky to remind you of the jang and clank of the world.

Recognizing abruptly the limitations of the automobile – not much better than the train, requiring a specialized surface – Nathan followed the blacktop to the southwest, vigilant for police. There were none, but he felt more concern than comfort in this. Who was patrolling this remote highway? Past Hurkett, Dorion, a turnoff to Pass Lake and Sleeping Giant Provincial Park, past the Terry Fox Scenic Lookout, on to Thunder Bay with its palatial grain elevators lapped by the whitecapped bay and the buttes of islands standing clear in the distance.

He drove down to the harbour where freighters leaned against the piers, hulls pressed into the frigid lakewaters. He gassed up, drove downtown, circled through its streets, parked across from the Ontario government building, a vast structure sided in pearlgrey aluminum. He sat looking up at it through the windshield, trying to make up his mind, then got out his cellphone, called directory assistance.

Thunder Bay, he told the automated voice. Ministry of Transportation.

He dialled the number, made his way through the pushbutton labyrinth, press four, press six, dial zero if you wish to speak to an operator, until at last he got her on the phone.

It's me, he said. Nathan Soderquist.

There was a long pause, and then she answered without emotion, Ah, Nathan. This is a surprise.

I'm in Thunder Bay.

A longer pause, then, What brings you here?

Passing through. Listen, I'm wondering if you want to meet. For coffee.

Meet? When?

Right now. He glanced up at the smoked windows, wondering if she was behind one of them. I'm parked on Red River. Across from your building.

You're lying, she said. Anyway, it doesn't matter, I can't right now. I'm working.

I see.

But hold on. What about tonight? Dinner.

No, he replied quickly. I won't be here that long. I've got to get on.

Well I can't just leave. I'm in the middle of something.

All right. I understand. I just wanted to say hi. So, hi.

There was a long silence and he said, Are you there?

She said, I wish you'd called earlier. Now's a really bad time.

All right.

I mean I finish at five. You can't stay until five?

I can't. Quiet again. Hello? Norah, did you hear me?

I heard you, she said. I just don't understand the rush. Why you can't stay a few more hours.

I'm just passing through.

A silence, a long sigh. Then she said, Fine, and hung up. Nathan held the phone to his ear as if expecting more, then folded it shut. Thinking that it had probably been enough, that he'd only wanted to hear her voice. And now it was done. He pulled away from the curb, began to drive, but felt agitated, needed air. He saw a sporting and army surplus store, decided to buy a utility knife, with scissors and a corkscrew and a Phillips-head screwdriver. Inexplicably convinced that he needed one. He parked around the corner and got out, saw as he approached the store a ragclad youth slouching against the storefront, his neck thrust forward and eyes closed beneath the brim of a baseball cap, but his face rose as Nathan reached for the door.

Hey buddy, the boy called. Spare some change?

What for? Nathan asked, stopping.

Eat.

What's that you're holding? Nathan asked, noting that the boy was pressing the palm of his right hand to his chest. The boy looked up now, straight into Nathan's eyes with an expression of hate, and Nathan took an involuntary step backwards, convinced that it was a weapon. The boy lifted his palm for Nathan to see that it was wet with blood. He restored the hand and dropped his head.

Hell, Nathan said.

Just a buck or two?

Nathan started to stride away, stopped. I'm going to get my car. I'm going to take you to a hospital.

No, the boy replied, softly but with conviction. I just need a buck. How bout a buck.

Nathan's fists clenched. He had to resist the urge to seize the boy and fling him over his shoulder. He glanced up and down the street. No one. He jogged to the corner, convinced that what the boy needed was a second opinion. When he rounded it he saw coming towards him at a brisk pace, heels clacking against the pavement, a slender brunette wearing a long coat and huge, silvered sunglasses in which the reflected world lay warped and bloated. She stopped when she saw him, seemed about to turn, then came on.

Nathan, she said breathlessly.

Norah.

I came looking for you. Didn't expect to find you. Still want to get that coffee?

I thought it was a bad time, he said.

It is. An awful time. But you have a few minutes? Before you skip town?

All right.

Norah stirred her drink, rapped the teaspoon against the rim of the cup as if calling for order. She set the spoon in the saucer and crossed her forearms, rested them on the tabletop.

So, she said, finally pushing the sunglasses up into her hair. He saw the sad slant of her eyes, their stonegrey irises. She used to wear tinted contact lenses of swimmingpool blue. Her skin waxy and pale. Her hair a deep, peaty brown, highlights fading at the tips.

So, she repeated. How are you?

Stress on *are*, attempting to turn the phrase sincere. Not just making conversation — she needed to know. He wondered if she felt complicit. Guilty. He was overcome by a sudden, jarring rage. I'm fucking pissed off, he wanted to say. You ruined my life! Tension rippled across his shoulders and chest, down his biceps, into his forearms. Veins stood out on the backs of his hands like cables. And to his astonishment she was studying him — his shoulders and chest, his muscled arms — and her eyebrows rose minutely. Nathan wanted to bash the table with both fists. He wanted to sweep the crockery onto the floor. What's the matter with you? he wanted to shout. They're dead! Do you understand?

Norah, he said, his voice almost a whisper, and she leaned forward.

But the waitress came, and Nathan turned and faced at eye-level her generous breasts, slung in the hammocks of a pushup bra with the creamy flesh exposed in the scoop of her t-shirt so they seemed offered to him on a platter. He cleared his throat and looked up but it was no secret to any present where his eyes had lingered. The waitress beamed, and Norah bent over her purse and searched furiously for something, her cellphone apparently, for she checked it and returned it to the bag.

More coffee? the waitress asked, and Nathan focused on her face; it was caked with foundation which had crazed like china-glaze around her eyesockets. She was pretty nevertheless, with wide, brown eyes and a bottom lip that pouted invitingly. The voluptuous opposite of Norah, and Nathan hated himself for comparing them. Stop it, he told himself, struggling to manage these mutinous thoughts. Turned to Norah and was struck with loathing for this bony, selfconsious waif whom he had kissed and touched on the eve of his wife's and child's deaths. It hadn't caused their deaths, he said to himself, as he had many times before. It had nothing to do with that.

I'll have more coffee, Norah said, and the waitress filled her cup.

Yes. All right, Nathan said, pushing the cup towards her and averting his eyes from the feast of her bosom.

I heard you were transferred here, Nathan said after the waitress was gone.

Yes, she replied. I needed a change.

Nathan was remembering with painful clarity how he'd come out of the washroom and found her, this pretty friend of Lisa's, quietly weeping outside the door.

What's wrong? he'd asked her.

Nothing, nothing's wrong.

All right. But you're crying.

Oh Nathan. I'm so lonely. You know Rick and I broke up a few months ago. I just can't seem to get over it. Not *him*. I'm long over him. Over *it*. Being alone.

Someone brushed past behind him and entered the washroom, shut the door, another of the party guests.

You're not alone, Nathan said. You have friends. Good friends who would do anything for you.

She let out a sob and Nathan folded his arms around her. She pressed her face into his chest, muttering.

What's that? he asked.

This is so embarrassing, she whispered, then broke away from him, pulled open another of the hallway doors, and drew him into the darkened room. Threw her body against his.

Nathan looking at her across the table, wondering still, after these many months, how much had been spontaneous, how much she'd planned. And just wanting her to go away now. He had to think. She began talking about her job, describing the paperwork, her co-workers, the stink of the new carpet in her office. Nathan clenched his teeth, tried to focus his energy on making her feel unwelcome. Didn't she have to get back?

Look at her, he told himself. Look at the temptation that ruined your life. Look.

The lips he kissed. In the room in a politician's house, beside the playpen in which his own daughter was sleeping. Indicting whispers carried on radiowaves, broadcast through the baby monitor on the dresser to the receiver, to Lisa in the livingroom.

Nathan imagines Lisa on the couch in the candlelight, the glow of the Christmas tree, submerged in the hubbub of drunk party guests and seasonal music. Imagines her sipping eggnog while some underachiever from the Department of Justice babbles restlessly to regain her attention, which, having heard odd rustlings, is fixed on the speaker within the little unit, now pressed to her ear.

Oh god Nathan. Do you know how long I've wanted to do that?

No, he'd tried to say, but she smothered the word with her lips. He was not pushing her away, not yet, he was dazed, his ego charged, he was suffering the pre-rational thrill from the novelty of tasting after so many years another's mouth. He was going to push her away. In a second, in the very next second.

Then Lisa bursting into the room, her hand slapping and groping the wall, for what purpose Nathan could not at the time determine, until the lights blazed on. Not even looking at Nathan and Norah as they drew apart, as Norah wiped the back of her hand across her mouth, Lisa making straight for the playpen in which Sydney lay, the girl waking instantly as Lisa drew her forcefully to her breast, child emitting a gasping wail, and Nathan's first impulse was to move towards the girl to offer comfort, halting dead a pace away as Lisa's face met his, her expression like the thrust of a dagger.

Nathan's universe, which for years had grown firm and hale, collapsing. Knowing he had no defence against years of her smouldering, groundless jealousy. Wringing his hands, he was actually wringing his hands as Lisa with their daughter in her arms strode past him and out the door, and he closed his eyes and attempted, without irony, with absolute sincerity, to will, by brainpower alone, to make time reverse itself by an hour, by ten minutes, was it so much to ask for, ten paltry minutes?

He didn't speak as he followed them to the livingroom, Sydney's wail like a fire engine's, opening a path through the intoxicated partygoers, some of them were dancing. In the foyer Nathan stood there, a dozen phrases summoned to his lips and then dismissed, standing in desperate silence, watching, powerless as Lisa packed the bawling child into a snowsuit, as she drew on her own coat and boots. Nathan watching, he would understand later, the genesis of their deaths. He said nothing, he said nothing at all, failing to determine a phrase, perhaps *the* phrase, that might've stopped her, or even delayed her by a moment, enough to evade the snowplough, to achieve the curve without spinning out. One word that may have set the future on a different path, nudged by some minute degree the domino of the moment so its effects propagated to results marginally different, yet sufficient to save their lives. That word – was it *stop*, or *sorry* or *don't*? There, at the front door of some government minister's country house, on December 21st at 10 p.m., he'd had a chance to change the future, to preserve the future.

He gazed across the table at Norah, who was still speaking, and he knew suddenly that the key word was none of those. The word that would have saved his world was *no*.

No, he said now, interrupting her.

What?

No, he repeated. No, Norah.

Norah looked at him, their eyes locking, and she glanced

immediately at her cup, averting her eyes from the threat. She looked up again, a doubletake, checking to see if her assessment was correct. It was. She lowered her eyes to her watch, tapped its crystal with a lacquered fingernail and looked up with a hopeless smile. I've got to go.

Nathan sat back on the bench.

Norah's eyes dropped to her wallet. She cracked open the changepouch, fished about, withdrew a dollar. Then she leaned forward, tapping the coin on the table, looked Nathan broad in the face and prepared to speak. Goodbye, she said, and rose, and was gone.

No, Nathan whispered. But too late.

CHAPTER 4

Standing outside the café buttoning his coat Nathan suddenly remembered the wounded boy. Hell, he whispered, and jogged around the corner, but the boy was gone, the only sign he'd been there a reddish stain the size of a coin on the cement. Nathan ran to the next corner, glancing across the street, looked each way at the intersection, but the boy was nowhere to be seen. Nathan returned to the spot and squatted, looking at the bloodstain, trying to assure himself that it wasn't much, certainly not a life-threatening amount. He stood and paced back and forth. He had gone for help, had been distracted by Norah's arrival. He stood, clenching, unclenching his fists. Feeling helpless. Decided to wait for the boy. He might be back. Nathan went to his car, got his notebook, and returned to the spot. He sat on the pavement with his back against the storefront, the bloodstain beside him, felt the cold cement through his jeans.

OCTOBER 10TH
Herringbone sky, frozen ripple from an event beyond the horizon, sheer cloud gripped by its edge and snapped like a bedsheet sending wave upon wave through the fabric.

It was no good, he wanted thunderheads, a tornado stabbing down, sucking man, beast, and structure into its cruel heart, where all would be wrecked and rendered and blended before the thing spewed it back to earth in a foul smut of all that had been.

A woman, maybe sixty, clicked past on heels too high, scowled at him. Derelict vagrant, shunned, maligned. Himself guilty of judgment of the destitute before Lisa chided him in her gentle way, reminding him again that the success of civilization depended on discarding the visceral, evolutionary reaction. They'd just emerged from the grocery store laden with shopping bags. Nathan had cursed a panhandler, grinned at Lisa. No drawnout lecture, simply this: Imagine, Nathan. Money gone. Family gone. Can't work. And then that's you on the pavement with your hand outstretched.

Hey, he called after the woman in heels. Hey!

Her shoulders stiffened, but she did not turn, increased her pace. Nathan drew his legs up and glared at the passing cars and trucks. He pressed his hand to his breast, the same spot where the boy was wounded. Pedestrian traffic increasing as five o'clock came. He was a street pariah. He rose and dusted himself off, shut the notebook, carried it back to the car and threw it onto the passenger seat. He was hungry, walked in search of food. He entered a cluttered convenience store, picked out a cellophane-wrapped sandwich that looked like styrofoam, got an applejuice, and went out into the failing light. He glanced at a newspaper rack in front of the store. Tuesday, it was Tuesday, and he was in Thunder Bay.

He wanted something lowkey, a bar, a murky den, not some family restaurant, no menu featuring herbal tea and Shirley Temples. He walked in an expanding spiral with his car at the hub, passed shops selling software, shoes, pornography, passed faded For Lease signs, floors littered with collapsed shelves and mouseturds. Getting dark now, and colder, and he finally found what he sought, a dingy club with a backlit sign, Ace of Spades, the view within obscured by opaque yellow foil.

He inhaled smoky air. It was a place of former glory with a nickel bar and a ceiling of stamped tin, the upholstery torn, the carpet bald at the door and along the walkway behind the barstools. Low light, bulbs missing from some of the cutglass lamps dangling from braided cables above the bartop. Nathan squinted into the back, made out shadowy figures hunched over beer and whiskey. Faces concealed beneath greasy bangs and the brims of caps. A middleaged woman sat across from a leering rake in a rugby shirt. She was wearing a pink haltertop, her flesh liverspotted and grey.

Nathan set the plastic bag with his juice and sandwich on the seat closest the door, hung his coat across the backrest. He sat beside it, brought his hands together on the nickel top, sitting straighter than usual, wanting to stand off from the desperate monads in the back. The bartender wore a studded leather vest over an ivory dress shirt, stitching on the forearms and across the breast, his mouth like the stroke of a knife across his jaw, eyes the colour of old pennies. Leaning on the bar, polishing a shotglass without irony. He eyed Nathan cautiously, glanced into the back as if seeking permission to move, then approached. The man's hair stiff with grease, swept over his ears in glossy arcs.

Get you.

Bourbon, straight up, Nathan said.

Someone came in, admitting a sweet gust of cool air. The bartender's eyes moved, watching the new patron pass, then returned to Nathan.

What?

Bourbon, straight. In a fucking glass, Nathan said softly.

This got the barman's attention. His face grew rigid, and Nathan knew he was one of those guys good with a suckerpunch or throwing a knife into a fistfight. But he was smallboned and squat, and Nathan lifted his shoulders and pushed out his jaw, and the bartender stepped back and guffawed, whether in defiance or resignation Nathan could not be sure, but in a moment he set before Nathan the shotglass he'd been rubbing. Then he whirled, seized a bottle of Wild Turkey from the bar, poured the glass full. Nathan nodded in a way calculated to acknowledge without necessarily thanking, and the bartender retreated to his corner and drew a new glass for buffing.

Nathan's cellphone rang twice before he knew what it was, and he patted his belt where he sometimes clipped it. Unsuccessful, he turned to the chair beside him, found the phone in a coatpocket.

Yes.

It's Mabel.

God Mabel. You always take me by surprise. He imagined her small and lean on a pressback in her farmhouse kitchen, the mouthpiece lodged between chin and shoulder with the cord running in knotted coils to the phone. Remembering her on the night of the accident. The one who found them? the cop had said to Nathan. Lives up there in that farmhouse. She's in here. The cop leading the way to the police cruiser.

Do other people call you? came her voice from the phone.

No.

Then why the surprise?

I don't know. I guess I'm surprised that you don't give up.

Ha. Well, giving up isn't something I'm disposed to. Nathan, where are you?

Thunder Bay.

You passed me by.

Yes. I guess I did.

I thought you might stop and visit.

Did you really think so?

No. I guess this is ground zero for you. Where the world ended.

Yes, he replied. Exactly.

Ka-boom. I hope you don't hold it against me.

Of course not.

If it were me I'd pretty much avoid everything to do with that night.

I'm glad you understand, Nathan replied, trying to forget that not an hour ago he'd sat across a table from Norah.

Will you ever be able to overcome that?

Someday.

Well, she said, her voice brighter. I'm glad about that. Because I could take care of you. I'm good at it. I've got six cows, thirty chickens, and a donkey. She laughed. I'm sure you're no worse than a donkey.

He was overcome by a deep gloom. It dogged him for a moment before he saw the bourbon on the bar and tossed it down in one swallow. The causticity of it made him hack and cough, and he knew in an instant that this was some inferior brand that had been poured into a Wild Turkey bottle. He heard chatter from the phone, which had fallen away from his ear.

Mabel, he said.

What happened Nathan? You were coughing.

I think I'm coming down with something.

You need my magic cold elixir. I use ginseng and honey and whiskey.

Make mine a double.

After a pause she said, Nathan, will you call me? When you figure it out?

Nathan laughed.

Will you? she repeated.

Am I trying to figure something out? I thought I was just, you know, driving.

Driving is only a manifestation of a process. It is not the process itself.

Where do you get these ideas? From novels?

Comic books. Stop laughing, I'm serious. Here's a question for you: if you were a superhero and you'd lost your powers, what would you do?

He laughed. A superhero? If I was a superhero? I don't know. Get a job? Is this a serious question?

You'd try to restore your powers, she said soberly. Why?

Because they're cool?

Because they're integral to your identity. Because you don't know who you are without them.

All right. I guess that makes sense. And what if I can't get them back? What if my powers are dead? What then?

Don't confuse your power with your wards.

My what?

Your charges. Those you pledged to defend. Just something to think about, Nathan. I have to go. I'll call you again.

I still don't understand.

In a few days.

All right.

Bye Nathan.

She hung up. He ordered another bourbon, said with some menace to the bartender, Let's try your premium brand this time. The bartender nodded mildly, filled Nathan's glass from a bottle from beneath the bar. Nathan turned back towards the room. A beefy man had come from the back, passed over the empty stools, taken the one beside Nathan. He nodded, fingering the vinyl cover of a binder. A big, piefaced man, dark hair mown back as far as his ears, pale cheeks wormed with bloodvessels. He wore a plaid shirt buttoned to the neck.

Good evening, he said in a voice which, though hushed, rang rich and clear, like a preacher's.

Hi, Nathan replied, feeling a blend of suspicion and goodwill. How are you?

I am pleased to meet you, sir. Pleased to meet you. My name is Dan. And yes, I am selling something.

Nathan gave a sidelong look to the man, then sipped his bourbon, which was decidedly smoother than the first. What? he asked.

Dan drummed nicotinestained fingers against the binder's cover. He wore on the pinky of his left hand a heavy ring of gold with an ornate *D* fashioned from onyx.

Well, Dan replied. I will show you once I've determined your, hum, let's call it receptiveness. No point in displaying my wares to a disinterested party. He drew a brass case from his shirtpocket and opened it to reveal a tidy row of cigarettes. Nathan accepted one, and Dan stuck one into his own mouth. He closed the case and rubbed his thumb against the cover, on which Nathan saw an engraving of a nude woman. Her legs were splayed and she was masturbating with a stout dildo, a look of ecstasy illuminating her features, which were decidedly Asian. Dan turned the box away then looked at Nathan, grinning with the cigarette between his lips. He searched in his pants pocket and came up with a lighter, also brass, and lit their cigarettes, and snapped it shut, then, leaning on elbows, held it before his face to study it.

Now how about that, he said through the cigarette. He drew smoke, plucked the cigarette from his mouth, and held it between two fingers while stroking the lighter with the pad of his thumb. Nathan leaned to look. An engraving of similar aesthetic, this of two naked women, kneeling before a standing man, one with his erect penis in her mouth, the other stroking with dangerously long fingernails his ample testicles.

Dan was watching him. He folded his hand around the lighter, put it back in his pocket. Care to browse the binder?

All right. Nathan imagined the pages laid out with every convenience: wallets, keytags, travel mugs, even blenders and toasterovens, all displaying similar artwork.

I must query though, and I'm loath to ask, but you're not connected in any way with law enforcement, are you?

What? You mean like cops? Hell, no.

I'm a cautious man. I have to ask that, he said, drawing open the cover.

Polaroids stuck into clear vinyl pockets, four to a page. Dan flipped slowly through it. Overexposed flash photos of women, some of them virtually girls, some in bikini tops and shorts, others wearing cowboy hats and tasselled jackets with rhinestones, one dressed in a yellow tutu, the cleft between her breasts a hard black rule. Her expression simulated lust, but below that, deep, concealed, Nathan saw contempt, desperation, fear. Most of them like that. Subterranean fury simmering beneath a veneer of arousal. Most of them white, with pale, untanned arms emerging from restrictive tanktops, skinny white legs; a few black women, some Asian. Near the back, one woman lifting with both hands a t-shirt to display the stark undercurves of her breasts, the blushing semi-circles of areolas exposed below the hem.

You're selling pictures, Nathan said.

Dan's laugh boomed through the barroom. I'm selling girls, he said, pushing the binder towards Nathan. Take your time. Ask me anything. That one there, for instance. She'll take it any which way you like.

Nathan's cigarette was almost gone. His windpipe felt raw and burned. He stubbed out the butt, wanted water but the bartender had disappeared.

He found himself paging through. Catalogue of humans. For sale. For rent. Not utter slavery, of course, not for more than a few hours, and not the person entire. Just mouth and tits, cunt and ass. Which seemed worse. A great wheel of nausea stirring in his belly, maybe from the food poisoning, maybe the bourbon. Maybe this. Hating himself for looking, for studying, for selecting. Hating the arousal building in his groin. This one with vast, brown eyes and heavy, red lips. Kissing. Do you kiss a whore? You can do whatever you goddamn please. Exciting, loathsome, the idea of utter compliance. Renting her body, her will. Buying her surrender. What an awful thing to ask of a person. His cock swelling.

He turned the pages. Overwhelming choices. Involuntarily sorting.

Last summer, Nathan's friend Conrad, yelling into Nathan's ear over the industrial boom of drummachines. They were at a downtown danceclub, Whiskey Saigon maybe, Conrad winnowing into simple categories – yes, no, maybe – the women gyrating around them, his judgment swift and unsentimental. Many no more than kids, nineteen years old.

The two men went to the bar, shouting into the ear of the semiclad barmaid with raccoon makeup, demanding more hard lemonade, and Nathan asking that Conrad not do that anymore.

What?

That thing, the sorting of the girls. The women.

Why the fuck not? You need a boost back on the pussywagon, my friend.

You misogynist fuck, Nathan replied, but so softly he hadn't heard it himself. Conrad touched his ear and Nathan just shook his head.

The candysweet drinks. Both men immensely drunk. As they re-entered the dancefloor the fevered throng swept over them, music thundering in a tribal drumbeat of such weight Nathan felt submerged to a great, subocean depth. They were into it, the moving bodies, parade of faces, a sweating man tanned and muscular, naked to the waist, a woman in a white undershirt, her breasts swaying as she danced, face lowered, wrists crossed as if bound, lifting them in a high arc. Bodies pressed against them as they regained their spot on the floor. Nathan moving then, eyes closed, letting the beat take control, shake him like a puppet.

Nathan flipped through the binder, forwards, backwards. Lascivious smiles. Their eyes accusatory. Involuntarily imaging Lisa in one of these snapshots. Or a grownup Sydney.

He clapped the binder shut, shoved it back to Dan.

Nothing you like? Dan asked. Nothing at all?

Nothing, Nathan replied, feeling his face flush.

Oh, come now, Dan replied, then guffawed. He opened the book. Her, he said. You like her, don't you? She's one lean little cocksucker.

Nathan snapped up his coat and stood, drew a twenty from his wallet and clapped it on the bar. Once on the street he realized he'd left the bag with the drink and sandwich inside. He reached for the door's handle, let his hand drop. A holocaust of rage in his chest. Fists balled.

He strode away, realized it was the wrong direction, came back.

Dan stepped out before him, drawing a jacket over his broad shoulders, cigarette dangling from his lip. He was clutching in one hand his binder, in the other Nathan's bag. Didn't see Nathan immediately, was studying the evening sky.

Gimme that, Nathan said, and Dan turned.

Was just coming out to find you, Dan said. You forgot this.

Nathan took the bag, checked its contents, looked at Dan's expectant face. Let me have a look at that binder again, Nathan said, holding a hand out.

Why, certainly, Dan said, lifting it.

Nathan snatched it and pitched it whirling into the street. A corner struck the asphalt and the binder cartwheeled into a far lane where an approaching car honked and slowed, steered so the binder passed between the wheels. A van narrowly missed it, and another car clipped its spine and sent it spinning into the centre of the lane.

Dan held his chin in one hand and smoked, gazing across the

street as if puzzling over how the book had come to rest there. Then he turned to Nathan and eyed him through a squint. That was a goddamn fuckish thing to do, he said mildly, and drew on his cigarette. Now I could split your face right here and peel it back like a lemonskin, or you could run like a good doggy and fetch my property.

Nathan forced his hands to relax, took a long breath of the cooling night air, imagined it dousing the heat in his belly. He turned his back on Dan, walked.

Hey, Dan said. Hey, you sulky son of a bitch.

Nathan heard footsteps behind him, braced himself but did not turn. A hand came down on his shoulder, and Nathan halted. He glanced at the hand, then looked over his shoulder at Dan's face, flushed purple. Cigarette still burning between his lips.

I could kill you, friend. It's not such a hard thing to do. This started off so well. Just fetch my book and we can part amiably.

Get your goddamn hand off me.

Dan pulled Nathan around and threw a punch into his belly. Nathan was ready, and the fist met the rigid slab of his abdomen. Nathan seized the wrist of the hand still planted on his shoulder and twisted, drawing Dan down to Nathan's rising knee, which struck Dan squarely in the ribs. Nathan felt the satisfying flex of the bone, heard Dan grunt as his heavy body fell towards the pavement, but Nathan hauled him back to his feet with one hand and punched his face with the other, once in the cheek below the left eye, the second time squarely in the nose.

Dan stood tottering on his legs, stunned. He fingered his nose, from which a thick gob of bloody mucous dangled, then felt his lips.

I believe my cigarette's gone missing, he said, eyes flicking from side to side, hunting the pavement. He spotted the cigarette, which had settled, still smoking, in the seam between two paving stones. He crouched to retrieve it, put it between his lips, and remained squatting, smoking while probing his nose.

Sir, I think you've broken my nose, he said. How does it look?

Broken, Nathan said. It's an improvement.

Oh my. Your wit worse than your punch. Give us a hand up, will you?

Dan extended a hand and Nathan looked at it.

Come now, a gesture of amnesty. You've beaten me.

The man crouching on the sidewalk, a hand extended, cigarette down to a stub between his lips, the wisp of smile on his face. Nathan stepped forward and extended his right hand. Their hands locked and Nathan started to pull the man to his feet. Nathan heard a tiny snick and the knife shot upwards in a blinding arc, its blade slicing through the leather of Nathan's sleeve. Nathan jumped back but Dan retained his hand in a crushing grip, and Nathan dodged outside the knife's reach as Dan thrust at his chest and belly, Nathan vaguely aware of the traffic still passing on the street, which seemed to have been retarded to a slowmotion crawl, as if the air had grown viscous, impeding their progress. Nathan swung Dan into a spin, letting centrifugal force aid in his avoidance of the knife, but then Dan threw the blade into the inside of Nathan's right forearm.

Nathan wailed. He struggled harder to escape and Dan punched the knife down again beside the first wound.

Think, goddamn. He will slash your arm to ribbons while you struggle like a dog on a chain. As Dan raised the knife to strike again, Nathan charged under the shining tip, drove his knee deep into the cushion of Dan's belly. The big man doubled forward and released his grip on Nathan's hand. Nathan staggered back and studied his wounded arm, saw red pearls of blood bloom from each of the two jagged entrypoints in his jacket sleeve. Flexed his fingers. The jacket's fibroid leather had impeded the blade, but he still felt an alarming tingle in his fingertips, and blood was surging from the wounds. He pressed a hand over them and looked at Dan, who was bent at the waist, panting, a palm on each knee, the knife still gripped in one hand. He raised his head and looked at Nathan.

If that doesn't educate you to respect the blade, I'm not sure what will.

Run, Nathan thought. Just run.

But before he could turn Dan rushed, the knife swinging in a long arc aimed at Nathan's throat. Nathan blocked Dan's wrist with his left forearm, and the blade stopped an inch from his forehead. Then a series of feints and cuts which Nathan flailed to avoid. When he emerged from the flurry he was cut above his right eye, a shallow nick. He felt blood run into his eyebrow, pushed his fingertips to the wound to stanch the flow, to keep it from getting into his eye. The cut curiously painless. The leather at the jacket's elbow dark with blood, and a constellation of blood-stains on the sidewalk beneath them.

Dan straightened before him, smoothed his free hand down the front of his shirt, then looked out at the traffic before returning his attention to Nathan.

It's still right there, he said, and in the syrupy murk of Nathan's thoughts he could not fathom Dan's meaning. Nathan turned to look, and he spotted the binder, still undamaged, lying in the far lane. It seemed hours ago that he had cast it there.

Dan pinched the bridge of his nose, and his voice was now filled with regret. There's still a chance to stop this ridiculous fighting. We can both return home to lick our wounds, and consider how wrong this day has gone. What do you say?

Nathan saw an image in his mind of Lisa, nodding, sweeping her hands forward, urging him to comply. Stop this. Just pick up the damn binder.

As Nathan opened his mouth to respond, Dan tottered on wobbling legs, seemed to crumple in a slow collapse towards him. Nathan heard a shoe slap the pavement as the man went over, but the fall was all wrong, and Dan's arm shot out and he jabbed the knife into Nathan's side. The blade glanced off Nathan's lowest rib and Dan's fall drew it into the soft tissue below it, ripping deep through the leather, for it had behind it the momentum of Dan's weight, and it sliced through the fascia and muscle of Nathan's side until it caromed off the bone of his hip, ripping free as Dan maintained his hold on the handle while he toppled to the pavement.

Nathan was running. Left hand inside his coat, curled along

his flank and pulled taut by the yoke of his shoulder. The wound's parted lips kissing his palm. Running. If he'd been uninjured he could certainly have outrun this heavyset pimp, but as he clutched the cut and raced along he could hear the footsteps behind him, could hear Dan's mammoth panting. The wound, his empty belly, yesterday's poisoning impeding him.

Gaining. Just one thing to do. A glance over his shoulder. Dan just behind him. Nathan slowing. Let him get closer.

Nathan halted instantly, and in one rapid motion doubled himself into a tight cylinder with his arms around his knees and prone, his forehead pressed to the sidewalk. Nothing Dan could do; he was too close. His legs struck Nathan's compressed form, and the man flipped. Nathan, winded by the collision, heard a smack he hoped was Dan's head against pavement. Nathan lifted his face, pushed his hands against the sidewalk, rose to a kneeling position. The blood on the hip and thigh of his jeans had chilled. Tried to unfold his legs to stand, but could not.

They were on a residential sidestreet, the light poor. Dan was down on his face, rolling, rising, his cheek and mouth bloody and ragged, spitting blood. He prodded into his mouth with fat fingers and fished out an eyetooth. Rolled into a sitting position.

You crafty son of a bitch. I'll remember that one. What's your name, friend? I'll call it after you. In your posthumous honour.

Dan rose, a hand splayed against his cheek, blood oozing between his fingers, his expression but tranquil. Nathan saw in the meagre light of streetlamps and porchlights that his other hand was empty. Dan lumbered about, casting his eyes in the grass beside the curb.

Fuck! he cried as he stood with one hand on his hip, the other pressed to his face in a expression of befuddlement. He straightened, regaining his composure. That particular knife was a favourite. I hate to see it lost. He stepped towards Nathan, stood over him as he drew forth the cigarette case. Worse still, he continued, is the repugnant chore of kicking a man to death.

Nathan wanted to rise but his legs had gone numb. He sat like a supplicant in a posture almost yogic, awaiting punishment. The first kick struck his collarbone but he didn't go over, refused to go over, knew that when he went down the kicks to kidney and groin would begin. He thought about Lisa and Sydney. Thought of them watching, anticipating his arrival.

Dan straightened his jacket with his free hand, swung his foot back for another stroke, when he abruptly lurched forward, and an instant later back, then spun, revealing the cause of this sudden spasm: a man – a police officer, Nathan perceived – on his back. When Nathan looked past the struggling pair he saw at the curb a cruiser with Thunder Bay Police on the door, and a second officer with his billyclub unsheathed, rushing forth.

Dan reeled and bucked like a bronco, shot an elbow back and caught the first officer in the ribs. But the cop held on, and the second officer moved in, raising his club. He brought it down with a crack across the crest of Dan's skull, but the pimp seemed unfazed, began to writhe and quake with vigour. The trio reeled backwards, the coupled men slamming against the cruiser's flank, but the first officer maintained his mount, and the second struck again with the nightstick.

Nathan let himself fall backwards, landed with his back on the grass, and through a titanic effort – while the three struggled voicelessly before him – unfolded his legs. He stretched them in the air, restoring circulation and sensation, while blood gushed from his side. In a few moments he was able to roll onto his belly and draw his legs beneath him, force himself into a crouch, then he rose and stood trembling like a drunk, watching the struggle as if it were nothing more than a televised spectacle. Then he moved off down the street, staggering, shivering now in the cold night air, wondering if shock was setting in.

He stepped into the empty street to investigate a glittering object. It was Dan's knife. He looked back at the fight still raging beside the cruiser, heard through the distance the occasional crack of the nightstick, and he picked up the knife and wiped his own blood against his jeans and folded the blade shut and put it in his pocket. Then he staggered along the street, past the raked lawns and porchlamps until he reached the end of the block and turned onto a thoroughfare, headed back in the direction of his car. Headlights of passing vehicles haloed and uncomfortably intense. He passed the convenience store where he'd bought the sandwich, closed, and remembered his bag containing the sandwich and drink, wondering where it had gone. He wasn't hungry but he was desperately thirsty and thought of the applejuice almost sent him back to the front of the bar where he was certain he'd find the bag. But then he saw his car parked at the curb waiting faithfully for his return. Dark inside but for the polygons of light projected onto the seats from a streetlamp. Get inside. Lock the door. Familiar scent, the smell, he decided, of his uninjured self. He lifted his hand from his side and held it before him and looked at it in the coppery light. A glove of wet and congealed blood with tracers of still wet blood even now drooling into his shirtcuff or falling against the seatfabric with the rhythm of a metronome. He replaced his hand and reached around into the backseat, felt the congealed blood at his elbow cracking, those little jabwounds now inconsequential, pawed through the silky laminate of magazine covers until he found his windbreaker, tugged it into his lap and wrapped it around his waist inside his leather coat, knotted the sleeves on his left side, drawing it tight. Water repellent, blood repellent? Better something absorbent, he thought, and again dug around in the backseat, then the floor behind the passenger seat. Found a small rag of fabric, wondered what it could be, pulled it forward. A barnyard scene in primary hues. Sydney's blankie. Forgotten memento he'd been carrying with him, lost beneath the refuse. He set it in the seat beside him, dug more, came up with nothing but a few Tim Hortons napkins. Jammed them beneath the windbreaker. Not enough. Suitcase in the trunk but he was too weak to move. He'd felt something else back there, fished about and came up with a halfbottle of grapefruit juice, or so it said on the label. The stuff inside had separated into a layer of sediment and a serum of clear fluid. He shook it, hoping to reconstitute it into something drinkable, so intense was his thirst, and opened the cap and without pause threw it down his throat. It had turned into a chunky liqueur that stung his throat and settled uncomfortably in his belly. Reached into his makeshift bandage and withdrew the napkins, which were flimsy and soaked with blood.

Hell, he whispered, and took the blankie from the passenger seat and crammed it into the cinched windbreaker against his wound. He needed antiseptic, stitches. When was his last tetanus shot? But at the hospital there'd be questions, and police. He started the engine, gripped the steeringwheel with his bloody hand. The wounds in his right arm had stopped bleeding, but an ache penetrated to the bone from shoulder to wrist as he reached for the gearstick and rocked it into first. As he eased into traffic he noticed trapped beneath a wiperblade a parking ticket. He uttered a curt snort.

Get on the road and find a clinic in some nondescript highway town where he could get sewn up and sent on his way without the law's intervention. Head west. At worst he could find treatment in Manitoba, where he wasn't the fugitive he was in Ontario. He knew his map lay somewhere among the detritus of the backseat, but if he recalled correctly the Manitoba border couldn't be more than an hour or two away.

At a red light he felt his left hand bonded to the steeringwheel with congealed blood, pried it off and when he flexed his fingers the skin of blood cracked at the fingerjoints and flaked into his lap. He glanced at the driver in the car beside him, a middle-aged woman who sat canted forward in her seat as if watching some suspenseful episode, and she seemed to sense his gaze so she turned and he let his bloodcaked hand fall to the base of the steeringwheel. He switched his eyes forward and gunned away from the light with a chirp of tires, followed signs leading to the Trans-Canada Highway, hit it and sped northwest, relieved to escape the hot barks of pain from every shifted gear. Traffic was moderate and he turned on the radio and drew a strong CBC signal and heard the tailend of *Ideas* and then the refrain for the 9 p.m. news. Fighting in Kandahar, an outbreak of waterborne E. coli in a town in Yukon, a labour dispute with civil servants. He increased the volume to crush thoughts of his condition but static began to erode the signal until it faded to a hiss. Panic weighing his gas foot to the floor, needing constantly to remind himself to remain alert, inconspicuous. Battling an augmenting fatigue, and cold now, teeth chattering, pushing the heater's levers to the stops, reducing them as the temperature rose and with it his weakness. Keep cool, stay awake. Stay alive. He tucked his right hand into the makeshift bandage, felt that the little wool blanket had swollen with blood, which was in a way good for it increased the pressure against his wound. So thirsty. Could he risk a drivethrough? Get a coffee. A diuretic, wasn't it, caffeine? Make him stop to pee. Better to get juice, to replenish, but he needed the stimulant. His bloody hands though, and how did his face look? What options? Part of him wanting to stop, to turn himself in. They'd help him, wouldn't they? But he'd heard stories too, Conrad once borrowed a Ferrari that was being used for a filmshoot on which he was assistant director. Pulled over for speeding, hauled down to the station where they shut him in a room and the constable who'd stopped him went in to beat him in the groin and belly while a sergeant stood guard outside. How would they treat him, who'd evaded them since Algonquin, who'd destroyed one of their cars? Not that he'd destroyed it, but they wouldn't see it that way. Victoria's gift of escape wasted. He thought of the unreadable manuscript in the seat beside him, wanted to touch it but feared staining it with blood. Kenora, 427 kilometres. Still Ontario. Hell.

Leave it in some higher power's hands. He would stop at a drivethrough, get coffee and juice, something sweet too, didn't they feed you cookies when you gave blood? Recharge. And if they called the cops, so be it.

After Finmark he drew into the lot of a doughnutshop, parked beneath a light standard and shut off the ignition. Angled his rearview mirror to study his face. Blood from the slice above his eye caked in his eyebrow, a smear on his cheek. His face alarmingly pale, but that was partially due to the light. He held up both hands, the left richly crusted with blood, the right less so. He licked away at the fingertips of the right, sucked away at the tangy membrane, tasting iron. In a few minutes the hand was passably clean, then like a cat he wet his fingertips with his tongue and pawed away the stains on his face. Studying his features he felt a suffocating wave of weariness and he sat back and shut his eyes.

The mad lust of thirst hoisted him awake hours later and he banked the mirror to view the takeout window, fearing its closure, but it was still open. He started the engine and backed out and turned and drew up to the speaker. He sat waiting and no greeting emerged from the aluminum grate and he waited with his hand gripping his sandblasted throat and was about to press the horn when a man's out-of-breath voice said, Sorry, sorry. I had to take a crap. You waiting long?

Nathan tried to speak but his voice lay like a broken relic in the pit of his larynx.

Are you there? Sorry, shouldn't have said crap. Maybe toilet. Or washroom. Or watercloset. Dig that. Sorry, I had to use the watercloset.

A laugh while Nathan pushed with mighty effort a grunt from his voicebox.

Or maybe not mentioned it at all, the voice from the grille mused.

Yeah, Nathan choked.

At least I didn't say I had to take a shit.

Ha, Nathan groaned. Then, Ha ha.

Yeah, okay. You're like, How about taking my fucking order, right?

Yeah, Nathan said. How about it.

Whatever you say. May I take your fucking order?

Large coffee, regular. You got applejuice?

Yes.

One applejuice. No, make that four. Four applejuice. And a halfdozen doughnuts. Anything. Mix them up.

Right. Your total comes to $11.60. Please drive up.

As he edged up to the window he hadn't considered that he'd need to fish his billfold from his back pocket. He lifted his bottom from the seat and a jet of pain ripped through his flank. He felt a gush of equalizing fluids but persevered, drew out the wallet, pulled a twenty from the fold, and leaned through the car window towards the drivethrough window, which remained shut and unoccupied. He waited, reluctant to move more, hoping to minimize the extent of the split he'd likely made in the scab on his side, waiting, waiting.

The face of the boy who came to the window gazed at him through a blear of drunkenness, a halfsmile on his lips as he shoved the window aside and took the bill, provided change, and handed down to Nathan, one at a time, four cold bottles of applejuice. He said nothing as he passed Nathan the carton of doughnuts, the coffeecup, and still that wry grin creased his features. As he was about to shut the window Nathan said, Wait.

Has the service been unsatisfactory? the kid asked with a broad grin.

You got booze back there? Nathan asked.

Jesus! the boy said, feigning outrage.

Give it here.

The boy hesitated, then hefted through the window a half-full jug of Jack Daniels.

Nathan held up the bottle. You drank this yourself?

With help from my associate, the boy said with a flourish behind him. Nathan looked through the window but saw no one. The boy leaned out the window, eyes fixed on the jug. What are you going to do with that?

Nathan unscrewed the cap, lifted the bottle, and took a long drink, shivered as the fire hit his belly. Unwise, he realized, but he needed courage. He took another swig.

The boy went to close the window and Nathan, still struggling to choke down the last hot mouthful, put up a hand to stop him, passed the bottle back. The boy tucked it slyly beneath the counter and shut the window, gave a thumbs up as Nathan pulled away.

He drove a distance down the highway, stopped on the shoulder, and put on the domelight. He drank two bottles of applejuice, the coldness salving his parched throat. He could've taken the other two, but he thought he'd let the quench lie to see what came of it. He cracked the coffee's lid and sipped and it tasted good. He drank half the coffee and set the cup into the cupholder. He ate three stale doughnuts, the last powdered with sugar and filled with sweet jam which oozed out the back and onto his hand as he bit into it. The wound in his side started to hurt like hell. It came in a sudden, expanding wave that left him stunned and flagging. He gripped the steeringwheel and took three deep inhalations and on the third felt the clotting unbind within the wound and a rill of blood begin, but the pain was diminished and the bleeding did not feel excessive. He got back on the road. The Trans-Canada split at Shabaqua Corners. Fort Frances straight on, right turn to Kenora.

He squinted into the dark as he turned northwest, saw a sign that told him he was entering the Arctic watershed. Now all rivers flow north. After Raith he crossed into Central Time, and though he didn't know the time it still seemed like a gift, an extra hour of life. Upsala had a nursing station, dark as he sped past. Then on along the straight, flat highway in a channel cut through raw forest, sipping coffee and piloting the wheels over the bodies of roadkill, beheaded skunks and raccoons pressed flat with their guts blasted through their necks. He'd hardly paid attention before, but this stretch of highway seemed rife with fresh kill, like some terrible wheeled juggernaut had thundered through, reaping wildlife. At English River an orange cat recumbent on the roadside as if sleeping but for its chin turned towards the sky and the cage of its teeth shining in his headlights. Nathan had struck his fair share during his journey – raccoons, and once a porcupine by night, groundsquirrels and chipmunks by day. And once to his horror a pair of white mourning doves had lifted off the road at his approach, and one veered into the lane and exploded against a quarterpanel in a mangle of feathers. Staring into the rearview mirror at the retreating scene, Nathan tried to recall if these birds mated for life. He thought it so.

Contrary to his expectations he felt powerfully alert now, plummeting into the night with a bellyful of raw matter, the processes of his marrow manufacturing fresh humours. He dreamed of a shank of rare beef on a plate, potatoes with hot gravy, green beans. Spreading into the pith of a steaming dinner roll a curl of butter. Mouth watering. Where to find such things in this bleak night on a strip of unpopulated asphalt?

Signs for Dryden and Kenora expressed diminishing kilometric distances. He turned on the radio, but the stub antenna caught only static. If only he had music. The cassette he'd been listening to when the tape player expired months before, just days off the used-car lot, still rested in the player's mouth. Nathan prodded it with fingertips until the mechanism drew it inside. And by god it began playing. He turned the volume knob, brought the throb of drums and the froth of distorted guitars into the cabin. Bachman-Turner Overdrive. He laughed loudly and raised the volume, remembered that the car's previous owner had installed a booster which Nathan never used because the sporadic and staticstained radio stations he could receive benefited little from amplification at the low end. He thumbed the power button and the system ignited, jewels of green erupting on the equalizer's sliders and music thundering from the woofers behind the rear seat, shaking the car to its frame. The song was called "Not Fragile."

He saw at the reach of his highbeams a lone figure staggering through the roadside gravel and this figure turned to regard the car's approach. It seemed to be some lost indigent marooned in the murk, a shaggy beard of pepper and salt and eyes ignited like kerosene beacons by the headlamps. This derelict opened his mouth to speak what Nathan imagined would be some curse but in a moment the car was past and the figure evaporated in the grainy dark. Nathan thought of the aspect his car presented to this spectator, a pounding, screaming machine boring through the pneuma of night, then hying past in a glare of headlights before it tunnelled into the distance, the residual bass pump sucked away down the highway in its wake.

Dryden came and went, bypassed by the highway, a little crown of light against the sky. He had music now, more guitar rock on cassette, Tom Cochrane, Neil Young, Tragically Hip, applejuice, doughnuts. And he'd won that fucking fight. True, his opponent had inflicted greater injury, but only by bringing a foreign object into the ring. And the police's arrival had trumped the deck. But who now languished in a jailcell with a split pate while his foe sped away into the night?

He cracked another applejuice and drank it in three swift gulps. "Boy Inside the Man." "Rockin' in the Free World." "At the Hundredth Meridian."

Cloudy moonless night spread over Canada like a black emulsion. He sensed the sun beneath the world at some antipodal depth over China, circling eastward across Asia, rolling towards Europe, the Atlantic. Nathan retreating at 130 kilometres per hour.

He slowed through Vermilion Bay and the highway beyond it grew more desolate, no light on the roadside to show habitation. Not even a gasbar, but the gauge read just past half and he was glad he'd fuelled up in Thunder Bay. The music drowning out those usual anxieties, clatter of the lifters and bustle of the rods and cylinders, pump and squeak of springs and shocks needing replacement, the gruff stridor of worn bearings. In Manitoba he will stop and have his body fixed, and perhaps his car too.

On, on, the phosphorescent crown of Kenora's lights visible in the sky ahead, sliding away to his left, straight ahead a bypass but an approaching turn would take him through town, told himself he needed it, a break from the pounding dark. He turned off the music and along the meandering road the town came as all towns do, increasing density of houses, stores, and gas stations dark and desolate in this northern night, and suddenly the bigbox stores: Canadian Tire and Walmart and between the two a stark, paved field, dead lamplit ground. Another never-to-be-conducted census for Sydney, how much of the planet have we paved to serve retail.

A traffic light that managed the exit to this paved savannah cycled to amber and red. Nathan considered running it, as there was no traffic anywhere in sight, let alone emerging from the lot. But he stopped. And there she was. At last, in this northern Ontario night in the trough of an unknown hour with the enterprise of branding on garish display while his blooddrained body sagged in the seat of a foreign sports car. Here she was, she who had evaded him for almost a year, now sitting, incorporeal, smiling at him from the littered passenger seat. He thought he should tell her of all that had happened since her death, the cataclysm of his regret, his departure from their halfrenovated home in Toronto's Annex, the roads, motels, diners, fistfights, the unconsummated seductions. He wanted to tell her but looking at her he realized she already knew. That death had granted her omniscience. That perhaps she was always in that seat and only now had the veil lifted. He wondered if he was dying.

Where's Sydney? he asked, but she did not reply, and he studied her expression for fluctuation, fearing that something worse than death had befallen their child, but her smile remained unchanged. The car shuddered and Nathan gripped the steeringwheel. A styrofoam cup skittered across the roadway, clattering hollowly.

He heard a squawk and thought it some fresh necromantic phenomenon, but caught reflected in his rearview mirror the pulse of red lights, and saw a Kenora Police patrol car behind him.

The traffic light was green. He didn't know how many sequences had passed while he sat there, but he raised a hand in acknowledgment and eased forward and accelerated to a reasonable speed. The cruiser drew up beside him and the cop in the passenger seat gave him a bored look before the car sped into the night.

That was close, he said to Lisa, but when he turned he was alone.

He drove through the town's heart, its antique red brick. A funeral home clock said 2:07. The road rounded a small bay above which stood a hospital skirted with trees, and below it in the water's still face its reflection. Ablaze with light, illuminated blue *H* repeated in the water. A gift from Lisa. The road arched closer, he was going to meet the entrance. Coming up on his left. Emergency. He put on the blinker. And drove past. The road banked and turned, crossed a bridge. He followed the Highway 17 signs until the houses and stores thinned and the road met the bypass. Reached to signal the turn and found the indicator still flashing, since the hospital. He made the left and accelerated while the highway stretched away beyond his highbeams. He drank his last apple-juice and ate another doughnut. In the cellar of his skull a new pain was developing; it felt like a corkscrew boring into the meat of his brainstem. And at the fringe of his vision things began to swim, manta rays, hammerhead sharks. He sped on. He had to piss. He strained his eyes when they saw at the verge of his headlights the retroreflective sparkle of each roadsign, and he prayed for one announcing the Manitoba border, but they only declared speed limits or the contour of pending road.

And then out of the darkness loomed an enigma, a sign of cunning simplicity, a blue square, and on it a single white question mark. Nathan suffered a bout of dread. What monster would place along the shoulder of a major expressroute such a thing, such a mystery, this object without explanation? He watched it flare in the headlights then whip past his window before the dark consumed it. He pitched forward with his chin above the steeringwheel and waited, breathless, for whatever that sign boded.

And then he saw it on the left side of the highway, beyond another question mark, and this one with an arrow marking the exit to a structure: Ontario Tourism Information. The question mark meant *information*. He knew this and yet it seemed outrageous. He chuckled and then recoiled at the abrasion of his laugh.

And then a sign shaped like Manitoba welcomed him to Manitoba.

He'd expected a border town with a hospital at the highwayside, lamps shining under the marquee of the Emergency entrance, but there was nothing here but asphalt, more highway escaping into the dark beyond his headlights. He closed his eyes for a second and fatigue pounced. It took an enterprise of will to open them again, but the damage was done, he knew now the depth of his exhaustion. He gripped the wheel and drove, wanting more than anything he'd ever wanted to simply shut his eyes and sleep. He began to take giant, round gasps, forcing oxygen into the cavity of his chest, but doing this aggravated his sidewound and brought breathtaking pain. But if he pulled over and slept he would never wake up.

He pushed the gas to the floor, accelerating, wanting to escape these thoughts, to escape death itself, knowing that this only brought it closer, invited it into the very cabin of his car.

It came then, but not to him. Hurtling through the highway dark at 160 kilometres per hour he perceived only a subliminal flash — like a single frame in the speeding thread of a motion picture — of the moose striding longlegged and burly from the scrub into his headlights. The car struck, and for an instant Nathan sensed a wash of droplets against his body. Like some tender anointment of rainwater. But it wasn't rain, or even water. It was a torrent of imploding safetyglass.

CHAPTER 5

He waited for the siren to approach or recede, but it remained constant and unending, and he grew annoyed with it, as he sometimes had in the city when Sydney was sleeping and the sound of police cars and fire engines shrieked endlessly in the distance to attend what could only be, judging by the magnitude of the wails, an apocalypse. He'd sometimes search for coverage of a disaster that would explain the dispatch of dozens of emergency vehicles, but only once – an inferno at an old paint factory – was the mayhem justified.

And still this siren howled, a penetrating *whoo-whoo* rising and falling like laboured breathing, and pain abruptly smashed through him like a torpedo, severing the ballast that had kept him submerged in unconsciousness, and he erupted through the surface of that calm pool, eyes launching open to see above him a trio of bright lamps. A bomb of pain was exploding in his right shoulder, and as he sucked for breath he felt like he was being skewered through the breast with a pitchfork. When at last he was able to tune his breathing to a manageable agony the air he inhaled was cool and soapy, with a faint chemical tang. His mouth and nose cupped by a plastic airmask. He wanted to rise, to change his position, to do anything to flee the pain, but he was buckled down, arms and legs and head and foot, to a wooden board. He tried to lift his skull away from that unyielding plank and a head loomed above him, backlit, the face indiscernible.

Sir? Sir, can you hear me? No, don't try to nod. In fact, I'll ask you to please keep perfectly still. You may have suffered a spinal injury. We've immobilized your body. Do you understand me?

Nathan nodded as best he could.

Don't nod! the paramedic cried. Do you understand?

Nathan nodded.

Listen, I just want you to blink to respond. Okay then?

Nathan nodded.

Oh for chrissake, the paramedic cried, and pressed his hand to Nathan's forehead. Please, I know it's hard, but don't nod. Just blink, okay?

Nathan tried to nod, but failed against the pressure of the paramedic's hand, and instead blinked once.

Very good. I'm Ron. Do you know your name?

Nathan blinked.

You've been in an accident.

I can speak, Nathan croaked, his voice tempered by the mask.

Okay. Okay, so that's good. What's your name?

Nathan Soderquist.

How do you feel, Nathan? What hurts?

Nathan spoke, but his words expired in a gurgle.

Take your time.

Everything, Nathan repeated.

First of all, I want you to know that you're all right. I mean you're banged up, but as far as we can tell, nothing life-threatening. Do you understand?

Nathan nodded.

Your voice, the paramedic cried. Please.

What's broken, Nathan said.

Okay, you have a concussion. You were knocked out. Your other injuries are on the right side. He leaned over and hovered his palm over each zone as he described it. You've probably broken some ribs. That's the pain when you breathe. Dislocation, possible fracture in your right arm. You've got lots of cuts and bruises. There's a pretty deep gash on your side, just above your hip bone. Can you tell me what else hurts?

That's it, Nathan moaned.

Your legs? Anything on the left side.

No.

Can you feel anything else? Can you wiggle your toes?

Nathan wiggled and Ron looked at his feet.

Just a little wiggle.

I am wiggling.

I see.

Ron wiped the back of his hand across his mouth, fingered the stethoscope slung around his neck.

Wheeling through pain. Not my spine. Let it be slight or much. If it's something from which I won't entirely recover, I want death. Dead at least he'd be with Lisa and Sydney, if he believed in such things. And if dead did not mean afterlife, it would at least offer the end to memory and pain. He most feared that tragic middle-ground of living damaged in body but not mind, with no escape. As long as he'd kept moving his spirit had remained spry. At the very least, he thought, leave me capable of suicide.

How's he doing? a voice called, and Nathan swivelled his eyes, but from this locked-down position could see nothing but the lights and ceiling and a portion of a cabinet.

He's conscious, Ron called.

Damn, the other voice called. That's good. That was some wreck.

Nathan was trying to manage the blue explosions of pain. If he could move he might writhe free of its grip. He strained arms and legs, wanting to ask if he could be released from this harness, from the mean plane of the backboard, knowing that he could not. Despite their contrary purposes, torture and medicine were sometimes indistinguishable. Different sides of the same street. Distract, distract. He tried to put himself on a beach somewhere, anywhere, but against his back the sand was a marble slab. The knifewound in his side dulled against the sharp new pains in chest and shoulder. A bead of sweat licked down his cheek, into his ear.

Hey, he said, but the paramedic did not hear him. Hey!

Yes? Yes, what is it? Ron asked, leaning close as if to take his confession.

How . . . how's the moose?

Ron blinked as he digested the question. Nathan wondered if he'd heard. Ron sat up, then laughed percussively.

What is it? the other voice asked.

Ron continued to laugh, his cheeks reddening, hands clenched across his belly, his face a mask of mirth. He sagged forward like a deflating toy, and Nathan feared that he would fold far enough to press his forehead to Nathan's belly, but then he inhaled and recharged his lungs with a rasping inhalation.

What? What is it? the driver called.

Ron bent again, cheeks shining with tears, and drew a smaller breath, and gasped through the fit, He wants to know . . . he wants to know how the moose is doing.

Then he leaned over and screamed into Nathan's face, The moose is fine! The moose is okay! The moose drove your car away from the scene. Last anyone saw he was headed north. Hey Ned, I told him the moose drove his car away.

Drove his car, that's good, Ned replied. More like: no thank you, I'll wear that home.

Yeah, Ron laughed, Yeah, latest fashion for moose these days. Toyota in dark blue. All the moose are wearing them.

Ron scooped tears from the wells of his eyes, rubbed his belly. Wow. That was some workout. I need to tell somebody that one.

Hey Ronny, the voice from the front called. We time this right we might be off by five.

What is it now, a little after four?

Yeah.

Thank you, Nathan, Ron said. Looks like you timed that perfectly.

Nathan realized that the siren had ceased, though he hadn't noticed until now. He could hear the roar of the engine, the beat of the tires against the blacktop. He hated that he couldn't determine their compass vector, was it east or west? Just his luck, to be shipped back to Ontario after everything he'd done to escape. He felt suddenly dizzy, felt the ceiling begin a slow, nauseating rotation, and he shut his eyes against the intensity of the lamps.

Just a few more minutes, Ron's voice murmured.

Nathan wanted nothing more than to curl his body around the pain. Get through it, he thought with each breath. Get through. He thought of Lisa in labour, her courage as she huffed through the contractions. To expel that object which at the time seemed foreign, an antagonist. But that was pain to achieve an end, a happy end, the birth of their child. Could she have taken it if she'd known that the child would live less than two years? And that they would perish together. Nathan's physical pain displaced by the emotional. Which was worse? He thought it absurd that there was a time in his life – a long time, the majority of his existence – that he had not felt pain. The gong of a hangover, a stubbed toe, some angst from a girl's brushoff. That was all.

He let his throat intone a low note, a hum, an om of yogic calm he'd sometimes heard Lisa use to calm her nerves, and it helped a little, a carrier wave on which the pain could ride out of his body.

In the far reach of his consciousness a voice screamed. It came in a long bilabial syllable, which sounded, until its completion made it otherwise, like mimicry of a cow.

Moose!

Moose. Such an absurd word.

There came a tremendous concussion and the board against which he was bound was flung against the lockers at the front end of the compartment. The deck of the ambulance started to tilt and there was a hard crash and a shudder which redoubled the pain in his arm and chest and side, and he guessed the ambulance had capsized and was skidding on its side. He saw through what he realized was one of the tiny side windows a frenzy of yellow sparks, the grating of the ambulance's shell against asphalt. The vehicle ground to a bonewracking halt. The lights flickered and went out. The gurney remained fixed to its floormounts, which left Nathan strapped to the vertical surface of the board and suspended above the paramedic's bench. The mask had ripped free of his face and dangled against his cheek, hissing menacingly. He tasted blood. He spit and drew a deep breath and it felt like someone was hammering railroad spikes into his chest. He smelled medicine and alcohol and blood and diesel.

He heard from beneath him a moan.

Hey, Nathan called, mortified that he'd forgotten the name. A single syllable. Jim? Don?

Ned. The driver's name. Ned? he called. Ned? Ron. Ronny. Ronny, are you okay? Ron, can you hear me?

He heard laboured breaths, then vague motion. The plink of dripping liquid. A creak as something sagged, then the mild tick-tick of the cooling engine block. For a long time nothing but soundless detonations of pain.

After a while he heard from the distance the sound of an approaching vehicle. Headlights illuminated the reticulate glass of back windows and polygons of light swept the compartment. Nathan cast his eyes about, at the shadows sluicing around him, saw Ron on his back beneath him among a litter of gear and glass, face bloody, arms clenched across his chest. Eyes open, craning about. They met Nathan's.

Outside, the vehicle slowed and stopped, the headlamps pouring white light into the ambulance. He heard a car door open.

Holy shit. Anyone in there? Hello?

They heard the sound of a telephone, three phone tones.

Nine-one-one, Nathan whispered.

I'm cold, Ron said, and Nathan was suddenly afraid for more than his own life.

He awoke with his mother in his thoughts. He lay in a private room, his body crisscrossed with bandages and the pain of his injuries veiled behind a scrim of drugs. Wanting to think lucidly, but a blue haze obscured his thoughts. He thought of his mother watching him and thought of her crying. Look at you. Look what you had, what's left. Nothing, not even a beatup Subaru.

Mom. It's a Supra.

Not even a notebook full of skies. Just blood, bone, and thoughts, if that. Is that why I made you?

I'm sorry Mama.

He wanted to hide his eyes, to cover them against the penetration of her stare, but his arms wouldn't respond. His right arm heavy and immobile, he could not determine why. Fearing that it was gone and what he felt was the ghost of sensation. He looked, but a sheet concealed it, and beneath the sheet a thick, rigid cylinder. Bronze light from a fluorescent light above the bed, filtered by a yellow gel. An IV drip, PVC sac of clear liquid and the instrument that regulated it humming and clicking competently on its pedestal. He gazed down at his exposed left arm where the vinyl tube burrowed into a wad of tape. A bruise of gunmetal blue above his wrist.

Someone entered and he closed his eyes and peered through the cage of his eyelashes as a nurse in yellow approached the bedside. Something pressed into his ear, clicked, chirped. She bent to study the intravenous regulator's display, punched keys, cursed under her breath. She went out, soles whispering on tile. Nathan gazed to the right and saw a window, and that it was night.

He'd been the first one rescued from the wrecked ambulance, still mounted to the spinal board like a stuffed trout, pulled free and set upon a gurney, but then they rolled him aside like junk, pushed him among debris torn from the vehicle, an augmenting pile, this dour crew of firemen, two paramedics, a trio of highway patrolmen. Ron was pinned beneath an equipment cabinet, but he was soon out, shrieking with pain, horrifying wails of every timbre and cadence, mimicking collected laments of past patients. An anthology of woe. Then, to Nathan's shock, the paramedic was packed into the new ambulance and whisked away. Nathan abandoned in a nebula of dieselsmoke.

He did not witness the labour to free Ned from the ambulance's cab but knew by the length of time it took, by the urgent rushing and collection from the firetruck of fresh equipment and the anxious expressions on the rescuers' faces that the situation was grave, and as Nathan lay beneath a mound of blankets watching the predawn stars reel past he heard the shriek of machinery and the shouts and oaths and the hollow pound of a sledge and the croak of pried metal and, after the calls and a chorus of grunts, a bonechilling shriek of agony. Then it was quiet for a long time, Nathan sweating under the blankets and grateful for the cold against his face. He heard a distant wail and the first ambulance returned, its taillights illuminating the scene, Nathan's breath escaping in vermilion huffs as the vehicle backed to where he lay and at last they hauled him aboard. But they did not immediately set off, and he lay in the truck's box, unattended, waiting, until at last they brought Ned aboard, slid the gurney in beside his own, the rescuers uncharacteristically silent. Nathan unable to move, his head still clamped in place, trying to read what he could from the extreme periphery of his vision. Almost certain there was a sheet drawn over the man's face. A paramedic named Chip climbed in beside Nathan as the doors were at last shut and the ambulance got underway. His vital signs checked. And then, en route to the hospital, Chip asked if there was someone they should contact. No one, no one. And the question repeated, as if this response were suspect.

He lay gazing at the objects reflected in the hospital room's window, the light above his bed, the green digits on the IV display. He shut his eyes and sleep poured over him.

It was still dark, or dark again, when he awoke. There was nothing to show the time but the level of the IV bag, which was almost empty. The IV machine was beeping in an urgent manner and the noise persisted until a nurse came in and prodded the keypad to silence the machine and went out and returned with a fresh bag. She worked methodically and only when she was done did she look at him.

Oh. Hello, she said.

Nathan wet his lips to speak but did not. She removed a thermometer from a pocket in her uniform, attached a fresh probe, and pressed it into his ear. She checked the display and smiled and met his gaze.

Normal, she said. She was thin, a little gaunt, streaks of grey in her black hair, a pocket of fatigue beneath each eye.

Good, he grunted.

How do you feel?

Sad, he replied, and her mouth gaped as if she meant to reply, perhaps suggest a remedy. After a bewildered moment she swung her attention back to the IV machine, tapped the junction below the regulator.

He slipped in and out of consciousness, his sleep a timeless catacomb from which he emerged in light or darkness, unprepared for the hour, always amazed when a nurse told him it was dawn or midnight or high noon. Pain circled him, a demon concealed by a veil of morphine controlled by Nathan's thumb against the button of the grip clutched in his palm. In boredom he played games with that beast, would resist pressing the key, allowing his allocation of the drug to accrue while the stuff in his blood dissolved and the pain increased by degrees. Just as the monster's face showed through that pale gauze and he could hear its snarl his thumb would strike once, twice, flooding his bloodstream with that sweet milk, throwing between him and the creature a barrier, sending his body into an exhausted spiral of sleep.

The ceiling was a grid of foam tiles and during wakefulness his eyes navigated the acrylic spacers. He imagined the streets of a foreign city.

In twilights of consciousness he was visited by a brownhaired physician who seemed through the haze of doped pain to be herself under the influence of some mood-altering chemical, smiling, her attention distant, her eyes laughing while her hands, detached from that mirth, prodded him professionally, his neck and abdomen, pulled the wad of bandages from his flank, or articulated his limbs, checking against his expression the level of pain each action provoked. He watched her while she worked, the view from his pillow as if from the bottom of a well, and yet her every feature magnified. She was in her late forties, plainfaced, with close-set hazel eyes, her thinlipped mouth fixed in that smile. Her voice on the rare occasions she spoke was raspy and jovial.

Late one night he woke and saw a cardboard box containing a copy of *Maxim* sitting on his bedside chair. From his car? He shifted painfully in the bed to gain a better perspective. He wanted to see what was under the magazine, reached out with his good arm and grasped the carton's rim and tried to haul it aboard the bed, but it was too heavy. He crabbed sideways, sheets entangling his legs, a profound ache radiating from his side, his shoulder, eyes tearing as he clutched and lifted and dropped the box, sweat erupting on his brow, filling his armpits. He drew the box towards him, trying to press it against the bedside and slide it upwards, but as he adjusted his position with his weight on the box's rim it tilted sideways and he jerked over, bolts of pain stabbing through his body as he toppled and began to slide out of the bed towards the tile floor where the box's contents were spilling. Even as he desperately pressed his arm to the chrome rail to keep himself aloft he was studying the mess on the floor searching for his spiralbound notebook. He saw magazines, the missing pocket thesaurus, his cellphone, a scatter of coins and pens, but that was all.

A chuff of footsteps in the hallway, and he croaked through the burr of his throat, Help. Help me.

The footsteps were receding, and he was starting to imagine the potential damage of hitting the floor when the steps slowed and began to increase in volume. The brownhaired doctor entered and stood openmouthed as if watching some tremendous acrobatic feat, and it was not until Nathan grunted with the effort of maintaining his position that she scooted forward and caught him and they grappled momentarily like wrestlers engaged in slow and tender combat until she was able to restore him against the pillows.

Are you okay? What the hell were you trying to do? she asked, her voice reprovingly maternal, and Nathan said nothing, because he could not. She regarded him sternly, but still with that air of cheeriness, before looking down and seeing Nathan's last worldly possessions scattered on the floor, and she bent and put them in the carton and placed it on the bed. Her gaze lingered on one of the men's magazines, cover photo of a model in a gown which plunged almost to her navel, revealing the plump halfmoons of her breasts, then she met Nathan's eye with her brow mildly furrowed, and Nathan wanted to speak, to apologize, but his larynx had seized. He drew the carton close and began to unload other magazines, stacking them on the mattress on the opposite side of the bed, and then examining the items that emerged next: the cellphone, which refused to activate when he opened it; a box of unsharpened pencils; a clear plastic satchel containing his toothbrush, paste, and shaving kit, as well as an unopened box of condoms; an ice-scraper; the thesaurus, its tissuethin pages like those of a pocket bible, thumbed and worn by a penitent.

A few audiocassettes. And there, at the bottom of the box, its cover freckled with blood, his notebook.

This, he whispered, hugging it to his chest. It was the only thing he had left.

He closed his eyes with that doctor standing there, and in his dreams she remained there, motherly, standing vigil, guarding not only against disease and infection but his other enemies: the law, defeated combatants, the moose, his guilt. Exhaustion overtaking him. Eyes shut, wondering if she was still standing above him. Churn of sleep. He wanted to ask her something, how she could always be so happy in this wretched world of pain and distress, but before he could speak he slipped into a pale fog and heard a hiss like surf blustering against a seawall, and slept.

The pain was worse the next day, propagating into new regions, flaming barbs radiating from the knifewound and across the muscles of his lower back, his groin, the ache in his shoulder worse. He saw his notebook on the bedside table and remembered his struggle to reach it, his near-plunge to the floor, rescue by the happy doctor. He told a nurse of the expanding pain and she granted him a pacifying nod and when he asked if his morphine dose might be increased a doubtful look crossed her face.

But you will ask the doctor?

Of course, and she was gone only a few minutes when she returned with a perturbed expression and she prodded the iv's keypad and told him to tap the button and asked how that felt, and the drug poured like warm honey into his veins, and he sighed gratefully and nodded.

A cub reporter came from Winnipeg to interview the man who in one night had struck two moose, and though Nathan tried to explain that for the second incident he was a helpless patient the reporter nodded and recorded nothing of this detail on the notepad. He was a chinless simpleton of twenty suffering a tremendous cold and obsessed with clearing his left nostril, and he pressed his right to seal it while blowing with such force that his face flushed. Nathan sat stoically, his head deep in the pillow.

Did it hurt? the reporter asked while blotting snot from his lip.

Did it hurt? Nathan repeated, suddenly alert and bristling. He'd been thumbing the IV button for some time now without effect, and he suspected that the nurses were restricting his dose. He'd have to tell the brownhaired doctor, though he hadn't seen her in days, and that added to his anxiety.

What part of having your shoulder blasted out of the socket by a moose's antler travelling at 160 kilometres per hour does not sound painful?

So that's a yes, the reporter said, writing. Okay, how about this: What do you think the odds are of person hitting two moose in one night?

You're asking for my expert opinion?

Sure.

Based on my experience.

Why not.

One in one, Nathan replied flatly.

One in one?

Sure, Nathan replied. I know that's anecdotal but it's all I got.

The reporter pondered Nathan's response, then wrote it down. Nathan shut his eyes and began to breathe slowly and evenly.

Nathan? the reporter asked. Yo, Nate?

Nathan continued to feign sleep, had to avoid the temptation to snore. He heard scribbling for some moments, then the sound of the reporter rising, donning his coat, and shuffling away. The footsteps stopped at the door.

You're an asshole, the reporter muttered, and Nathan smiled, but the footsteps were already retreating down the hallway.

Nathan paged the nurse, and it took some minutes before a voice blared from the speaker behind his head, Can I help you?

Something wrong with my IV, Nathan reported.

Be right there.

And still he waited a lifetime, fifteen minutes at least, his veins itching. He was perspiring, wiping sweat from his forehead. It was Bun who arrived, or so Nathan had named her, for she always wore her hair in a brown knot at the back of her head, her real name Noreen or Nancy or Nicki or some other N name, spoken at introduction and never repeated, how long ago now? Days? A week?

Is that thing working? Nathan asked, nodding towards the machine.

Bun hunched her stubby form over the display, punched keys, summoned from it a dreadful yawp.

Sorry. I don't know why it does that. It seems to be okay. What's the problem?

Well, Nathan replied. I do this – and he raised the button and tapped it repeatedly – but the pain. I mean I don't feel any difference.

Bun lifted his chart from the wall caddy, examined it.

Your dose was lowered. It's natural to feel the effect.

Lowered? Who lowered it? I thought it was just raised.

Yes, it says here that Dr. Gooding requested an increase three days ago, but then Betty, the head nurse, had it lowered again.

Why did she do that?

She thought it too high. You can talk to Dr. Gooding if you like.

Where is she?

On leave for a few days.

Leave? What's that mean?

Family business.

Nathan struggled to understand this, the idea that a doctor could abandon her responsibility to her patients to cope with some kind of domestic snit. It sounded illegal, and if it wasn't it should be.

Who is this Betty? I want to talk to Betty.

She cannot increase a dose. Only decrease. That's hospital policy.

Then who's my doctor while Gooding is out?

Dr. Farge. He's on rounds right now. He'll pop in shortly. Is there anything else? Mr. Soderquist? Mr. Soderquist, is there anything else?

No. No. Nothing.

She went to the window, began to draw the curtain to shut out the sunlight.

No, he grunted. Leave it open.

Are you sure? It's getting warm in here.

Leave it.

She exited and Nathan fumbled for the bed's controlpad, raised the head of the bed and pawed the sidetable, lifted the notebook onto his lap and spread it against his raised knees. He drew a pencil from the coil binding. Shoulder aching, side sore. Sniffling, wondering about the reporter's cold. He imagined viruses crisscrossing the airspace like Stukas. And then slowly, carefully, lefthanded, the words a scrawl of canted or inverted or backwards characters, he wrote.

OCTOBER ?

Through hospital glass a sunsoaked day, drifting cloudtubes like lathed granite cores, pocked and mottled with quartz and obsidian. Moving east, moving slowly east they might be stone missiles arcing towards Toronto, Ottawa, Montreal, their tails ablaze with the candescence of their exhaust, nosecones packed and primed with ordnance. Occident and orient, boreal and austral, what keeps the hyperborean tribes from annihilating each other? Does night hate day, or is repulsion a requirement for existence? Love makes the world go round, but hate keeps it from collapsing. A dream of smooching antiparticles. Pale warriors in the sky. Their huts slowly shrinking. Cirrus circus. Iridescent amoebas. Hatted homunculus. Whittled alpenstocks. Deckled scrimshaw.

When he awoke he would see at the tail of this passage a senseless scrawl of characters followed by a thread of graphite that curled and twisted like the path of a plummeting jetliner. Off the page and onto the bedsheet.

Three days after the interview he was sitting up in bed thumbing through an issue of *Road & Track* he'd sent a candystriper to buy in the giftshop when someone lifted his wrist to check his pulse, and when he looked he saw it was the brownhaired doctor. It took him an instant to recognize her, for though she was superficially unchanged, she moved and acted with a heaviness he'd not seen in her before. There was emanating from her, he realized, that tang of grief he'd detected from the towtruck driver he'd fought. A dialect known only to some, and in which he was fluent. She completed her examination without once making eyecontact, and when she left Nathan sat stunned with the magazine open on his lap, the distress from his injuries, which he had thought waning, suddenly renewed. It was in this state that he listened to a phone ring six or seven times before he discovered that it was the one on his bedside table, and he picked it up and answered, Yeah?

It's me.

Mabel, he said. How did you find me?

I tried your cell, but there was no answer.

It's broken. I was in an accident.

I know. The moose. Two moose. You're in today's paper. The *Globe*.

Hell, aren't they supposed to be reporting news?

Are you okay?

I'm terrific. A broken arm, dislocated shoulder, shattered ribs.

Minor injuries, they said in the paper.

Still hurts like hell. Is that how you found me? Did they mention the name of the hospital?

Yes. What were you doing, Nathan?

Just riding along in an ambulance.

I mean the first one. The first moose.

Driving.

Too fast.

Probably.

You're in such a hurry.

Sometimes.

What if you stopped for a while?

I might have no choice at this point.

Well that's good. You'll need someone to take care of you.

Right, he replied.

I mean it, Nathan. Don't try to do this on your own.

Do what on my own? I'm just living.

That's what I mean.

Mabel. You are aware that I'm an adult, right?

No you're not. You're a hurt little boy.

What the hell?

It's true, Nathan. Isn't it true? Right now? You're helpless.

Damn you, Mabel.

Don't say that.

Damn you!

Now it's the drugs talking.

It can't be the drugs. It can't be the drugs because they're cutting my drugs. So damn you. Damn everybody! Why the hell do you call me, anyway?

I call because you need me to.

Damn you!

You're repeating yourself. I'm serious Nathan. You're going to stop moving now. And whatever's chasing you is going to catch up. So you're going to need help. You can be angry with me and you can curse me, but that won't change these facts.

Nathan was silent.

Now, what about your cellphone. Nathan, stop pouting and answer me. Your cellphone.

It's busted.

So I won't be able to reach you. You'll need to call me once you're out of the hospital. Do you remember my phone number? Nathan, do you remember my phone number?

Of course. All those fives and sevens. Impossible to forget.

Good. That's good. It's time to rest. Rest now. Okay, Nathan?

All right.

I will call you in a few days.

Fine. Goodbye, Mabel. Mabel?

Yes.

He hesitated, then said at last, Thanks for calling.

He hung up. Felt a gulf of loneliness widen in his gut. Remembered trudging through snow towards the police cruiser. Her small face in the lens she'd rubbed in the fogged glass. His first thought that this was a mistake. A runaway teen, gaunt and scared. Too insubstantial to be witness to their deaths. He would learn in latenight phonecalls shortly after the funeral that she was almost thirty and widowed four years, husband claimed by brain cancer. Running the farm alone. The secrets he revealed to her, and she to him, in those calls. Until he recognized the impropriety of this so soon after the burial, and he'd stopped calling, thinking she'd get the hint. But she hadn't, or had simply disregarded it. So he'd stopped answering. And even that hadn't worked.

A sunbeam poured blinding light into the room and he clenched his eyelids to shut it out.

Nathan sat on a barstool, boots against the fulcrum of a brass rail, and he watched delivery trucks and pickups cruise to and fro, laden with snow. Those heading eastward struck the lip of the iron bridge and quaked and snow fell from them in powdery gobs. He sat turning his beerglass on a coaster listening to the drone of tires on the bridge's grating. The river a wreck of buckled iceplates the colour of antifreeze.

Soda, someone called from behind him. Soda!

He turned his head and Blair fingered one of the beertaps. Ye want another?

Nathan lifted his glass and tilted it in the dull light, gave the inch of beer a swirl. Sure, he said, and knocked it back.

When he looked out again it was snowing, fat, slowmoving flakes like something shredded, wisps of detonated cloud. He'd been here a long time and when the beer came it was his fourth. Blair collected the empty glass and pressed the new one onto the coaster. Filled to the brim and there was almost no head to speak of.

Thanks, Nathan said, and lifted the glass and sloshed beer over his knuckles before bringing it to his lips for a long swallow. Blair hesitating at his elbow, until Nathan turned. What?

Well. How's it working out at Doc Gooding's? he asked, his eyes on the passing traffic.

It's good. Weird house, but comfortable.

You know, Hugo built that place with his own hands.

Hugo? Who's Hugo?

The husband. You know she's got a husband, right?

Of course.

Comes in here sometimes. Out of town right now. That room they rent out. Haven't in a while. Usually foreign students.

Nathan studied the man, the small eyes and nose, the buckled chin bristled with stubble.

Like Chinese guys. Or from Peru, Blair added.

I'm from Toronto, Nathan said. That foreign enough?

Sure it is, Blair said with a laugh. Maeve was calling him from the cashregister, and he nodded to her, began to move away before he said, They . . . she been through some rough stuff. Recently.

Like what?

You know, family stuff. He looked away, straightening. Thought you should know.

He moved away before Nathan could ask more.

Snowfall and coming night were diminishing the light and he thought to check the time but didn't. She'd be home soon and his rent included meals, though with her shifts he usually found himself reheating something. Soon the beer was done and when he ordered another it was darker yet and a din was rising in the barroom behind him. He thumped his right arm to the rhythm of the western song on the jukebox, and his cast boomed on the counter and when he struck hard the final note, glowworms of pain erupted from the fissures he pictured deep within the bone. He turned and surveyed the room and returned nods and saw in the glass eye of the stuffed falcon on the bar some critical spectre and he turned back to his beer. He was halfway through it when Blair appeared beside him proffering a cordless phone, his hand covering the mouthpiece.

It's her, Nathan said, and Blair nodded. Tell her you couldn't find me. Tell her I left.

I won't lie. She's good people.

Blair elevated the phone and Nathan accepted it.

Soda here, he said.

Are you coming home, Nate? she asked. I've got your supper ready.

I'm just getting my coat on, he lied.

Hurry, it'll get cold.

He hung up and sat gripping the phone, staring at his beerglass, thinking that he should finish it and after that order another and then another. Galled by the boarding arrangement, this obligation to comply with a schedule. Knowing that Blair wouldn't serve him any more, he fished bills from his wallet and at the bar the falcon watched him pass these and the phone over the heads and into Blair's outstretched hand. The barman tried to make change but Nathan waved it away and negotiated the crush to the door while patrons muttered their farewells, calling him Nate or Soda, and in a moment he was standing on the sidewalk with the door closing behind him and the bar's jolly rumpus silenced. Snow falling in the headlights of cars and trucks. He sank his left hand into the coat's cavernous pocket and pressed the other in its fibre-glass shell against his breastbone within the coat's rank interior. The coat was made of dead things and he felt Lisa's censorious glare. He bent forward and walked across the bridge. He watched through the steel grating as moirés of light rippled across the plates of broken ice below and disorientation blended with the alcohol in his blood to brew a crude analgesic, so that the ache in his arm diminished to a throbbing pang that swelled and shrank with each heartbeat. Oversized boots booming on the grate, he reached the far side, a channel of footsteps beaten through the snow on the roadside. In a few minutes he turned up a sidestreet, one without sidewalks, and he plodded down the road's centre, stepped aside when light from cars approaching from behind pooled around his feet and cast seething shadows on the plough tailings lining the roadside. He rounded another corner and looked up into the flurry of snowflakes falling from the lit sky, saw the darker clouds beyond the houses where the town ended and countryside began.

Pain in his arm surging now and the wound in his hip joining the chorus. Past bungalows, some with modest garlands of Christmas lights along eaves or girdled about the waist of a towering balsam. Then the great wooden house, a misfit towering over the meek dwellings of the street, this polymorphous structure at once sailing ship and castle, hewn from logs and raw planking, designed and constructed by a twisted and scattered master. Nathan's eyes rose along its varied frame, passed over the gothic finials of the porch eaves, the balcony the stern of a Spanish galleon, then above it braced precariously on handcarved joists a kind of crowsnest, and beyond that gables and the belfry and a wind compass of a sperm-whale yawing in the uncertain wind and the snow all coming down into the spotlamps which illuminated the strange and perilous structure.

Nathan mounted the steps and entered a panelled hallway, smelling beeswax and pine and woodsmoke and the lusty oxide scent of seared beef.

Hello, he called.

Is that you? came her voice from the kitchen.

It smells good.

Leave the boots on the mat.

He stepped out of the hide boots, shed the coat, glad to escape its animal odour, and he hung it by its furlined hood on a peg. Stood a moment in the house's warmth, studying the woodstrip walls, the ponderous baseboards and doorframes, sensing the weight of the house, feeling like a woodboring beetle that has chewed its way inside with no appetite to eat its way back out.

In the powderroom beneath the stairs he pissed and when he was done he closed the toilet's lid and sat on it and looked at his glum reflection in the mirror. The pains in his arm and hip and lung keen and penetrating, impeding his concentration. The pain had become part of him, like a fundamental component of his being, a new organ, essential, definitive. He was that pain. Packed lightly now in a cold brine of alcohol.

A knock on the door.

Nathan, are you okay?

He rose and flushed, rinsed his good hand, pushed open the door.

Dr. Avery Gooding stood there in the low light, a crease of fatigue or concern on her brow. Her brown hair loose and she was wearing bluejeans, a sweatshirt. Without her physician's frock and stethoscope she seemed smaller, less authoritative.

Did you wash? she asked. Your hands?

Yes. Hand, he said, showing the right one to remind her it was wrapped to the knuckles in an acrylic cast. .

With soap?

What are you, my mother?

Do it again, with soap, she said. I'm a doctor, remember? Infection control.

He turned to the sink, worked the handsoap pump into his left hand. Now what?

She came forward, pushed up her sleeves and washed his left hand, rinsed it. As she was drying up on the towel he buffed his hand on his pants.

Use the towel, she said. The towel.

This is ridiculous, he said, rubbing his hand on the towel.

It's there for drying. What's ridiculous?

I don't know, he replied. This arrangement.

That's enough, it's dry. Dinner's getting cold.

He followed her into the diningroom where they sat at the heavy wooden table. On Nathan's dinner plate, brown rice, steamed broccoli, garden salad, thin strips of panfried beef. A glass of milk. She sat across from him and picked up her fork, looked at him.

What? she said.

This looks so. Healthy.

It's good for you.

And why do I have milk when you get a glass of wine?

Because you need to heal. Your bones. Anyway, you probably had a drink at the Falcon.

Probably, he replied, and began to eat.

How about asking about my day?

Oh hell, really?

It's polite.

How was your day?

It was crazy, she said eagerly. Some guy got a concussion tobogganing. Hit a tree. His fourteen-year-old daughter got him into their car, drove him to the hospital. He had a laceration from here to here. An elderly woman with Alzheimer's wandered off, her sister found her three hours later with frostbite on both feet. She'll lose at least one of them. The usual cases of chest pain – only one was a real infarction. And of course the rounds. Round and round. Oh, and twins born this morning. Boys, identical. In good health. I haven't seen them yet, but I'll look in on them tomorrow.

Ah, he replied. Twins. You know, this isn't half bad.

Flattering, she replied. There's one more thing. The hospital received a phonecall today. From the Thunder Bay Police.

He felt instantly alert, tried to register no reaction.

Did they? he said.

They've been calling around to hospitals. They're looking for someone in connection with an incident. A fight that resulted in a knifing.

A knifing? he asked, looking at her. What, you mean like someone being stabbed?

Yes.

Does that kind of thing still happen? It sounds like an anachronism. I thought everyone shot each other.

Oh knives are still popular. Happens more than you think.

So why are they calling hospitals?

They wondered if we'd treated anyone for such an injury.

And have you?

I don't know.

You don't know? How could you not know? he asked, trying to manage the hostility he heard in his own voice.

Well, she said. You can't always tell. I mean a knifewound is simply a laceration inflicted by a keen edge. If you take for instance a car accident. Well. There are sharp edges all over the place. Lacerating your victim. Nathan, are you okay?

He was breathing carefully to manage his responses, placed his hand on the shell of the cast, took a deep breath and said with a wince, My arm. There's been a lot of pain today.

She shifted back in the chair, pushed the rice on her plate into a little mound. Yes, well. Of course there wasn't any choice, the bone had to be reset. But it's only four more weeks.

Nathan suffered a pang of conscience at milking her guilt for setting the bone incorrectly in the emergency room. An x-ray last week had revealed the error, and an orthopaedic surgeon had come from Winnipeg to break and reset it. A setback which seemed to affect all his healing, his shoulder and ribs and knife-wound. Wanting to touch his side at the thought of the latter, but fearful it would reinvigorate the topic of the stabbing.

Are you taking the Percocet?

They don't work. I get dreams.

This was true. He suffered intolerable dreams, violent episodes, the moose smashing through his windshield and body, but it wasn't a moose, it was Lisa standing on the roadside in a camisole, bare feet on the frozen asphalt, skin pale as soap, abruptly striding across the highway, fixated on some goal on the far side as Nathan's Supra flies out of the darkness. The car ploughs through her; she is insubstantial, a vapour, a ghost, but the car is nescient of this fact; it folds around her; it collapses inwards around the imploding grille, and he is sucked into a vortex of glass and steel, it batters him as he swirls within it, the left side of his body unscathed within its torpid eye while his right swings through the arc, unprotected, shredded by the storm of debris. This dream three or four times now, with variation: Sydney crossing the blacktop, or Lisa holding Sydney. Waking, sweating, the drug clogging his brain's capillaries like a cold wax. Trying to winnow truth from dream, are they dead? Did he kill them? And the settling pall of grief, momentarily fresh, that instant he swept the fog from the passenger window of Norah's car, recognizing the Prius crushed and inverted against the snowplough's blade.

Avery's fork clacking against her plate. I'll get you T-3s. Codeine.

You can do that?

I'm a doctor. Why is that funny?

Nathan covered his grin with his hand, cheered by thought of the new drug. He glanced at her, watching her press the rice flat with a fork. One of Lisa's regrets, that she hadn't become a doctor, given her life to Doctors Without Borders. Vaccinating Sudanese orphans while warlords clash outside the canvas.

Organic yogurt with berries for dessert. When they were done Avery cleared the dishes while Nathan sat silently at the table, trying to conjure a topic far from police and stabbings. Finding none, he sat studying his cast. Wondering if he should allow people to sign it, if adults participated in that ritual.

Do you want some tea? Avery asked through the window to the kitchen as she filled the kettle.

He shook his head, said, Got anything else to drink?

Like?

Bourbon.

She frowned, said, I have chamomile or decaf chai.

Come on, he replied. I'm in agony here.

She put the kettle down and gave him a weary look. I think there's some cognac.

Anything else? Scotch? Jack Daniel's?

Just cognac.

Cognac it is, he said.

Go to the livingroom, she said. I'll bring it.

He sat on the easy chair next to the fireplace. She'd built a fire but it had died down. He lifted a chunk of birch from the woodbox and threw it into the embers, generating a splash of sparks. He nudged it into position with the poker, the bark crackling. Avery came in, handed him a snifter of cognac, sat heavily on the couch. He was surprised to see she'd poured one for herself. She sat with her hand cupped under the bowl, swirling it slowly, lost in thought as she stared into the fire. Nathan sipped from his glass. It was like drinking hot silk. He gulped more, felt his cheeks blush.

Tell me about Hugo, he said.

What's to tell? she replied wearily. He's my husband.

Where is he?

He's got a cabin in the woods. His favourite place in the world. I've only been once.

Tell me about it.

Not much to tell. Single room with a bed, a woodstove, a table. That's it.

Electricity? Running water?

Neither. You know, he actually built this house after my visit. I'm starting to realize he meant it as a joke. Like the opposite of the cabin. Or an exaggeration.

Isn't it cold out there alone? Don't you think he's cold?

He's always got an intense fire going, she said. In the stove. A pile of logs beside it. He opens the door, he tosses one in, he shuts the door. That's as complicated as it gets.

Sounds like hell.

You said it. I thought this town was dead. But there. Oh god the quiet. The darkness.

Why does he go?

It's how he copes with stress.

How do you cope?

Not well, she said, and lifted the snifter to her mouth, sipped.

Your job must be nothing but stress.

It can be. It was worse in the emergency room in Winnipeg. One reason I moved.

You met your husband here?

She nodded.

When will he be back?

No idea.

She looked into the fire, took a few quick sips of cognac.

Nathan shifted in his chair, trying to find a comfortable position, said, I'll have to take a couple of those Percocets tonight.

No you won't, she said, and he looked up to see her gaze fixed on him.

What?

Not after the cognac, she said. Oxycodone and alcohol are contraindicated.

But the pain.

I don't relish the idea of hosing your greymatter off the pillowcase when your brain turns to goo.

Just one. I'll only take one. Okay, a half.

No, she said, sitting forward on the couch. Do I have to go upstairs and take away the bottle?

Of course not. He sat back in the chair, looked into the fire, refusing to meet her eye and glad she didn't know how much beer he'd had at the Falcon. Four pints, or was it five? He downed the last of his cognac, set the glass on the sidetable, and stood.

What are your plans, Nathan?

I'm going to bed, he said.

I mean tomorrow. I'm on shift.

Oh. I'll probably spend a bit of time exploring. Then see what's up at the Falcon.

She sighed with something like disapproval, said, I'll make sure there's a dish you can microwave for supper.

All right.

Good night, she replied. Pleasant dreams.

He climbed to the second floor, from which he had to mount a steep wooden staircase to his room in the loft, hauled himself wearily up, casting his eyes into the dark hole from which cold air fell. He rose through it and in his exhaustion sank to his knees on the floorboards. Blue light from the window sketched out the room's features: the squat box of the dresser, the towering armoire, a bed with head and foot fashioned from birch limbs. A faint yellow from the nightlight in the bathroom. The wind blew and the room quaked in its timber braces, and he rose and pulled the chain of a driftwood lamp and sat on the edge of the bed with the buff ovals of Percocets in his palm. He took two, went into the bathroom and gulped them down with tapwater. He drank a second and a third glass, conscious of alcohol's diuretic effect, something he hadn't known about until well into his twenties. How many hangovers he could have mitigated. Brushed his teeth and drank another glass of water. Sat on the toilet to piss, mistrustful of his ability to stand and aim. Then he stripped to his underwear and climbed beneath the covers, lay there listening to the buffeting of the wind, waiting for the terrible dreams, and as he drifted off he suffered a sudden panicked vision of his body, naked and bound, a sacrifice on a stone awaiting the garlanded priest with his prayerbook and dagger.

He awoke in the murk of dawn flat on his belly with the sheets peeled back and his skin chilled, his consciousness so gummed and smoked that remembering Avery's warning about taking the pills he raised his head to check the pillow for evidence of dissolved greymatter. He pulled sheet and quilt over himself and collapsed into sleep.

He woke next on his back with the slant of sunlight on him, which meant the day was mostly spent, for his room faced west and the winter solstice was approaching. The house silent. He pushed away the sheets and blankets and let the sunshine warm him. Seduced by an optimistic euphoria he raised his head and felt instantly like he'd been clocked with a frypan, and he sank slowly back to the pillow and rested there, panting. He turned his head as if it lay in a nest of bees, saw the halfglass of water on the bedside table, took it down and tried to drink without raising his head, felt the cold water dribble down his chin and into the creases of his neck. He finished the glass, closed his eyes, and let it go to work.

Opened his eyes somewhat later to underlit clouds, their bellies burning orange as the sun threw the last of its light from beyond the horizon. He had to get out there. When he raised his head experimentally the pain was bearable. He twisted to land his feet on the floor and dressed as fast as he could with his handicaps, and when he'd started down the stairs the clouds were cooling to pink. He had to climb again to retrieve his notebook and he thought to write the entry here propped against the dresser with his forehead at the glass, but didn't.

When he finally reached the bottom floor and had girded himself for the cold and made it outside and around the back of the house, all colour had drained from the air and the cloudheads hung in the sky with texture and shade he thought infinitely more dramatic than the preceding sight. He sat on the minced top of a woodsplitting stump and smoothed the notebook against his thighs and wrote.

DECEMBER 18TH

Charred sky, narcotic soot floating in dusk, rich and toxic, a woolly nightmare propagating in slow smoky tempo against the starry depth, unveiling even as it occludes, spreading new reality like a blanket over the old, the old itself a deception which in turn smothered some lie of reality more ancient still. Timelapse roll of charcoal sky, a pendulous gas blooming and rolling in burnt pockets of doom, stirred by the tines of naked treebranch and prickly pine.

He spent ten minutes in the waning light correcting his damaged handwriting, rounding o's and straightening t's, brushing pink whiskers of eraserdust into the snow. He looked at the sky above the trees and it was a dark smear now, and he waited for the snowflakes but they did not come. Waiting too for Lisa's presence in the aftermath of the writing, but she also refused to arrive. The moment's stark ruin. He looked into the forest beyond a wire fence, the treetrunks like flexing dancers in a tableau, and he stood and set the notebook on the stump and walked past the rustling husks of dead milkweed and into the forest. When he turned his gaze upwards he saw the margin between the citylit clouds and their darksome kin in the east. He walked further to leave that borderland behind and the snow came to his knees and each step sucked a new packing of snow into the boots, but he persisted and when he looked behind him he saw his footsteps stretch out to the fence's opening like fumaroles from which he expected at any moment to witness a Plutonian glow. Boles almost obscuring the house as he crept deeper into the wood. Ache of exertion, his breath in steaming scuds. He should've thought to bring some Percocets, he should turn around, for if he fell into a drift he might never rise again. Lie struggling in the snow within sight of the house and freeze to death, and to evade such a pathetic outcome he stepped deeper into the forest, escaping the house's proximity. The ground began to descend steeply and he flailed his left arm for balance.

Twilight deepened but the landscape sustained a radiant glow as if the snow itself were luminescent.

He continued down the hill, passing among fir and maple, the leafless scrub piled up on both sides so he knew he'd found a path, but if it was product of animal or human footsteps he could not determine. Soon he heard a low gurgle and it grew louder as he descended until he reached the valley's depth. He crouched and heard the creek running beneath the snow, rested an elbow on his knee and put his chin in his hand. The burble stronger from downstream, and he stood and took a few steps towards the sound's source and found a dark aperture in the ice. He knelt in the snow and peered into the hole's depth. Reached into that opening and felt the sting of the icy water sluice through his fingers. Realized that this impulse to put his hand in rushing water was new to his life, as if he needed to feel the world's circulation. Fluids pumping, the Earth alive. It struck him that everything that was Lisa and Sydney was still present on this planet. Death is nothing more than a reorganization.

He worked his way downstream, found a spot where the ice opened to reveal a foot-high waterfall, its base littered with rocks large enough to step on. He crossed in three swift bounds.

He fell one time as he mounted the opposite slope, twisting as he toppled so he landed on his back, and he lay in silence and stared at the sky. Through the bones of the trees he saw the night-glow of the town of Krillbane in the west, and he struggled to his feet and continued away from it, fleeing into darkness in great, spiderlike strides, extracting a leg from its borehole, throwing it forward to jam it down, then drawing out the other leg. Panting deeply, each breath like inhaling a cloud of burrs.

And then in the gloom, rising out of the snow, a low concrete wall, and set into its flux an ironwork fence of crosses joined by the fat links of a chain, and within this spare enclosure a handful of antique gravestones. Nathan halted and looked about as if seeking a comrade with whom to share this finding, but when he looked back through the forest the lights of the street's houses were still visible, and he knew that his discovery was unremarkable. He began to circumnavigate the little boneyard, found an archway on the far side and stepped beneath it and into the compound. He could see that except for rodents and fieldmice which had dimpled the snow with their footprints he was the graveyard's only visitor of late. Tombstones rose from the snow, and he moved forward with caution, appreciating that smaller stones might be concealed beneath. The first monument rose to his waist, a simple granite slab with an arched top, and he crouched before it and excavated its face until the inscription was revealed, but in the darkness he could not read it.

He moved through the yard checking headstones and found near the back a low stone of pale marble. The year 1911 and a surrounding filigree of ivy were cut deeply into the face just below a ridge in the gravestone's crown. He scooped snow from the stone's face and kneeled, feeling the cold through his jeans. The marble seemed phosphorescent in this darkness so he was able to read of Elizabeth Jane Chapterwood, July 3, 1883 – December 23, 1911, and Carolina Margaret Chapterwood, March 20, 1909 – December 23, 1911, interred here together, souls conveyed into the merciful embrace of our Lord Jesus Christ. Mother and daughter, dead a century. Nathan settled back in the snow while breath poured out of him and the cold which had begun to intrude upon his concentration seemed to retreat. The desire to tilt forward and touch the stone came once or twice but he remained motionless. After a few minutes he rose and backed out of the graveyard and using his own stepholes made his way down the slope and across the creek and up the hill back to the present.

He returned to an empty house. He was hungry, opened the fridge and saw perched on the rack under cellophane some grilled chicken, a Tupperware drum of rice. He ate these cold while flipping through an obstetrics textbook he found on the diningroom table, staring at the illustration of a placidfaced fetus resting inverted in its mother's womb, before he clapped it shut and pushed it away.

He realized that caffeine withdrawal might be responsible for his headache and started a pot of coffee, and rested on the couch before the cold fireplace while it brewed.

He awoke at the sound of Avery's arrival home, could tell by the plod of her steps down the hallway that she was exhausted. He thought about telling her how he had survived the oxycodone and alcohol, but fearing she might be apprehensive about him with codeine – which he hoped she'd brought tonight – he said nothing. He did however clutch his eyes shut in a wince and pant slightly when she came in. She passed him and went into the kitchen where he heard her bustle about before she returned. He felt her standing over him and he kept his eyes shut. She let out a little sigh of what sounded like pity and he felt her lift his left arm and press something cold against the crook and when he opened his eyes and looked down she was sliding a needle into the vein.

What is that? he asked, and she pushed the plunger, and a hot wave of euphoria poured through him and he exhaled to the root of his lungs and looked with what he hoped was deep gratitude into her eyes. It seemed some minutes before he could gather the energy to inhale, but they passed without panic, and when he'd refilled his chest he sighed deeply like someone resurrected.

Anxieties, uncertainties, pain, all were washed away in that tsunami of morphine, and he sagged into the cushions like some ponderous drone, not himself but an effigy, a ballast Nathan, sinking by slow degrees into the foamrubber, drawn unstoppably towards the Earth's core.

When finally his eyes opened Avery was still there, and Nathan was stunned to see her, for he felt certain that days had passed since the injection, and her life must've continued through this fugue: she had risen and eaten supper and watched television, gone to bed and slept through a night, arisen, returned to work, spent a twelve-hour shift tending patients, returned, slept, worked, countless days, yet here she was, unchanged, kneeling on the floor beside him, a hand gripping his wrist.

Better? she asked, and he nodded and called for the musculature of his face to smile, but it was a long time coming.

I'm glad. You look so much better than when I came in. I'm going to make myself something to eat.

He considered the idea of panicking at her departure, because detached now from his body he felt unbearably alone, far more than he had during his solitary driving, his illness in the cottage on the Superior shore, even in the Annex house in the weeks after the funeral.

He heard her puttering in the kitchen, then she set a plate on the coffeetable and laid newsprint and kindling into the fireplace's grate, struck a match against the fieldstone, nursed the fire to life. She lifted the plate and sat in the wingback beside the couch and ate. Nathan stared at the pinestrip ceiling and rode the swells of euphoria. The effect was becoming manageable now, more pleasurable. He felt as if he was surrounded on all sides by walls, walls formed not of stone but blankets and pillows. Like lying in a bassinet. He shut his eyes and felt immediately like he was rocking to and fro. He opened his eyes and found himself on the couch, motionless, heard the crackle of the fire, the scrape of Avery's fork on the china plate. Startled at the fidelity of the illusion of lying in a cradle. He shut his eyes and it came again, stronger, more vivid: he was a baby nested in receiving blankets, drifting off to sleep.

He awoke in the same spot the next day, alone, shivering, for though there was a blanket spread over him the fire had gone out and his veins ached for what his liver had destroyed. He drew up his legs and turned onto his side and quaked, cursing what she had done to him, but adoring her too, and most of all needing her, hungry for her thumb against the plunger, for the hot rush of the drug. Sleep would not come and he imagined himself ransacking the house to find her cache, unconvinced that what she'd brought home last night was a single dose she'd requisitioned from the hospital. He clutched his eyelids shut and screamed this truth to his edacious nervous system, but the need persisted, grew sharper, and he clenched his teeth, muscles growing rigid until his hands closed into balls and his right arm strained against the rigidity of the cast. He finally rolled and threw his feet on the floor and stood. He called Avery's name a few times before accepting that she had left for the day. Embarrassed at the tremulous whinny of his voice.

He went into the powderroom and though he had to piss badly what emerged was a painful, reluctant drizzle. After several false finishes he zipped his fly and bent over the sink to splash water from a cupped hand into his mouth and across his brow.

In the hallway he donned winter gear and set out for the Falcon, though he stopped before the iron bridge and looked at the grey sky, annoyed to discover that it failed to disclose the hour. He continued across the bridge and stood in front of the bar's door and saw that there were people inside, families, and they were eating breakfast, an elderly couple at the window each with a stack of pancakes and on the plates' rims the stout turds of sausages. His stomach churned and he reeled away, continued briskly along the street, noticing that exertion allayed some of the craving. He walked past storefronts, his coat unbuttoned until he discovered by the way other pedestrians were bundled and hurrying to get indoors that the day was viciously cold. He buttoned the coat, passed the shoe store and public library and grocery store, threw a longing look into the drug store, though he felt reasonably sure that their stock did not include anything as potent as what he needed.

Heroin.

The thought stopped him dead before the plateglass of a furniture store. He bent his head and looked at his boots on the pavement while he considered a potential source in this town, and when he looked up his own reflection looked back at him from the glass, the cylinders of the boots around his ankles, baggy bluejeans, the great gamy coat buttoned to his neck, the right sleeve dangling lifeless at his side, the ridge of his mending arm behind the buttons, his stunned expression on a stubbled face, sweating, eyes bloodshot, addict, addict, here was an addict, paleskinned and stunned. Heroin, he said aloud, for the voyeuristic thrill of seeing himself say it. You fucken junkie. He drew the furlined hood over his head and tilted his face down to repel that image, turned and walked back towards the bridge. He lifted his eyes at the Falcon and saw beyond his chagrined reflection Billy Pepper, one of the tavern's regulars, beckoning to him, and Nathan stopped and lifted his good arm in a shrug. Pepper waved him inside and met Nathan at the door.

What is with you? he asked. Sick?

Yeah, pretty, he said.

Can't that doctor do nothin?

What time is it? Can we get beer?

It's not even noon yet, dumbfuck.

Is that a no?

Shit. Let me buy you a coffee. You hungry? Christ what a face. Coffee then.

Nathan sat agitating his coffeecup watching over Billy's shoulder the television, a soundless CNN anchor babbling with a halfsmile on her lips while text he could not comprehend scrolled across the screen's foot, and Billy went on at some length describing an interview he suffered the previous day for a stockboy position at the IGA.

You're like to need a degree these days for work of every kind. Soda, could you just listen to me for five seconds?

Nathan's eyes moved with some reluctance away from the TV and Billy looked at him with irritation. He was a big man, wide shoulders, the left one jacked permanently forward, by injury or habit Nathan could not tell, and he had a wide, soft chin and skin freckled so finely he looked sandpapered. Eyes like brown beachglass, and a pale crop of hair concealed beneath a wool cap. He'd driven for a local courier company until his truck slammed into a car that had run a red, killing the woman driver, clearly not his fault, in fact the coroner had concluded that she'd been suffering an epileptic seizure at the time, but still the company didn't want him on the road. He'd spent his severance on a ramshackle bungalow near the CN switchyards and now lived on welfare cheques, for which he endured considerable guilt.

Government money, he'd moaned. Sucks the joy out of beer and cigs.

Which didn't stop him from buying either.

Nathan looked into his coffeecup. He hadn't much more than sipped it, and when Billy's breakfast came the feared nausea did not rise, and he considered the possibility that he was hungry, so he ordered a western.

While they were eating, Billy's friend Elizabeth arrived and stood at their table slouching with her hands in her pockets and delivered in a monotone voice the weather forecast: Cold today with a high of minus eighteen, overcast with a fifty percent chance of flurries in the late afternoon. Temperature dropping to minus twenty-eight tonight, winds light from the north at seven.

Elizabeth, do you want to sit down? Nathan asked when she paused for breath. She was a pale woman, with glossy skin, her cheeks rouged from the cold, and she wore her hair yoked back into a ponytail. She appeared honoured at his invitation, and shucked her arms out of a canvas backpack and dropped it to the floor before cramming herself into the booth beside him. Billy fixed her with a critical stare which made her wilt, so Nathan cranked himself towards her and said, You know, you have a very flexible name. You can be Liz, Lizzie, Eliza, Beth. Or do you prefer Elizabeth?

Everyone calls me Elizabeth.

But what do you like?

I like "Nate."

That's my name. You can't have it.

No, I mean I like calling you Nate. Why do they call you Soda?

Soderquist. My surname.

Oh, she said without comprehension.

It's a riff. Soderquist. Sodaquist. See, it's kind of "soda" in the first four —

I think she gets it, Billy stated with some hostility.

Nathan's western arrived and while he ate Billy and Elizabeth chatted about television. Nathan's eye swept the room and he saw at a table near the door a two-year-old girl in a boosterseat dipping homefries into ketchup. Her quarrelling parents inattentive of the mess on her fingers and chin. She had curly red hair and cheeks like apples. The bar's TV drew Nathan's eyes, now a commercial showing a car negotiating a winding highway, now the ads of various bigbox retailers imploring shoppers to spend generously, then some minutes of news until a screen showing celebrity birthdays, and Nathan noticed the displayed date.

Is that today? he said loudly.

What? Elizabeth said.

The nineteenth of December.

Oh yeah. Hey, almost first day of winter.

Shit, he said.

Yeah, Elizabeth replied. It hasn't even started yet.

And already it's freakin cold, Billy laughed, and Elizabeth joined him, and Nathan realized with some annoyance that she was watching Billy with something like admiration. Billy met her stare and something clicked, and Nathan smacked his coffeecup down with such force that it cracked the saucer.

Whoa there Soda-man, Billy said. Winter's something you gotta accept.

Nathan shovelled the last of his homefries into his mouth, and when Maeve came with the coffeepot he said, Gimme the bill.

Hey hey, Billy said, his voice gruff and threatening, then to Maeve, Sorry, Soda just got wind that winter's coming.

The redhaired girl was halfway out of the booster and climbing to the floor when she slipped, banging her forehead against the table's edge, and her mouth opened in a silent yawn of pain. The mother scooped up the girl and wrapped her in her arms. When the cry finally came it was desperate and breathless and Nathan saw on the face of her father the constriction of fear as he repeated over and over, Is she okay? Is she okay? until the mother bawled, Of course she's not okay! At that the man rose and lifted the girl's pink coat from her chair and began to work it onto the girl's arm.

What are you doing? the mother cried over the girl's wail.

Get her to the hospital.

Wait. Just wait.

The father stopped then, and stood hunched, holding the coat in place on the girl's arm while the mother stroked the girl's head and cooed and the crying subsided. The parents each stared into the girl's eyes for signs Nathan remembered well – glazed look, uneven pupils – and he saw by the slackening of their shoulders that the girl was all right. She looked over her mother's shoulder at Nathan's stare and he winked and she buried her tearstreaked face into her mother's neck. The old pain – relentless, more substantial – flared in his breastbone and filled his belly and limbs with bile that soured the food in his gut so he thought he might puke. He placed his left hand on his thigh and squeezed until his fingernails bit into muscle. When he looked up the girl was staring at him and her face blanched and she whispered something into her mother's ear and the mother turned and shot Nathan a venomous glare and he looked away.

Maeve was still hovering with the coffeepot chatting with Billy about music-sharing websites when Nathan interrupted by asking, Hey, where do you get drugs around here?

A momentary silence, then Maeve, her old face pinched into a scowl said, No drugs in this place, friend.

Just some weed, Nathan said. Just some fucking weed.

Nobody I know, Billy said, his voice deep and very soft.

In this town. There's got to be a guy in this shithole town who sells weed.

Everyone was shifting uncomfortably now, and Nathan said, Jesus Christ. Let me have my bill, Maeve. I got stuff to do.

Maeve gave him a hard look, then went off.

You got to mind manners, Billy said.

Maeve's nice, Elizabeth muttered, then dropped her eyes.

I need out, he said, and she stood fast, stumbled over her backpack. Billy's hand shot out and he steadied her, and Nathan said, Sorry. Just hate winter.

Things you gotta accept in life, Billy muttered. Death, taxes, Manitoba winter.

Bye Nate.

Bye Lizzie, he replied, and she blushed.

Nathan got to the cash and leaned on the counter and looked at the bill. In Maeve's dark scrawl was the tally, and beneath it,

Shut your fucken mouth, then, in smaller print below that, Come to back kitch door.

Maeve didn't meet his eye as she punched the total into the register, and Nathan looked at the top of her head, the coils of platinum hair thinning near the crown showing a blue scalp. She gave him his change in the same manner, without acknowledgment, and he pressed a five into her hand. Once on the sidewalk he raised his hood and rounded the tavern by negotiating a series of snowbound steps which ran between the river's bank and the summer patio, chainlocked tables and chairs under tarps.

At the rear a plot where the snow lay packed by footprints and littered with cigarette butts. The back door was a slab of unpainted steel propped open by a fire extinguisher. Nathan stood beside it with his forehead near the cinderblock wall, peering inside, but there was nothing to see but a concrete floor and a stack of cartons. He heard the clatter of crockery and the hiss of a tap. His left hand grew chilled in the fierce cold, and he held it to the opening. Then he knocked loudly and stood back, waiting. The sound of the tap ceased and Maeve came to the door. She gave him a penetrating look, frowning, her irises the colour of zinc, then she glanced behind her before pushing the door open and stepping with her brown loafers into the snow. She drew a cigarette pack from the pocket of her sweater and offered him a cigarette, which he declined. She lit it and pressed one arm across her breast, smoking with the other.

This shit cold, Maeve said.

What have you got? Nathan asked.

Ah, to business, she replied, her smile showing an eyetooth of silver. There's no weed to speak of these days with all the growop raids, or nothing worth selling, but I got this last night and you're the first lucky gets to check them.

She got out an unlabeled pillbottle and held it up between thumb and forefinger.

What is it? Ex? Nathan asked eagerly.

No, she laughed. No, not Ex. It's uh . . . uh. She plucked at the chapped skin of her upper lip. God dammit I know the name. These medicine names.

Amphetamine? Quaalude? His heart quickened and he asked in a whisper, Morphine?

No. I'm pretty sure it's better than that.

Valium? Ativan? Xanax?

Shut up, I can't think. She was shivering now, teeth chattering.

Hell, Nathan said. Just give them to me. How much do you want? He began to draw out his billfold.

Percocets! she cried, stabbing at the bottle with her cigarette. Percocets. Percocets. This is some fine shit. Painkiller. They give it when you have your teeth out.

Nathan pushed his wallet back into his pocket and took a step back.

What? she said.

Not interested, Nathan replied.

Not interested? Shit on you not interested.

Nathan turned and stumbled up the steps to the street while Maeve bellowed after him, I'm freezing my ass off here for this. Soda. Hey, Soda! Come back you son of a bitch!

Nathan reached the street and started walking. Moving felt better, the cold tempered by the coat's thickness, his face's depth in the furlined cave of the hood granting him anonymity, exertion heating the muscles of his legs. He crossed the bridge and where he should've turned onto Avery's street he walked straight, continued along the roadway past houses, gas station, convenience store, the buildings thinning. The hood's fur around his mouth rimed with frost. The waist-high snowbank along the shoulder forced him close to the roadside, and the passage of vehicles accelerating as they neared the edge of town thrilled him with the knowledge that if one struck him he'd be propelled forward at high speed and die instantly on impact with the road or, better still, an oncoming vehicle. His last moments spent airborne. Motes of snow suspended in the air before him, too light to fall, buoyed on gusts from the traffic. Passing a chainlink fence now, the town's scrapyard, smashed and rusting vehicles stacked three or four high, snow ploughed out in the aisles and pushed against the lower wrecks, obscuring some to the rooftops, the ground muddy and unfrozen where fluids immune to cold – antifreeze and coolant and motoroil – were churned into the earth.

He stopped when he recognized in one of the stacks a blue Toyota Supra. Nathan climbed over the snowbank and pressed his face to the fence. It was his. He looked up at the fence's top and saw a strand of rusting barbed wire no worse than what he'd conquered many times in his youth, and he reached with his left hand above his head and gripped the icy chainlink, but when he raised a foot to jab a toe into the weave it was clear that the boot's toe was too large. Not only that, with his right arm incapacitated there was no way to haul himself hand over hand. He moved along the fence until he reached a sheetmetal hut, paint peeling in flakes and a backlit sign: Kelly's Scrap, Cash Paid 4 Junkers. There was a screendoor and he pulled it open and stepped into near-darkness and the scent of enginegrease. The walls were lined with shelves all crammed with automobile parts: steeringwheels, hubcabs, pipes, crankshafts, pistons. A tower of radiator cores stood by the door like a stack of greasy waffles. At the back a row of old bicycles. Every surface of the room smeared with machine oil including a worktable with paperwork spread across it, a desktop computer, a fluorescent worklamp. A cluster of cigarette butts crammed into an ashtray that had been pulled from a car's dashboard. A parabolic heater stood behind the desk, its coils aglow and casting a mild orange light onto the floor. A Dutch door stood with the top half open into the yard, and Nathan unlatched the bottom and stepped outside and closed it. He stood in a yard where a new Cadillac of pearlescent white stood in the mud, its hindquarters crushed until most of the trunk was crammed into the rear seat. The rest of the car was intact, fresh and faultless as if from a showroom floor. There were other cars in various states of demolition, recent arrivals, and he moved past them and walked across mud littered and stirred with bolts and cotterpins until he reached a broad avenue crisscrossed by impressions from a bigtired truck. He walked along glancing down each aisle until he spotted the Supra, its doorless and destroyed right side sagging into the lane, the floor of the car resting at chest height atop a crushed Lincoln, and on top of it a Jetta which looked undamaged except for the significant corkscrew twist to its frame, a corpse with a broken neck, only the head askew. He approached and stood looking into the remains of the Supra's front seats. The passenger backrest was a mangle of foam, shredded fabric, and twisted springs. Rustcoloured blood stained the remnants of the car's interior, whether of moose or man or a blend he could not tell. He saw similar gore on the driver's seat, and he knew that much of that was his own, spilled before the accident. Part of the steeringwheel was missing, seemed to have been cut away with a blade. Of the windshield there was nothing but a jagged shred above the instrument cluster, and the right side of the hood was peeled back and what was left of it folded across the driver's side in a rusting curl. He reached out and touched the front wheel, which hung free, tried to give it a spin, but it was seized, the brake callipers fated to obey forever his final command to them.

He rounded the row to approach the driver's side, saw immediately by the flared edge of door and frame that some pneumatic instrument had been used to pry him out, and try as he might he could not recall by what trademarked name such a device was called. He reached up and tried the doorhandle but it would not budge, though when he tugged the door it came to anyway, and he pulled it wide and stepped up to the doorframe and leaned inside. Old blood and here and there frozen gobbets of what he hoped was only moosemeat. Flakes of paper scattered about, bloodstained. He lifted one, studied it, saw a curl of violet ink. Victoria's unreadable message, destroyed. He let the paper go and it fluttered off on the wind. Looked back inside the car and saw a little bunched rag on the floor, stiff and brown with congealed blood, an end wrapped inexplicably around the clutch pedal. Sydney's blankie. It drew a knot of sorrow in his chest, and he considered liberating it and taking it with him, but he thought that with the quantity of his own blood soaked into its nap it more resembled an obsolete organ of his gut than the little rectangle of textile that once solaced his child. What would he do with such an artefact?

He looked at the steering column, the slim gap between its hub and the backrest, studied the jagged points of shredded and wrenched metal, thought about the head and forequarters of a thousand-pound moose penetrating the car's passenger compartment at 160 kilometres per hour. Stepped back and saw the car as it almost had been, a steel sarcophagus. Why hadn't he died that night? For such a thing there must be a purpose. He clutched the car's chassis near the hinge and berated himself for such nonsense. Purpose. Things happen − or, less eloquently, shit happens. That phrase had always sounded flip and meaningless to him. Now he understood. There is only cause and effect, and effect becomes cause and the cycle renews. Effect does not anticipate consequence. There's no plan.

But you can find purpose. Create purpose. Or so Lisa had told him. And so he had made her, and then Sydney, his purpose. But now they were gone. He thought of Lisa as she had appeared in the passenger seat while he bled and waited for the traffic light in Kenora. Later, that moose's head had torn right through the seat. He recognized in that instant that she really was gone. Waiting for some new grief at this comprehension. But numb.

As he stood looking into the car he saw a glint of light on metal and he stepped forward and put his hand under the driver's seat. It emerged clutching a little oblong of brass, on which was engraved an illustration of a woman straddling a supine man, her vagina impaled upon his penis. Another man halfsquatted behind her with his phallus penetrating her anus, her head thrown back and her expression exalted. Nathan touched a stud on the handle and the blade popped out with a snick, the sound of it launching a bolt of anxiety through his gut, and just then he noticed a bustle of motion at the fringe of his vision and he turned and saw two dogs racing towards him. In a moment they were upon him and only when the jaws of one of them clamped around the shank of his boot with bonecrushing force did he perceive their threat.

He kicked at its head as he felt the flesh of his calf compress painfully against bone, and while he staggered about on one foot the second dog bit into the hem of the coat, pulling him in a sidling hop along the alley. He knew that he must not fall down, must not bring his throat into their reach. They were some kind of brindled mutts, with aspects of pitbull and Doberman, and each was frothing as the three danced in the aisle in a strange choreography of canine and man. Nathan continued to kick with his boot to no effect, and the tug of the second dog on the coat drew it open with such force that Nathan heard among his gasps and the dogs' grunts the ping of the buttons pelting the steel of the cars stacked before him. It took a splash of daylight across the knife's blade to remind Nathan that he was in fact armed, and he instantly put the knife to use, jabbing it swiftly into the hindquarters of the dog on his leg. It barely penetrated into the muscled haunch, but the dog responded by releasing Nathan's boot and curling like a shrimp to inspect the incision. Nathan's casted arm fell free from the open coat, and he swung it downwards, the hard acrylic connecting with the other dog's skull with a keen crack. He heard the dog yelp through its clenched jaws but it did not relent, and he had to pound it repeatedly before the jaw slackened enough for Nathan to pull free. Then, by no action Nathan could recall or reconstruct, he found himself perched on the lip of the Supra's driver's seat, the dogs below braying canine oaths as they leapt and snapped at his dangling boots. He'd have laughed at them if he hadn't recognized the depth of this conundrum, alone and hunched in the wreck of the car that had nearly killed him, a pair of rampaging hounds circling like sharks. The one he'd stabbed was bleeding lightly from its haunch but seemed oblivious to the wound as it stood, momentarily bipedal, gnashing its teeth below Nathan's foot. Nathan sliced the air with the knife and to his surprise the dog quailed and dropped to all fours.

Not as dumb as you look, he said.

A whistle pierced the air and the dogs flinched as if stung by bees, and they ducked their heads and retreated towards the fence as a figure in a hooded oilskin coat strode down the alley towards them gripping a length of steel pipe. The hood concealed the face, and the man whistled again with such power that Nathan winced and drew himself deeper into the car's cabin. The dogs came forward as if jerked by a chain, and moved around the figure, cowering, their baying suppressed. The figure stepped swiftly forward and kneeled beside the injured dog and drew off a mitten and pressed a palm against the wound. Then he pulled down the hood and his hair was cropped and brown, and he turned his head to face Nathan. But it was a woman, and not quite twenty, who looked at him.

You fucker, she said.

I was defending myself, Nathan replied.

You're trespassing.

Well. Forgive us who do that, they used to tell me in church.

You do this? she asked, lifting her hand to reveal the wound.

Look, you should have a sign on the door about the dogs. I came through the office but there was no one there.

Are you hurt?

No. Not from the dogs anyway. Nathan lifted the cast.

Come on down.

Not sure I can.

She stood and came to him and offered up a hand. There was dog blood on her palm. He shut the knife against his pantleg and put it in his pocket and accepted the hand, but descending was more complicated than simply being pulled down, and the woman had to guide his feet into toeholds on the Lincoln's frame so he could descend. The dogs shivered where they stood a few paces behind the woman but remained sitting.

Let me see that knife, she said once Nathan was standing before her.

He hesitated, looking at her open hand, then gave it to her. Nathan cleared his throat to explain, but had nothing to say. She had tawny eyes and a severe expression with patterns of freckles on both cheeks as if they'd been applied with a spraygun, one squirt per cheek. She was petite, barely to his ribcage, and he didn't know how he could've mistaken her for a man except by her walk and the agonized compliance of the dogs.

She turned the knife handle so that the engraving caught the light and when she saw what was etched there she muttered, What is this shit, then pressed the stud to release the blade. Then: There's old blood on this.

Mine, he said.

She looked at him but asked nothing, fingered the tip and said, Point's broken.

What?

Tiny bit of the point. See? Snapped off. In you or her?

I don't know, Nathan replied, feeling in his wound a cold prickle.

It's an old break, but I guess we better find out.

She folded the blade and pushed the knife into a pocket. He was going to ask her for it, but then she whistled sharply and waved the pipe down the aisle, flushing the dogs forward as if by remote control. Nathan walked some steps behind the girl to put her body between him and the dogs. She looked back once to make sure he was following and they rounded the aisle's end and made for the shed, the dogs accelerating until they broke into a run. A sharp whistle from the girl brought them to a halt before the door.

Hell, you've got quite a hold on them, Nathan said.

She turned and whistled at him in the same way, waved the pipe, and Nathan almost obeyed. She smiled but it was a sour smile. She let the dogs inside and held the door for him and though he didn't relish the idea of being penned inside with them he trusted her control and he followed her in.

She gave a low, descending whistle, and both dogs stopped where they were and sat, panting, glancing about. Then the injured one twisted and lapped at her wound.

The girl opened a desk drawer and drew out a steel box and opened it and withdrew a tube of salve and a gauze pad and a spool of tape.

Is that for people or dogs? Nathan asked.

What's the difference? the girl asked.

She went to the dogs and kneeled behind the injured one.

You hold her head, she instructed, and Nathan didn't move. Come on. You did this.

Nathan squatted in front of the dog, its face a hand's breadth from his, and seeing him there it stopped panting and gave him a speculative look. Head like a cinderblock.

Good girl, he whispered.

A harrowing stillness came over the dog.

I only got the one hand, he said.

That'll do. Just rub the side of her head. And say good girl.

Nathan brought his hand to the dog's cheek and the dog's expression seemed more curious than aggressive and he felt beneath the fur and belts of muscle the massive hinge of its jaw. The dog blew from its wet nostrils and Nathan stared into the pits of its eyes and began to rub. The other dog sat watching like a voyeur, its head askance. The girl stood and took down the desklamp and set it on the floor, flexed the stalk until it illuminated the wound. She told Nathan to be ready. He could not fathom how he could accomplish this except by tightening his muscles and bracing for attack. She prodded the wound with her fingertips and the dog tensed and whined but the girl whistled and the dog relaxed.

It's not deep at all. Can't see anything. Lucky for you. Okay, ready again. She squeezed ointment onto her fingertips and swabbed them against the wound and the dog did nothing but blink. Nathan relaxed marginally and his slackening seemed to cue the dog to emit a bark like the boom of a cannon. It blew Nathan backwards against the front of the desk and he thought in a moment the dog would be upon him so he brought the cast up to protect his head.

The girl laughed and said, That's called cowering. You're cowering.

I'm cowering, Nathan admitted.

She drew a strip of tape from the spool and fixed gauze over the wound, taped it down, wiped her fingers against her coat. She got up and returned the lamp to its place and put the kit away. Then she turned the chair so she was facing the computer. She punched some keys on the keyboard, muttered to herself, then said aloud, Oh, you asshole. You asshole.

Who? Nathan asked, rising, keeping an eye on the dogs.

Nobody. My dad. He can never give me the dirty jobs to my face. She reads from the screen in a choppy monotone: Hey Dora, just your dad checking in on this cold day. Hope everything is okay and you're keeping warm. That spaceheater doing the trick? Yeah, she growled, blowing into her hands. I can almost feel how fucken cold I am. Reading again: Anyway, I don't know if I mentioned but Ken Doke from Harmony wants the front seats out of the yellow Mustang. Can you see about cleaning them up?

Front seats? What's to clean?

What the paramedics didn't load into the meat wagon.

Who was in there.

Three kids. Joyriding.

And they were . . . they were . . .

Unlucky, she replied. That your car? she asked, and befuddled Nathan looked about as if she was referring to an object in the room.

Yes, he replied after moment. The Supra. Yes.

You're the moose guy. Two mooses.

That's me.

You want to see the ambulance?

Not really.

Fourth row, about three quarters back.

The car was about enough for today. I better get going.

Okay.

Sorry about the dog.

Not my dog.

How will you explain her injury? To your father.

Not like they don't get cut up all the time on scrap.

Should post a sign.

Yeah, he should.

He went to the door to the street and opened it.

The dogs got up and moved towards it but a hard whistle from the girl brought them up short.

It's Dora, right? I'm Nathan.

Hi Nathan. Bye Nathan.

Bye Dora, Nathan said, and he stepped out and closed the door.

It felt colder now and the sky had darkened to a smoky grey, snow falling heavily, cold and dry like ash, and as Nathan made his way back towards town he began to feel that the feat that had launched him from the jaws of the attacking dogs and into the Supra's front seat had not been achieved without penalty, for the pain in his side and lungs and throughout his entire body began to resound enormously. He bent forward in the heavy coat, his left arm braced across it to keep its buttonless front closed across his chest and broken arm, cold and distance and deep snow collaborating to make the journey more arduous. Stopped short, realized he'd left the knife behind in Dora's pocket. Stood trying to decide if he should go back and retrieve it. Didn't matter, he didn't care to keep such a thing or even see it again. He pushed on, traffic throwing wind and snow into his face. He looked down at the crimson fingers of his left hand pinching the coat shut and realized he could not feel them, that they were like something other, flesh of a foreign creature, or not even blood and bone but something manufactured, a springloaded claw like the kind Lisa had used to clamp her hair in place. The distance greater it seemed than he'd come, but at last here was the gas station and the houses and the street down which he turned and hurried at a staggering halfjog which only enhanced the pain in his limbs and trunk. When at last he was mounting the steps he could not liberate his hand and direct it to the keys in his pocket, and he stood near the wall, sheltering the hand from the wind and working the muscles, hoping to pry it open, and only after considerable effort, his bulging bladder joining the chorus of his discomforts so he feared he might pee his pants right there on the porch, did he free the hand and plunge it into the pocket, where he left it to warm before it would obey the command to close around the keyring. Shaking violently now, wheezing. He wrangled the key into the lock and cranked it open, staggered into the house's warmth. On the verge of tears. Trodding with sloppy boots across the hardwood until he got to the toilet where he pissed long, tears filling his eyesockets. He had completed the struggle to stow his cock and was zipping his fly when a voice at his elbow said, Hello. He crumpled to his knees, the final store of energy depleted. He'd not closed the door and Avery was beside him helping him not to his feet but to a reclining position with his legs out the door and his head beside the porcelain moon of the toilet bowl.

Nathan, what is it?

He wet his lips and tried to answer but his larynx only fluttered.

Do you want to lie here for a minute?

He nodded and she settled against the doorframe. She lifted his hand.

Oh! Your hand is like ice. No, don't talk, just lie there.

She sandwiched his hand between her palms to warm it, and he was filled with a rush of helpless affection for her.

Did you eat something today? she asked. At the Falcon? He nodded again. I hope you didn't spend your whole day there. You need to get strong again. I can't imagine you got any exercise today.

Thinking of his fight with the junkyard dogs he raised his eyebrows and nodded emphatically.

Well, she said. That's good. Even if it was just walking around town. You need to eat, you need to exercise, and you need to rest. Get strong.

They were both silent for a time, Nathan looking up at Avery, who was staring into space in thought. Then she looked at him and said, We had another call today. This time it was someone from the Ontario Provincial Police. Dr. Farge took it, I'm not sure what he said to them. She waited for his response, then asked, Nathan, is there anything you want to tell me?

He gave her a puzzled expression, shook his head.

Because, she said more quietly now, as if conveying a secret, it's important that we trust one another.

He lifted his eyebrows, nodded.

We do trust each other.

He nodded.

She was still looking at him critically, but after a moment her features softened. She patted his hand, said, Well. I think I know you, Nathan. I know you want to be good. You try so hard, don't you. They sat that way for a long time, Nathan staring up at the bathroom ceiling and Dr. Gooding warming his hand in hers. At last she said, Let me fix you something to eat. Then we'll see about giving you another shot.

He loved her. As he watched her rise to her feet, reach down a hand to help him up, he knew he wanted to tell her everything, of the fights, of the knife, of his crime that killed his family. But as she was hauling him to his feet, he thought she might punish him by withholding the drug. And this he could not abide. As he stood he remained mute, maintaining on his face an expression of frank innocence. Realizing behind this benevolent mask that not only did he love her, he hated her too.

CHAPTER 6

Rattle and click of saucers of glass and the waxen sticks clattering inside the fabric bag as Nathan made his way through deep snow. The woods' silence amplified by heavy falling snowflakes. He was listening intently for the babble of the creek, was surprised when he reached the foot of the hill and found only a thick shell of ice. He knelt and drew back his hood, admitting the sting of cold air, and tilted his head, straining to hear. Somewhere far off the softest burble, like the pump of blood through an artery. He wondered what it would take to stop it altogether, an embolism of ice, what kind of postapocalyptic cold. He stood and continued up the slope. The landscape was a fierce, muted blue, as if viewed through welder's glass. It was midwinter's night.

Up ahead, the wall, snow cambered against it and snow piled atop each link of the iron chain. He rounded the wall and stood below the arch of the cemetery's threshold like a graverobber, suddenly uncertain about the legitimacy of his plan. He decided it could hurt no one but himself, and he stepped forward, kicking a walkway to the white gravestone. He stamped out an area in the snow and kneeled and dumped the sack's contents. Candlesticks and holders, plundered from Avery's kitchen hutch. With his mittened hand he cleared away the snow from the face of the tombstone. From the pile he lifted a beeswax candle, and he pressed it to his nose and sniffed, but the cold had so immobilized its scent that what he smelled came only from memory, the sweet, honeywarm tang. He drew a box of wooden matches from his pocket, struck one against the stone. The flare of the head burned a dimple of white into his retinas, so for some moments afterwards every blink brought a green facsimile of the match's ignition. He lit the candle and it threw a corona of light around him, repelling the dark and forming a compact cavern of illumination, so when he brought the flame to the inscription he imagined himself an archaeologist deep in a subterranean vault, studying the lost intaglio of an ancient race. He moved the flame along the inscription of names and dates, shadows flitting through the grooves left by the burin, Elizabeth Jane Chapterwood and her daughter Carolina. He thought of the mouldering bones below, long ago pillaged by worm and bug.

He put the candle on the headstone and sat back on his boots, but the stone's overhang cast a shadow across the inscription so he sat looking at a backlit monument wavering in the candlelight. He saw the menagerie of candles heaped in the snow in front of him, reminding him of his plan to mount them on every stone, to flood the yard with candlelight, but now in the solemn dark with the flame throwing shivering shadows against the tombstones the idea felt excessive and disrespectful, so he sat unmoving with his eyes pressing into the darkness of the stone's face.

He sat with a hand in his lap. He tried to cry but he could not cry, and then he tried to pray, but who was he praying to? He hoped there was a God and an afterlife, but he also recognized Hope's poor record when it came to inventing Truth. Maybe he should pray to Lisa, but he thought she was still angry about the kiss, and he didn't blame her, for hadn't it killed them? He could pray to Sydney, but this was strange and insincere, because what would he ask for? Forgiveness, he thought, but he knew that if she could she would have granted it already. It was not something toddlers withheld for long.

And so he sat, legs growing numb from cold and immobility, face lowered. A wind came once and tugged at the candleflame until Nathan thought it would be torn from its wick and extinguished, but the wind died and the flame recovered. He thought of Lisa watching him, criticizing him for this impotent act of remembrance. Her response when a cousin had died of AIDS was to establish a fund in his name to fight the disease. Spend your energy on action, not remorse. Grief concerns the past, which is unalterable. Only the future can be manipulated, and only through action in the present.

At this thought he began to load the candles and holders into the sack. He stood and walked a small circle to restore feeling to his legs, and he left the graveyard and made his way along his own tracks down the hill towards the creek. He looked back once and saw the candle burning like a star in a blueblack sky. As he crossed the frozen creek a train of wind howled through the trees and rolled over him and he turned in panic realizing that the graveyard lay in its path and he saw the candle stutter as wind roared through until it seemed that the flame was out, but when the invisible boxcars and caboose had subsided into the night the flame straightened and burned brightly again.

He climbed the hill, casting back occasional glances, and the flame remained potent and clear in the cold distance, and he knew it meant nothing, yet it consoled him.

He came to the backyard where a floodlamp with a motion-sensor came on, and even under this illumination he could see if he moved his head to find passage through the trees and branches that pinprick of yellow light, the sun of a distant solarsystem.

He entered the house and peeled off the winter gear and found Avery in the chair beside the dead fireplace, a book spread on her lap. She wore reading glasses and a lavender robe. The room was cold and she sat with her arms pressed to her sides, the book's margins clamped in each hand.

I heard you go out. I was worried.

A year ago tonight my wife and daughter were killed in an auto accident. It was my fault.

She blinked but gave no sign of hearing. He thought to repeat it but the words which had emerged a moment ago with surprising fluency lay stoppered in his mouth. He and Avery faced each other for a frozen halfminute, until Nathan swallowed. This action seemed to free Avery from paralysis, and she set the book on the sidetable and stood and lifted her arms, a gesture that reminded Nathan of a heron preparing for flight. He expected next a downbeat of wings, but she stood there, arms splayed, offering an embrace, and still he could not move. He said instead, I need a shot.

She did nothing but blink, and so stark was the silence in that room that Nathan actually heard it, the wet tick of her eyelids. Her arms fell until they drooped to her sides, and he saw that the robe's sleeves fell below her fingers, so she looked childlike in her exasperation. And for an instant Nathan did consider the simple comfort of a hug. Not to receive that comfort, but to grant it. She was moving towards the kitchen and in a panic of need he opened his mouth to call out and stop her. A sudden physical recoiling halted him. Terrified she might misunderstand, that he would take the hug in lieu of the drug. He shut his mouth and followed her to the kitchen.

She opened a cupboard and removed the lockbox that contained the vials and syringes and when she turned and saw him staring at her she paused and seemed uncertain. Then she unlocked the box with a key she kept on a lanyard around her neck. In the livingroom he lay down on the couch and clenched his eyes shut as she prepared the syringe, hating these moments before the injection not just for the feverish anticipation but because he felt so absolutely vulnerable. It had occurred to him more than once the ease with which she could murder him, leave air in the syringe, push it into his bloodstream. An embolus of gas navigating his circulatory system until it lodged at some critical juncture and choked off the bloodflow and killed him.

He cracked his eyelids and watched her suck the drug into the syringe, and instead of the look of pained compliance she usually wore at this moment, her expression was calm, almost pleased in its resolve. She looked at him and nodded, smiling. The syringe's cold bodkin penetrated his vein, and she drew a coil of his blood into the vessel, thumbed the plunger.

Oh, he heard himself say as he tumbled into a cyclone of bliss. He heard the *chiddup chiddup* of sparrows and wondered vaguely how they'd gotten into the room, thought he felt their wing-beats as they leapt from the mantle and passed across his face and landed on the couchback. They opened their beaks and emitted a chorus like singing monks, a slow, hypnotic chant which poured like warm honey into his ears and pooled in the bowl of his skull.

He exhaled to the bottom of his lungs and paused there, his chest empty for some minutes, waiting for his body's petition for breath, but after a long time he grew concerned and inhaled, and the fresh oxygen united with the morphine in a pleasing hybrid that lifted the corners of his mouth. He thought Avery must still be watching him and he opened his eyes to see her reaction to this smile, but she'd moved to the easy chair where she sat hunched, the robe's sleeve scrolled past her elbow and her arm bent. Nathan suddenly realized that she'd always worn long sleeves, and saw for the first time on the inside of her forearm a tattoo showing an open straight razor, its blade inked so it appeared to be embedded in her wrist, summoning a drop of blood. The needle went in; the drug raced through its bore and into her body. She withdrew the barb and slumped back into the chair and let out a heavy sigh.

Nathan lifted himself on his elbows. He could see now that the tattoo razor was gripped by a gloved hand, like a surgeon's, and on the blade a blue caduceus.

Hey, he said.

She lifted her chin and glanced around searching for the voice's source.

Over here, he called.

She turned. Ah, Nathan, she said softly. I've wanted . . .

Nathan waited, but that was all. She lowered her head and shut her eyes. Nathan watched her, waiting for each breath as one watches a stormy sky for lightning. Here was one. And sometime later, another. Then with effort she rose and came to stand before the sofa. She sat on the floor crosslegged, facing him.

Nathan turned onto his side to look at her. Her pupils were pinholes, the textured discs of her irises explicit. As if they'd been flayed open for dissection. She watched him, her lips pursed with a look that seemed disapproving. It made him uncomfortable, so he closed his eyes and fell instantly into a dream. He was walking across a prairie, and though the scenery trundled past he thought he was making no progress at all – rather, it seemed his foot-steps were propelling the world beneath him, like a treadmill. He suddenly realized that he'd assumed an awesome responsibility to keep the Earth turning, and if he stopped walking the progression of day and night would stop forever, and one face of the planet would scorch in the sun's eternal glare while the opposite perished in the icy pall of an endless night. So Nathan. Keep walking.

He awoke, mouth dry, body stiff, his arm dead beneath him, and Avery gone. He rolled onto his belly and worked his fist, flexing the muscles, trying to restore circulation and feeling. He felt wretched, wondered vaguely where she had gone. Relieved to be alone, but then he heard a low gurgle and slid himself to the couch's brink and peered over the edge, saw Avery lying on her back on the floor beside the couch, her mouth ajar and a clot of phlegm gurgling in her throat. Her body seized as she tried to cough but nothing emerged except a high, increasing whine, like the recharge of a photographer's flash.

Nathan slipped clumsily to the floor beside her, but he forgot about his broken arm and the cast crashed against her sternum, and she jerked upwards as if electrocuted. He hoped that this concussion had been enough to dislodge the gob of fluid in her throat, but no such luck — she stretched out again and the gurgle became a croak like a dog choking on a chicken bone. He sat watching her, certain that somewhere in the jelly of his mind there was a solution to this predicament. When it came he spent moments chastising himself for taking so long to reach it. Then he seized her wrist and rolled her onto her side, delivered several savage blows with the heel of his hand to the middle of her back. The fifth or sixth stroke brought a greenish foam to her lips, though still she didn't cough. Her breath came in soapy gasps, so he lifted her to a sitting positing and kneeled behind her, drew her back against his chest and, gripping her around the torso with his fist pressed below her breastbone, gave a swift compression, a procedure with a name he could not at this moment recall. The Hindenburg Manoeuvre? The Heineken Manoeuvre? She barked and sucked a long breath, then rested against him, gasping, but Nathan couldn't tell if she was awake or asleep. When he looked over her shoulder he saw a wad of sputum on the knee of her robe with the hue of things that glow in the dark. He held her for a long time, until his back ached and he could think of nothing more appetizing than a bed, alone, cool sheets, sleep.

He awoke on the floor, his body curled around the vacancy left by Avery's body. The house silent. He pushed himself painfully into a sitting position before he stood and searched the main floor. Through the front window he saw grey morning light, which would make it almost eight. He wondered if Avery had a shift today. He climbed to the second floor and found her sprawled facedown on her bed. Ankles overhanging the mattress edge, slippers lifted from her heels and hinged at the toes, gaping crocodiles. She was snoring softly. He sat on the bed and looked around the room. Honeycoloured panelling. The bed's headboard a conglomerate of branches pegged together in a high arch. Sidetables of pine, and on this one a glass of water on a coaster, a vase of dried flowers, an antique clock showing 8:20. Its tick so meek he could hear it only when he faced its dial. Above the headboard a curtain of brocade interwoven with silver thread. The theme of wood pervading the paintings too: trees, forests, log structures. The ceiling trussed with timbers. At his feet a hooked rug showing settlers paddling a hollowed-out canoe with outriggers. Wood floor. He was a prisoner in a wooden box.

He'd been sitting for some time when he looked up and saw filling the doorway a man wearing a great coat of stitched pelts, his beard a clotted hoary shag, eyes the colour of teak, mildly crazed, though after regarding him for a time Nathan thought his expression serene, smug even. A ghost, perhaps.

Nathan rose to greet this apparition who even now was stepping forward and then without a hint of malevolence the figure lifted his arm and clubbed Nathan across the jaw with the back of his hand. Nathan spun and went to his knees, his cortex and nerves and muscles mustering their retaliatory power until he flopped forward and lay still, eyes open and seeing under the bed resting on its side among the dark and dustbunnies a yellow pillbottle.

He awoke in a new attitude, his head sagging backwards and

the walls and decoration moving, inverted, past his eyes. Being carried, he was being carried along almost tenderly, as if he were a sleeping child.

Then he recognized that his porter was climbing steep stairs, breath labouring, and it was the stairs to the loft. When Nathan looked up he saw the approach of the woodstrip ceiling adjacent the attic hole, thought he would as punishment have his face slammed against it, but at the last moment the man swung Nathan's body upright and carried him adeptly through the opening and set him on the floor. Then Nathan watched the man he'd seen at the threshold of Avery's bedroom rise calmfaced through the opening and step onto the attic floor. Then the feet, Nathan watching the man's enormous feet clad in woolly socks jig about on the floor before the bed, and Nathan thought he might be making it up, straightening it, tucking in sheet and quilt. A moment later the man lifted Nathan onto the open bed, resting his head against the pillow, and he felt a blanket drawn up. The light clicked off, the creak of descent.

Awoke to a still house. A mild ache in his jaw and in his bones that craving. He turned onto his back and listened, heard the pelt of snowflakes against the window, a sough of wind.

He got up to get dressed and found he already was and collected soap and towel and shaving kit and descended to the second floor where he stood for a long time listening at the foot of the staircase. Moved along the creaking floor past the bedroom, where Avery no longer lay but the covers were peeled back and the bed in disarray. He continued to the bathroom, where he closed the door and stripped off his t-shirt and shaved and undressed and showered, trying to keep water out of the cast and washing tenderly beneath the bandage in his side, where the meat of his abdomen met in a yellow seam.

He heard the door open. Stood rigid in the hot cascade of water, listening. A shadow moved across the showercurtain, then he heard a low grunt, and the sound of a urine stream stirring the toilet water. A long piss. A sigh. The toilet flushed then, and

Nathan was so preoccupied listening that he did not brace for the hot blast, squirmed out of the flow, cursing. The door closed again.

He finished and towelled off and wrapped the towel around himself, opened the door and glanced into the empty hallway. Climbed and dressed and descended to the second floor, then down the stairs to the first.

The man was sitting at the kitchen table reading a newspaper. He wore an earthbrown sweater and rested on his elbows with his forehead in has palm, reading.

I'm Nathan.

The man did not reply, instead raised his index finger and read for a moment longer before looking up.

I am Hugo.

Avery's husband.

Yes. You're boarding here, Nathan?

Nathan could not place the accent, thought it might be Scandinavian.

There's nothing between your wife and me. He'd been planning to say this since he'd awakened, but didn't think he actually would. But there it was.

Is that factual? Hugo asked.

Yes.

Then why does she tell me otherwise?

What do you mean?

This opium thing you are doing together.

Morphine.

Ah. Ah, so you know what I mean.

It's for the pain. She gives it to me for the pain. She only injected herself once, yesterday.

Oh, so you're an expert on her life.

I didn't say that.

I guess I needn't tell you she has had such a problem before. It's why the first fetus was lost.

The first . . . the what? Nathan became vigorously, painfully alert. The what?

I receive blame because of working as a radiologist. She blames x-rays and beta particles.

You work at the hospital too?

It doesn't matter. The problem is from her. She puts drugs into her own body. A doctor should know the harm from these things. Especially a doctor who wants a baby.

Nathan felt himself sway, and he grabbed a chairback for support. Hugo was paging through the newspaper, didn't notice.

You say there's nothing, but there is something between you. There is morphine between you. She feeds it into your blood, is this factual?

A few times. As I said, it's for the pain.

Pain comes for a reason. Pain reminds you of your errors. What's this object on your arm? How did you become hurt?

A moose.

You received this injury from a mouse?

A moose!

How does such an animal attack a man?

I was in my car.

Driving.

Yes.

Carefully driving on the highway. And then the moose. And then, boom.

Yes.

Hugo looked at him, not a stare because he glanced periodically at the newspaper. Then he rose, said, We shall drink?

No thank you.

You won't drink with me? You sleep in my house and share drugs with my wife and you won't drink with me, your host? We drink cognac. You like cognac?

No, Nathan replied.

Come. We drink cognac.

The liquor hot in Nathan's empty belly, rapidly assimilated. Hugo slouched in the chair beside the fireplace, snifter balanced on his thigh as he described in low tones how he'd recently killed a wolf with an axe. He'd been splitting logs, the wolf had come at him from behind, bitten his calf.

Very unusual behaviour for a wolf, was it perhaps rabid? Hugo wondered aloud.

Nathan watching him through a boozy haze, trying to focus. Well, he said. Was it rabid?

I don't know.

But it bit you.

Yes. Here, Hugo replied, and drew the cuff of his pants to his knee and twisted his leg to reveal a parabola of violet punctures. It's much better now.

But did you get treatment? Nathan asked, trying not to sound shrill, failing.

Why? It's healing.

But rabies! You might have rabies.

I feel fine. My body would fight such a thing. Let me tell the rest. Hugo placed his glass on the coffeetable, rose to his feet – a little unsteady now from the cognac, but maybe, Nathan thought, due to the swarm of rabies microbes reproducing in his body, moving along the network of his nervous system towards his brain. Hugo said as he fanned his hand over his calf, The dog here, biting. I lift – and here he kicked the leg forward – There is dog hanging from my leg. And with this axe I swing . . .

He made a motion with his arms, simulating an arc of the axe to swat the wolf away. With the side, he said. Not the edge.

Why not the edge? Nathan asked.

I might cut his head off and it stays clamped to me. When he falls I run at him quick and cut his ribs and belly and head, chop him dead.

Hugo flailed his arms as if working the axe, grunting with each chop of the blade, until he staggered towards the cold fireplace, almost fell into it. Then he sat and drank from his cognac, looking at his glass, muttering quietly.

They heard the front door open and Avery enter, both looking expectantly towards the room's entrance, but she went out again, and they heard bags and paper sacks carried in and set on the hallway floor. Nathan thought about rising, to go and help, but he looked at Hugo heaped in the chair, fixated on his drink, and thought, I am just the boarder.

But he heard the front door slam, and he sat up abruptly, thinking about morphine. The urgent plaint of his nervous system. Was rising to go and help her when she came in, stood in the doorway with a bag in each hand, looking at Hugo, then the cognac bottle and glasses on the coffeetable.

Here is my frau, Hugo boomed.

Merry Christmas everyone, she said with a hint of sarcasm. What are we talking about?

Life, Hugo replied, then added, Wildlife.

What does Mr. Soderquist think of your wilderness adventures?

She looked at Nathan, and when she saw his expression her manner changed entirely. No, Nathan, she said. No, no, no. I'm sorry. There won't be any more.

Nathan not moving, looking at her, his hands clamped to the chair's armrests. Trying to force his mouth to say, I wasn't going to ask.

Stepping through snowflakes falling slowmotion in the blue orbs of the bridgelights, hum of snowtires on the decking as Nathan made his way across the frozen river. The day's light only recently retracted and he moved along, face lowered with the hood pulled over his head, body bent as if the coat held the world's weight. He looked up expecting to see the warm glow of the Falcon's windows and familiar faces smiling in greeting but it was dark and the glass carried nothing but reflection of the headlamps and streetlights and approaching it his own bedraggled shape. He tried the door and it was locked and he considered some family tragedy of the owners forcing early closure when he saw taped inside the glass a sheet of stationary showing a listing of holiday hours. Closed 3 p.m. Christmas Eve. Closed Christmas Day. Open 9 a.m. Boxing Day for Breakfast. He tried the door again and let his hand drop. Not realizing until now he'd been planning to talk to Maeve about drugs. She'd been cold to him lately but he had a scroll of cash in his pocket. Lisa and Sydney's money. The hot want in his blood. Panic coiled in his gut like a cobra.

Walking quickly down the main street, a few shops still open and within them the desperate: the husband at a jewellery store counter, hand pressed to his mouth as he surveys a tray of earrings, and in the toy store next door a mother dredging frantically through a bin of stuffed animals. Victims of capitalism. What gift for your wife and child tonight, Mr. Soderquist?

Up ahead Rainbow Donuts, Open 24 Hrs. He stepped into its fluorescent interior and shook the powder from his coat, got to the counter where a Filipina girl with a posy of mistletoe clamped to her collar asked him what he wanted. He studied the doughnuts in their alcove, greasestained paper lining the wire racks. He wanted morphine, opium, heroin. Give me crack or crystal meth.

I'll take an extra large double-double, and a halfdozen doughnuts. Mix em up, he said, jolted by the steadiness of his own voice.

He took a seat in the front window facing the street and drank the coffee hot and finding himself famished ate two doughnuts one after another and then ate a third. The urgent plumpness of his bladder sent him to the men's room where he pissed trying to prevent the tears from escalating into fullscale sobbing, saw in the mirror while washing his hands a smear of icing sugar on his upper lip and the rim of one nostril. Someone stepped in behind him, squeezing through the narrow gap between Nathan's back and the tile wall and in the mirror their eyes met and it was a highschool kid he didn't know and he had a shiner, his hair tucked beneath a black beret and they nodded to one another before the boy went into the stall. Nathan returned to his seat and ate another doughnut.

Hey, someone behind him said, and looking in the reflection in the glass he saw the highschool boy.

What, Nathan said without turning around.

The kid stood with his hands in the pockets of his varsity jacket and he shook one hand to produce from the pocket the rattle of pills in a bottle.

Nathan turned. Sit down, he said.

The boy took the chair beside the window and leaned forward, his hands on the tabletop, fingers laced.

You want a doughnut? Nathan asked, opening the mouth of the sack, tilting it towards the boy, who reached inside and took one and ate it.

I got codeine, the kid said, his mouth full.

I need morphine, Nathan said.

I got codeine, the kid repeated.

How'd you get that, Nathan said, nodding to his bruised eyesocket.

Somebody hit me. A suckerpunch.

Well, Suckerpunch, Nathan said, leaning back. I need morphine.

It's all junk. Same source, the kid said. Crystalline alkaloids derived from opium. Morphine, codeine, heroin.

How the hell do you know all that?

Wikipedia.

Wiki-what? Never mind. How much?

Fifty.

Fuck off.

Okay, the kid said, rising.

Forty, Nathan said, knowing he'd pay fifty, knowing he'd pay five hundred.

Forty-five, the kid replied.

Nathan was imagining the boy's mother or aunt or grandfather panning frantically through the medicine box for the pillbottle even now making its way beneath the table into Nathan's palm. Fuck them, he thought. I need this. He fished into his pocket for the bankroll, and concealing it in his jacket peeled off the cash, pressed it into the kid's hand.

Go on, Nathan said. Get lost now. Happy holidays.

The boy rose and shuffled out the door. Nathan sipped his coffee, attention focused gigantically on the bottle in his pocket, the tablets which he sat pondering, conjuring them in his mind. Were they round, oval, oblong, scored for easy division? Pink, blue, canary yellow, roseate, luteous, tawny? And what company's name stamped into each? Pfizer, APO, Upjohn?

He would not take them here. He did not know their effect, how rapidly they might deploy to his tortured nervous system. Curiously, he felt no urge to rise, to head for the door. Not yet. Savouring the craving. Not convinced of their efficacy, and perhaps fearful they would do nothing. Opening the bottle and finding vitamins, thumbtacks, marbles – choking hazards, as such things had come to be known in his household. There was a vocabulary, a reality, that opened with parenthood. It included an awareness of a broad section of our society to which the childless are oblivious. Daycare centres in office buildings. Nursingrooms at the mall. Diaper change stations in washrooms. Meanings altered. The casualness with which he once took the death of a child in films or books or on the nightly news turned to horror, to outrage.

What other worlds exist parallel to this one, visible only to the affected? The handicapped, the aged, the devout. The addicted.

At this thought he turned his head slightly to survey the shop, those lone figures hunched over tables with their spent coffees, suffering under the cold haze of the fluorescent lights. An old man near the door might be an addict or just senile, thin lips slick with spit, muttering silently while his hand worries a bald spot on the cuff of his army coat. By the door two girls with their clownish makeup, harlots looking to turn a Christmas trick. Stubs of cigarettes in the ashtray between them stained red with lipstick. It was not a cheery nation to which he'd gained admittance.

On the vacant table beside him, a heap of newspapers. He leaned and collected them, pushed aside his empty coffeecup. Thumbed through, discarding flyers proclaiming last-minute deals and a Boxing Day nirvana to come. It was the *Globe and Mail*, yesterday's, sports section, classifieds, business. He skimmed the funnies, which weren't. Someone ill with flu came in and ordered coffee and in the confines of the shop his coughs sounded like field artillery. *Woof-woof. Woof-woof.* Nathan turned the page and saw an obituary for a respected newspaperman and the photograph was his father. Resisting an impulse to turn the page again. Knowing he can make it unhappen by choosing not to see it. The pagecorner pinched between thumb and forefinger, turn it, just turn it. Reading about his father. His dead father.

Found himself in the street. Lone figure in a whirlwind of closing stores, of people scampering homewards for Christmas Eve. Wind rising as if to usher them along, down the street, into vehicles, cleansing them away. Slam of car doors, rev of engines. It seemed over in a matter of moments, the stage cleared after the encore, and suddenly he was alone on this town's main street, a lost figure standing against the wind and blowing snow in front of dark shopwindows and a trafficless avenue. Pivoting slowly to regard this ghost town. Wind lifting to horizontal a stinging barrage of snowflakes. He turned until it met his back and he heard the flakes pelt against his raised hood and he saw them flailing away down the street leaving in his lee a cutout of his onearmed figure until they merged downstream as if obliterating all trace of him. Howl of the powerlines and a restless *clank-clank* of a yoga studio shopsign overhanging the sidewalk, straining against its lugnuts. The naked trees in their concrete basins all hung with pinlights clatter like muted chimes. A snowplough rounds the corner and pauses, its blue light sweeping the street as if searching for prey. Nathan stands his ground as it edges forward and passes, the blade scraping at the film of dirty snow and pushing it into an inchhigh berm beside the curb and leaving a stink of dieselsmoke before the whine and clatter of the steel bridge and its palpating engine retreats into the night.

There was no one to fight. This thought coming fast on the realization that he'd like to hit someone. Hard, in the jaw or belly or balls. And be hit back, again and again, until he folded, until he fell and the kicks came one after another.

He was walking. His boots on the bridge. Wind in his face, snow in his eyes bringing tears which he blotted with a coatsleeve. The only image of his father Nathan could conjure had the man at his desk in his study, and he was saying, No. Not withholding permission for Nathan to attend an event or own some kind of merchandise. A more substantial no.

Soon Nathan was standing before the door of the wooden house, pulling his key from his pocket.

The house was quiet. He found tucked and folded inside the jacket beneath his broken arm the scroll of newspaper with the obituary. He put away coat and boots, made his way into the livingroom, balled the newspaper and set it among the ash and char on the fireplace grate. He saw by the clock on the mantle it was almost ten. Hours gone, evaporated. Santa inbound.

He was hungry and he went to the kitchen hoping for some leftover morsel, expecting none, but there was inside the fridge a plate for him wrapped in cellophane with mashed potatoes and roast beef and steamed beets and green beans with carrots. A yellow note affixed to the plate's rim: rolls in the breadbox.

He thought to dash it to the floor. The sound of shattering crockery bringing them both downstairs to find him dancing on the food, kicking it into the corners. A kind of patient rage was waiting for him to say the word, waiting for him to relinquish control. He lifted the plate and put it on the counter, stripped away the plastic, stuck a finger into the potatoes and smeared it on his tongue. He thought about his mother. He put the dish in the microwave and pressed Reheat Meal. Found the rolls, buttered one. Horseradish. A re-corked bottle of pinot noir on the counter, one perfect glassful left inside. He sat at the table with cutlery and a cloth napkin and sipped the wine. He did not know if it was good or bad, but he liked it. He ate the food, mopped up the gravy with a second roll. Pushed the plate away with his thumb and leaned on the table. There was a mouthful of wine left in the glass and he brought it to his lips, but stopped before draining it. He studied the sanguine liquid in the bowl. Then lifted the glass a fraction towards the empty chair across the table, and drank.

Early the next morning he lay on his back on the floor in the bathroom off his room with his head beside the toilet and his feet sticking out the door. The codeine bottle upright on his chest. He did one slow, painful stomach crunch, lifting head and shoulders towards the ceiling, keeping the bottle balanced, belly muscles constricting. At first he thought it was good, the familiar tensing around his midsection, the hardening of his abdomen, but then a lance of pain ripped from the sidewound and radiated through his body. He flopped back so fast his skull cracked against the floorboards. The bottle dropped to the floor beside him and he rolled slowly onto his side facing it, too close to focus on the label. He didn't want to know whose pills these were. They were no one's. They were his. He unscrewed the cap, shook four into his palm, and held them there, chalky white talismans like ovals of bone.

CHAPTER 7

- - - - - - - - - - - - - - - -

It was a dark, tenacious winter, but spring came anyway.

Nathan built the fire on the ashes of previous fires and sat looking into flames translucent in the sunlight, and then he lay back on the mossy earth and raised his arms, brought his hands down over his head and closed them around a rock the size of a firelog. He let out a breath, and then, inhaling, lifted his upper body and the rock in a belly crunch of such intense effort motes of light bloomed at the periphery of his vision. He lowered the stone but did not rest, repeated the motion, rising, gasping, the muscles in his belly and biceps clenching. Again and again, muscles burning, throat raw as his vision of the sky pinched shut in a narrow focal-point of distilled cobalt. When he felt himself flagging he began to summon objects of rage to fuel the effort of each crunch: grief for his losses; persistence of his injuries; want of narcotics; dependence on Avery and Hugo, and at last, with such hideous effort he thought blood would spring from his pores, a single, black summation of selfloathing, his weakness in all these things, in failing to regain purpose in his life. His belly muscles screaming at that last, torturous flex. He flopped back on the ground and released the rock, lay wheezing and sweating, paralyzed with fatigue, his recently healed wrist, shoulder, ribs, and side throbbing, unable for a time to bring his arms to his sides. After a few minutes he sat up and peeled off his soaked t-shirt and lay back, panting at the fire-side. Wishing he could cry. He thought this often, how if he could cry – something he hadn't done even at the funeral of his wife and child or at news of his father's death, hadn't done since some hormone-charged rejection or breakup back in adolescence – all this terrible constriction might be released, his eyes flushed clear by tears, so he would at last be able to see a way forward, a way out. He'd tried forcing it, sitting alone in his loft in the wooden house: he'd clench his face, he'd shake and sob in a weak counterfeit of crying, but the effort was dry and futile, and that terrible hydraulic pressure filling his head would not abate.

If he didn't do something soon by will he would do it by impulse, and that thought terrified him.

From where he lay he glanced around at the halfdozen stone cairns fashioned from rocks he'd scrounged from the hilltop and the surrounding forest. He'd stacked them into shapes and figures; most were meaningless monoliths, but one was meant to be an abstract representation of the house he'd left in Toronto, and the last and largest was a figure that though he hadn't meant to make it his father was his father. Tall and lanky, slightly stooped as if in a moment it might lurch forward and lumber down the hill towards town. A slab for the shoulders and arms set atop a slender torso, wider chunk for hips which stood balanced on a pair of stocky legs set upright on the hill's crest. The figure still headless.

Krillbane lay in the west, obscured by hills and scrub and forest. There was good sky today, all wisp and cirrus, a look of clean, brushed cotton, skeins of fibre unravelling in the slipstream of the westerlies. Or so he would have written if his notebook hadn't lain a two hour-walk away in the house within which he lodged with a corrupt physician and a mad Norseman. The armistice there was about to end. He could feel it, a bomb's fuse burning down to its root.

When they'd heard about his father's death they'd adopted him. It was the only way to describe the household's dynamic. There was no mystery to the psychology of it, this couple wanting children but the clockwork of their bodies running down, failing, and here he was for them, a man reduced to boyish dependence by injury, grief, and addiction. Hugo thrilled in the power of paternalistic dominance, but in truth it was Avery who ensured Nathan's acquiescence by continuing to supply him with pills: oxycodone, codeine, hydromorphone, and there was always the unspoken possibility of morphine. What she didn't know was that he'd stopped taking the pills, had discovered that intense exercise (not the lax rehab he'd been prescribed) was his antidote to chemical addiction.

He put hands under his head and looked into the sky's soft twill. It was time to head back. The sun crawled north, days lengthening by minutes, and he knew that if he left now he would step through the backyard gate just as the last light drained from the sky. But he could not move. Despite the sunlight, the song of a phoebe, the boughs of white pine exuding an aroma of citrus and spearmint as they emerged from the melting snow, he suffered that potent dread. The wind coming up, chilling him, sunlight weak on his forearms, his right wrist where the skin was still bleached and scaly from the cast.

He rose and began a slow circuit below the hill's summit, scouting for a head for his father. There were plenty of rejects, this one too irregular, this one too small, this one with a split along one edge and likely to crack. But here was one he liked, blocky and monolithic, with a ridge along one side like a brooding browline. He'd looked at it before but thought it too heavy to move, though that was almost a month ago. He stepped forward and drove his arms beneath it, feeling its chilly underside. Closed his eyes and lifted. The rock's shift so surprised him that his eyes popped open and he let it fall. He shut them and lifted through his knees, up, up until he was standing almost erect, and he staggered back with it cradled in his arms, its cheek against his bare chest. He stood briefly, swaying, computing the stone's balance and bulk, and then he climbed, carrying that brick − fired in the Earth's kiln four billion years ago − up the slope to the hill's crest and that headless inukshuk. Sweating now, watching his biceps bulge against the stone's ridges, right arm whining within its jellied core and healed ribs throbbing, but he persevered, taking one shaky step at a time until he was standing beside the figure, which awaited its gift of a head. Nathan feared for an instant that if he set it in place the thing might come alive, and of course it would be cruel and ruthless, as a thing of stone inevitably must be, and he the one responsible for unleashing it upon the world. He stood quivering, trying to determine the orientation that would best accommodate the rock, enjoying the crisp irony of it all, the urgent need for balance to complete this statue of his unbalanced father.

This thought jarred him just enough that his foot shifted and caught on an outcrop. All at once he was falling. His elbow came around, struck the figure's shoulder, and the thing seemed to pause as if stunned before toppling backwards and sliding stone by stone downhill. The rock in Nathan's arms meanwhile pitched sideways and he shot a foot out and with his remaining strength launched it away from his body to keep from falling with it clutched in his arms and suffering grievous injury. It struck another rock with a shuddering crack and then split, and the echo of its cleaving reported back from each of the neighbouring hills in different timbres like a rumour returning altered to its source. He rushed forward and dropped, kneeling in front of the stone with his hands on each side of the break, panting hard and feeling white ricochets of pain in his elbow and back and ribs. Then he leapt to his feet, and in a surge of fury delivered a series of roundhouse kicks that destroyed all of the cairns and left nothing but a few artless mounds of stone.

It was long past dark when streetlights came into view and he crunched through refrozen snow past the moonlit cemetery, crossed the creek and continued dodging shrubs and low branches up towards the house. A resonating chorus of aches from the exertion of carrying and then hurling that stone. He came to the opening in the fence where the motionsensor saw him and energized the floodlamp. It shined hot into his eyes, leaving the rest of the world black and impermeable.

He found them both in the livingroom looking towards the room's entrance as if at an insolent teen arriving past curfew. Avery on the couch, agitated, legs crossed, her foot jiggling. The fire in the hearth at its normal excessive pitch and Hugo in the chair beside it, hands flat on his thighs. Both of them looking from him to the coffeetable on which lay the knife used to inflict his sidewound.

Nathan stood in the doorway and folded his arms across his chest.

Someone brought this thing here, Hugo said, opening his hand towards the object on the table.

The girl from the scrapyard, Nathan said.

Yes, Avery replied. Dora. She said it was yours.

It is, Nathan replied. Someone in Thunder Bay gave it to me.

Gave it to you, she said.

Yes. A gift.

Avery drew from the pocket of her sweater a clear baggie which looked at first to be empty. She held it up as one would an item of courtroom evidence.

Hugo was sitting forward now, panting as he lifted the knife from the table. He pressed the release and the blade flipped out with a snick. Nathan tensed at the sound, felt a flux of energy ripple through his tortured muscles. His mouth went dry and he straightened his frame to full height. Hugo was oblivious as he waved to Avery for the baggie, but she'd met Nathan's eye and perceived the threat in his stance.

Give it here, Hugo said impatiently, and she broke eyecontact with Nathan, reached out and handed the bag to Hugo. The man drew it open and reached inside, fished about for some moments with his fleshy hand, and having captured whatever minute object lay within, let the bag drift to the floor. Now he held the knife at arm's length, and squinting severely, forgetting his reading spectacles pushed up into the snarl of his ashcoloured hair, he held whatever the baggie had contained, so small that it was concealed within his fat digits, and attempted to mate it with the blade's tip. He frowned blackly as he reoriented the piece several times to no satisfaction until he slapped both blade and chip onto the table and barked, Baa, sat heavily back in the chair and stared into the fire. Avery rose and collected both pieces and then, her eyes mildly crossed, aligned the metal fragment with the blade's broken end.

Nathan stood, waiting impatiently. She let the blade and its tip drift apart, the knife falling to her side but the chip, that tiny, inconsequential delta of stainless steel remained the focalpoint of her attention.

Well? she said, and looked at him.

Do you have a point? he asked with a tight smile.

I dug this out of you, she cried, deaf to the pun, holding aloft the knife's tip. That night in the ER you rolled in on the gurney all smashed up. I knew when I saw it that it didn't look right. That it was suspicious. Not part of a car at all. So I held on to it. And then those calls from the police.

So what.

So what. So what? You broke my trust! she cried. I asked you about this more than once. Gave you opportunities to confess. And every time you lied to me. You lied to me!

Yes, he replied. I lied.

A stunned silence at the calm with which he'd responded. Hugo combing his fingers through his beard said softly, There will have to be a consequence.

Yes, Nathan said. A consequence.

In the pause that followed Avery cleared her throat and started to say, Well. I think now that things are out in the open we can get back to –

Nathan recognized all at once the indecorum, even criminality, of the ways she'd manipulated and controlled him with her apparent compassion, and the corruption of that virtue aroused in him a tremendous fury. No! he shouted, his hands balled into fists. There will have to be a consequence!

She looked at Nathan in startled recognition that he was no longer weak and injured and, more significantly, no longer addicted. Her control had waned and now the restraints were gone. A wild animal unleashed.

Very well, Hugo said, unaware of the danger now present in the room. A severe consequence. What do you suggest?

Evict me.

Avery sucked in a breath.

Let's be reasonable, Hugo said.

There was a massive wooden bookcase beside the doorway and Nathan lifted a foot and kicked its side so it trembled and spilled books onto the floor.

Hugo finally brought his gaze up and saw for the first time the fury present in the room. He gave a weak smile, seemed to glance about at the rest of the room's furniture, and a look came into his eye as if, Nathan thought, he was seeing it all dashed to flinders. Nathan knew he was incapable at the moment of anything of the kind, that the kick had drained the last of his reserves, and he could not name one part of his body that wasn't achy and flagging. But he maintained a ready stance, concealing his weakness.

Very well, Hugo said at last. I evict you.

No, Avery said. You can't. He's our guest. He's paid until the end of the month.

You can stay until the end of the month, Hugo said. And then, you will go.

Unless . . . Avery started to say.

No, Hugo barked. He goes.

But where? Avery asked Hugo hopelessly. Wait, she then said, bringing her hands together and looking at Nathan. There's those little bachelors over the laundromat. I know who owns them, he's an anaesthetist at the hospital. Hugo, you know Cliff Chan. He rents those rooms, doesn't he?

Avery, you're out of your mind if you think I'm going to stick around in this shithole, Nathan said mildly.

Wait, she said, stepping towards him. You wouldn't actually leave Krillbane, would you? Listen to me. Listen to me, Nathan. I'll get you more. You know I can get more.

He fixed his features to prevent any hint of interest from showing. He said, But I'm cured, Dr. Gooding.

No.

Yes. You cured me. I'm cured. And for that, I thank you. I thank you both for your hospitality, warmth, and support. You've made me see it's time to leave. So, as per your wishes, I'll be gone by the end of the month.

He spun and left the room, returned to the foyer and donned coat and boots, which were still Hugo's coat and boots. He heard sputters and hisses from the livingroom and left the house. He walked with a sense of triumph, marching along trying to manage the ache in his muscles and bones, then realized with a sudden burst of despair that he had nowhere to go. It brought him up short, the old griefdriven punch in the gut, and he stood, swaying in the keen equinox evening. After a moment recognized he was facing west, the direction he'd been travelling before meeting the moose. At that thought he began to walk again, seduced by an urge to go and keep going in a westerly direction, but then he felt the weight of the coat, heard the boom of the heavy boots on the grate of the bridge. These were not his things. He kept on, and as he passed the Falcon hands rose in greeting behind the glass, but he passed by, continued along the street and discovered the Salvation Army store open, it didn't close for another halfhour.

He found a denim shirt and a longsleeved plaid shirt and some t-shirts adorned with faded logos, Coke, Serious Moonlight Tour, Run for the Cure, and he put into his cart two pairs of jeans and a midweight coat with a tear in the lining and a dozen pockets and a zipaway hood. He found a big hiking backpack. On a battered shelf he found books, he collected a halfdozen, two Steinbecks, something by Agatha Christie, and two by E.M. Forster, plus *The Good Soldier* by Ford Madox Ford. He brought it all to the cash, where a tall Indian wearing an eyepatch rang up the purchases, and Nathan paid and declined the offer of bags and stowed everything inside the backpack and went out with it on his back and crossed the street to a clothing store, where he bought underwear and socks and undershirts. The discount shoe store was closing when he arrived, the clerk was Calvin Peach, who Nathan knew from the Falcon. Calvin, a chubby middleaged loafer who wanted to be liked, unlocked the door and turned the lights back on and Nathan found a pair of cheap Chinesemade runningshoes to which Peach applied his employee discount. They walked together to the Falcon, Nathan in the new shoes with Hugo's boots in a plastic bag. Peach held the door but Nathan said he had something to do. Peach said he'd see him later and went in while Nathan walked on and crossed the bridge. He thought to return to the house where tonight he would sleep but instead continued past the street and along the highway past the gas station and convenience store until he saw the glare of spotlamps above the junkyard where his wrecked car lay. He gripped the chainlink and looked at the cars, trying to see if there was anything that might be salvaged, and he moved past rows, observing in the cold light his Supra, and continued until he reached the shed from within which he was surprised to see light. He went to the door and tried it and it was open. The girl sitting at the desk, doing homework.

May I help you? she asked, rising, flustered. Then she recognized him. You. This about your knife?

No.

I heard you were living with that doctor and brought it there.

I don't care about that.

Thought it might have sentimental value or something.

Do you sell cars?

Like what? Like cars that drive?

Yes.

No, no. Just parts.

What time is it? Why are you here?

I got this project for school. I like working here.

You should lock the door.

Yeah. You're from a big city, eh?

Don't bad things happen out here?

Sure.

Well you should lock the door.

I let them handle it, she said, and nodded to the corner where the dogs lay, one asleep, the other, the big bitch he'd stabbed, panting, watching him.

Nathan felt his kneehinges loosen and he lifted a hand at the dog as if to hold it at bay.

They remember you or would've killed you by now, she said, smiling. She whistled once and the dog came forward, and Nathan backed towards the door but when the dog arrived it stopped and looked up, huffing, its tongue lolling.

Pet her, the girl said, and he did. So, a car, eh? There's Harmony Motors about two klicks down the highway. They're closed now but tomorrow you could go down. They got this Mini I sort of have my eye on. Navy blue. Hands off.

Uncomfortable silence as he glanced around the room, at the scree of carparts on the desk, floor, shelves, organs for donation, harvested from the dead. Arrayed against the back wall, those dozen bicycles.

What are those? he asked, stepping towards them.

Bikes, she said. You heard of bikes?

Are they any good? I mean do they work?

Yeah. They work. They're salvage too. Rebuilt from junk. My dad's project. No one ever looks at those.

He was standing above them, studying them. They were a mixed lot, mountain bikes and road bikes, frames of steel and aluminum, scratched, some rusting, pitted, Raleigh and Giant and Supercycle. He squatted to get a look at their accessories, the pedals and derailleurs, calliper brakes, spokes and tires. All the tires were flat. But the bikes themselves seemed reasonably good. He singled a larger one out from the bunch, a Raleigh hybrid painted metallic green.

Can I look at this one.

Thought you wanted a car.

I thought so too. Let me see this one.

So look.

He shifted the bikes in sequence, opening enough space to admit the pedals and handlebars of the Raleigh so he could roll it into the space before the desk. He tested the brake levers, watched the callipers close on the rims, lifted the front of the bike and spun the front wheel, watching it turn, seeing if it was true. Almost no wobble, no bind from the brake pads, which were new and glossy black. Tires almost new. He pounded the seat, felt the piston in the shaft give, bounce back. Walked around the bike, sighting it from every angle.

You got an air pump?

For what?

The tires. I want to take it for a spin.

She sighed loudly. There's a compressor hose hanging on the wall outside, she said, tossing a thumb over her shoulder.

Out in the yard under the blue lamps he set the compressor dial and filled front and back tires, rolled the bike inside.

Can I take it for a spin? he asked her.

Sure. Watch for moose.

Funny, he said, and rolled the bike outside onto the gravel, stood with the seat resting against his hip waiting for a lull in the traffic. It was suddenly busy on the road. When a break came he pushed the bike forward and swung a leg up, landed on the seat trying to remember when he last rode a bicycle. He thought it might be fifteen years ago. But the aphorism about never forgetting held true, and though the seat was too low and the handlebars too high his feet landed on the pedals and he rode out onto the asphalt with only a mild waver of the front wheel. Rattle of the dry chain as it tried to mesh with the drivegear, and he put his thumb on the shifter – when he last rode, shifters were mounted on the handlebar stalk – but found that he couldn't make a fine adjustment, this was indexed shifting, locking into each of the three positions but never landing the chain correctly onto the corresponding gear. The best he could manage was second, the chain chattering against the chrome guide. The rear derailleur was better, engaging each gear smoothly, though unable to drop the chain onto the smallest sprocket. He was making his way eastbound on the highway's margin, occasional traffic roaring past inches from the handgrip, he had no lights and he felt woozy and vulnerable with the night wind in his face and a sense of motion, of moving, yes, he was moving again, and now he remembered how important it was to remain in motion, to keep going.

It was with reluctance that he stopped on the roadside and looked back, amazed at the distance he'd covered. The junkyard was lost behind a bend, and the territory here was foreign, he'd not seen it before though it was in the direction from which he'd come into Krillbane, in the back of the second ambulance those many months before. He was breathing hard, and this seemed right – that he work to escape, that pressing an accelerator did not qualify as a sufficient expender of effort to grant him peace, and he knew then, standing with his hands still clutching the grips, puffing, traffic hying past on the highway, that he'd found his mode. That tomorrow he would move on, and this was his transport.

He walked the bike across the highway and into the opposite lane, mounted, and returned to the junkyard shack, where he bought the bike for $85.

He realized as he pedalled for Avery and Hugo's house that without a destination, speed didn't matter. Motion was his medicine, and this twowheeled instrument served that purpose as well as a car. Better, because part of this exercise was exercise, rebuilding his health, bringing strength back to his body.

He stood before the wooden house and found himself holding the bicycle before him like something earned or won for which he anticipated praise. Waiting for Hugo or Avery to step out and congratulate him. Such a ridiculous, poisonous notion, he thought, scooting the bike along the side of the house and crossing the backyard, igniting the floodlamp which cast his shadow and the bike's together across the dead grass and the shed. He passed through the fence and into the forest, the wheels tilling the earth and crackling through patches of frozen snow, frame and handlebars plying through branch and twig until he reached sufficient depth to conceal it. When he returned to the frontyard a glance revealed their bedroom light was off – shiftwork often sent them to bed early – and using his key he entered the house and went upstairs, creeping silently past their bedroom door, mounting to his room where he collected his things from the bathroom, toothbrush and toothpaste and razor and shaving cream and a bar of soap in the package and a stick of antiperspirant. He put these on the bed, then removed from the backpack his recent purchases, and arranged them on the bed, set the bag there too, placed among them the notebook and a handsharpened pencil, his wallet with his credit and bank cards – still tapped into insurance and house sale money – and his keyring. The keyring. He picked it up and threaded the house's key through the coil and put it on the bedside table, was about to set the ring on the bed again when he saw the spare Supra key, realized that it and the others collected over the years – from lost padlocks, old apartments, obsolete luggage, the Annex house's garage – were now irrelevant, and he closed his fingers around them to feel a last bite of their teeth before he tossed them into the wastebasket. Then he stripped off the clothes he wore and balled them and threw them into the corner. Stood naked before his worldly possessions, looking at them in the yellow light from the tablelamp, bleak shadows of the stacked clothing casting shadows across the comforter as in a moonscape. Floorboard creak as he shifted his weight. This was all there was left of him.

He unwrapped the underwear from its cellophane and tissue-paper and pulled on a pair and peeled from the socks the adhesive label that bound them across the cuffs and put them on, and put on jeans and the plaid shirt. He stowed everything else in the bag and put the bag on the floor and lay on the bed, flinching at the *cheep* of the bedsprings. Lay looking at the pinestrip ceiling, then reached and groped for the light's chain and tugged it, closed his eyes against the darkness, and slept.

Awoke with warm breath against his ear and thought it the sigh of a woman, her limbs lashed about him in the cold dark. Lifted his head and was alone, shivering atop the comforter with a strong erection, groping to preserve the dream but it fell away like water through splayed fingers. He did not know whose breath. He reached for the comforter's edge to pull it down and climb under but stopped and swung his feet to the floor and crept to the window, unable to suppress the squeak of the floorboards. The room faced west and there was no way to know if dawn was a breath or hours away, but high in the sky beyond the fanned treetops a belt of cloud blushed orange. He turned and looked at the bed in the dark, sensed only its bulk but felt its lure, like a lover beckoning.

He bent and cast about the floor until he found the bag, gripped its handle and swung it onto his shoulder, stepping now with the gait of the furtive but accompanied at every step by the bleat of the floorboards. He couldn't fit through the opening to the staircase with the pack on his back and had to dangle it from one arm as he descended.

He reached the floor and stood panting, eyes trained on their bedroom door. Not knowing why his escape required stealth, why it was an escape at all and not simply departure. He was a free man, truly disjoined from all responsibility, achieving what he had secretly pined for those days and nights he'd played the perfect husband and father. Though he'd been totally committed to wife and baby, he'd been simultaneously overcome with a wild lust for freedom. Even while he was congratulating himself on his paternal competence and solicitude, he found himself envying shit dads everywhere, at card games, on weekend fishing trips, at the office seven to eleven, missing every diaper change and feeding, never once jigging a screaming infant around the nursery at 3 a.m. trying to ease her back to sleep. Deliberately insensitive to the ordeal of parenthood. Men with the courage and cowardice to say, Fuck your career, honey, mine is the important one in this household. Not my fault you were the one born with tits.

He sprinted past the door, expecting it to spring wide, to be accosted before he reached the staircase, Hugo with a fatherly bearhug or Avery stabbing him with a syringe full of morphine, but he made it past and down the stairs without incident. He opened the front door and stepped in sock feet onto the porch and pulled the door shut, unzipped the bag and removed the shoes, sat on the decking and felt the cold through his jeans and pulled the shoes on and laced them, got out the coat and put it on and stood, his breath in the porchlight hanging visible in the windless air. Swung the pack onto his back, cinched the straps, then padded down the steps and onto the path. Jogged down the side of the house, hearing in the near-silence the sibilant brush of dead grass against the treads of the shoes.

It took some minutes of thrashing through the brush, panic rising at the idea that the bike had been stolen, until he found it. It felt fragile and insubstantial in the dark, incapable of bearing the weight of him and what was left of his life for any distance, and he bordered on abandoning it and setting out on foot before he let reason prevail, and he wheeled it into the yard and along the house, the *tick-tick-tick* of the drivecog echoing from the plank wall, until he reached the driveway. He'd decided he would not look up at their bedroom window and did not, but then did. She was there. For some reason he'd expected Hugo, not to bid farewell but to supervise his departure, the threat that Nathan represented to his superiority never acknowledged until this instant. But it was Avery in the window, watching him with a neutral expression. She lifted a hand and held it there, and he looked back at her refusing to grant a reply, watching her impassively, trying to feel outrage or rage or disgust at her behaviour but feeling nothing except – he was shocked to discover – pity. For her childlessness, for her cold and rustic husband, for her addictions and the fact that her boy was leaving home forever. Her hand still suspended, she watched him, a still life of woe all the more woeful for her expressionlessness. He turned away from her, threw a leg over the saddle and pressed his shoe to the pedal and went. And before he rounded the corner beyond which he would vanish from view he threw his chin over his shoulder and saw her there still, hand lowered, watching him go. He looked away, forward, into the direction he was travelling. He lifted his left arm, bent at the elbow with his hand extended in a gesture that would've been a cyclist's handsignal for a right turn, and so he told himself it was, except that a moment later he turned left.

By the time he reached the highway a plumcoloured light filled the eastern sky and the light set in silhouette a pair of tractortrailers thundering into town, their jakebrakes hacking as they passed the speed limit signs. Nathan waited with one foot on the gravel for them to pass, then followed in their cold wake with the taste of dieselsmoke in his mouth. He pedalled hard, running up and down through the stuttering gears trying to find a natural cadence, and when he crossed the steel bridge the oscillation of the hard tires on the grating shot through the frame and into his skeleton and set his clenched teeth abuzz like they were being powersanded. It let him know to relax his jaw, and the going was easier after he left the bridge and followed the mild downgrade through the town's core. He looked at his florid knuckles as he passed under the streetlights, pressed his ears alternately to each shoulder trying to warm them. He needed gloves, a hat.

Everything shut tight. He stopped the bike and dismounted, stood blowing into his hands. His toes, the insides of his thighs chilled. The cold was boring into his ear canals, making his braincase constrict and spawning a headache. The Falcon opened at 6:30. He might get some breakfast.

No. Enough of easy. It was time to go. He didn't want to say goodbye to anyone.

Traffic on the main street starting its dawn increase, and he saddled up and rode, the whole sky above him and into the west peppered with small clouds, each catching against its eastward cheek the flush of sunrise. He pedalled up a grade, stopped at the red light at MacDonald Street and jammed his hands into his pockets, flexing them back to life. His cheeks and forehead on fire with cold. Cars and trucks moved past his shoulder, and he looked up and saw the green light, curled his hands around the grips, and set off. In a few minutes a service station, cars at the pumps in a haze of fluorescent light, rapid business of customers in and out the door of the convenience mart, people emerging with paper cups, nodding to one another. Nathan rode across the lot and to the door, realized he had no way to lock up the bike, laid it against the glass and went inside.

Swift enterprise at the counter, a brown man in the store chain's red and white uniform taking cash and debit cards, pulling cigarette packs from the rear display, bagging microwaved croissants with a tight grin and stating with formal aplomb to each departing customer, Goodbye, sir, or, Nice day, ma'am. Lifting his eyebrows to Nathan, who was passing towards the coffee urns.

Nathan filled a cup and wrapped his hands around its heat, blowing steam from its oily surface, eager to suck some warmth into his body. In the chrome trim of a displayboard his own face reflected, a fat red blush. He shuffled through the store, passed among the twinkies and soup cans, antifreeze, beverages, the milk fridges, consciously taking in the store's ambient warmth, storing it for his ride. He might see someone he knew from the Falcon or the hospital, but he seemed already in a different town, a different world, one populated by another species of humans, those who dwell in the dawn hours, away from late nights soaked in lager and bourbon. He rounded a shelf and found a basket of miscellaneous winter gear, said aloud, Ah, and began to paw through it one-handed. There were lots of earmuffs in neon orange, purple, yellow, and tiny childsized gloves, and bandanas, also purple, yellow, and he began to despair until he unearthed a toque machineknitted from acrylic wool the colour of green tea, and then, of similar hue, mittens. He kept digging, hoping for gloves, but there were none that would fit his hands. He broke the acrylic tie that united the mittens, and put one on, crooked his fingers, folding them against his thumb, remembering a snake puppet with which he'd entertained Sydney in her bath. Look out Syd, here comes the Woolly Taipan! Her shriek of laughter as she evaded its snapping jaw.

He brought the items to the cash, the checkout clerk with a halfsmile pressing his lightgun to the barcodes. Nathan accepted his change.

Farewell, Soda, the clerk said with that semigrin, and Nathan looked up, but the clerk had already swung his attention to the next customer, Pump six yes? Thirty-six please, on Visa, very good.

By midmorning he felt better than he had since New Brunswick. He was moving again, the world awash in sunlight, a vernal tang to the air, an old dial thermometer hanging outside a feedstore showing a temperature in the mid-50s. He had shed the toque long ago, and unzipped the coat to release the vapour of his sweat, maintaining an even rhythm on the pedals. He'd stopped an hour ago at a Home Hardware in Rennie and bought a tin of machine oil and a kit of small screwdrivers, had managed through trial and error to tune the front derailleur so it no longer clattered against the chain, at least on the middle sprocket. It had taken him some time to grow accustomed to the bikeseat, its geometry built contrary to male anatomy, but he found that if he sat further back, pushing his buttocks higher onto the padded domes, he could alleviate the numbing of his loins.

He bought a tuna sandwich at a convenience store and sat outside on a bench and ate it, and hunger forced him inside to buy another, and when that was done he resisted the impulse to go in and buy a third. As he sat finishing a gingerale he looked at the bike propped against the wall and decided that he didn't yet feel affection for it. But still enjoying the endorphin charge of the exercise. When all was done and he had crushed the soggy cellophane in his palm he sat in the sunshine smelling the air, which carried a faint scent of green, succulent after winter's necrosis.

And then on again, cruising the highway's margin in a haze of labour, the focused action of muscle and tendon carrying into his cortex a soothing quietude. He suddenly remembered, as if it had travelled through a time wormhole from his desk in a highschool English class, the word "nepenthe." From the Odyssey, a mythical drug that cured grief. Exercise his nepenthe.

He thought the highway traffic should annoy him, the stream of semi and SUV, cars and pickups, thinking of Lisa's antipathy to the perpetual consumption of a finite resource and the interminable exhaust of greenhouse gases and pollutants into an atmosphere upon which depends not only the climate but our moment-to-moment survival, the constant four-minute margin between existence and braindeath. But it didn't, and he knew why. It was because he was allowing himself like the majority of the population to enjoy the thrill of mobility, of our technological prowess, and as no immediate threat to our wellbeing was obvious from the railroad of traffic roaring past, he could maintain his high spirits as he pedalled westward.

He saw the back of a broad sign on the highway's opposite shoulder, and as he rode past he turned and saw that the distance to Krillbane, the distanced he'd pedalled since dawn, was forty-one kilometres. He stopped and dismounted and resting the bikeframe against his thigh looked at the sign and then down the highway along which he'd come, the pavement through each lane's centre white with pulverized salt. He turned and looked at the stretch he was about to cover and it seemed in every way identical to where he'd been, the same cracked blacktop stretching into the distance, a little hazy, and on both sides of the highway conifers and leafless trees crowding together against a litterstrewn buffer of dead grass. The triumph of forty-one kilometres fading. And does this fucking traffic ever fucking stop? Can we really keep doing this for fucking ever?

He got on the bike and pedalled furiously now to consume distance, smug in his appreciation that he was travelling – unlike those combustive monsters ripping past in both directions – without causing harm to anyone or anything. Pedalling for Lisa, for Sydney, for the whole ungrateful planet.

He laboured for a while at this clip, until his breath grew hoarse and whorls of light began to fizzle across his eyes, and when he reached the crest of a hill he stopped again and set his feet on the gravel, his legs straddling the bikeframe. Ahead stretched the highway in its awesome monotony which he knew would become only more so as the land flattened into prairie, after which he'd hit Winnipeg and there pick up the Trans-Canada and follow as it bored arrowstraight until the foothills of Alberta pushed him towards the sky. And after the terrible effort of climbing those mountains and navigating their rare, cold air he would begin his long descent to the Pacific. And then what? He could not think what he would do when he found himself pressed against that endless sea. Waves washing over his bare feet, the bike's tires sunk into sand. The journey complete, for what?

Moot. That question utterly moot, for here he was in the middle of the continent with this little footpowered machine beneath him. The highway offering a simple binary choice: east or west. He'd already tried east. It had been a disaster. And that mainspring of need wound up tighter than ever in his gut, ready to break or unravel violently.

He remounted the bike and went on, it was three in the afternoon now, the sun a quarter down the sky and very warm. He stopped again and took off the coat and stowed it in the bag and rode on, his sweat cooling in the spring air. Rode west, consuming kilometres as his legs pumped him thoughtless towards evening.

Not long after dark he came upon a roadhouse, its glass adorned with neon of every hue with signs for Corona and Blue and brands of beer unknown to him. He took the bike around to the back and stowed it behind a dumpster and came to the front passing a halfdozen vehicles, mostly with extraprovincial plates, and he went in. Stood by the Wait to Be Seated sign, still puffing and inhaling vapours of hot meat and vegetables. A chalkboard on an easel beside the vacant hostess station listed specials in coloured chalk. It was steak and seafood and backribs, every dish striking hunger into his belly, and when the hostess at last arrived, a small brunette in her midteens with hair in a bun and cheeks caked with foundation he feared he might not be able to speak with the saliva filling his maw. Luckily he only had to hold up an index finger to indicate the number in his party and he followed her to a table against the wall beyond a row of booths – a lone diner, concealed from the room. But as he leaned to draw the chair closer to the table he smelled himself, a blunt, musky scent of sweat, and he drew in his arms to seal his armpits. Then he rose and went to the men's room. It was a single room and cold, with a grate in the wall blowing outside air that smelled of the day's nascent greenery. He locked the door and took off his shirt, hung it on a peg and wet a papertowel, mopped his chest and armpits and the back of his neck, squeezed a dollop of pearlpink soap from the dispenser and washed himself, then with a new papertowel wiped away the soap and with a fresh wad dried himself. Wishing he'd brought the stick of deodorant from his bag. Then he washed his face and slicked back his hair with wet hands and put on his shirt and pissed and washed his hands. He returned to the table, pulled out his chair and sat, but as soon as he relaxed he recognized the error. For he was unbearably, heartbreakingly weary. His legs howling with fatigue and the room dimming beyond an eclipse of exhaustion. He rested his forehead in his palm and let the menu blur until it nauseated him enough he had to shut his eyes.

How are we today? Can I get you a drink? a voice asked, and

Nathan looked up to see a short dandy of a man dressed in a starched shirt and black slacks. Nathan ordered coffee and drank it and called for a refill and drank that. It seemed to do nothing but bring a sharpened awareness of his fatigue. He ordered steak rare and it was thick and bloody and good, and he ate the mashed potatoes and steamed vegetables and a basket of bread and ordered pecan pie and ate that and still was hungry. Was waiting to ask to see the menu again, then someone was shaking him, saying, Sir are you all right sir? Nathan lifted his head, blearyeyed and groggy, to see the waiter standing over him. For a moment remembering waking openmouthed in the dark of the nursery, head back in the rockingchair, the blue nightlight like some faraway beacon signalling to him ambiguous warning, not a red light, not yellow or green. Blue. Startled now in this Manitoba restaurant to recall that snowploughs, snowploughs carried blue warning lights.

I fell asleep, Nathan said, blinking the room back into clarity.

Anything else, sir?

A bourbon. Straight-up. A double.

Is that a good idea?

Look, I'm not drunk. I just rode a bike in from Krillbane.

Today?

Today, Nathan said. So bring me a damn bourbon. Please.

The waiter returned with the drink and put down a napkin and set the glass upon it and winked at Nathan and when Nathan lifted it he saw liquor poured to the brim. He drank it fast wishing he'd taken it before eating but the volume was enough to achieve the desired effect and by the time he paid his bill and asked the waiter about a motel room his head was whirling pleasantly.

He wheeled the bike into the room and propped it against the wall, crashed onto the bed.

Awoke late morning beneath an excruciating weight, thought that someone was on top of him, pinning him down. His mouth slack against the pillow, a cold tarn of drool against the linen at his lips. Tried to rise but could not. Wanted to call for mercy but could not. It was his knapsack, still strapped to his back. He was pinned beneath his pathetic worldly possessions.

Lay there beneath its weight, clawing out of what felt like anaesthetic sleep. No sense of time's passage, just the fugue of unconsciousness and now awake, the clocks turned forward and the planet craned about on its axis. His legs taut, sinews humming like harpstrings. Lay there watching the sunshine creep across the carpet.

Nothing worse than someone who refuses to be who he is.

Nathan started from a halfsleep at his father's voice, lifting his head, expecting to see Logan Soderquist himself seated in the chair by the window. Fearing it, yet disappointed when he saw the chair empty. Wondering what the man would think, sitting there, studying his son pinned by the sum of his belongings to a motel mattress. Not disappointed. Not sympathetic. Satisfied. Vindicated. For Logan's sentiment – that everyone should select for himself a particular character and stick to it – was immutable.

At the suppertable, his fork swinging like a conductor's baton to the rhythm of his rant. A colleague's sudden resignation for a change in career. Some woman's departure from her family to pursue singlehood. His own son's transformation at age fifteen from pedant to hooligan. But at the time Nathan had known who he wasn't: studious achiever, teacher's pet. He was a lover of fun, a budding womanizer, a connoisseur of Blue and hashish. Relieved suddenly of that girdle of responsibility, of caution and consideration, of studiousness. It had been a terrible effort to maintain this rank, a greater effort still to make it appear effortless. When he'd attempted to explain this to his father, there seemed no way to make it sound right, and when he'd finished, his father tilted back in his deskchair and mused a moment before replying, So in your heart you're a loser. A cog, a gear. No, Nathan had wanted to reply. I still care about books and ideas. I just don't want them to get in the way of fun. But he knew that would get him nowhere. Standing there on the hardwood planks of his father's study. Like a chess player considering his response to a provocative move and seeing that all courses led to defeat, and just wanting to minimize the time he would have to stand there (he had a girl to call or a rendezvous with a friend and a bottle) he replied, Yes. And then, with conviction, Yes. A loser. Knowing it was a response his father could not protest. Nathan was being who he was. The speech, the assertion his father would cast at any other reply, that people's grief comes inevitably from trying to be who they are not, and only by finding not your calling but your true caste could you achieve happiness, that unbearable lecture could be repelled by instantly delivering the response it was intended to solicit. Yes, Dad. A loser.

Logan Soderquist had then rocked his chair forward and rolled to the desk, seized from the cluster of family photos Nathan's own portrait, pulled open a drawer, and dropped it in. He then glanced at his youngest son, said, Go then. And as Nathan turned and pulled open the door he heard the drawer shriek shut on its rollers.

And fourteen years later he stood on that same spot and told his father he was done. Careful not to say he was changing, that he'd been wrong, he wasn't a cog. Rather that he'd exhausted a particular ambition, reveller, gamboller, skylark, libertine, and was ready to pursue another: husband, philanthropist, father. He was going to marry Lisa, quit his job as chainsaw man with the city's park department, and take a paycut to work for a not-for-profit, and have a child. Children. As he was explaining all this Nathan was certain his father would cast his mind back fourteen years earlier to the day his son abandoned scholarship and responsibility, and be pleased with this decision, thrilled that Nathan was returning to worthwhile pursuits. Withdraw that photo of a gawky teen, if he still had it, and set it among the cluster of portraits. But no, it was as it always was, his father unwavering in his philosophy and remaining fastidiously consistent.

Logan had stared at him for a long time before he'd stood and said, No. You can't. Your apparent success as a loser leads me to believe that this is in fact your calling. Your true nature. You will be who you are.

You don't have a say in the matter, Nathan had replied.

No, his father said. I don't. You can choose what you want, but nature will prevail.

A black rage had filled Nathan's heart and he'd stood there again calculating responses and projecting replies, knowing that his father was implacable, that to try to contradict this particular conviction, of the unstoppable predilection of each human character to follow a single commandment, Be Who You Are, was to argue evolution to an orthodox Christian, that mode of thought wearing a trench so deep in the psyche that its walls are unscalable and no amount of reason or proof can boost the victim free.

The day after the accident Nathan's brother Rex came to collect him from the hospital where his wife and child lay cold in their trays in the basement morgue. It was a sunny day and the rolling snowfields were dazzling, and as he drove towards Toronto Rex tried relentlessly to get Nathan to talk, stirring in Nathan a vicious anger he felt no obligation to curb. When Nathan appealed for silence Rex responded by filling the cabin with sighs and murmurs.

And then the inevitable arrival home, the reunion with grieving grandparents, and the dark days where Nathan could bear little more than viscid, blinding sleep and his mother's pea-soup, and always thoughts about going home to his own house where Lisa and Sydney must be waiting for him, before memory's violent correction. His mother begging, imploring him to cry, frustrated that he wouldn't, or couldn't, certain that it would help, or rather that there was great peril in his refusal to, and she feared she would lose him too. And how he could barely look at his father, could not meet his eye with the threat of that retributive stare hanging between them, and when finally it became too much Nathan launching across the dinnertable his fiercest glare, daring that look, and his father when he met it set down fork and knife and rose from his chair and rounded the table, and even as Nathan sat there in his defeat his father drew out the chair and lifted his son to his feet and folded his arms around him in a firm yet somehow unsentimental embrace before he returned to his seat to finish his meal. Nathan standing there shellshocked, feeling not comforted but beaten, physically abused, as if that hug was meant not to console but to wound.

His consistent father, who never strayed from what he was: drunk, disenfranchised reporter, then later, editor, and always failed novelist. A failed Hemingway.

Strangely dead now. The inevitable transformation. Curious to think of his father's dissatisfaction, his annoyance, his highstrung ambition and endless failure, all of this to be now complete.

His mother. Alone. Wondering where her son is. Filing past the coffin, all of them, his mother, Rex and Hester. The grand-children. His father's friends, associates, rivals. The old man rests in the casket, eyes glued shut, the undertaker's paint hiding the spiderweb of burst bloodvessels beneath the flesh. All the guile gone from his face, and where, Nathan was thinking, where does it go? Disappointment, rage, vexation, all of these are a kind of energy, and energy cannot be destroyed, so where do these emotions go? Fall away from the dead like cockroaches, scattering for dark recesses.

Mama. Thinking of his mother at the kitchen table with her teacup. Eyeglasses resting beside them. Quietly grieving. Wondering where is her littlest son. He swivelled his eyes to the telephone on the bedside table, an old rotary dial made from beige plastic. Only the weight of the pack preventing him from rising, lifting the handset, dialling.

With a great surge of his arms he jacked himself up, worked his way towards the foot of the bed until he could slip to the floor where he pushed himself upright, tottering on palsied legs. Wondering if he could ride again today or if he should stay another night, resting. So much time already wasted. Yet nauseated at the sight of the bike against the wall. Hating his frailty. He had to get strong again. He shucked the bag onto the floor and sat on the bed, turned on the television. Flipped until he reached the Weather Network, saw that it was closing in on 11 a.m., the temperature seven degrees Celsius. Rain moving in. The day half done. He was hungry as hell. Let that hunger rage. He took a shower and halfway through had to sit on the rim of the tub so weary were his legs. And when he couldn't get up he lowered himself to the floor of the tub and sat with his arms around his knees and let the water rain down. Watching it corkscrew down the drain until the stream at last began to chill and he figured he'd depleted the hotwater tank. Turned it off and sat shivering on the cold enamel, wondering how he would negotiate the slippery sides and get out. After some minutes he tried and found the strength in his legs somewhat restored, and gripping the soapdish managed to haul himself to sit again on the tub's lip and swing his legs onto the linoleum. Pulled a towel from the towelrack and dried himself, then shoved the towel beneath his bottom and pulled down another to wrap around his shoulders. He thought he might crawl to the bed, but this would be pathetic. Sat for a long time and got down on his hands and knees and crawled to the bed.

When he awoke it was raining, the room's light a muted grey. Hunger gone. He should get up and eat, but then he decided he was fasting, and fell asleep. Awoke at 3 a.m. The rain stopped and moonlight on the carpet the colour of bone. He got up and wrapped the towel around his waist and went outside, stood on the curbstone and watched a truck rip past like a comet. He went back inside and got his notebook and pencil and filled a glass with water and stood in the doorway drinking, glanced at the lamp on the wall outside with its old spiderweb and the author of the web herself desiccated at its hub, a spiderhusk trembling in the prairie wind. Nathan sat on the curb and opened the notebook on his lap.

MARCH 21ST

Cold night. The moon floats at the hub of a xenon aureola, a pearl in a belljar. Rags of lucent cloud, the smudges of fingerprints. Or are they nebulae fixed upon a deeper stratum, the speckled pane of the Milky Way? Stellar incubators within which the fetuses of solar systems nourish and grow. Worlds under construction. Soul forges.

Minor quakes of shivering rippling through his body. Teeth clenched at the cold soaking through the towel from the concrete, chilling his ass. She really was gone. He was alone.

He went inside and got dressed, packed the bag, put on his coat and mittens and hat, threw his key on the bed, wheeled the bike outside. He crossed the highway and stood a moment on the gravel looking across the fields and listening to the wind's susurrant voice through the sagegrass. Then he mounted the bike and rode.

CHAPTER 8

- - - - - - - - - - - - - - - -

He squeezed the brake levers and steered the bike onto the slim shoulder where he dismounted and walked it down a narrow footpath to the root of a lone cottonwood and its oasis of shade. He heard a whine of tires on the blacktop but it took a long time for the pickup to appear and after it passed in a wow of tiretreads it took another era for its sound to be spent southward under a vast sky populated by schools of brasscoloured cloud. He lay the bike in the knapgrass and sat with his sweating back to the tree and drew his waterbottle from the holder screwed into the bikeframe and drank. The water hot, tasting of plastic.

The sky. He was through with it, he swore that now, this goddamn fucking sky. Four months had passed since he'd left Krillbane, and it was difficult to account for his activities during this span. He'd begun with the intention of continuing westward, but somewhere he'd become sidetracked, went north and kept going, seduced by solitude, by relief from the suffocating dominance of Avery and Hugo, seduced by the sky. He spent days at a time riding in one direction, only to erase his progress and return to his starting point, taking off on a new vector. Sleeping outdoors or in motels, eating in diners, sometimes spending weeks without speaking a single word of consequence to anyone. It was the sky that held him, the intoxicating, addictive sky. Its infinite textures, sudden transformations, psychotropic capriciousness. It made him write, and writing seemed to be the thing he ought to be doing, his obligation after the paralysis of Krillbane. He zigzagged across Manitoba, Saskatchewan, crossed briefly into Alberta before heading back east. It was a world of pure sky, and he cowered beneath its endless curve, never reaching the rim, and he'd filled most of the notebook with accounts which became one upon the next more desperate, rampant, rash, as he plundered the language of every serviceable metaphor

lustrous cauliflower carbuncles racked in serried battlements all fluorescing with a wanton phlogistic pyrexia

and had lately turned when English failed to offer adequate diction to inventing words

transgriffic jackbars plonting through the happitic gulf of spanrous ochre, spreading north-south in a long, uninterrupted atragat, slungsherried with battered hapgars.

But it was no good. His writing couldn't summon Lisa anymore. He'd given up. The impulse to write exhausted. His energy given over to motion. There was a single word left in his vocabulary, and it was *go*.

He was in a new country. There'd been a sign with an arrow showing the way to the United States, and hungry for change, he'd followed it. He was at the breastbone of the continent, had emerged not an hour before from the lower right corner of Saskatchewan, a silent highway through rolling pastureland, passing lone prairiedogs standing on the shoulder like spectators. Ducks marooned in snug reservoirs, the wind doleful as it passed among blond wheatheads.

He'd crossed the border at Port of Regway, expecting a town or at the very least a dutyfree, but there was none of that, the Canadian station stranded on the prairie and just beyond it, somewhat smarter in smoked glass and aluminum, the American port. There were no personnel in evidence as he passed the Canadian office and when he cruised the curve to the trio of vacant booths at the U.S. side he imagined some apocalypse he'd not heard about which had prompted the abandonment of the bordercrews. Thought of passing through and into the new nation when he considered the potential consequences of getting caught. Glancing about he saw an airhose stretched across the tarmac. He circled back and dismounted and stomped on it, heard a bell ring inside the building, arrived back at the booth and plucked off his sunglasses, hooked them on the neckband of his t-shirt as the agent emerged, a slight codger with a trim moustache and steelframed specs. Nathan sensed during the interview the agent's weariness at having to maintain a perpetually suspicious air, and after a few minutes another agent emerged from the booth, a young, plump fellow, then another, a widehipped woman with curly hair. They asked about his job (fundraiser), his bike, where he came from, the purpose of his visit, how far he intended to go, then his job again (fundraiser), all of it seeming more to salve their boredom than unearth his involvement in a terrorist plot. In the end they gave his bag a cursory search, seized a clear sack containing two apples which were more applesauce than not.

As he rode south he was irked to find the countryside unchanged, had perhaps expected a dramatic difference, those mythical Rocky Mountains of Montana. But these lay seven hundred miles to the west, miles, he repeated to himself, the one tangible change since he'd entered America, the speed signs now in miles, varying limits for cars and trucks, for day and night. The country rolled on in long, wearying rises followed by swift descents, and if there was a shoulder on which to ride it was pure rumblestrip. Virtually no traffic.

He made Plentywood by sundown, ate pizza at a restaurant with purple walls and vinyl tablecloths, the lighting fluorescent and the servingstaff all girls of around fifteen, and he chatted briefly with a local man who couldn't stop praising the French for abandoning socialism. At mention of a drive-in theatre Nathan rode out through the east end of town like an archaeologist eager to view an ancient temple, and he stood on the roadside watching the silent previews on the screen only a moment before beating a hasty retreat back to town, pursued by a cloud of mosquitoes. He slept at the Sherwood Inn while a thunderstorm raged outside, but when he emerged into the sunshine the next morning the pavement was bone dry. He bought coffee and apple fritters at a bakery filled to capacity with chattering bluehairs and pallid old men, rode west through the cloudless morning. It was forty-two miles of hard, hilly country to Scobey, and on the outskirts he rode two miles along a fence decorated with yellow ribbons, reminding him this was a nation at war. It was 103 degrees Fahrenheit. He ate two enormous plates of mac and cheese in an aircondialed bar, drank a light beer and a huge quantity of water, filled his pack with cold bottles and candybars, and pedalled south another fifty miles on shoulderless road. Saw his first white cross in that state, a sign of a traffic fatality. He'd seen other such markers in his travels, lurid shrines and dead wreaths, once a glass box with four dry roses inside, and this one a lone white marker mounted to a steel rod driven into hot Montana soil. Stood with the bike against his hip and cap in his hand, thinking of how he would put up two crosses, big and small, on the side of that Ontario highway. How the snow would bury them in winter.

He remounted and laboured hard through crests and dips, made it to U.S. Highway 2, the Hi-Line, which runs clear to the Pacific Ocean. The traffic heavier, weaving motorhomes piloted by seniors, transport trucks, pickups, suvs, and this shoulder no wider than an ironing board. Six miles to Wolf Point, a motel room where he stood shirtless twenty minutes above the airconditioner, his palms flared against the window, trying to reduce his body's core temperature. Went to sleep splayed on the stripped bed, woke at three shuddering with cold. He tugged the blankets to his chin and awoke late morning convinced it was winter outside. Went to the window and gazed through his palmprints at the conflagration of day outside. Drank a coffee and ate four doughnuts and rode.

Since leaving Krillbane he'd frequently seen other cyclists but rarely interacted with them, for most on long hauls were riding east with the prevailing wind. Sailing past at speed they sometimes shouted across the highway, Wrong way, you're going the wrong way! and if there was time he'd yell something like, I hear the plague hasn't hit the western states yet! and hunker down over his handlebars, labouring furiously into the breeze. Today however he was blessed with an aggressive tailwind, and he made it to Malta, a distance of 119 miles, almost 200 kilometres, for an average speed of almost thirty kilometres per hour. He was exhilarated by the ease with which this was accomplished, pledged to exceed it tomorrow, and at a squalid bar bought a round of drinks for the wary locals, none of them under sixty. The country seemed bereft of the young.

He left at dawn the next day with a hangover, the day windless and low stretches of road still in shadow until the sun came up and slammed the countryside. Twenty miles out of Malta the highway crossed the Burlington Northern Santa Fe Railway tracks which had paralleled the highway since Wolf Point. Long trains of COSCO and Hyundai containers, but in this flat land you could see them end to end, chugging serpents thundering along the rails under a drifting coil of dieselsmoke. Now the tracks slipped beneath the highway and disappeared north. Soon after, he hit a span of construction, the asphalt dropping to oily gravel, immensely punishing to Nathan's headache, no workers in evidence, the machinery silent along the roadside, a Bobcat nestled like an infant beneath the boom of a Kubota excavator. It went on until the next town, and though he thought to stop for water he felt the press of lost time and went on, crossed the Milk River, picked up a mild tailwind, ran an endless stretch past Fort Belknap where again he thought to stop for water but did not. The tailwind stronger now and visions of breaking yesterday's distance propelled him past Harlem. Four miles out he drank the last of his water. He was certain there was another bottle in his pack, and he rummaged furiously but it was not there. He looked back the way he'd come and then into the west and lastly at the fierce gem of the sun, traffic soaring past in both directions while he waited for something, he wasn't sure what, maybe an oncoming cyclist with a bottle to spare. Then a train ripped out of the east, he'd not realized the tracks had returned from the north, and he immediately mounted and followed it westward. It was soon gone, bluish boa of smoke hanging above the ties in the now windless noon. He grew immensely thirsty though he'd only just finished the last bottle. He knew that as a last resort he could flag down a motorist but he'd grown to loathe the traffic and thought it a kind of surrender to seek a driver's aid. He pressed on into a mounting headwind, squinting into the distance hoping to pick out the cone of a watertower, that frequent first sign of a town on these unremitting plains. The highway before him unbearably straight. He fixed his gaze on the vanishing point, and in the cushion of moisture padding the distance saw two vertical objects swaying against the rule of the horizon. He pawed the sweat from his brow and rode on.

He chased them for half an hour before he'd made sufficient progress to verify that they were cyclists. He wet his chapped lips and pedalled, urged by thirst, until he could see that they were both dressed alike in yellow-and-black tunics and black bikeshorts and silver helmets. Elegant panniers bracketed their rear wheels, and one bike towed a singlewheeled trailer with a yellow PVC bag lashed down with bungeecords. As he closed he saw that the riders were a man and a woman, each lithe and fit, a long braid swaying beneath the woman's helmet, and as he watched their bums lift off the seats and pump while they laboured up a small incline he felt a voyeuristic thrill. He pursued them for several minutes before the approach of a truck brought their heads around and they saw him through their mirrored shades. The truck was hauling hogs and left behind it such a stench the riders turned to show to Nathan their expressions of disgust and soon they were slowing until he'd caught them up.

Hello, the man called as Nathan drew alongside and Nathan looked them over. They were both in their twenties and impeccable in their slick outfits with brandnames stitched into shoulder and thigh. Their matching bikes were Gitanes with slender bright frames, the wheels narrow and sparsely spoked. He saw the man glance at Nathan's bike with a playful sneer which almost made Nathan point out that despite their machines he had managed to catch them, but as he looked past the man to the woman, eyes obscured behind silver sunglasses, he grew convinced that the man would lay blame on her. He didn't want to start a quarrel for fear it would delay the slaking of his thirst. He said, Water?

Eh? the man called back.

I need water. I'm out of water.

Merde, the man replied. Are you crazy? His accent was thickly French.

A little, Nathan replied, trying not to wince. Un peu, he added.

Okay, up ahead. There. We stop. He spoke to the woman rapidly in French. He called her Madeleine.

Guardrails rose on each side of the highway where it crossed a creek with cottonwoods and willow along its banks and they followed a path down into the shade and dismounted. Nathan dropped the bike and threw off his knapsack and the man hunched over his pannier and came up with a pack of cigarettes and lit one in his mouth and passed it to the girl, then got one for himself and lit it before offering the pack to Nathan.

Water, Nathan said through gritted teeth and the man tongued the cigarette into the corner of his mouth and fished around in the pannier until he came up with a bottle of water which he handed to Nathan who wrenched off the cap and drank deeply. It was cold and it immediately mitigated his headache. The woman spoke in French and took off her sunglasses and helmet and wiped the sweat from her forehead and she was very pretty with her brown hair drawn into a complex braid and her slim body lovely in the skintight riding gear. The man handsome, his skin tanned and a fine stubble on his sharp chin, but he was smallboned, shorter than she – his wife, Nathan guessed by the matching wedding bands. The man strutted about surveying the spot as if seeking its flaw. He went down to the river and Nathan looked at Madeleine who stood with the cigarette in one hand and a waterbottle in the other alternately smoking and drinking, looking at him and then not looking at him and then looking again and he said, My name is Nathan. Are you from Quebec?

She looked at him and shrugged, and he said again, Canadian? France, she replied.

He stepped forward, his hand extended and said, Nathan. Canadian.

Madeleine. France, she replied with a tepid smile, and gave his hand a shake. She halfturned and drank and smoked and drank.

The man returned from the river, agitated, spoke with

annoyance to Madeleine and they bickered for a moment before she kicked off her shoes and went down to the water.

I'm Nathan.

Albert, the man replied, and stepped forward and shook Nathan's hand. You are a Yankee? he asked.

Canadian, Nathan replied.

C'est ça, I thought you were different. You ride far on that thing? He jabbed his cigarette at Nathan's bike.

A thousand miles. Maybe more.

Albert frowned. I hear your gears from half a kilometre. Clacking like maracas. He went back to his pannier and returned with a canvas pouch which he splayed on the earth beside Nathan's bike and slipped out a multitool. He lifted the bike by its seatpost and with the cigarette clamped in his lips ran the crank with one had and shifted the fore gear and cranked again until the chain engaged on the largest sprocket. He made an adjustment to the derailleur and shifted and cranked again. He toiled on with stolid preoccupation while Nathan sipped water and after a few minutes went down to the river.

Madeleine was sitting on a rock with her feet resting on a stone above the water, which frothed and churned with a brownish effluent.

Dirty water, she said as if in apology.

Chemicals, Nathan said. Roundup or some shit.

Merde, she said.

Probably poison, Nathan said. He looked at her feet, which were small, the nails painted red, and she caught him looking and wiggled her toes. Nathan looked away, across the creek to dense brush on the far side, then towards the bridge beneath which rocks lay submerged, wigs of green slime fluttering in the current.

He is fixing your bicycle? Her voice was childlike where it rose to make the interrogative.

Yes.

He is always fixing things. He never stop fixing. It makes him crazy when something is not perfect. I like things they are a little bit broken.

Nathan said nothing and he didn't look at her and she sighed and he saw from the corner of his eye her fold forward and rest her cheek against her knees, watching him. He finally looked and she touched her hair and ran her hand along the length of the braid.

You are in good shape, she said, looking him over. You have travelled far?

He got up and walked to the bridge, rested his hand against a wooden pier and ducked his head beneath the span, listening to the fall of water echoing within the dim chamber. It smelled of creosote and organic decay and something else, a highstrung metallic scent, complex organic molecules in suspension, and when he looked into the water he saw speckled tadpoles wriggling beneath the surface, the crowns of their slimy scalps pressed against the water's surfacetension. A transport truck roared by on the highway above and the chamber boomed.

Nathan, she said, and when she said it it rhymed with Satan, and he turned to look but she only watched him with her mouth ajar, which made her look childlike and vulnerable. Little girl. He had a flash of how good it would be to hold her, but retreated instantly from the idea.

He went back up the hill with a sudden hollowed-out feeling in his gut, stopped and watched Albert spraying the chain of the Raleigh with a snubnosed aerosol can. He was engrossed in the task and Nathan climbed the embankment to the highway and stood on the shoulder looking east and west, squinting into the sunbaked distance. Far to the south a green tractor stirred a plume of dust from a field and forktailed swallows darted about overhead. Nathan walked across the bridge looking at the ground and lifted from the gravel a smashed tireguage. He tossed it away and looked into the brush below the road, saw something shiny and stepped over the guardrail, descended into the weeds and shrubs which grew lush in the river's influence, found it was a Mercedes hubcap. He turned it over in his hands, raised his eyes and looked through the brush and across the river, and saw Madeleine still sitting with her feet on the stone watching the water flow past. She didn't see him and he watched her for some seconds, was about to call to her when she yawned hugely and stood and stepped to the water's edge where she pulled down her bike shorts – nothing underneath, there was suddenly the carefully trimmed chevron of her pubic hair – and turned around and squatted and pissed into the creek. She remained there for some moments studying her fingernails with the shorts around her ankles, and there was a tattoo he could not discern at the base of her spine and her bum was as smooth and elegant as the contour of her bikeshorts had promised. She tossed her head over her shoulder, ran her gaze rapidly over the shrubs and trees, then tugged up the shorts and climbed the slope. Nathan staring at the vacant glen. Replaying the motion of her gaze, it was like she was searching an audience for a familiar face. He wondered if she'd seen him, or if she'd sensed his presence. And if she had, what it meant. Sex had been so far from his mind for months he was unsure how to respond. He should've found it erotic, he supposed. That perfect French ass presented – perhaps offered – for his study. The eroticism hinged on that, on her intent. He decided, as an exercise, to imagine that she knew he was there, that she was showing herself to him. But there was still nothing. No sexual response. More specifically, no physical response. He closed his eyes, summoned in his mind a series of erotic images and situations involving the woman. Nothing. He opened eyes at a sudden, tormenting thought: the bikeseat had disarmed him. He tried to remember his last erection and couldn't. He put his hand against the front of his shorts and tried to stir a reaction but there was none. He shoved his hand down the front of his shorts and briefs, felt the flesh hot there but as much as he handled his cock, rubbing his thumb against the underside of the glans until the skin began to feel raw, he could not bring it to life. Cupped and stroked his balls, then at last probed with fingertips that place of the saddle's constant pressure, his perineum, massaging it to encourage bloodflow and the restoration of sensation.

He looked up and saw Albert on the bridge astride Nathan's bicycle looking down at him without expression. Nathan withdrew his hand and called up, That bikeseat. It's rough on the plumbing, don't you think?

Albert did not reply, pedalled the bike away and Nathan climbed to the highway's edge and watched him ride down the road and turn and come back. He stopped in front of Nathan and dismounted.

You try, Albert said. Much better, you will see.

Nathan began to explain himself but stopped when Albert leaned the bike into reach. Nathan accepted it, settled onto the seat but lifted with sudden aversion. Saw Albert's exasperated look and settled back down, harrowed as he imagined the terrible consequence of it all. But as he began to ride he grew distracted by the bicycle's transformation, the former chatter and gnash of gears replaced with a silky hum. He shifted through the cogs, exhilarated as the chain gripped instantly and precisely each sprocket, bringing confidence to his pedalling, the resistance to which he'd grown accustomed now annihilated, granting the bike a sprightly power. He bent forward and drove the pedals fast, shifted through the gears higher and higher until the chain engaged the top sprocket at both crank and axle and as he rocketed forward there was in the motion a sudden synergy between flesh and steel, the taut bands of his leg muscles impelling the pedals forward and the bike responding in a feedback loop which augmented the strength of calf and thigh until he was careening along the blacktop, hair streaming in the wind and all of it with an effort that seemed negligible. When he looked back Albert was a distant matchstick mirrored in his own mirage and had Nathan not left his knapsack behind he would've continued westward leaving the Frenchman and his wife far behind, never to catch him. But as it was he had to stop and when he touched the brake levers the callipers gripped with such force both wheels locked, sending the bike skidding along the asphalt in a dreadful yaw until he let off and straightened, applied subtler pressure and came to a stop. He got off and regarded the bike and felt abruptly the affection he'd been withholding all these months, confident now in its ability to propel him to the Pacific. But a glance at the saddle reawakened the spectre of impotence. He hammered it in annoyance and looked back down the highway where Madeleine must've joined

Albert, for two points now stood there, shimmering in the heat, and Nathan wondered if Albert was describing how he'd caught Nathan with his hand in his pants, and if so was she connecting it with her exposure on the far bank. Telling Albert about it, or not telling him. Nathan was flushing with embarrassment, now he really wished he could ride away, thinking about which of his possessions he could abandon. He ran through the list, decided nothing was irreplaceable, and just about took off. Then thought about the sky journal. He hammered the seat again and as a transport roared past he shouted an oath into the thunder of its exhaust.

He got on the bike and lowered his bottom delicately to the saddle and rode back while maintaining minimum pressure. He slowed as he drew near the couple, bedecked like a pair of yellow-jackets, watching their expressions to try to discover what they'd been discussing. Albert jogged forward to meet him.

So, he said, beaming, hands spread. Better?

Hell, Nathan replied, hopping off. It's really fast.

That is the best I can do with such a machine, Albert said. You must understand the design has limitations.

Can you fix the seat?

Albert stepped forward with an expression of concern. The saddle? This is a very bad saddle. Ah, he said suddenly, looking at Nathan with a wry smile, nodding, lifting a finger and shaking it. I know your trouble. It's choking your rooster. He turned to Madeleine and spoke rapidly in French and she put a hand over her mouth and cackled and said something that irked him. He barked a few harsh words that squelched her merriment and sent her tramping off the highway and back to the camp. Albert turned back to Nathan and said, A little adjustment can help. A little rocking forward or back. Come.

Nathan sat on the earth beside the bike feeling greatly reconciled with it now that Albert had tuned the saddle's pitch, throwing the point of bearing backwards to his buttocks and reducing pressure on the perineum. Albert kneeled beside him performing endless and minute adjustments to his own bicycle while the two men chatted about their countries and America. Madeleine had pulled a mat into a clearing downstream, hoping to sleep, and Albert was jolly and relieved at her attempt. He explained that the girl had suffered terrible insomnia since arriving in the U.S. nine days ago. The day held few remaining hours of daylight and Albert was considering making camp but they weren't carrying enough food to make a meal. Unfolded a map and found that the next town lay nine miles to the west, and he wanted, while Nathan remained at the site, to ride there and get food to bring back so they could eat and camp and leave in the morning.

Nathan was eager to try his enhanced bicycle, ride himself weary before flopping on a motel bed, though he did carry in his pack a foam pad and sleepingbag for nights outdoors. The spot seemed as good as any, but he was uneasy with the idea of spending the night with the couple, embarrassed and horrified about his dysfunction and the fact that they both knew about it. But Albert was adamant that Madeleine not be interrupted as she pursued sleep.

I will be gone one hour, Albert said. Please, monsieur. Then, in a fierce whisper: She is a goddamn fucking bitch without sleep and if she sleep maybe I enjoy this holiday. You just need to stay awhile and go when I return. Or you are welcome to eat with us and sleep here tonight. Just stay for now and protect her. Please.

Nathan finally assented and Albert was giddy as he prepared to depart. He warned Nathan in a condescending voice not to disturb Madeleine, then unhitched the bike trailer and wheeled the bike up the footpath to the highway. Nathan wondered if he should see him off but didn't want to appear eager to have him gone. He got *The Good Soldier* from his backpack and sat against a tree and began to read.

He'd finished a page when Madeleine stepped from the weeds smoking a cigarette, her hair unbound from the braid and fanned across her shoulders. She squatted in front of him and said with her hand extended, What are you reading?

He gave her the book and said, I thought you were sleeping.

I wasn't.

You didn't sleep at all.

I can't in this country, she said, flipping aimlessly through the pages.

Your husband went to town to get dinner.

I'm not hungry, she said, blowing a jet of blue smoke.

What do you want?

She squinted for a time at the cottonwoods fanned above them and said, It's strange. How everything looks like a dream. Shining with light around it. Une auréole. She lowered her eyes to him. And people. People look like angels. Natan, are you un ange? She looked at him imploringly, pupils so enormous they consumed her irises. He thought she must be drugged, had taken some narcotic to help her sleep. Her eyes left him, drifted aimlessly over the landscape. He studied her, looked at her tiny, pinched nose and small frowning mouth, her skin flushed and utterly smooth. His heart aching.

Madeleine, he said, hearing the panic in his own voice. You have to sleep.

Je sais.

You have to try.

She rocked back and sat on the earth, elbows on knees and staring at the ground with an expression of defeat. His body seemed to absorb that weariness, it reached him through the air like a contagion, forcing him to adopt a like pose, wrists atop knees and hands dangling, slouching like a puppet abandoned by its master. He fought it, surged to his feet and called her name, but she did not stir. He stepped forward and stamped the earth to rouse her, and when she didn't respond he bent, thrust his hands into her armpits, lifted her. She was torpid and lightweight and her body folded bonelessly around his, chin upon his shoulder, a slumbering toddler. He cradled her buttocks and her legs went around his waist as he carried her away from the highway, back to the pad fifty paces downstream. He set her upon it on her back and when he moved away her eyes were shut and he thought she was asleep. He kneeled and studied her face and the world seemed very far away, like he was adrift, cut free of gravity.

A light, hot breeze ruffled the leaves of the cottonwoods and a procession of cars and campers tore past on the highway, the *pum-pum* of their tires hammering the bridge's expansion joints. He shifted his eyes to the hardpacked earth, cracked where stalks of weeds had broken through. Was she asleep? He mustn't look. He was about to rise, tiptoe back to his book, when she whispered, Natan.

What? he said, still not looking.

Aidez-moi.

Help you?

Make love to me.

It winded him like a punch in the gut. Still he did not look at her, studied the sky, a fine bluish spray of icecrystals rippled like a sandy riverbottom. He suddenly wanted his notebook.

Do you hear me? she asked with an edge of annoyance, and he finally looked at her. A mistake, because she was striking, her eyes lifted to watch him, and he could for an instant think of nothing else but running his hands over the lycra within which her body was packed. Drawing the zipper, peeling it away like a fruitrind to get at her flesh and juice.

I can't, he said with something like a cough.

Can't. Or won't, she asked almost gently.

Both, he thought, wanting desperately for something to stir in his loins, to feel even the hint of an erection, horrified that though his mind was stepping resolutely and with explicit clarity through the steps that would lead to a union of their bodies, the narrative was totally unaccompanied by the expected – and at one time imperative – biological response. And, almost as harrowingly, unsure that if he was able to perform, would he be making the correct choice.

He got up and ran. Ran as if trying to escape thought and knowledge and the torture of abandoning such a lush and nourishing temptation. In a moment was up the path and at the highway, squinting into the long distance hoping to see Albert returning, but though there were cars and campers and trucks, he saw no sign of the cycling Frenchman. Nathan thought he should get on his bike and leave, but he wouldn't abdicate on his pledge to protect Madeleine, and he would surely encounter Albert as he pedalled west.

He jogged back to the clearing where his bike sat, kneeled in front of his pack and rummaged around until he pulled out his notebook. The image of the sky as a rippled riverbottom in his mind. Flipping through to the next blank he lifted his eyes and what he saw now in the sculpted cirrus running down the sky was the flat and muscular belly of a woman. Stretched taut, the elongated navel bracketed by ridges of muscle. Tensed, on the verge. He remembered kneeling between Lisa's widespread legs, her face constricted with concentration as she flicked with fingernails at her own nipple while he worked his index and middle fingers rapidly against her G spot, at the same time stroking with the ball of his thumb her clitoris, roving his eyes over her, watching her face constricted in deep focus, taut and all of her attention directed to those densely nerved zones as she fought to conquer that final, elusive summit beyond which lay the kinetic ride into orgasm. Ecstasy a breath away and above the blond thatch her belly, pale, rigid, flat, her navel long and dark with shadow, and he bent forward and stabbed his tongue there, a move and sensation so unexpected it threw her over the edge, and he heard as he buried his face against the hot skin her startled yowl as the orgasm crashed through her.

He was hard as steel. Almost weeping with relief at the sensation, the swollenness of his cock bent uncomfortably within the tight jeanshorts. He yanked the pencil from the coil and wrote and wrote, pressing hard and leaving on the page a dark scrawl of explicit detail. Gripping the book he read it back to himself, consulting the sky once or twice, making corrections until it was perfect. Kneeling on the earth, the book in his lap, his penis still hugely hard. His mind wandering involuntarily to the zipper on Madeleine's lycra top. Oh god, to see a woman's belly tense like that again.

He stood, reached into his shorts and adjusted himself, trying to find a comfortable position, then trotted down the pathway to where Madeleine lay.

She was awake, watched him arrive, and he was certain he saw her eyes alight on his groin, where his erection was plainly visible.

When he was a pace away he stopped and kneeled on the ground behind her head and opened the notebook. She tilted her head back and looked at him, her eyes swivelling upward, so she was seeing him kneel upside-down above her. She wet her lips and watched, almost smiling, and then he imagined Albert returning, what this would look like, the staging of a ritual perhaps, the woman laid out, the man kneeling at her head with an erection and a notebook. Reading to her:

Coral sky, alight in an ocean shallow, unfurling anemone toe, probing into the atmosphere, reaching reaching to stroke the trembling vanes of a jellyfish, pulsing fluidfilled sacs, those clouds with their rudimentary nervous system, benevolently watching . . .

Paging randomly:

Transient swelling mountain range, highspeed tectonics in massive motion, burgeoning into the whiteblue gulf, fluid, wrenched transformation of landscape, a billion years in five minutes, time is a whisper and a shout, a shot and a kiss . . .

. . . sooty ceiling corroded oozing pipes a subway cavern the low throb of trains and drip-drip like of a slow sewage leaking condensed wet collecting in drops running together in clear rivers pooling at the pockmarked intersections . . .

. . . a UFO flotilla; armada of bloated white starships, silver-topped, blackbellied; coming slowly from beyond the horizon; massing; deploying . . .

. . . sun a pale, wet blister hanging in a bitter pipesmoke heaven . . .

Recognizing that Madeleine likely understood little of his writing, his esoteric words and trite images, he modulated his voice, as one does when reading to an infant, hoping to lull her with the music of the language:

. . . foul black stalactite oozing free from a coalblack dome, dropping, descending, filthy vortex rainpowered by cubic miles of cloud heaped above it, constant bloom of electric filaments crackling, spasmed veins of bluewhite light, constant rolling thunder boom, an appendage reaching down through atmosphere longing to touch the planet, a slick sable worm drilling down as if ardently reaching, stretching, extending towards Earth a sooty snout . . .

He read for four or five minutes and when he looked up she was asleep. He thought at first that this had been too easy, that he needed to reinforce his labours, and went on, after a time swept up by the outrageous scope of his own words, settled back on his knees and read:

blue liquor sky, black liquor sky, gold liquor sky, green liquor sky,

white liquor sky, pale liquor sky, hot liquor sky, blood liquor sky,

slave liquor sky, day liquor sky, quaint liquor sky, fuck liquor sky,

eye liquor sky, lick liquor sky, lump liquor sky, bump liquor sky,

sweet liquor sky, fern liquor sky, hunt liquor sky, taint liquor sky,

spurn liquor sky, blind liquor sky, blond liquor sky, scar liquor sky,

ink liquor sky, monk liquor sky, zinc liquor sky, drunk liquor sky.

. . . his erection long faded and when he looked up again the sun further down the heavens and Madeleine still sleeping with a mild expression on her face. He wasn't inclined to explain things to Albert – he thought it either too intimate or too ridiculous that he should have wooed the man's wife to sleep by reading aloud his own words – so he left that clearing and walked back up the highway to survey the distance and see if Albert's arrival was imminent. There was nothing but cars and trucks up there and Nathan returned to where his bike and pack lay, and he leaned against the tree and stowing his notebook in his bag returned his attention to the Ford novel.

He awoke to Albert kicking the sole of his shoe. It was an hour before dusk, sunshine the colour of brass cutting through the riverbank trees and illuminating the Frenchman standing above him, sweatdrenched and clutching in each hand a plump paper sack adorned with Chinese characters. He was grinning hugely, holding the bags aloft like the heads of vanquished foes. He whirled and took off down the path to the camp, calling Madeleine's name, announcing, Chérie! La nourriture chinoise! Nathan knew Albert had reached her when his voice suddenly hushed. In a moment he returned, tiptoeing, face constricted with caution. He squatted beside Nathan, set the bags on the dirt and whispered, She is asleep!

Is she.

Oh yes. I can't believe it. He clapped Nathan on the shoulder, emitted a suppressed chuckle. Oh Natan, this is good. Now the holiday begins. Maintenant!

He rose and produced from the trailer a compact stove, set alloy pans on the gasrings, reheated the food, stirfrying chow mein and peking duck. He brought out bottles of cold beer from his pannier, and he and Nathan clinked them together, toasting Madeleine's sleep, and drank, Nathan wanting to tell Albert how he'd read the man's wife to sleep but feeling, for what he'd done and even the temptation he'd evaded, vaguely guilt-ridden.

They were each on their second bottle by the time the food was ready and Nathan felt a knot of inebriation forming between his eyes. Albert by dint of his recent exertion more acutely affected, laughing giddily at Nathan's jokes. At dusk the mosquitoes attacked and Nathan helped Albert set up a complex geodesic tent and drag Madeleine inside. Her eyes opened once and the men froze in the flash of her gaze, and then her eyes closed and the men set her gently on her sleepingbag. They built a fire in the twilight, sat drinking third and forth and fifth bottles, Albert growing maudlin until he was squatting on his hams swaying dangerously above the flames enumerating Madeleine's exorbitant faults, her insomnia at the fore.

Almost the only thing that gives her sleep, he said, slurring, his eyes swivelling lazily in his skull as he watched the fire, What always work is when she jouit.

What's that mean?

You know. If she fuck and come. Then she sleep. This always works. Albert seemed momentarily flustered by this confession, and he said after a long moment of contemplation, Or if she is very tired, like today.

Nathan fixed his stare on the fire.

It is not always a nice thing for me. Madeleine, she is slow. In French we say frigide. It is much, much work. He took a long draft of beer, wiped his mouth, gazing into the fire. After a moment his eyes shifted. I see you wear a wedding ring, he said, stretching his bottle out and tapping the band with its neck.

She's dead, Nathan said almost viciously.

Morte?

Yes, Nathan replied. Morte. You should treat your wife better.

Treat her better? I treat very well. Like a princess. What do you know? Madeleine is not easy. She is beautiful but she is a difficult beauty.

Treat her better, Nathan said with a dismissive shake of his bottle.

Albert inhaled as if to argue the point but all at once gave up, grunted, stared into the fire. The chorus of cricket and frog filling Nathan's ears like a whine of machinery. He squashed a mosquito on his knee, its gut had been plump with his blood and left a stain crisscrossed by the dead bug's own snout and limbs. He spied motion to his left, thought at first Albert was taking a swig but he was falling, pitching forward towards the flames. Nathan shot out a hand, caught him by the shoulder, and as he listened to his own beerbottle glug into the dirt where he'd dropped it he eased the Frenchman back onto the dry earth.

Sleepy time, Nathan whispered in the way he had when it was Sydney's bedtime, now holding the Frenchman upright, and Albert's eyes wheeled sluggishly about trying to find a target, his mouth warped into a faint sneer. Nathan helped him to his feet and with an arm across his shoulder guided him stumbling to the tent. Nathan zipped it open and pushed the man inside. He may have collided with Madeleine, for she spoke an imprecation then was silent. Nathan waited outside listening to Albert's flails and the sough of the tent's fabric and then silence, broken a moment later by Albert's snores.

Nathan awoke in the night to the long doppler yawn of a transport truck's horn on the highway above the camp and he lay looking at the stars salted across a background sky very nearly black, wondering what had prompted the warning, the truck cut off by an erratic driver or an animal crossing the highway, and the latter possibility made him fret, as he always did when he slept outdoors, about bears and skunks and feral dogs. It was too dark to see anything of the camp but he knew that the French couple's tent sat a halfdozen metres off and he was glad that Albert's snores had ceased at last. The night was warm, and the consequence was at first mosquitoes of a ferocious tenacity, but now the insects were gone and the night was silent but for infrequent traffic on the road and the trill of frogs and the ruffle of wind through the cottonwoods. He lay with his hands behind his head contemplating the heavens. It was just stars and he felt no impulse to write about it. He was drifting off to sleep when another horn sounded, this one a car's, and it was accompanied by a chirp of tires on the macadam as if the vehicle had swerved around an obstacle, and as it raced on it honked three times, the third a long, fading clarion, an invective. Nathan sat up, looked towards the tent. Albert, he called in a whisper. Then he thought again, recognizing the danger of waking Madeleine. He struggled out of the sleepingbag and felt about in the dark for his shoes, put them on. It was colder when he stood up, for he was just wearing shorts and t-shirt and the ground was radiating heat from the day's sunshine. He moved cautiously towards the highway embankment, bent forward while sweeping his hands before him to keep from tripping over his bicycle which lay somewhere close by. He met the weeds at the clearing's edge and pawed through them until he found the footpath and it was possible to discern the berm against the starry sky. He walked along the path and was soon mounting the slope and standing on the gravel shoulder. The highway a pale river running to each horizon. The winking ruby on a radio mast thirty kilometres to the south. Nothing else. He squatted and touched the warm asphalt. Rolling kernels of gravel between his fingertips. The sky larger here without the trees, and as he rose he staggered with vertigo. He looked into the sky's deep bowl and perceived after a moment the traffic of satellites on their sundry vectors, and then a meteor ripped out of the east and flared for an instant before it broke and sputtered halfway towards the horizon, leaving a green afterglow on Nathan's retinas that followed his gaze and was renewed by each blink until at last it faded.

Hell, he said aloud, for it seemed the only response to that awesome, quaking vault. As a child he would have said, Wow. As a teen, Fuck. And one day, he thought, if he ever found himself in old age, at the door of death, he might say: God.

A grunt from the east – the bray of an animal, he thought at first – spurred his heartbeat until he saw an advancing white light. It was a long time coming and after some minutes it split into a pair of headlamps, and he felt mild anxiety as they bore down on him. Nathan shuffled to the centreline and watched those lamps race towards him, letting a suicidal thrill grip him before he continued across to the highway's south side and stood watching them come. He lowered himself into the weeds relishing that childish fear, the diesel engine assertive, the truck travelling very fast, beads of orange lights deployed along the cab's roof and the headlights dividing again into standards and highbeams with the illuminated road before the prow looking itself like a fixture of the truck, a ram. The jewels of smaller lights now visible and Nathan thought with a rise of panic about a movie long ago in which a character mistook a UFO for a transport truck. It seemed to come faster now, the roar of its engine loud and brawny, and it wasn't twenty metres away when something appeared in the plough of its headlights, bony and sprawled on the blacktop and a moment later seized by the truck's bumper and dragged in a fan of blue sparks which lit the undercarriage for two hundred metres down the highway. The truck slowed, jakebrakes stuttering and then tires sliding while its box slewed sideways and came about as if it intended to pass the tractor and go on without it. After a few seconds the truck stopped and sat idling on the highway, its taillights aglow like embers in the dark, and then Nathan saw like stars fallen from the sky glowing fragments of metal scattered in its wake. In a moment they were gone, cooled to black.

The truck's door opened and a thickset woman climbed onto

the runningboard and hung into the night air looking up and down the highway before she stepped down and rounded the fender to move into the spray of the headlamps. She glanced about and stepped behind the cab. A minute later she emerged on the truck's far side hauling a skeletal wreck in her arms which she hurled into the dark before she dusted her hands and rounded the truck's prow and stepped up and grabbed the truck's doorhandle. She paused and looked down the flank of the rig directly at him, but when he looked down at himself he could barely perceive his own faint form in the taillight glow, as if he were incorporeal. Then she swung the door open and climbed aboard, revved the engine and put it in gear, and the truck shuddered and moved off, stepping through the gears as it accelerated away into the dark and in minutes was gone.

Nathan expected at any moment Albert and Madeleine to appear at the roadside to investigate the commotion but they did not. He walked along the highway to where the truck had stopped and stood smelling dieselsmoke and hot rubber, studying the ground where he saw the glitter of starlight in a random spread. He bent and took up a hot washer from the roadway. He held it in his palm and smelled it and it smelled like nothing at all. He stepped to the road's shoulder and found laying in the gravel a bicycle wheel like an orange slice torn open at the rind, and he descended the slope slowly probing with outstretched hands like a blind man through the weeds until he found near the foot of the embankment the mangled bicycle frame. He ran his hands over its skin and they found the sheared ends mushroomed with bladed extrusions and very hot and he groped more until he found the handlebars or a part of one and wrapped his hand about the rubber grip and it seemed to mesh with his palm as if grip and hand had been machined for this union. His bicycle. He sat there awhile with it sprawled before him in the sagegrass and if he felt anything at all it was peace. Then he stood and picked up the frame thinking that he would bring it to Albert to see what could be done, to see if that wallet of Allenkeys and spokewrenches might offer a remedy. And when he recognized the absurdity of this idea he thought Albert might want to see it anyway, this velocipedal curiosity that had wandered off by its own volition and perished on the highway like an escaped housecat. He stood for some time holding it before he let it fall. Astonished to only now comprehend what had happened, to understand that Albert and Madeleine were gone. And still he mounted the slope to the highway and jogged east and across the bridge and scrambled down the footpath into the clearing and stomped about in a rage cursing and grunting and he still thought he might fall over the tent where the couple were sleeping but they were gone and yet unconvinced he hoped he'd find their bikes so he could similarly dispatch them as they had murdered his own but of course the bikes were also gone and he was alone. Then in panic he groped for his knapsack certain it would be missing but it was where he had left it at the foot of his sleepingbag. Unzipped it in panic until he felt the spine and cover of his notebook.

He stood panting in the darkness and was soon overcome by such fervent rage he saw light flare at the periphery of his vision like something was exploding behind him. He imagined lifting the couple, one in each hand, and dashing their heads together, their skulls splitting like pumpkins and spilling a red and grey mash. Strode to where the tent had been, kneeled there skimming with his palms the oval depression, and then he smashed his fists into the sand again and again, the earth resounding with each punch, clods of sand bursting around him until there was grit in his mouth and eyes and still he battered that earth as if by rage alone he could transcend time and deliver his punishment three hours into the past while their bodies still lay in that place. When this was done he sat in the dark, sweating and panting, his mind free of anger and even thought. Sat crosslegged like a Buddha, hands resting against the turned soil, the earthworm scent rising into his nostrils while time passed unmarked. He may have slept. When he was again conscious he felt cold and he thought about climbing into the sleepingbag to finish the night but that thought was preposterous beside his predicament. And his need for revenge. No, not revenge, for this was something Lisa would abhor. Justice.

He would not hurt them, he would request reparation. And if they refused then he would hurt them. His anger surging again, it brought him to his feet and without thought he was dusting the sleepingbag and rolling it and cramming it into the knapsack. He fretted over leaving something behind or finding something valuable left by the couple but it was too dark and the only thing of import, the bicycle, his dear green friend, was gone. If he set out now he might catch them. This was his thought, that perhaps they'd stop in the town Albert had visited last night which was only nine miles away and if he set out now he could apprehend them before they made their getaway.

He caught up the bag and swung it onto his back and glanced futilely about in the darkness before he climbed to the highway and set out at a jog westbound, made out on the shoulder the lone bicycle wheel and glancing in the dark down the slope where the carcass of the bike lay invisible.

He did not get far jogging, was dismayed at how quickly he was winded considering his fit body. Running couldn't approach cycling for efficiency – all that coasting energy lost with each step – and his distress grew when he looked back and saw the eastern sky grey and the trees of the campsite still visible in the distance.

Why? he shouted suddenly. Why why why? It didn't make any sense. What had he done to them? Was it because he'd told Albert to treat Madeleine better? Or because he'd read his wife to sleep? Did he think he'd slept with her? Thought it was the only explanation for her achievement of sleep? Or was it because he hadn't slept with her? Had this angered her enough to make her tell Albert that he had? Or angered Albert that Nathan should turn down the offer of his perfect wife?

Perhaps he'd offended the Frenchman in some way, said or did something of which he wasn't even aware. Saved him from pitching facefirst into the fire. Dragged him into the tent. Maybe there was some reason even less fathomable, it was because he was taller, or couldn't speak French, or was caught touching his balls.

He stopped walking, clutched his head in his hands, feeling such a torrent of rage he thought he had to grip it to keep it from detonating. A convoy of trucks was racing past and he wailed furiously into their wake, his entire frame atremble with anger. What a thing to do. And why, why?

And then he pivoted his body at another thought, had she been complicit in his bike's destruction? Did she know about, suggest it, aid in its agency? These were answers he needed, answers he would have.

He was running again when he heard the songs of awakening birds and knew that dawn was imminent. He slowed and turned and stepping backwards saw a blush of light pilling over the horizon which only drove him on and he turned and trotted at a halfjog along the highway. Whine of tires on blacktop and he stepped aside to let a car pass at high speed and then another came from the opposite direction, the birds twittering as they came and went along a wire fence and he could make out cattle in the field to the north while a row of grain silos grew distinct beyond them. The light increasing rapidly, pouring westward and laving against a bulwark of clouds building in the southwest.

A farmhouse with a ramshackle barn and quonset moved along on the southern field and there was a cattlegrate at the foot of the drive with those southwestern clouds duplicated in the water filling the ditch. Huffing as he jogged, slowing to a walk to catch his breath before running again. And here was the hamlet called Zurich, nothing to it, an informal collection of structures on each side of the highway, certainly no Chinese restaurant, so he knew Albert had gone further to get dinner, and Nathan would have to walk to the next town where he would surprise them.

He stopped suddenly at a pang of enormous loss which though it chiefly encompassed Lisa and Sydney now included the bicycle which had carried him since late winter all through Manitoba and Saskatchewan and Montana, and aside from a few flat tires and the frequent collapse of the chain onto the pedal hub had never failed him. He felt doubt at leaving it behind, roadside trash to be collected by some itinerant crew of felons and hauled off for scrap or maybe left to rust, the steel frame and chain anyway, he couldn't imagine how long the aluminum wheelrims and chrome accessories might last, centuries perhaps, to be buried beneath loamy soil, relic of our age. He thought back to the Supra in its graveyard and saw his descent from car to bike to foot as something alarming, and he couldn't help wondering if he might shortly regress to crawling or even scooting about on his belly like a worm. The one thing he knew was that he had to keep moving, keep moving.

He saw beyond the yellow hills the cone of a watertower and soon after spotted the tops of grain elevators, and it was still forty minutes of plodding along while trees and houses came into view before he passed a green sign which read Entering Chinook. He marched on until he stood with his back to the elevators, his legs humming at the workout which seemed to tax muscles immediately adjacent to those used for pedalling. Looking across the highway at a bakery-café and an insurance broker and a Chinese restaurant and a squat, windowless casino, waited while a pair of motorhomes from Iowa each towing a car sped past before he crossed and followed one of the streets into the town. He wandered its gravel roads glancing left and right seeking the French couple or their bicycles. He spotted a flash of yellow up a side-street, but it disappeared before the figure or figures could resolve and Nathan sprinted in pursuit and as he came around a hedge he startled an old woman in a yellow windbreaker walking a white terrier.

Mercy, she said, her hand on her breast.

Sorry, Nathan said. I thought you were someone else.

Well, she replied. I haven't been chased like that in years.

Nathan was backing away, preparing to turn, and she called, Who are you looking for?

Oh. A French couple on bikes. Wearing black and yellow.

Friends of yours?

Y-yes. I was supposed to meet them here. But my bike got. Damaged.

I haven't seen them. If they stayed the night it might've been at the Big Sky B&B. You cross Missouri Street and go two blocks south to 5th. It's right on the corner.

He was already running and when she called, I hope you find them! he raised a hand and turned the corner.

He ran into the rising sun and found the sidestreet, ran fulltilt until he was standing before a bungalow. The Big Sky B&B sign sat in a bed of impatiens beside a plastic deer, and he stepped to the side of the building seeking the bikes. There was a closed garage at the end of the drive where they might be stored. He went to the front door and pushed the doorbell. No one came and he waited a few moments before he pushed it again and he was just turning away when a middleaged woman in a pink housedress opened the door and said through the screendoor, Yes?

Is Albert here? And Madeleine?

Her look was perplexed and he knew she'd not heard those names of late so he said, French. Any French people here?

I think you have the wrong house, friend, she said. Do you need a place to stay?

What motels are there around here? he asked.

Well other than me there's just the Night Light Motel. On the west side of town. But it's closed coming on two years.

CHAPTER 9

They were miles, hard, mean American miles, hot and unc-
tuous, archaic, arduous, not at all like the lean efficiency of
European kilometres in their polished thousand-metre incre-
ments, these were miles, every one of them 5,280 feet. Strewn
with liquorbottles and beercans and waterbottles and newspapers
and broken glass and used condoms and audiocassettes and plastic
bags and husks of blownout tires and mufflers and roadkill like
racks of jerky with the meat suncured on the bone. There was a
bathtub which appeared to have been hurled from an immense
altitude against the rockcut where it lay, squashed like a paper cup.
A shoebox spilling pornographic videos, the cardboard sleeves
with lurid images split and torn and the ink sunbleached to leave
pale apparitions of ghosts sucking and fucking, a halfmile of roadside festooned with ferromagnetic tape, snagged on a wire fence
and rippling in the wind.

Nathan trudged on, sunburned and sweating, and in the limbo
between towns swore he would in the next place buy a bike or a
car, but when he arrived he forgot this promise or if he remembered it there was nowhere to buy such things so he crisscrossed
streets panning the scenery hunting the French couple or some
sign of them or someone to ask.

By a railway siding in Havre where he'd stopped to eat a sandwich in the cheatgrass with the railcars groaning past he was set
upon by three youths in filthy clothes and high laceup boots. One
of them had a swastika tattooed on the back of his hand, and one
had a paring knife and the third a pair of vicegrips. They wanted
his sandwich and his pack. They were mangy and hungry and
angry and they loathed not just him but one another, and Nathan
set them against each other by choosing the weakest of the bunch,

a frecklefaced redhead with split lip, explaining that he wanted to be beaten by him and no other, for he was clearly their leader and superior to the others in every way. The whole time his heart thrashing in his chest, thinking how stupid it would be to die here at the hands of these rotten youths and not to have found Albert and Madeleine.

He almost laughed aloud when Swastika punched Red in the ear. The kid went down screaming, and then the other kid with greasy skin and head like an earthenware jug brought the vicegrips down on Swastika's forearm. In a moment they were all fists and flying boots, and Nathan lifted his pack and ran, but he only got ten paces before he turned to watch, listening to the percussion of their blows and the grunts and panting, and then he shucked off the pack and stepped into the fray, set about beating them methodically, starting with Swastika and working his way through Jughead and finishing on Red until they were all laid out on the ballast panting and bleeding and cussing while railcars shunted and clattered on the next siding, the booms of compressing hitches ripping down the length of the train and the ground quaking. Nathan himself was cut across one ear, and he'd taken a blow to a testicle which ached in its interminable way, but other than that he felt lusty and keen. He went to the pack and brought out a loaf of white bread and a jar of peanut butter and set to making sandwiches for the boys, and he gave them cans of warm cola and they sat in the grass eating zealously. They were from Oregon and they'd come riding boxcars and lumberflats and had been trying for days without luck to catch a westbound freight.

Nathan told them about his wife and child and his infidelity and their deaths, and travelling and the accidents with the two moose and hospitalization and morphine addiction and riding across the border and the destruction of his bicycle, and by the end of the story the three were in awe and Red said how cool it would be to father a kid and have the kid die, and Nathan slammed his sodacan into the side of the boy's skull, sending an arc of cola across his crown and into the weeds.

Don't be an idiot, Nathan said as he collected his bag and stood.

Jughead picked up the loaf of bread and handed it to Nathan and Nathan said, Keep it. And go home.

Then he walked away, following the rails until he met a level crossing where he jogged down to the highway and set off westward past casinos and steakhouses and out across the prairie.

He spent the night in a motel on the east end of Kremlin run by a fastidious Korean couple, the room painted cobalt blue, plastic peonies on the table. He shaved and took a shower and washed and still wrapped in the towel lifted the paper hood from a drinking glass he found by the sink and he filled the glass from a quart bottle of bourbon he'd bought that afternoon. Then he sat on the bed which had an extraordinary mattress or maybe it only felt that way after all his nights on the hard ground. He watched a western on the widescreen LCD and then he watched a rerun of *Seinfeld*, his lone laughter stark and hysterical in the room.

He drank the glass dry and it was like the old days with the Supra for he was clean and had a bed to sleep in and booze to drink. He slept and dreamed he was driving a car that both was and wasn't the Supra, for it was new and shining and ran flawlessly. Lozenges of streetlight whisking across the dashboard and seats.

He awoke late in the morning, lay a long time in the havoc of the sheets, staring at the ceiling. Recognizing his absolute disjunction. Wife and child dead, father dead and mother abandoned, brother and family alienated, and he had probably become a sociopath, smashing potential bonds, the pretty minister, the generous pimp, the kindly doctor and her rustic husband, barroom pals, the French couple who had rescued him from thirst.

He rose and picked up the phone, dialled rapidly and without thought the number with all the fives and sevens he'd seen so frequently on the face of his old cellphone.

Yes?

Hello Mabel.

Nathan. Nathan, is that you? It's been a long time. God Nathan, what's happened?

Nothing.

Something's happened. You sound different.

Nothing's happened.

He recalled her at the front door of the Annex house, that abominably empty house, a week after he'd stopped answering his phone. She'd driven from Hastings, panting on the doormat as if she'd raced there on foot to deliver a bulletin. Tiny under the porchlamp, eyes enormous, and he'd invited her inside, immediately convinced that she had a message from Lisa, some insight or confession made in the moments before her death. He led Mabel to the sofa, put a cup of hot tea in her hands, and sat across from her, perched on a chair, waiting. She sat birdlike on the cushion, darting her eyes about at his things. Their things, his and Lisa's. And Sydney's. Her eyes landing on a toy rockingchair on the floor beside the fireplace, and in it a goldenhaired doll in a floralprint dress. She'd looked then into his eyes, and he realized she'd come to rescue him. From his grief, from his loneliness. From this.

Now, far away, she said into the phone, Then something's going to happen.

Yes.

You can't stop it, can you.

I don't think I can.

Hesitation, which for her was unusual. Then she took a breath and said, I'm certain it will be all right.

I don't think so, Mabel.

It will, Nathan. Have faith in yourself.

Why?

Someone has to.

What about you?

I have faith, but I'm too far away to make a difference.

I didn't call you to hear that.

It's the truth.

Why didn't you do anything, Mabel? When you found them.

Now he expected a pause as she considered this question but she responded directly, There was nothing to be done. Your little girl was already gone.

I didn't know that.

And your wife was barely conscious. From all the glass. She tried to speak but her throat −

I know.

And she had lost so much blood −

I know! he shouted.

Then why do you ask me? Nathan. Nathan, are you there?

Do you know the spot where it happened?

Of course. It's practically at the end of my driveway.

How long before you called for help.

I called when it happened. I saw it from my kitchen window. Saw the plough's blade roll the car. I was on the phone in the next second.

Would you have done anything differently?

I wouldn't, Nathan. Would you?

His hand tightened around the handset. He said: I have to go.

Nathan, please. Don't go.

I have to.

Will you call me again? Nathan. Will you call me again?

Why? Why should I?

Because you'll need to.

He said nothing, lifted his eyes to the gap in the curtains, saw cars and trucks whisking past and above them a fragment of low, fastmoving cloud the colour of graphite.

Nathan, I'm just a voice. I can give you truth, but it's up to you to use it. Call me afterwards. You'll need to call someone.

I won't.

That's your decision. Just know that I will accept whatever you do.

What if it's a terrible thing?

Even so, you will do it for the right reason.

Why?

Because that's who you are.

In the gap between the drapes something yellow and black flitted by, launching him to his feet. He barked, Goodbye Mabel, and hung up. He pulled open the door and looked. The view west occluded by the motel office. He would stride to the highway's edge were he not naked. Instead he kicked through his clothes strewn before the bathroom door and pulled them on, gathered in one armful his toiletries and dumped them in the pack and jammed his feet into his shoes and with them unlaced and the back of one crushed under his heel strode to the roadside and looked west. Nothing, nothing but the headlights of oncoming vehicles accelerating as they came out of town and the taillights and brakelights of others heading west, but the distance was hazy and a few spits of rain came out of the sky like stinging things sent to dissuade him. He fixed and tied the shoes and jogged past the office and threw his key into the mailslot and ran. The rain increasing, gusting into his face as he jogged through the town where a few people regarded him from doorways and beneath awnings. As the rain began to lash him he walked with his head down to keep the water from his eyes, watching raindrops hammer divots into the dust but the dust still reluctant to yield sent them skittering about like marbles. By the time he'd got his slicker out of the bag he was drenched and most of his things too, but he pressed on knowing that if it was the French cyclists he'd seen they'd have to stop in this downpour and that would be his opportunity to spring upon them. When he'd been at it fifteen minutes a pickup drew onto the shoulder ahead of him and he looked at it warily as it idled there, its tailpipe smoking, and as he was passing by the passenger window came down and the driver, a young man in a stetson called across the seat, You want a ride mister?

Nathan leaned his head into the window and replied, Thanks, but I'm all right.

You sure? It's no trouble at all. I can take you as far as Chester. Now don't you worry about getting these seats wet, this is a old truck and got plenty worse than rain in the fabric.

Nathan gazed out at the fog and rain listening to the truck's wipers sweep across the windscreen, convinced that the French couple would seek shelter from the weather, and that in the front seat of a speeding vehicle he'd certainly miss them. He was in fact expecting to presently fall upon them huddled in some grotto perfectly surprised by his arrival. What happened next he could not foretell, and he thought it best to leave this to spontaneity. He leaned back into the window and said, You're very kind, but I need to walk.

Suit yourself, the man replied, and he pinched the brim of his hat and Nathan stepped back as the window rolled shut and the truck drew back onto the asphalt and sped away. Nathan ran to make up for lost time, still glancing and spinning to check for what hiding spot he might have missed. He walked for an hour and then another as the rain continued, and still he went on with cars and trucks and motorhomes passing in clouds of steam. When he looked at his hands the fingerpads were corrugated with wet. He was shivering, his nose running. Around noon he passed a diner, a neon Budweiser sign in the window and yellow lights within, all of it reflected in puddles riddled by raindrops. He was thinking about hot coffee, a corned beef sandwich, onionrings, coleslaw. He stood there a long time before he set out again. He would catch them. He was going to catch them.

His shoes and calves were muddy and the pack having absorbed much water grew ponderous, bending him forward so that he plodded along like a chimp, yet if he straightened up the weight threatened to snatch him backwards, and he imagined himself on his back like a tortoise, treading against the air until rain inundated his mouth and nose and he drowned on a Montana plain. Longing for the punishing heat of previous days.

Then he was on his knees in the mud. Listening to the patter of raindrops on the slicker he thought perhaps he'd blacked out because he had no recollection of falling. He lifted his head, peered through the procession of waterdrops creeping along the slicker's hoodbrim and watched the vertical blitz of rain beating down from the sky. Each raindrop seemed in its trajectory to leave a persistent trace, a javelin stuck in the ground, and all of them together erected before him an impassable barrier. A warning perhaps, a divine telegraph recommending that he go no further. He cranked his head about, the coat's rubber creaking, and looked the way he'd come, saw far to the northeast that a hole had dilated in the cinereous cloud to admit an immense pillar of sunlight illuminating pastureland and field cultivated in oat and barley, the wet roofs of cattlebarns gleaming in the sunshine. Obviating the previous message, certainly a sign that things would shortly improve. He would wait here on the highway's brink until it arrived to warm and revive him. He turned back to face the crash of rain and closed his eyes, listening to it chatter against the slicker. Car and truck flailing past. He waited ten minutes and turned, expecting imminent sunshine, but it was gone, the cloud fused without suture, leaving storm and rain as if there never was nor would ever be anything but.

He stood, tottered a moment on his legs which hummed and prickled from being crushed beneath him, and lurched forth into the storm.

It was long past dark when the rain ended. The sky remained cloudy but after a time Nathan could see openings scattered across the wide vault through which stars scrolled past. The road descended into a country of naked hillocks under the waxing starlight, and all about the mineral stench of wet earth. No barnyard lamp or porchlight or any sign of human occupation. He tore off the slicker and balled it and tossed it into the ditch. After a few minutes his wet clothes and flesh chilled in the cold air and he realized his error, but he would not turn back. Enormously thirsty – he hadn't had a drink since . . . since last night's bourbon. Certain that he'd absorbed through the skin more than his daily requirement in rainwater, but his throat was painfully dry. Like he'd ingested a caustic powder which had begun to burn through the ribbed flue of his throat. He tried to swallow but there was nothing to swallow and he gagged and coughed. He saw stars reflected in muddy puddles but thought it hazardous to kneel and drink, for he might never rise again. He staggered on, not knowing if the next town was five miles or fifty. No traffic now, and he wondered if in his delirium he'd strayed from U.S. Highway 2 onto a branch road. Drifting towards a deeper wilderness. Thought that if so then he'd surely miss Albert and Madeleine. Pausing in his steps at the thought of them, braced for that fury, but finding it decomposed by his thirst. He walked on.

A nebula of light showed above the hills ahead, revealing that the landscape lay beneath a layer of diffuse fog. And then he focused on the light, the pale crown of it beyond the hills. Light meant water. A house, a whole town beyond that crest. Springwater, lemonade, fruitpunch, sodapop, icecold beer. Propelled now by willpower alone. Throwing a leg forward and planting it on the ground, pivoting over the ball and socket of his hip as he cast the other leg ahead, repeat, repeat, the process reduced to its raw mechanics, like he was some ramshackle robot completing its final mission.

Treading the centreline now he could see as he rounded a hillock that the light shined across the road's surface, illuminating the hills opposite, hills banded in strata of pale and dark. He seemed to be entering a kind of arena filled with hazy light. Next he saw the flat of a gravel lot with a rusted pickup truck parked at the corner of a building and then he walked a storefront into view, its windows aglow with fluorescent light and a sign perched on an iron pole which said Night Owl Supplies, a winking owl, and beneath it glowing red, Open 24 Hours. Nathan stopped and licked his lips. An apparition perhaps, but he would not let that keep him from getting a drink. He took a step to cross the lane and was thrown back by the blare of horn from a car that tore through the curve. His heart smashing beat upon beat in his breast and he was certain he could not remain upright a moment longer but he did. Once past him the car slowed and he feared a confrontation he was too spent to handle, but then the brakelights cooled and the car charged away into the night. He moved to the shoulder and stumbled along, hyperventilating, until he stood at the gravel infill that crossed the ditch. He stepped through the parkinglot and pulled open the door and entered. A severe chill inside, airconditioned, the light so intense that Nathan stood dazzled by the lustrous excess it illustrated. A shallow room, but the aisles crammed with merchandise, with the rear wall lined with glass fridges gorged with bottles and flasks and jugs. Cashdesk immediately to his right with trays of lottery tickets and two registers backed by a pageant of cigarette packs. Vacant. He stood before it for many moments as if awaiting permission to enter. Then he made his way down the left aisle towards the fridges and all those sweet bottles of juice and pop and water. When he got there he hesitated. It seemed ludicrous but he could not decide. He thought perhaps something carbonated, with sugar. Then he thought plain water. Then fruitdrink. Or something milk-based. When he swallowed, his throatvalves rasped together like sandpaper. He reached for a doorhandle as light swept over him and he saw headlights reflected in the fridge's glass. He thought it might be the car that almost struck him, it had turned around and brought its occupants back to quell their outrage. He let go the handle and stepped behind a tall shelf of cans and croutons and boxed pasta and jugs of cooking oil, found a spot where he could peer through an aperture between shelfposts. A woman entered and just as he had she hesitated before the empty cashdesk. Then she made a slow rotation, scanning the store.

Nathan's mind reeled as he looked at her, and he stopped breathing. She was immensely, staggeringly beautiful. The floor seemed to pitch and rock like a ship's deck in a typhoon, though his head like the compass mounted on its gimbal remained upright and inextricably oriented towards her. She was still now, and with her head askant she called towards the back of the store, Hello? Nathan tried to reply but could not, and each second he didn't made his presence and the steps by which he must reveal himself increasingly awkward. In a moment she would be gone. He thought to cough or sneeze or sigh, but then she turned and planted a foot on the shelves of candy and trinkets on the face of the cashdesk to lift herself onto it. She kneeled on the acrylic shield beneath which lottery tickets lay row upon row and she reached into the button cluster of the cashregister and punched a key. The machine rattled and pinged and the drawer rolled open. She scooped bills from the tray and was turning and cramming them into the sidepocket of her jeanjacket when the steel door in the back opened with a squawk and a young man in bluejeans and a black t-shirt stepped through. He saw the woman and as the door sighed shut he paused as if he knew her but then Nathan thought he must be contemplating her preternatural beauty, and he said, Can I help you? in a voice of remarkable calm.

She smiled and looked sideways in a gesture that was no less beguiling for the fact that it appeared rehearsed, and Nathan thought he might just give to this woman anything she asked. His money, his clothes, his eyes. She reached both hands behind her back and seized the hem of her jacket, drew it down, straightening it, and when her right hand rose it was gripping a handgun the colour of a blue wasp. Nathan stepped back from his spyhole as if she might see him through it, then put his eye back, watching to see if she would shoot, or make a demand, or just walk out, his heart slamming in his chest as if to remind him his own life was in peril as it never had been before. She stood with her arm extended and the barrel trained on the man's chest and nothing moved. They were three people in a room, and as long as time didn't advance he was safe. But time is never so obliging, and she said with an amused smile, Anything in the other one?

The other what? the man replied, he was really just a boy, crewcut, a trim goatee, schools of polychromatic tattoos flaring up both his muscled arms, and she was older, early thirties, ten years his senior, and they both played their scene with such confidence, as if it was something they'd rehearsed again and again.

The other till, she replied without impatience.

Nathan tried to see the car outside to determine if there was an accomplice, but the light within the store was too strong and projected the interior against the tall windows like an antistore in which an identical drama played itself out. He saw himself standing bent in his hiding spot and felt panic when he realized that if either the woman or the man looked at the reflection they would see him.

No, the man replied. It's empty.

Show me, she said, flicking the gun.

He moved fearlessly past the barrel and rounded the desk and she stepped up again onto the counter to ensure that the boy didn't press an alarm or pull a weapon from beneath the counter.

The boy fumbled with the cashregister. It was the first time he seemed flummoxed as he punched keys and the machine uttered a loud and extended tone which he tried through more prodding to silence. She was calling him klutz and dumbshit when Nathan heard a familiar squawk and someone – another boy of the same age, cleanshaven, with his baseball cap's brim cranked around to the rear, stepped through the door saying, Aidan, how many times do I have to teach you –

He was silenced as the woman turned and put the gun on him, and he said, Shit, oh motherfucking shit, just as the other boy brought up from behind the counter a shortbarrelled assault rifle and in one swift and practised swing clubbed the stock into the back of the woman's head with such force Nathan felt the concussion rend the air. Her eyes rolled up in her head and she dropped the handgun and it clattered to the floor and she slid from the counter ripping away one of the plexiglas partitions spilling lollipops as she dropped to the floor, where her skull cracked against tile.

Holy shit, holy shit, the second boy said as he strode towards her. Fucken bitch, he said, and then again, shouting, Fucken bitch! He kicked her gun and it went spinning across the floor. How's that, bitch? he screamed, and he was bringing his boot back again to kick the woman's face when the other boy barked, Craig!

Craig stopped his foot and seemed to straighten without thought, and Aidan came around the counter holding the assault rifle with ease across his abdomen. He went to the door and peered outside then lifted the gun and pushed through the door swinging it from side to side peering over the barrel. Craig meanwhile had squatted beside the woman and was looking her over and as Nathan watched it seemed such a very long time since he'd taken a breath and still he dared not. The other boy was outside scouting the parkinglot and Nathan thought he'd see inside so he bent to hide behind the shelf and felt for all the adrenaline pouring through his system unbearably weak and he sank to his knees on the floor and looked at the array of oil jugs on the shelf before him and tried to swallow but there was nothing in his scorched throat to swallow. He heard the front door open and Aidan say, All clear. What the fuck you doing?

Checking if she's got other weapons, Craig replied.

You think her fucken tits might be loaded, the other boy replied with disgust. You never change.

Hey, my first white one, Craig replied. Fuck you should feel these.

Nathan put his hand against his mouth and hugged himself and bit into his palm to suppress a shout. He was looking at those bottles of canola, the golden oil and on the labels fields of yellow flowers under a cerulean sky, and he was trying not to listen to the boys' barbarous debate on the features and uses of the woman's body. His thirst forgotten. He had to get out. Doors in front and back, both in open view. Studying those impotent groceries on the shelf before him seeking some property to give him an advantage or opportunity. Dehydrated potatoes, Kraft Dinner, tins of lima beans and tomato sauce, his eyes returning to the canola oil. Then quietly, quietly, he drew a jug from the shelf and unscrewed the cap and peeled the seal and tipping the jug so air could enter the spout without glugging he poured its contents onto the floor beside him so it ran in a yellow pool flowing with the floor's mild slope towards the foot of the refrigerators. He eased the empty bottle back onto the shelf and opened another and emptied it too until a puddle as broad as a stride filled the aisle adjacent the fridges.

He heard footsteps and the lights went out but for a single faulty tube above the steel door in the back, the plasma within it writhing, casting a jittery, inconstant light.

What're you doing? Craig asked.

Closing up. Don't want a customer come in and see that. You take her in back and get started. I'll go out front and kill the sign.

Wait, Aidan, wait, Craig replied. Let me get mine.

What for?

In case she's got friends. Someone might show up we better be ready.

More like you're scared she'll wake up and kick your ass.

Shut up.

Kick your sorry little ass even with the straps.

Shut the fuck up!

I'll wait. Go get it. Go!

Nathan heard the door to the back open and a few seconds later Craig returned. He said, Hey babe, why don't you suck on this. Then the ratchet of what sounded like a pumpaction shotgun. Aidan said, Craig. Be careful this time. I want a piece too and I'm no necro.

Is that an order? Craig replied.

At's an order.

Nathan had during this talk been easing his arms out of his backpack's straps, and though he worked with infinite care the pack was heavy with wet so that when he settled it on the floor it heaved a damp, forlorn sigh.

He heard instant, frantic motion. They were moving his way. He lifted himself onto one knee, fingertips on the tile like a sprinter in the blocks and he let them see him at the end of the aisle before he launched himself over the oily pool and into the corner at the end of the last aisle, trying to lure them into it so they'd slip and fall and he could run. It wasn't much but it was all he had.

Freeze, motherfucker, Craig said, and Nathan looked up to see the boy at the head of this last aisle, shotgun raised, bores like a pair of narrowset eyes looking him over. On the floor! Hands where I can see them! he shouted, and Nathan complied, kneeling, arms raised. The boy crabbed down the aisle with the shotgun fixed on Nathan's head while Aidan stood back covering with his rifle.

Got him? Aidan asked as Craig put the shotgun's muzzles to Nathan's throat. Let me secure the perimeter.

It was almost two minutes of the creak of Aidan's shoes as he methodically navigated each aisle and then checked the back, and at last he arrived with the assault rifle pressed to his hip. He fished in his pocket and came up with a strip of white plastic, handed it to Craig who put it in his teeth, seized Nathan's t-shirt, and yanked him to his feet. Craig drew Nathan's hands behind his back, and Nathan felt the strap close around his wrists, heard a zip and felt the plastic tie cinch painfully about his wristbones. Craig gave him a rapid frisk and pushed him to his knees, moved back. Aidan stepped in front of Nathan, asked, You with her? Nathan stared at the floor, panting, and Aidan shouted, Hey fucker, I asked a question. Are you with her?

Nathan shook his head.

Is there anyone else here?

Nathan smelled the hot stink of whiskey on the boy's breath, shook his head again.

You lying sack of shit, Craig cried, jabbing the barrels into Nathan's breast. There's only one car out there. What, did you just walk here? Nathan was nodding but Craig had turned to Aidan, barked, I say we waste this fucker right here.

Aidan laid his hand on the shotgun and said, Craig. This ain't Al-Fallujah. It's your dad's store. You think your dad appreciate you painting the corner with this guy?

Craig chewed his bottom lip, muttered, Naw. Naw, guess not.

We're in a civilized country now.

Sure.

There are rules.

Yeah. Yeah I know.

So take this, Aidan said, and pulled from his belt a handgun and turned the grip to Craig. Take this and bring him out back and do him there. Way out back in the soft duff where we can dig a hole.

Right. Okay, man. Sir. Okay, Craig replied, accepting the gun. Thought you were going soft on me.

Semper fidelis, my friend. Aidan turned, said, Aw fuck, and they all heard the crunch of tires on gravel as a pickup swung into the parkinglot. Nathan thought to make a break but Craig held the pistol on him. I'll go wave them off, turn out the sign, Aidan said, striding down the aisle. He flipped the rifle onto the checkout desk and pushed through the front door, waving, yelling, Closed, we're closed!

Craig squatted beside Nathan to keep out of sight, and they could hear Aidan talking to the driver, couldn't make out the words.

Then tires on gravel and the headlights swinging away, a toot on the horn as the truck pulled onto the highway and accelerated.

Let's go, Craig said, grabbing Nathan's shirt and yanking him to his feet, pressing the pistol into Nathan's spine between his bound wrists. Nathan stepped across the front of the fridges and lowered his foot in front of the puddle of canola oil and took a broad step to clear it. As he reached the other side and Craig dropped his boot into the stuff Nathan stumbled, bringing the boy up short with surprise before he slipped sideways, smashed his head into a fridge handle, and he went down into the oil with a grunt.

Nathan ran past the fridges and the steel door and turned down the first aisle he found, head ducked below the shelf height, saw the woman, lying at the end of the aisle, hands clasped primly on her belly, feet together, unconscious or maybe dead. He heard Craig scuffing about in the oil. Nathan kneeled on the floor beside her, swung his wrists into the back of his knees, and sat back on the tile while lifting his thighs to his chest. Forcing himself to take his time he drew one leg and then the other through his bound wrists. Saw in the dim light that he was bleeding around the plastic bands. Heard Craig gaining his feet, heard him panting and cursing. Nathan rose and stepped over the woman and was reaching for the rifle on the counter when something clove the air in front of him and in the low light he saw a pack of cigarettes behind the cash buckle and explode in a dash of shredded paperboard and tobacco. He was hearing even as he saw this the tremendous concussion of the gunshot and through unconscious impulse he dropped to the left and scrambled away, head down, and stumbled and crashed to the tile. The air blown from his lungs as he tried to get up, ears ringing and all a blind panic in the trembling light. He got to his knees and crawled, and was appalled to find in his thoughts that prediction he'd made after he'd lost his bicycle, how on this odyssey he'd descended from driving to cycling and then walking, had here at the threshold of death finally come to crawling, to the place where he would meet his end. He could hear Craig coming up the aisle and he smelled the gunpowder and it brought him back to an intensely happy memory, fireworks on a hot Canada Day evening, they were at the water-front, he was with Lisa and Sydney, Lisa's hand around the girl's, which gripped the wire stem of a sparkler as they whirled and flicked it, the corona of sparks and the hot core within creasing Nathan's retinas with streaks and coils.

There came a crash he mistook for the gun but it was Craig going down into the shelves, the soles of his boots yet oiled, and for this last insult Nathan felt glad, forced himself to feel glad, for he wanted his last emotions to be anything but dread and fear on the offchance there was an afterlife and into it you carried your final emotion for all eternity.

He crawled, a tripod of knees and lashed hands, rounded a shelf and found lodged against the base of it a semiautomatic handgun. Realized it was the woman's, kicked here by Craig, concealed from Aidan's sweep by the overhang of the shelf. Nathan took it into a hand and thumbed the safety hoping there was a round chambered because with hands restrained he could not pull back the slide, and he scurried down the aisle, the heavy weapon booming on the tile each time it struck, and when he rounded the end where cases of Miller High Life were stacked he saw Craig standing at the intersection of the next aisle lifting the shotgun to his shoulder. Nathan climbed to one knee waiting for the flash of the muzzles, waiting for the onrush of hot lead to blast through his body and carry his life away with it. The boy stood there swearing so Nathan thought that being cursed was the worst he might endure, until he saw the boy swab his hand against his jeans, return it to the trigger where it must've been still too oily to pull so he wiped again, and all at once it occurred to Nathan that his death was not inevitable. He lifted the pistol and fired.

His hands shuddered with the blast, and some kind of activity which he could not immediately discern occurred in the space between them, as if some sleight of hand had been performed too quick for comprehension, leaving him to regard only the aftermath: the boy on his back on the floor, a wet wheezing like that of a bathtoy, a rubberduck squeezed underwater, the air expelled and water sucked back in.

There was no time to contemplate any of this, for the front door was opening and he saw Aidan's shape stepping through and Nathan ran forward, skipping over the dying boy and the dark penumbra spreading beneath him, and he was somehow through the steel door and into the back of the store, momentarily dazed by unshaded lightbulbs hanging from the rafters casting stark shadows on the stock, crates and cartons of Kellogg's and Heinz and Coors. He seized the stack and shoved it against the door, was casting about for more when he saw syringes and spoons and a length of rubber hose scattered on a countertop. A thump on the door and then three rapid blasts, and a trio of holes at the level of head, chest, and groin opened in the grey metal, accompanied by that same perception of objects obscene and supernatural splitting the air, shockwaves from the rifle rounds. They struck a second door in the back, shattering a window and leaving two divots in the wood below it in a line perfectly vertical. Nathan forced himself to step into their wake, throwing his hands through the window and bringing the plastic tie down on a shard of embedded glass. Heard the door behind him slam against the stacked crates as he sawed his wrists back and forth until the tie separated and his hands flew apart. And then he was outside in the dark and startlingly capacious outdoors. He broke left running crouched as he'd seen soldiers do in warzone footage and was soon mounting a hill the soft earth flying from his soles and just as he reached its summit and dropped down the lee side he heard the rifle crack three times behind him. He ran left towards the road but realized he'd have no cover there and cut right and thought no, his pursuer would expect that, and in his indecision did worst of all and ran straight out from where he'd descended the hill. The moonless night almost completely dark. He waited for the rifle's report but it didn't come and he thought and hoped Aidan had given up to tend to his fallen comrade, for this would be better for everybody. He crouched panting behind a clot of weed, eyeing the hill he had just crossed. Looked at the pistol in his hand and thought of its owner.

The woman. Not better for her if Aidan broke pursuit. What would he do to her if he went back? Though she might already be dead. He hoped she was dead, which seemed the wrong thing to hope, but he hoped it anyway. Better for all if she were dead.

And then he saw her in his mind as she had walked in, before she'd committed no crime, but only stood with the intention in her heart and that gun in her belt but still innocent. If only he had spoken to her. Broken the sequence about to unfold.

He stood and shouted with his ragged throat, Hey, Aidan! Come and get me, fucker! He waited trying to listen above his own panting but heard nothing, cupped his hands and screamed, Craig was easy and you're fucking next!

Nothing, and then a shape skylighted above the hill and three shots as before in quick succession and he saw the muzzle flash and heard the bullets whiz past in the night air and he ran, straight out again across the rough ground praying that he wouldn't encounter pit or bog or wire fence. He splashed through a shallow puddle, and sooner than he'd expected it heard Aidan's own noisy transit through that water. He wanted to run faster but there was nothing left in him. A long bench of land ahead which he thought if he climbed would reveal his location against the stars but there was no choice if he hoped to lure the boy away. He ran and scrambled up the slope and found it topped with rails and gravel with the scent of creosote, crossed railroad tracks one set then another and three shots again and he saw from the corner of his eyes the spark of a bullet clipping the rail's crest, and then he was over and sliding flailing down the far side falling forward and slamming his face into the wet earth. He lay for a moment spitting dirt pawing it from around his mouth certain he had a few seconds, Aidan couldn't have caught up now, but beside him and not two paces away came a hard thump and there was Aidan rolling and expertly righting himself and sprinting off on the trajectory Nathan had been following. Nathan lifted the gun and aimed at the boy's back but didn't shoot. He waited as Aidan retreated into the dark. Then he pawed about along the earth until he came up with a stone as big as his fist, stood, and with all the might and technique of his out-fielding days threw it to the left of Aidan's track. He dropped again listening while the rock spent five heartbeats in the air before it struck with an appreciable crash of shrubbery followed instantly by a whump against the earth. He scrambled west hugging the berm trying to find a place farther along where the boy was less likely to look and he heard a burble of water and found a swollen creek rushing under a trestle of stone and wood. He swung beneath it stomping through the fast cold water feeling the suck of the current as he ducked beneath the beams until he emerged on the other side and sprinted through the mud and brush until he met the highway. He looked west, dreaming of escape, and turned and ran eastward, into jeopardy, sprinting down the centreline of the road, the waterlogged shoes threatening at each footfall to burst while he wondered distantly that if she weren't beautiful would he be racing back into peril to save her. There was no time to properly consider the question before he came to the darkened store which looked in the night to be peacefully vacant. He passed the woman's vehicle, a dark Ford Escape SUV, its nose at the glass, and he re-entered the store and smelled gunsmoke and an iron tang that reminded him of the butchershop of his childhood where great bloody hanks hung in the window. The woman was laid out in front of the cashdesk, and he saw that they'd bound her wrists and ankles with plastic ties. He kneeled beside her and as he felt past the tie to her wrist for a pulse he saw framed at the foot of the aisle the other boy, faceup in his lake of blood. He jammed a hand over his mouth, trying to reassemble the events that led to this impossible situation, a person dead and Nathan the killer. He tore his attention away from this thought, recognizing that all he could do now was mitigate things, save this woman's life, escape. But he couldn't find her pulse and was about to bail when he heard in the silence a slow, even breath which he thought from the boy but then realized was from the woman. He felt her throat, moved his hand along the ripple of her windpipe and up to the base of her jaw and there was nothing. Resisting the sense of impropriety which could've allied himself with the dead boy down the aisle he slipped his hand inside her jacket and rested it gingerly above her left breast and closed his eyes focusing the span of his senses into that one hand. Snatched it back as if stung. He'd felt it, the slow pump of her heart, the meagre rise of her chest. He jammed the gun into the front of his belt, realizing after it was done he should've set the safety, then slipped his arms around her waist and lifted her from the floor, alarmed at the flop of her neck, thinking of newborn Sydney and the constant anxiety of cradling her head, and he staggered back against the cashdesk as he brought her body against him, lifting, feeling her bend at the waist, folding across his shoulder, the fireman's carry. He teetered momentarily under her weight thinking he might fall and cause her graver injury yet, and as he was steadying himself he heard a squawk and the steel door opened. Nathan drew the gun from his belt with his left hand and waving it towards the door pulled the trigger three times. One bullet struck the drywall above the door, a second shattered the glass of a fridge, and the third caught Aidan across the upper right quadrant of his skull and blasted it away, carrying the gore into the room behind him. There were the pings of the casings striking the floor and the boy stood a bare moment and then slid down door like a machine deactivated, plug yanked, but then he seemed to sit up with renewed intention. Nathan raised the gun, ready to shoot again before he realized the hydraulic piston had drawn the door shut and forced the boy to sit up.

Nathan had meant only to warn him off. Hadn't he?

Get out. There was only one thing, one person, to salvage from this situation. He set the safety and stuffed the handgun into his belt with the barrel hot against his groin and he carried the woman outside.

He thought hours must've passed since he'd arrived at the store and that dawn was imminent, but as he carried her around to the suv's passenger door and pulled it open and lowered her into the seat it was still deep night.

He drew the seatbelt across her shoulder, had to thread it between her lashed wrists. He found in her left jacket pocket a perfume sampler and in the right the scroll of cash from the register, which he pushed back inside. But he found no keys and though he hated to do so he drew her legs straight so he could feel into the pockets of her pants, but they held only a few coins and the wrapper from a candybar. Then he glanced at the steering column and saw them there, in the ignition. Ready for the get-away. He stepped back and closed her door, was rounding the hood when his thirst reasserted itself. He looked at the store.

He went in and stepped left keeping his eyes off the dead boys who had fallen less than three paces apart, went to the fridge and stopped at the spot where he'd concealed himself when the woman entered. His found his pack here, drew it onto his shoulders. The small, jarring light of the fluorescent tube. He was about to step to the refrigerators when he remembered the oil, which when he looked down he saw had been smeared along the aisle where Craig had first fallen. He reached across, careful not to step in it, and pulled open one of the fridge doors and took down a bottle of mineral water. The seal crackled as he uncapped it, and he drank without pause to the bottom of the bottle. Then he wiped his mouth with the back of his hand. Suddenly picturing himself there, a killer with his victims lying a few paces away. Enjoying a post-rampage drink. It wasn't like that, he thought. I'm not like that. He'd tried to conjure the horrors they would've committed to his body. To her body. It was no good, it reinforced the horror rather than cancelling it out. He pushed all thoughts away, emptied his mind. Took a long breath, inhaled until it hurt, let it out slowly.

He looked down at the oily floor wondering what the police would make of it.

The police. He hadn't thought that far. This wasn't over. Crime scene. He suddenly perceived the store for what it had become, a crime scene. Detectives. Forensics. He looked at the polyethylene bottle in his hand, held it up to the light. Fingerprints. The bottle of canola he'd opened at his feet. The handle of the fridge. The doorknob on the door to the back, the cartons he'd used to barricade the door, the handle of the outside door behind the store. His mind navigating his route, footprints in the mud. And back to the front door, its aluminum grip. A process to follow. A meditation to escape the horror.

He found a carton of dishcloths, tore it open and rubbed down the bottles, fridge handle. He stepped to the door in the back wall, careful to evade with his feet the black pool spreading about the dead boy, but though he averted his gaze from the open skull he saw splattered against the unpainted steel the blood and pulp and then hoping he was mistaken but knowing he wasn't a gobbet stuck there sprouting from it a cluster of short hairs. Nor could he evade breathing the tinny stink of blood and brain. He buffed the doorhandle and stepped back, not looking at the dead but thinking again of his route. He went to the aisle at the far right of the store and dropped a fresh cloth and pushed it about with his foot, the water still pulsing from the seams of his shoes aiding in the enterprise as he washed the strip along which he'd crawled with the pistol before he'd shot Craig. And now it seemed so distant, as if it was something that happened years ago and today he'd returned to vivify the memory.

He went outside glancing through the car's tinted windshield at the yet unconscious woman and went to the store's back door, pulled it open, shaded his eyes from the stark lightbulbs. A mess of blood and bone spraypainted across the wall adjacent the inner door. He did not look much but twined the cloth about on the inside doorknob and let it close.

A low growl. A car, truck on the highway on the opposite side of the store, and he froze. Growing louder, he heard it from the east building rapidly and sending tremors through the ground, then out of the dark a trio of white lights followed by the thrumming slug of a locomotive and then another and another moving swiftly along the elevated tracks and then the sound retreating into the west while car after car clattered past, dark rectangles against the starry vault.

He ran around the building to the SUV, recognizing that he had spent too long here, had to get away, get away before someone stumbled upon this carnage. He opened the tailgate, found it crammed with a wrecked suitcase and an overstuffed canvas bag, threw his on top, slammed it. He got into the driver's seat and pulled the still-warm gun from his belt and pushed it under his seat, tossed the soiled cloths to the floor and looked at the woman who had not moved and could yet have died while he tidied the evidence but it didn't matter now, he had bound himself to her by murder. Turned the key and the engine started and he backed it out and threw it in gear, set off down the highway westbound, trying in his head to justify the direction from some tactical perspective but realizing that westbound had simply become habit.

Drove the speed limit, or slightly above, as was custom. He glanced at her from time to time but she did not stir. His mind on his footprints in the mud. Nothing to be done.

Like remote control. The gun. Push a button here and something happens there. Nothing so complex and banal as changing a channel. The termination of a life.

He'd thought little if at all about guns since crossing the border, knew that Lisa would've been obsessing about them, as she had in Las Vegas and when they'd holidayed in Florida. Suffering the idea that everyone was armed and ready at a moment's notice to shoot.

He'd mocked her. People had them or they didn't, but people were people, Canadian or American. His friend Conrad had one, not strictly legal, but fun to shoot nevertheless. Just another toy or appliance.

But then he thought of the events back there. Subtract guns from the equation, and everything collapses. Replace them with something else, with cleavers, with broadswords, and the outcome is utterly different. If the scene plays itself out at all. Imagines the woman standing there after plundering the cashregister, Aidan enters, and instead of the gun she draws a dagger.

He was shaking. He didn't see it coming, was just driving, watching the dotted line ride out of the dark and pass on his left and into the taillight glow, and his legs began to quake. It spread rapidly into his gut and chest, down his arms, his shoulders seizing as he gripped the steeringwheel with both hands trying to catch his breath, trying to keep the road steady in front of him.

No, he said, then gritted his teeth, and then again, louder, No. And then he shouted, a great primal shout, with all the power and volume he could muster, No!

There came from behind him a thin, white wail. He thought at first it was the siren of a police car, and his eyes darted to the rear-view mirror, expecting the beacon of a police cherry. Vacillating between stopping and pushing the gas to the floor. But there was nothing there and the whine was closeby, something inside the car. It stopped but after a small but determined intake of breath it started again. Nathan turned his head to see a pale shape elevated in the backseat behind the woman and only when he passed a yard illuminated with a bluewhite lamp did he see in the rhombus of light that swept the car's interior the baby in her carseat, and then there was a great rattle and bump and he swung his head back and hauled at the wheel to bring the car off the rumblestrip and back onto the highway. The crying continued and Nathan looked at the speedometer to see ninety miles per hour. He forced himself to let off as the baby cried and cried. Not a baby, he thought, for the wail had authority and coherence to it. A toddler. He drove as it bawled and he glanced several times at the woman beside him, hoping that the cries would rouse her, for wasn't she its mother? He slammed his fist against the steeringwheel wanting to shout at her with all the rage and fear continuing to mount in his gut, Why? You're a goddamn mother! Seeing her again in his memory brandishing the pistol as she pocketed the cash, and her shape was completely altered now, identical but in every way changed.

The child's wails increasing now in a spiralling, mounting whine.

It's okay, he said quietly, craning the rearview mirror about, trying to find the child in the dark. It's okay. There now. Everything's okay.

And still the crying built, each successive wail followed by a gulf of desperate silence as the child drew a lungful of air with which to deliver the next bawl.

He pulled over and got out, rounded the nose of the car, the headlights flaring across his thighs, and went to the back door, opened it. He saw her now in the domelight glow, the baby, the toddler, a girl with curly brown tresses, her mouth a cavern as she sucked air and then delivered with everything she had her cry, face soaked with tears and her eyes clenched shut as if in concentration to deliver the next broad yowl.

He said, Baby, baby, don't cry, his hands pressed to his sides and then he saw the pacifier clipped by a cord to her sweater. He lifted it and put it into her yawning mouth but she didn't even know it was there, so wide did her mouth open, and then he touched her tongue with it, interrupting the cry and making her recoil and twist away and cry harder.

Instinct and experience told him to touch her, to unbelt and hold her, but this wasn't his child, he was a stranger and he'd scare her into worse wails, though how she could achieve something surpassing her current pitch he did not know.

And then he was releasing the harness, operating the clips with ease, the upper bracket across the chest, the pushbutton between her legs, drawing limbs from beneath the belts and he had her in his arms, the weight of the child, her arms gripping him so familiar, stirring such memory of Sydney that he felt weak and disoriented as he stared across the shell of the roof which reflected the starry sky, while he jiggled and cooed. When this had no effect he thought to put the girl into her mother's lap but suddenly the girl went quiet, whimpering a little and shuddering with each inhalation, moulded against him with her head on his shoulder and arms braced about his neck. The familiarity of it incubating a terrible grief. He held her for a long time, making a slow revolution as he tenderly jostled her, looking out into the blackness within which he and this child found themselves. When he was sure she was asleep he put her back in the seat and enclosed her in the harness, got back into the driver's seat and drove, drove through a night which seemed without anchor or hamlet, town or oasis, as if the highway had been pried from the Earth and cast adrift in space. He knew that the woman he could barely see slouched in the seat beside him needed a doctor, knew that after severe head trauma she shouldn't be sleeping, though he knew it to be more than sleep, and he drove until the sun rose and cast on the road before the vehicle its own elongate shadow.

The fresh light in the cabin reignited her numinous beauty, and as he drove the compulsion to look was irresistible. For moments at a time he found his gaze fixed on her face, which as she sat sprawled in the chair was angled towards him, eyes closed, expression peaceful. The chug of tires on the rumblestrip or the blare of an oncoming horn would revive him, and he'd look forward slightly aghast to discover laid out before him a highway and he moving swiftly along it, but in a few minutes her face would lure his eyes back. Her loveliness seemed to wound him in some indescribable way, and as the sun climbed he expected its light to illustrate her flaws but instead it only enhanced her splendour. The girl in the backseat woke and cried again this time with less zeal and Nathan knew she was hungry and so was he. He didn't want to stop but the girl's cries were persistent, and then she began with Mama Mama Mama, which Nathan again hoped would rouse the woman, but she showed no sign of anything approaching consciousness. He wanted to put more distance between themselves and the crime scene, had vague ideas about exiting the state or even the country. But the cries were mounting, the girl adding Hungy, hungy to her implorations.

He pulled over and got out, his ears ringing in the abrupt silence, opened the back door. The motion distracted the girl from her wailing but when she saw his face she started up again at a different timbre, thrashing in the restraints and calling more plaintively, Mama, Mama. He saw a satchel on the seat beside her and zipped it open, found inside a vinyl kit decorated with teddybears and opened it to reveal plastic tubs of biscuits, goldfish crackers, orange wedges in a ziploc bag, a sippy cup of applejuice. He held the cup out to the girl and she seized it, sucked noisily from the spout, paused for breath, drank more before she lowered it, panting. She did not resume crying but looked at him warily while he spread a handful of crackers on his palm. She took one and ate it, took another and another, not meeting his eye. He ate a few himself, they were salty and tasted manufactured. Sydney had never eaten such things. He had to stop himself from gobbling the lot, he was so hungry. The sun higher now. He put the tub into the girl's lap and got back in the driver's seat, drove on.

Ten minutes later they reached an intersection where an arrow pointing left indicated the way to Highway 2. It was true then, he had left the Hi-Line during his deluded wandering. He took the turn and in a few minutes they reached Highway 2, and they rolled west among the tractortrailers and motorhomes. They weren't on the road ten minutes when Nathan spotted up ahead, labouring along the shoulder, garbed in yellow and black, a pair of cyclists. Rage flared in Nathan's chest, but after the night's traumas there was little fuel for it. Their speed also offered no opportunity to contrive appropriate reprisal, and the best Nathan could do in the circumstance was swing close to the road's edge and at the instant they passed sound the horn. When Nathan looked into the sideview mirror at their bumlebee figures retreating into the distance he saw one of the riders raise a fist and shake it in outrage. The mirror's convexity obscuring if the gesture had been Albert's or Madeleine's. And for a moment he thought it might've been two men riding. Plus neither was towing a trailer. But he was eager to free himself from the obligation of revenge, and as the truck sped on the anxieties of the present wiped the business from his mind.

Town after town, Lothair, Devon, Dunkirk, most of them insignificant, some on the verge of extinction and he excused himself for not seeking a doctor where he thought there would be none, but when he reached Shelby he forced himself to follow the turn into the business district. He drove along the empty street with its vintage storesigns aglow with neon, but he found neither clinic nor doctor and he got back on the highway. Cut Bank was next, they passed an enormous concrete penguin erected before a motel which made the little girl hoot and crow, then they went on through town, Nathan whipping his head about looking for anything medical but soon leaving the buildings and descending into a gorge where the bridge was under repair and a great red crane rose spar upon spar above the span, the parcel of I-beams on its cable swaying in the haze. As they crossed the bypass bridge he glanced up the eastern rockface and saw overlooking the cutbank a wooden cross and beside it a rusting sheetmetal Jesus, his arms spread and palms upturned as if testing for rain. Nathan looked at his own hands on the steeringwheel, his own stigmata of scabs across his wrists from the plastic tie. They sped up the new asphalt on the west side and accelerated to highway speed. Quiet from the backseat and he bent the mirror to see the girl asleep again, which both relieved and troubled him, for he couldn't imagine Sydney in her carseat this long being so slumberous and compliant.

The air ahead a leaden grey despite the sunshine filling the east. After a time he saw through this haze a cloud's isomorph of dirty white stamped into the sky. It was snow. The peaks of mountains growing evident beyond that murky veil. The highway banked and they entered Browning, passing motels and Indian souvenir shops, and he vowed to find a doctor here. There was risk of course, but the woman had been unconscious too long, and as they rounded a curve and faced the mountains he wondered at what point unconsciousness crossed the threshold and became coma. This thought brought panic, and he turned onto the next sidestreet, began a frantic search for a doctor's practice. He found one at last in a secondfloor office above a florist's. He got out and ran to the door, found it locked, read the text on the glass, Dr. Shane Albright, Office Open Daily 8:30 – 4:00. Twenty minutes. He smelled woodsmoke. He got back in the car and watched the street, waiting for the doctor's arrival, but dozed a little and woke with alarm to see it was 8:40 and he scrambled out of the car and tried the door but it was still locked. He stepped back into the street and looked up at the window but there was no sign of occupation. Tried the door again and rapped on the glass with his knuckles, rapped until the glass shook in its mount and the wound on his wrist throbbed. He stepped back and scanned the street but it was empty and he got back in the car. Pressed his hand to the woman's forehead. It was warm, that was all.

He turned on the radio, nothing but twangy country music, ads for roof repair, renditions of scripture. Watching the clock, wondering if he'd crossed a timezone in the night. At 9:00 there was local news and he listened with dread and there was talk of forest fires in the south but nothing of any shootings. Where was that damn doctor? Sports next, scores from across the continent in baseball and standings in the Tour de France and some mild scandal in golf and he was in the twilight of sleep when he heard about the murder of a Texan baseball pitcher, the coroner concluding he was killed by a single pointblank gunshot through the heart, Nathan wondering what kind of advanced medical training one needed to reach such a startling conclusion, when the reporter added that police were still seeking for questioning the player's wife, former Houston Texans cheerleader captain Miranda Belle, who had disappeared with her thirty-month-old daughter shortly before the man's body was discovered in their Houston condo. Nathan looked at the woman, then into the backseat at the girl, who was now awake and watching him in a kind of awestruck daze. She whined a little, splaying her hands, and Nathan craned about in his seat and peeled open a tub of cheerios and gave it to her. After a brief hunt he found the woman's purse on the floor behind the driver's seat, rummaged among the agglomeration of coins and tampons and a dead cellphone and a makeup kit and her wallet. He opened it and found nothing but a halfdozen one-dollar bills. He drew out her driver's licence, surprised to see it was issued by the Province of Alberta. A little stir in his belly that she was Canadian. An address in Calgary. Felt stupid at his relief seeing her name was Hannah Mitchell. He said aloud, Hello, Hannah. Her date of birth was 7 January 1975. He felt intrusive looking through her things, stowed everything back inside and dropped it in the purse. A thought at something he'd seen, went back in and retrieved a nailclipper, and with it snipped the plastic ties from her wrists and ankles. Touched the welts on her wrists, and then his own.

He saw in his sideview mirror a suit jacket and bluejeans approaching and he got out and confronted a native man wearing tiny goldrimmed spectacles and carrying a briefcase.

You're late.

For what?

You the doctor? Nathan demanded, nodding towards the door.

Do I look like a doctor?

You don't not look like one, Nathan replied, and the man blinked, decoding this sentence.

He's closed Sundays. You sick?

Not me. My . . . my wife.

Doc be at church now.

Where?

Church. Mister, are you okay? You don't look too good yourself.

I'm all right, Nathan said, wanting him to be gone. I appreciate your help. Goodbye.

The man stood uncertainly a moment before he continued on his way, passing the truck's driver side where he glanced within and went on. As Nathan walked back to the truck he saw mounted on the hatch a Texas licence plate. It slowed him only momentarily before he was back inside starting the engine. He put it in gear and drove by no conscious decision westbound along sidestreets until they could go no farther and had to move south and resume the main drag. It was quiet with little foottraffic and only a few cars and trucks until they neared a church with its doors thrown open and parishioners in their modest finery streaming inside. He slowed to allow a couple to cross the road, the man in a tan stetson, the woman in a dress of faded poplin. When Nathan glanced into the backseat the child was looking through the window at the passersby, a hand resting in the empty cup, and she glanced at Nathan and pressed her lips together before returning her gaze to the pedestrians.

They sped towards the mountains, and the haze – which he now recognized as woodsmoke – began to thin, revealing a broad range of craggy and snowy peaks, dreamlike and improbably beautiful, an ascendant nirvana set below a sky scratched with contrails. Salt-rimmed cattle tank in the field beside the highway. It was at this point that Nathan committed the error of assessing his exhaustion. He calculated his food intake and sleep over the last forty-eight hours and came to a meagre sum, and this cast over him a hard and relentless fatigue. He almost wept at the realization that there was no immediate remedy. A part of his mind tried to reason that without food or sleep he was liable to do something rash, a notion to which he laughed aloud as he thought about those two boys who even now were being discovered dead.

They crossed the Two Medicine River and the trees began, ponderosa and lodgepole standing plumb straight on the slopes. At East Glacier the fuelgauge forced him to pull into a station where a bearded giant began fueling the tank while Nathan went inside to buy microwaved burritos, bottles of juice, a carton of milk, a bag of Oreos. While waiting for the clerk he added a newspaper to his purchase, and when he came out the attendant was leaning against the car redfaced with the spigot in his hand, easing the price up to a round number. The girl shrieking and thrashing in her seat, her face a deep carmine and soaked with tears.

What did you do? Nathan demanded of the attendant while pulling the door open and unbuckling her, gathering her into his arms.

Nothin. I looked in the window and waved.

That's all?

Made a funny face.

The girl was calming, but after Nathan paid and pivoted back to the truck the sight of the attendant over Nathan's shoulder sent the girl into a new bout of affliction. Nathan whirled away and set to comforting her anew. Only when the man retreated to his booth with a grieved expression did she settle.

The highway meandered and rose, each turn revealing a new and more astonishing vista, and when the girl began to whimper he knew she was reaching her limit in that seat. A moment later she began a thin, defeated wailing, and it occurred to him she needed a diaper change. The idea brought considerable dread, and he jostled the woman beside him hoping to wake her, but she jiggled bonelessly, which stirred in him a flux of annoyance he knew was unreasonable.

After the Marias Pass and the Continental Divide he drew into a rest area, parked away from the minivans and motorhomes, and found inside the satchel a supply of diapers and wipes and though there was no changepad there was a beachtowel which he laid in the grass beside a picnic table. The girl's crying diminished as he lifted her from the seat and carried her to the towel and placed her there, expecting her as Sydney had to resist and try to rise but she did not. Nathan loosed the snaps of her sleeper and only then smelled the stench. He recoiled in a way he never had with Sydney. He pushed on and brought a wipe to the ready as he tugged the tape and opened the diaper to reveal a minor apocalypse of shit the colour of curry. He sat back for fresh air then went in with one moistened wipe after another. She was rashy and he daubed zinc oxide into her creases and put on a fresh diaper, then by habit tucked the dirty wipes into the old diaper and rolled and taped it expertly into a rank little bun which he pitched into the weeds. The girl had stopped crying and was looking at the sky, the blue reflection overlaying the cooler blue of her eyes. All her lush brown hair.

Sky, Nathan said, looking up at it and back at her. Big blue sky.

Boo, the girl said.

Yes, blue.

Mama, the girl said, looking at the car. Mama.

Nathan looked, wanting to see the woman's face at the window watching them, look how good he is with my daughter, but he could see through the tinted glass only her shoulder where it had always been, for she had not moved.

Do you want to walk? he asked. Walk?

Wa, the girl replied.

Yes, walk. He lifted her onto her feet and released her, but she stumbled and he caught her, righted her. You can walk, can't you? he said, and tried again, but she could not. He wondered if she only needed time to recover from being so long interred in the carseat. He stood and holding her hands marched her about on the grass, watching her diminutive goosesteps, and he continued to experiment with releasing his grip but she could not walk and she would barely stand. He had perhaps overestimated her age due to the lushness of her hair, and he reduced his guess, thought she might be a little over sixteen months, though very large for her age.

In his exhaustion his own legs were not much stronger and

after a few minutes he put the girl back in the truck, pried the lid from the biscuit container, and put it in her lap. He was about to climb in when he waded into the weeds and collected the dirty diaper and opened one of the bearproof trashcans and threw it in. It was the first he had thought of Lisa in some time. Since he wrote about the belly of the sky.

He turned on the radio and panned the dial until he found news, already in progress, about a suicide bomber killing twenty-four Pakistanis and hysteria about the final Harry Potter book. The focus shifted to issues local and the first story was of two store-clerks murdered last night in a robbery. Identification pending notification of next-of-kin. A halfhour later there was more, they were Aidan Stewart and Craig Fordice and they'd each heroically served several tours of duty with 'L' Company of the 3rd Battalion, 5th Marine Regiment in Iraq. It was easy while listening to this report to disassociate himself from the incident, to shake his head as other listeners were shaking their heads wondering what this world was coming to when a pair of young war veterans could be murdered on the job and for a handful of twenty dollar bills. He glanced at the woman in the seat, thought of the cash scrolled in the pocket of her jacket. Wanting to snatch it out and throw it through the window. And now a thought of great urgency, to get over the mountains, to cross the stateline. He knew this notion to be foolish, expecting immunity in Idaho. Ah, but Canada, he thought. If they could cross into Canada. He began to weigh the risks against the possible benefits, grew immediately aware of the difficulty of re-entering the country with an unconscious woman and a child not his own. A child whose name he didn't even know. Idaho, then. Beyond the mountains.

He awoke to a violent shudder, steeringwheel jerking in his hands, opening his eyes to see the highway lifting off to his left and gravel under the tires, and he grunted swinging the wheel back the rubber thudding on the rumblestrip as he swerved into the lane. Looked in the rearview and saw the Greyhound coach behind them violently flashing its lights in reproof. He had to get off the road, he desperately needed food and rest. The girl luckily was agreeable in the backseat, almost alarmingly so as he considered how Sydney would've reacted to such hours trapped in the restraints. But where to stop, there was nowhere to stop. On through West Glacier, Hungry Horse, crossing the Flathead River into Columbia Falls, casting looks of longing at strip motels with their creaky beds and floral comforters but all of them with parkinglots like galleries open to the highway, thinking about that pickup truck that had rolled into the store's lot before Aidan waved it off, someone he knew, a witness who'd seen this black Ford Escape parked at the glass shortly before the murders. Glad for the model's ubiquity but squeamish nevertheless to park it with its Texas plates in plain view. Still thinking of a hospital, clinic, doctor, certain to find these in Kalispell, now cruising the strip stopping at a traffic light while a couple with two boys in a tandem stroller, all of those people just as Madeleine described in her insomniac fugue emanating that celestial glow, angels promenading, shopping for bargains. Green light and go, ahead he will make a stop, but didn't, and at the next lot he'll stop, but didn't, the town diminishing, open highway again, mountain and forest all of it sharp and almost painfully distinct, needle and leaf, limb and pinecone each calling out to him remember me remember me before falling behind in a blur of speed and oblivion. Under cloud and lightning, a bout of rain rinsing dust from the windshield, throb of thunder in the lee of the engine's hum, then clearing and brilliant wet highway glaring in the sunlight, an endless strip of chrome. At the apex of a curve he took too fast he imagined as the tires slid on the wet pavement three white crosses on a post, for him and the woman and the child, but as he threw the wheel hard to the left he wondered if in fact his cross would share with the pair a single mount, or if his would be set apart, a way's off, forever alone. The thought haunted him long after he'd regained control and sped on.

They were on a one-lane road crowded by brush and branch and in the rearview the pall of dust yellow in the sunlight penetrating the canopy of leaves, so he supposed it hadn't rained here.

Surprised that addled though he was by exhaustion he was still capable of such penetrating reason. Now that he has decided to stop he is desperate to stop, but this random road too narrow to pause and tears verging about the rims of his fatigued eyeballs as he seeks anywhere to park and embrace half an hour of sleep. They'd passed driveways marked by handmade signs, The Jacksons and Wilbur and Edith Kent and Swan Villa, a swan painted on still water. There were none for a time and then one called Breathless Point, a cable spraypainted fluorescent pink across the driveway's mouth and then the road ended at a turnaround where he could stop but did not, instead brought the car about driving slowly over the rough surface and paused at Breathless Point. He got out, found the cable fastened with a swivel bolt snap, unlatched it and dropped the cable to the dirt. He got back in and drove down the hill until they came to a cabin clad in brown siding with a moss-covered roof and a satellite dish. He paused, the engine idling, eyes fixed on the cabin's back door waiting for someone to emerge to whom he would apologize before he turned around and left, but no one came and he killed the engine and got out. The silence like deepsea pressure against his eardrums. He followed a deck around the cabin's side calling Hello? Hello? and came to the front to see a grassy slope falling to a lake reflecting the clean blue of the sky. An overturned rowboat beside a dock. A pair of mergansers moving across the water, their motion painting behind them in the lake's cold glass a widening vee. It was cool even in the sunshine, a product of the altitude. Sun falling towards the Cabinet Mountains. He turned and went to the high windows lining the deck, cupped his hands against the glass and peered inside. Couches and an easy chair but otherwise vacant.

He heard from the cabin's far side a high shriek of outrage from the girl. He rounded the cottage and tried its rear door but it was locked and he kicked with his heel until the frame splintered and the door swung inwards. He went to the truck and opened the back door. The girl threw her arms up at him and flexed her hands but he backed away and she began to bawl. He opened the passenger door and undid the woman's seatbelt. He smelled urine and thought the girl needed a fresh diaper – he'd stopped and changed one an hour ago – but when he bent to lift the woman he found she had pissed in the seat. He hesitated, straightened, and stared at the distant mountains, wondering if this was good or bad. He leaned inside and with a kind of reverent tenderness turned her head, studied her face while the world seemed to pitch and yaw, unhinged by this taste of her prodigious beauty. Attempting a clinical indifference he lifted one eyelid and peered at the iris which languished unshifting upon the white jelly of her eyeball. He had no notion of how to interpret the result of this diagnostic. When he let go the lid closed only partially and he had to prod it into place with a fingertip. The girl wailing in the backseat. He slid his arms beneath the woman's back and knees, carried her across the threshold and into the cabin. He kicked open a few doors until he found the master bedroom and he laid her on the bed, adjusted her body until she appeared comfortable, pulled off her pumps and set them side by side at the foot of the bed. He opened the drapes to reveal glass doors to the deck and sunshine poured in and illumined the woman and she was like a goddess slumbering upon her divan. He backed out and shut the door and went to collect the girl, who was only blubbering by the time he returned to the car. He carried her in and when he set her down in the livingroom he realized it was warmer inside the cabin than out, which he at first attributed to the sun shining through the windows, but when he touched the woodstove he found the metal warm. He panicked, and only his supreme fatigue prevented him from evacuating the cabin and racing away. He stood trembling, ears piqued to the sound of a returning vehicle while his mind sought, for reasons of necessity, to pacify the flight impulse. Today was Sunday; the stove was warm because the cabin's owners had just departed after a weekend visit, and as weekend visitors they would theoretically be gone until Friday. Not that he intended to remain here more than one night. The girl was sitting on the rug where he'd left her, glancing cautiously about while rubbing her tearstained face, and he realized there were advantages to her immobility.

In the kitchen he found dishes stacked in the dryingrack, a bead of rinsewater reservoired within the pedestal of an upturned wineglass. The fridge stocked with condiments, eggs, pickles, coffee cream. In the freezer cuts of steak in styrofoam trays, frozen vegetables, meatpies, loaves of white bread. He took a loaf out and opened the bag, pried off slabs of frozen bread and put them in the toaster. He got eggs and a block of butter, found a castiron frying pan, set it on the stove to heat, dropped in a chunk of butter and skated it about with a spatula, scribing oily glyphs on the hot iron. From the livingroom he heard a terrific crash and he rushed in to see that the girl had toppled a tower of CDs. Seeing him she began to cry and as he approached she threw her hands up and howled louder as she scrambled backwards until she struck a chair and shrank bawling hugely while twisting away in a mournful cower.

Wait, wait, he heard himself saying as he kneeled on the rug a few paces back, advancing slowly. It's okay, it's okay. I'm not mad.

But as he neared her her wails multiplied and he sat back on his heels not knowing what to do. He could smell the hot butter, and fearing fire he went back to the kitchen and cracked four eggs into the pan. The girl's crying fading beneath the hiss of eggs and the urgent plea of his appetite, the smell of toast and cooking eggs bringing to his body a plaintive euphoria while he watched mesmerized the eggwhites rippling in the hot butter. He had to force himself to return to the livingroom where the girl's cries had subsided but upon seeing his approach they rose again to a fevered shriek of terror. He bent and scooped her into his arms bracing himself for her assault as he carried her into the kitchen and she did resist but only momentarily before she succumbed to his hold, her head pressing with such force against his windpipe it gagged him. He clutched her with equal ferocity, his eyes pressed shut as he tried to evade the stark realization that had Sydney lived she'd today be about this size and weight, and he muttered calming phonemes which when he listened to himself were nothing more than syd syd syd. As she clung to him he freed an arm and salted the eggs and then with greater difficulty put toast on a plate and crushed the hard butter into its grain. Soon she dropped her head and watched him scoop the eggs out and lay them on the toast.

Are you hungry? he asked and her head nodded against him and she said, Hungy. He pulled out one of the mismatched chairs and set down the plate and then he sat with her in his lap and he carved the toast into strips and used them to pierce the sunny domes of the eggyolks. He fed her these yellowsoaked pieces and she ate many. Then she said, Mik, mik, and he realized he'd left her cup in the car. He carried her to the sink and filled a glass with water, tasted it – it was very cold and tasted of iron and he had to resist downing it himself before he held it to her lips. She drank, spilling a great deal down her chin but most of it fell into the sink. He finished what she didn't and refilled the glass and drank and refilled and drank. Then he returned to the table and using his free hand he ate it all, using a final stub of toast to mop the plate clean. He could not see the girl's face, her cheek pressed to his bicep, but he knew she was asleep. He thought to put her to bed but in his own exhaustion he could not rise and so he sat in a kind of exultant silence, still hungry and weary beyond anything he'd ever experienced, waiting for something to commence or complete, until at last he rose and carried her into one of the bedrooms at the rear of the cabin where he put her on her back close to the woodpanelled wall. She woke and whimpered and turned onto her side and fell asleep again. He curled the crocheted quilt over her body and stepped to the doorway where he turned and looked at her while he clutched the doorknob in his hand ready to shut the door, but then he realized she might roll off the bed. He thought perhaps to hunt for pillows to arrange beside her but he was already walking to the bed and pitching himself down beside her as a barricade. In a breath he was asleep.

CHAPTER 10

Hunger woke him in the pitchdark from a dream on a tropical beach where he and a brownhaired Sydney romped together in the surf. On the beach just beyond the throw of the tide Lisa asleep on a beachtowel. He'd called to her but she did not wake. He lay in the dark pondering all this, but of course it was no puzzle. He saw through the open doorway a faint light he thought might be dawn but when he got up he saw it was the glow of a nightlight. He used the bathroom and washed his face, studied it in the mirror. He looked old, new lines around his eyes, and he needed a shave. Went to the kitchen and ate a piece of dry bread, then another. Checked cupboards until he found a bag of cookies and ate a few. Crackers next, saltines. The clock on the stove said it wasn't yet eleven.

Faint light from stars and moon reflecting off the lake filled the master bedroom, and in this cold illumination Hannah looked dead. She hadn't moved. He sat on the edge of the bed and turned on the bedside lamp and lifted her hand and held it. It was warm. The room smelled of urine and he thought he should do something about that.

He brought in from the car his own knapsack and the satchel with the girl's things, as well as a small overnight bag which he opened and found packed tightly and without organization a woman's things, a pair of jeans, blouses, a bra, a few pairs of panties. Kneeled before the open case a long time wondering what to do. At last he lifted out a pair of panties, crushed them in his palm, and moved to the bed's edge. He cleared his throat and leaned over and looked at the woman's face.

Hannah, he said. I've got to do something.

He stood and turned off the lamp so the only light was from

the window, and then he kneeled beside the bed and loosened her belt. Paused, then used both hands to work open the button on her pants, and he set the underwear on her belly, and undid the button and pulled down the fly. It was when he pushed his fingers into the waistband to pull them down and he felt the warmth of her skin against his knuckles that he had to sit back and regroup, not from a libidinous reaction but from a clout of profound woe. He looked at the outline of her body in the darkness, overcome by a flush of distress at his powerlessness. All he had to offer was comfort, so he pressed on, seizing her pants by the beltloops and with effort working them off her long legs. He tossed them aside, his eyesight growing accustomed to the low blue glow so he could see her panties almost luminescent in their whiteness and askew from the removal of the jeans, the smell of urine stronger. He pulled them off, hunted about on the floor for the box of baby wipes, found them and tugged out a few. He drew her legs apart and towelled between them and along the insides of her thighs. Plucked the panties from her stomach and was about to put them on her when he realized she would likely pee again and he'd have to repeat this process. He considered this problem for a moment before he retrieved a diaper from the girl's satchel. Girded the woman's loins with it, but it was of course too small and he left the tape hanging. Then, working rapidly, he put her feet through the loops in the panties and drew them up, lifting her to tuck the diaper beneath her bottom and to set the waistband in place. He stood then, lifted her torso, drew her arms out of the jacket's sleeves and threw it on the floor, lay her back down. He pushed his arms beneath her back and legs and lifted her, set her on the rug, drew back the bed's quilt and blanket and sheet, set her onto the cool bottom sheet, covered her. Her head jacked unnaturally to the left, and as he was setting it straight he felt through her hair a soft depression in the back of her skull and he recoiled, stood at the bedside panting and looking at her face in the blue light. Heard a low moan and thought it was her, realized it was his own voice. He had to get her to a doctor. This was not an injury that rest could cure. He thought they should go now, now, right now, find the nearest town, find a hospital. Damn the consequences. He would go to jail for what he did, for killing those boys, but he'd had no choice, surely everyone would understand he'd had no choice. He walked a tight circle on the rug banging his fists together trying to manage the dread that rolled over him. Wanting to ask Lisa what to do, what would Lisa do? But that answer was easy, she'd not have killed those boys in the first place. But then she'd be dead. He'd be dead. If he hadn't killed, he'd be dead. He thought at first this recognition would absolve him of guilt, but was startled to feel a potent flush of remorse. Reviewing his actions in that store, trying to determine if there'd been some other way to escape, to save himself and the woman and child. But even now, away from the ferment of panic, he saw no option. Perhaps to wound the boys instead of killing them, but they were both armed and trained and committed to murdering him. If Nathan had administered to each a bullet in the arm, the leg – never mind that he hadn't the skill to target so accurately, even without the incursion of fear and haste – they'd still shoot back, and without reciprocal mercy. He'd been lucky to hit them at all, lucky they'd been stoned and drunk. But he didn't feel lucky.

He froze. Is this what his father had meant? That you can't escape your destiny, that you must be who you are? Was Nathan a killer?

Picturing their bodies, Craig flat on his back in blood, Aidan propped against the door, skull agape. Somebody's children, that's what Lisa would say, they were somebody's children. Whatever life had made them into, they were at one time babies, toddlers, kids, teenagers. Loved, or maybe not. But deserving of love. As are we all.

He'd done what he had to do, and still it was wrong. There was no reconciliation to this quandary. It was a paradox of practical morality. That two things could be simultaneously right and wrong.

He turned and looked at the woman on the bed. It was time to go. Take her to the hospital, where they'd summon the police. He would go to prison. His sentence dependent on whether or not he could convince a jury he'd acted in self-defence. He was fairly convinced Montana embraced the death penalty. But he could not let self-preservation kill this woman. He kneeled and began cramming her clothes back into the suitcase, and then heard a hard thump. Thought at first it was someone arriving at the cabin, was despite his thoughts of a moment ago prepared to fight or flee, but a moment later a wail rose from the next room. He was on his feet and already inside the other bedroom before he'd determined that it was the girl, bawling loudly now. He'd almost tripped over her where she lay sprawled on the floor, and he gathered her into his arms and held her tightly saying, Shhh, shhh. She would not be soothed and he took her into the livingroom and paced about the floor jiggling, trying to hush her. He thought the sight of her mother might calm her so he went into the master bedroom and turned on the light and showed her the woman in the bed but the girl was oblivious, her cries went on unabated and he took her back into the livingroom and made circuits of the room patting her back and pleading with her to hush. He tried her pacifier which she spit out and he went into the kitchen and tried to give her some water, a cookie, and then some coffee cream in a glass, all of which she violently rejected. He was back in the livingroom lapping the couch when he spotted a remote control, and he poked buttons until the television came on. It was satellite television and he impotently jabbed the buttons trying to tune the station away from a black and white movie, hoping to find children's programming, though it was almost midnight. At last he was able to change the channel, found more movies, latenight talk shows, and he floundered about trying to find something age-appropriate, realized a moment later it didn't matter, the girl's cries were diminishing, she was blubbering a little now, and he felt about on her head for a bump, cursing himself for not taking enough precaution to secure her in the bed, and thinking of her mother's own skull, dished in by the butt of a rifle, thinking that it was time to collect their things and go, to make for the hospital. He set the girl on the sofa, moved back, expecting protest and rage, but she was mesmerized by the screen and he went to the master bedroom and finished packing the bags. He pulled off his t-shirt, which smelled of sweat and fear, and while rifling through the damp interior of his backpack came up with his spiralbound notebook. Thumbed through the tattered artefact, longing for those days of easy vagrancy. The pages were wet, the rules had run and faded, but his pencilled observations remained clear and dark. He detected from it the faint tang of mildew and despairing for its corruption shoved it back into the pack. He got out a clean t-shirt, thought he should take a shower but it was impossible with the girl awake and unsupervised, and he felt deep regret, figuring it would be his last private shower for some time. He changed his underwear too, turned modestly away from the unconscious woman, put on a pair of jeans, socks, already nostalgic for his own things, his own choices. The girl was making noise now, calling softly, and he listened. She was saying, Mama, hi Mama.

He went into the livingroom and the woman's face was inset on the television screen beside an announcer, a bespectacled man in a tie and jacket. Nathan was disoriented at first by the statistics scrolling along the foot of the screen, the crest on the announcer's coat, realized this was sports, and he fought for comprehension, grabbed the remote from the coffeetable and thumbed the volume key.

. . . for Owen's wife, thirty-two year old Miranda Belle, who, along with their two-and-a-half-year-old child Brittany, has been missing since the day of the killing. At Wrigley Field today the Cubs and Astros stood silent for two minutes in honour of the fallen player. The Cubs went on to beat the Astros seven to six and sweep the series. In tennis today . . .

Nathan turned slowly to the girl, whose eyes remained fixed on the screen, her face slack. He said softly, Hey. Hey, little girl. Hey little one. Then he said: Brittany. The girl raised her eyes to him and he kneeled, put his hands on her knees and looked into her eyes. Is your name Brittany? he asked, and she watched him before she replied softly, Britty.

He sat back on his heels and pressed a hand to his eyes, studying the bright fissures between his fingers before looking at the girl again. He followed her gaze to the television, where attention had shifted to tennis scores.

Nathan changed the channel, scoured the cable news stations, but there was nothing else. Then he remembered the newspaper he'd bought at the filling station that afternoon. He found rock videos with their dazzle and thump, looked into her eyes fixed on the flickering tube before he jogged out to the truck and got the newspaper, then sat on the floor beside her.

It was the *Glacier Reporter* from Browning, the Saturday edition, yesterday's, published before the shootings at the store. He paged through, found in the sports section a headline, "Astros to pay tribute to Owen," and beneath it a photo of Owen's face, beefy, shaggyhaired, and bearded, not unkind, a dazed smile on his face.

Owen was found dead last Sunday in his Houston condo with a single gunshot wound to the chest. Police are still looking for his estranged wife Miranda Belle, also known as Hannah Sharon Mitchell, who disappeared along with their 30-month-old daughter hours before a neighbor discovered the body. Belle's parents held a press conference Thursday at their Calgary, Alberta home where they called for Belle to give herself up, a plea they retracted when Houston police chief Max Tanner announced at Owen's funeral yesterday that her surrender would not change his intention to recommend the death penalty.

Friends of Belle allege that Owen was abusive to both her and her daughter, and that she feared for their lives. Witnesses reported Owen roughed up both his wife and the girl on a Denver street last May.

Owen, who had just graduated from the Galveston police academy when the Texas Rangers picked him in a late round of the 1994 draft, was traded to the Astros in 2001. He's best known for his career-high 66 home runs during the 2005 season. He was 33.

Nathan pressed his hands to the rug, trying to steady himself as the room began to whirl. To save her, to save Hannah, for what?

So the state of Texas could run a tube into her arm and murder her. The girl an orphan.

She'd been making for the border. Cross into Canada. Get back home. The Canadian government would not extradite a citizen to the U.S. to face capital punishment. But she couldn't get across. Trapped here against the ceiling of America, waiting for an opportunity, running out of cash until she became desperate enough to walk armed into that store in the middle of the night.

He sat up suddenly, thinking of the gun beneath the driver's seat. The same gun that killed Owen? Why not? And now it had killed two more, those boys. Forensic tests would determine that, connect the crimes. He'd seen it endlessly on TV. Ballistics, grooves on the bullet hulls. He couldn't help imagining a character from one of those TV shows in his latex gloves roaming the aisles with cool detachment, picking up a spent shell and muttering a cocky quip. Nathan had neglected the shells. Not that it much mattered.

He wanted to run. Gather everything and get them in the car, and drive, drive north. But they'd have no chance at the border. Safer to stay here. For a few days, let the hunt cool. Get out before the owners returned. There was still a chance she'd recover. Probably better not to move her if he didn't have to.

He struggled against that furious impulse to flee. To save them. To save the mother and daughter. This time.

He bent forward, pressed his head to the rug, smelled its fustiness as he formed within the shell of his body a dark cavern, his hands pressed to the back of his neck as he hyperventilated. He wanted to weep, thought it might relieve some of this awful tension. Hearing from the TV inane lyrics endlessly reiterating the same dozen words and sentiments.

He got up and went outside, it was a cold night and he stood swaying in the dark looking at stars scattered above the lake and reflected in its mirrored finish. Immense silence, through which trickled the sound of the television. He wrapped his arms around himself, listening to his own life move through him, his lymph and haemoglobin, the flush of antibodies and platelets.

At 2 a.m. he carried Brittany's sleeping body back to the bed, stretched out on his side against her, a cordon, wide-eyed, his mind howling with thought. He slept shallowly, woke near dawn, and built around the girl a balustrade of pillows and blankets, and for extra measure liberated the couch's cushions and set them on the floor below the bed, adjusting them carefully to ensure protection if she fell again. He went into the other bedroom and stood in the doorway as light doused the western mountains, filling the room with blond light. He watched her there, wanting to believe she was only sleeping, knowing that this was a place far from sleep. The anteroom of death. There was a scent of decay and he opened the sliding door to the deck, admitting crisp morning air, then sat crosslegged on the floor beside the bed, watching her. He recalled stories of loved ones prattling to the comatose, coaxing them to abandon the netherworld and return home, but he didn't know what to say. His backpack lay nearby, and he crawled over and opened it, rummaged within its rank interior and withdrew his notebook. The paper showed pinhead blemishes of mould and the scent of blight was stronger. He rifled through it trying to find an appropriate passage, read silently, paged, paged again, but the words made him horribly weary and he closed it, pulled it against his chest, trying to feel every moment it contained, records of his head craned upwards as he attempted desperately to express himself to Lisa in ways he never had when she was alive. He couldn't give it away to this woman. As he had to Madeleine. Look what had happened. These words were Lisa's. They belonged to the dead.

He could smell the wetness of the paper, sensed the impending corruption of it. He carried it onto the deck and fanned it and slung it by its spine along a slat of the deck's railing for treatment in the air and pending sunshine. Then he went back in, stood uncertain at the foot of the bed. Stepped forward, sat on the edge beside her, noted that as the springs sagged she rolled a little towards him, her placid faced turned upwards as if in anticipation of his words. And he did speak for a long time in a low voice, but what he said to her he forgot as soon as it was done. He had a vague notion: descriptions for their future. Audacious promises of an exotic life full of pleasure and delight. The girl with them of course, he called her Sydney at first, had to correct himself, Brittany, Brittany, our dear child, always protected, loved with all the love he could muster.

And as the light grew he begged her, begged with his flesh and blood, with bone and sinew, begged with the very quiddity of his existence for her to come back, come back to this room filling with dawn light, and be with him, and be with Brittany. He promised her Earth and moon and sun and stars and every manner of celestial phenomena he could recall, comets, asteroids, pulsars, novae, he promised her everything.

He placed his hand on her forehead as if granting a benediction, moved it to the side of her face and cupped her cheek. The warmth of her flesh bringing a blusterous sorrow into his breast. He moved his hand down and placed it on her heart, closed his eyes to detect its slow pump. It was there, but unbearably mild and slow. Beating not with vitality, but obligation.

He heard the girl wake with a thin, shocked cry, and he went to her and at first she shrank from his touch, backing into the corner and flailing with arms and legs, fending him off while he pleaded with her, hands outstretched, trying to suppress his growing frustration, until at last he left her and she cried louder and when he returned she threw herself into his arms.

He put her in a fresh diaper and clean clothes and fed her and by then the sun was high, the lake dazzling and the air warm. He took her outside and they played games of chase during which he encouraged her to walk but she would not, so she evaded or pursued him on all fours like an animal. He thought of those allegations of abuse mentioned in the newspaper, wondered if that could have delayed her development, made her volatile. Thoughts like this made him lavish with his affection, with his permissibility, until he realized that indulgence was also no good. He forced himself to be tenderly strict and relentlessly consistent. The effort was exhausting, but after a few hours he thought he saw the intensity of her outbreaks lessening, and she seemed more ready to accept his comfort.

She liked to crawl to the water's edge, to gaze into the shallows, the bottom rippled by wave action, and when he asked if she wanted to go in she looked at him with something like awe.

Just your feet, he said quickly, because he wasn't much of a swimmer and was concerned about safety, his own and hers.

He went in first with his jeans rolled to his knees, and when he stepped into the water he had to suppress a gasp, it was so cold.

All right, he said. It's really cold. You're probably not going to like it much. She was sitting on the dock, and he tried to roll up her little sweatpants but her legs were so short he couldn't raise them high enough for the water's depth. He finally removed them completely so she wore just a onesie and a diaper, and he lowered her carefully into the water, expecting a squeal, prepared to lift her out, but she only giggled, and when she was standing on the sandy bottom she shook off his hands and stood triumphantly in the cold shallows, her expression rapturous. When she took a step he swept forward to save her from pitching into the water but she remained upright and looked up at him, beaming.

They pranced awhile in the shallows, Brittany walking about as she wouldn't on dry land. She fell a few times, but instead of bawling she howled with laughter, and soon she was soaked and so was Nathan. As they played he tried to teach her his name, but she only called him Nay-Nay, and he couldn't get her to call herself anything but Britty.

After a time she grew weary and with it came petulance and rage, to which Nathan brought every resource of patience he could muster, dodging blows as he carried her into the cottage. He put her in dry clothes and a fresh diaper and then to bed, and she fought and screamed, throwing herself from the bed until at last Nathan had to hold her down, cooing at a near shout to overpower her wails until at last, close to an hour later, she fell into a fitful sleep. He stayed with her for another twenty minutes, until her breathing became slow and even and her brow softened.

He went to the master bedroom to check on Hannah. The bed was empty. He stood frozen in the doorway as he looked at the disarrayed blankets, blinking as if to correct some error in perception. He spun and looked in the kitchen, checked the other bedroom. Then he thought, the truck, the truck, and ran to the rear door, but the SUV sat vacant in its parking spot. He crossed the clearing behind it, started to jog up the slope to the road, but turned, rushed back inside to the master bedroom and rounded the bed, found her on the floor, legs tangled in the sheets, eyes splayed wide.

Hannah, he said, reaching down and touching her shoulder. As soon as he made contact he knew she was gone. He squatted and looked into the bottomless depth of her eyes. Hannah, he said, softer now. He put his hand on her cheek and it was still warm, but not warm enough. He should have taken her to a hospital, why didn't he take her to a hospital? But then thought, what difference would it have made? To preserve her for the executioner? After the ordeal of the trials, the appeals, after four, five, six years, bringing Brittany to an age when she is conscious of it all, trapped in the media scrum, harried by camera lenses. No, it was better the girl not remember her mother at all, or remember her only vaguely, a creature from a dream.

Wondering now how the woman got to the floor, if there was a moment of consciousness, if she'd awakened. And he and the girl outside. Maybe she called out for her child. Unlikely. She must've suffered some kind of paroxysm, which had either caused or resulted from her dying.

He stood and flipped back the covers. Lifted her, and he imagined there would be some difference from when he'd carried her while she was unconscious, but there was none, and he thought it best to think of her as having died on the floor of that store after the fatal blow from the rifle's stock. He put her in the bed, drew the diaper out from between her legs, rolled and taped it and tossed it onto the floor. Then he arranged her carefully on her side, knowing that rigor mortis would soon hinder his ability to manipulate her pose. Make it look as if she'd been awake, had lain here, and died. He kneeled at her face, still unbearably lovely, but pale now, with a bluish cast, eyesockets dark and her eyes a little sunken, lips violet. Agents of death already busy. He put his hand on her cheek, whispered, Hannah. I will take care of her.

And then he got to work. It took him two hours, and mercifully the girl slept through.

He woke her, ready to carry her away that instant, but knew she had to see, felt that closure was necessary, that it would be unhealthy to deprive the girl of a last look, a last touch of the woman who'd borne her. He set her on the couch and kneeled on the floor clutching her hands, said, Brittany. It's time to say goodbye to Mama.

Mama, the girl said.

Mama's gone, he said. You have to say goodbye.

Bye-bye Mama.

You can give her a kiss. Then we will say bye-bye.

Bye-bye Mama.

Yes, bye-bye. Come, he said, and he put out his arms. She looked up at him and didn't at first move, then raised her hands, palms open, and he lifted her. He carried her into the bedroom and set her on the floor near Hannah's face. He had shut the woman's eyes, but one lid now stood ajar, and he thought to press it back into place but did not. Brittany looked up at him and then back at her mother. He was about to urge her forward, to encourage a kiss, when the girl stepped forward, and put her face to the woman's, and kissed her cheek. She turned and looked up at Nathan.

Mama cold.

Yes, Nathan said. Mama is cold.

Blankie.

He was driven now, eager to escape, but fought the impulse to seize her and go, instead went to the other bedroom and returned with a quilt. He tossed it on the bed, arranged it over Hannah's shape.

Blankie for Mama, he said to her. His mind awhirl. The girl's clothes, her diapers and pacifiers, a few snacks and sippycups, some toys collected and stashed in his knapsack, and those items he couldn't carry, the carseat, an umbrella stroller, removed from the car; he'd taken them as deep into the woods as he dared go, where he'd set them ablaze. His nostrils still rimed with the stink of burning acrylic and PVC. Wearing a pair of dishgloves he'd found under the kitchen sink he retrieved the gun from beneath the driver's seat, heavier than he remembered it, and like everything that would take a fingerprint he'd rubbed it down, polished it clean, then he'd put it in Hannah's hands, moved her fingertips over the barrel, the stock, set her index finger against the trigger. He'd polished the contents of her purse, stowed the gun inside, put the purse in the bathroom. Touched her fingertips to the TV remote, cutlery, crockery, a glass he filled halfway with water and set on the bedside table. Made the cottage look as if she'd been its lone occupant. He knew there was other evidence he could not erase, hair follicles and whatnot, but he hoped that Hannah's presence here was simple enough that the police would not investigate too diligently, not summon a fullfledged forensics team. He'd even flattened his and the girl's footprints on the tiny beach and in the sand of the shallows. The last thing he'd done before waking the girl was check his wallet. He knew it was there, but he looked anyway, rubbed his thumb across the certificate's blue intaglio. Soderquist, Sydney Jayne. Date of Birth, 3 July 2004.

He stood watching the girl, who had lost interest, was now regarding the lamp, about to reach for the chain to turn it on.

Brittany, he said, capturing her before her fingers could make contact. He held her gently for a moment, then turned her around, gathered her in his arms.

Did you want to say goodbye to Mama now?

The girl looked him in the face, and shook her head. He thought he should urge her on, was about to bring her close to the woman again to provoke a farewell, but then he knew it wasn't necessary. The girl had finished. He carried her out and through the livingroom, took one final assessing glance. He would carry the girl to the highway and then along the highway. The next town, Libby, Montana, maybe a dozen miles. There they could board a bus. Head west, and then, when it was safe, north.

He closed his eyes, drew a lungful of air, and moved. But as they were passing through the rear entrance the girl shot out a hand and seized the edge of the door, and Nathan had to brace it with a foot to keep it from swinging shut on her fingers. Mama, she cried as he tried to dislodge her and carry her through, but she gripped fiercely, launched her other hand to join the first. Mama! she screamed, bawling now as Nathan pulled, drawing her out horizontal, arms stretched and her fingers bloodless on the door as he saw her tears falling like fat raindrops to the floormat. He pulled, certain he would in a moment overcome her grip, but she held on, shrieking again and again, Mama! Mama!

Nathan reached out and pried her fingers from the door, but when he got one hand free and started on the other she reattached the first. The struggle went on in this manner for minutes, until Nathan gave a frustrated tug which tore her free, changing her woeful cries to those of pain.

He had the dishcloth he'd used to erase fingerprints in his pocket, and he tugged it out and buffed the door where her fingers had touched. He rubbed the doorknob too, pulled it shut against its splintered jamb, but it sprang open as soon as he released it. Leaving it open could admit animals, raccoons, possibly bears and mountain cats, which would ransack the place for food, and worse still, maul and ravage Hannah's body. The idea filled him with dread. But animals would destroy evidence. Earlier he'd considered burning the cottage down, but feared that smoke would attract attention, accelerating discovery of the dead woman, spurring a premature hunt for the missing child. As it was they might have a four-day head start, until Friday, when the owners returned.

Hannah was dead. Nothing worse could happen to her.

He let the doorknob go, heard the door creak open as he carried the girl up to the driveway, kneeled beside his knapsack, and held her while she continued to wail. My little girl, he whispered, Oh my little girl. She calmed and after a time he set her on her feet and peeled off the gloves and stuffed them in his pocket, picked up the knapsack, put his arms through the straps and snugged it in place on his back. As he was finishing the girl bolted for the cottage, but in two steps went down on her face in the gravel, and Nathan scooped her up, tottering under the weight of the pack. There was blood on her lips and teeth and she opened her mouth to draw a huge, silent breath before unleashing a terrible howl. Nathan dabbed at the blood with the dishcloth as he carried her up the hill to the road, the girl clawing towards the house, hands snapping at the air while she shrieked.

At the top of the drive he used the cloth to latch the painted cable across the driveway's entrance and stepped back, studying the surrounds. The cottage invisible from the road, and nothing amiss here to send anyone down to investigate. Unless neighbours came to water the plants. But he hadn't seen any plants.

They set off down the road, Nathan treading the grassy peak between the wheeltracks to keep from leaving footprints. In a few minutes the girl stopped crying, and then she slept, her head on his shoulder, the tearsoaked skin of her cheek against his neck. She was heavy, but he could carry her forever. Sydney, he whispered into her ear. Now you are Sydney.

He looked up and when he saw the sky through the over-hanging branches he felt for the first time in weeks an impulse to record his impression. Then he stopped walking, realizing with shock that he'd left the notebook on the deck's railing. He'd looked at it more than once while arranging their depar-ture, never quite overcoming the inertia that socked him when he thought to go out and retrieve it. The book held everything needed to incriminate him in murder and kidnapping: his finger-prints, his handwriting, his route conveyed in dates and weather conditions, even his blood sprayed across the cover. But he knew of no records on police file to match these against, so he would have to live an unsullied life, ensuring that the need or opportu-nity to collect that kind of evidence never arose. Unredeemable folly he knew, to leave it behind. But it was with Hannah, and somehow – maybe because she was now dead, as Lisa and Sydney were dead – that made it all right.

He would start a new notebook, today's sky the first entry. He'd have no problem remembering, for the observation was simply this: The sky is blue. He was surprised that the eyes he imagined reading these words weren't Lisa's. It was the future, and the eyes that read his words belonged to a young woman with the name Sydney Jayne Soderquist. His daughter.

He walked on, felt a sureness of action he hadn't felt in a long time, years it seemed, and the relief it brought from doubt so over-came him that he began to weep, tears spilling down his cheeks, salty on his tongue. He cried for a long time and then stopped and looked around and it was as if his tears had cleansed the landscape, because the leaves and pineneedles reaching out to him across the road's margins seemed fresher, their green enhanced, while the air carried new scents, a tonic of pine and balsam and cedar. Not far down the road he could see a stopsign, and just past it, the highway.

OCTOBER 5TH

The woman in her navyblue uniform squats before the girl, grips her arm and asks, Say your name again. Tell me your name.

Britty.

My head throbs as the blood oozes through constricted vessels. Confession filling my mouth.

Oh, the woman replies. Oh, you certainly are pretty. But what's your name?

The girl looks at me but before I can coach her with eyes or words she looks back at the woman.

Sydney? the girl says.

Ah, the woman replies, glancing at the card in her palm. Thank you, pretty Sydney. And can you tell me where your mama is?

Mama cold. Mama gone.

Yes, the woman says, lowering her eyes. You can go back to your daddy now. Go on.

And she comes to me and I fall to my knees and hold her.

You can go now, sir.

Thank you.

Welcome back to Canada. In future when you travel be sure to bring along her mother's death certificate. And you'll be wanting to get her a passport for next time.

We go outside and there are rifts in the clouds through which bars of sunlight shine down on the Georgia Strait. We get in the car and drive north through White Rock and park under a cluster of maples shedding leaves in a great, red cascade. I hold her hand and we walk down the sand and take off our socks and shoes and put our feet in the sea.

The sky is a girl and her hair is a cloud. Her eyes are both suns and her mouth is the moon and all the words she will ever speak are stars falling one by one out of night.

At ECW Press, we want you to enjoy this book in whatever format you like, whenever you like. Leave your print book at home and take the eBook to go! Purchase the print edition and receive the eBook free. Just send an email to ebook@ecwpress.com and include:

- the book title
- the name of the store where you purchased it
- your receipt number
- your preference of file type: PDF or ePub?

A real person will respond to your email with your eBook attached. And thanks for supporting an independently owned Canadian publisher with your purchase!

ACKNOWLEDGEMENTS

- -

Kathleen, Lucas, and Galen: my family. Love you all so much.

Margaret Booth, Christine Fischer Guy, Kathryn Kuitenbrouwer, Teri-Ann McDonald, Neal Panhuyzen, Kathleen Sandusky, Deanne Sowter, and Glen Synowicki. Thank you for reading drafts and providing valuable feedback.

Nathan Stretch, your car carried me across the continent. Glad we could help each other out.

The Canada Council, the Ontario Arts Council, and the Toronto Arts Council provided grants that supported the writing of this book. Huge appreciation.

The people at ECW Press, listed here in order of appearance (to me) during this excellent process: senior editor Michael Holmes, sales and marketing director Erin Creasey, art director/cover designer Carolyn McNeillie, managing editor Crissy Calhoun, copyeditor Peter Norman, publicist Jenna Illies, text designer Tania Craan, production manager/typesetter Troy Cunningham, and proofreader Kathryn Hayward. Thank you everyone for your kindness and attention.